Praise for
The Shadowglass

"A worthy conclusion to a story that is, at
its core, about love and letting go."
—*Kirkus*

"Head-over-heels romance, terrifying curses,
political intrigue, and epic magical battles will
appeal to fantasy enthusiasts… A must-purchase."
—*School Library Journal*

"Required reading for fans of the first two novels,
whose many questions will finally be answered."
—*Booklist*

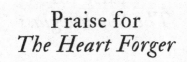

Praise for
The Heart Forger

★ "In this spectacular follow-up to the rich *The Bone Witch*, Tea's quest draws the reader further in, setting them on a more dangerous yet intriguing adventure."
—*Foreword Reviews*, starred review

★ "Rin's beautifully-crafted world from *The Bone Witch* (2017) expands in this sequel, which joins Dark asha, Tea, on her crusade of revenge. Dark and entrancing with a third volume to come."
—*Booklist*, starred review

"A wonderfully original tale—even better than the first."
—*RT Book Reviews*

"A sequel that builds in both thrills and enchantment."
—*Kirkus*

"Chupeco has crafted a glorious world for her twisting, turning plot, rich with magic, exotic beasts, romance and treachery. A mesmerizing tale, this sequel is even stronger than its precursor."
—*Shelf Awareness*

Praise for
The Bone Witch

★ "Mesmerizing. Chupeco does a magnificent job of balancing an intimate narrative perspective with sweeping world building, crafting her tale within a multicultural melting pot of influences as she presses toward a powerful cliffhanger."
—*Publisher's Weekly*, starred review

★ "Fantasy world building at its best."
—*Shelf Awareness*, starred review

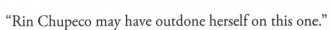

"Cupeco delights. Exceptionally written from beginning to end."
—*Buzzfeed.com*

"Rin Chupeco may have outdone herself on this one."
—*Bustle.com*

"Chupeco craftily weaves magic, intrigue, and mystery into a captivating tale that will leave readers begging for the promised sequel."
—*School Library Journal*

"A fantasy lover's fantasy, with a rich history and hierarchy of its own."
—*Foreword Reviews*

The
SHADOW
GLASS

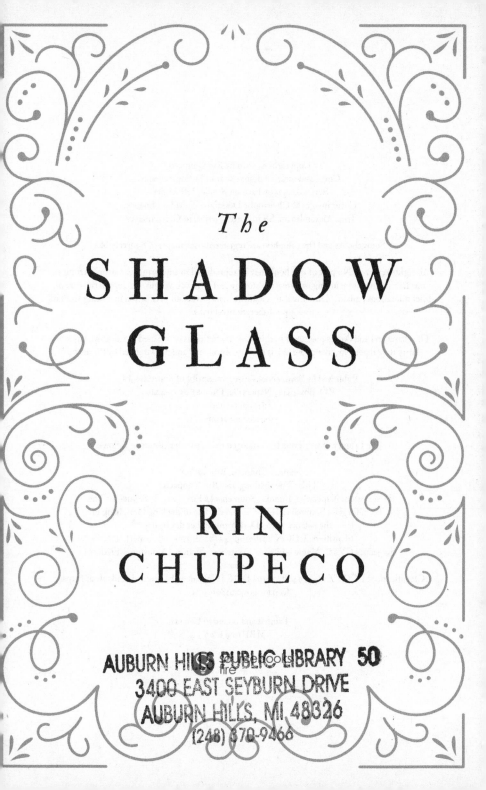

The

SHADOW GLASS

RIN CHUPECO

Published by Sourcebooks Fire, an imprint of Sourcebooks
P.O. Box 4410, Naperville, Illinois 60567-4410
(630) 961-3900
sourcebooks.com

The Library of Congress has cataloged the hardcover edition as follows:

Names: Chupeco, Rin, author.
Title: The shadowglass / Rin Chupeco.
Description: Naperville, Illinois : Sourcebooks Fire, [2019] | Sequel to: The
heart forger. | Summary: Tea's life, and the fate of the kingdoms, hang in
the balance as the Dark grows in her day by day.
Identifiers: LCCN 2018010904 | (hardcover : alk. paper)
Subjects: | CYAC: Magic--Fiction. | Witches--Fiction. | Monsters--Fiction. |
Fantasy.
Classification: LCC PZ7.C4594 Sh 2019 | DDC [Fic]--dc23 LC record available at https://
lccn.loc.gov/2018010904

Printed and bound in Canada.
MBP 10 9 8 7 6 5 4

To the lovely people of Japan,
for inventing ramen,
the best damn thing on the planet.

THE WORLD

OF THE BONE WITCH:

THE EIGHT KINGDOMS

*H*E WORE HER UNREAD LETTERS *like an amulet. They were tucked into his coat, folded carefully over his heart. Sometimes he ran a hand over where they lay hidden, reassurance that they were not figments of his imagination—that she still lived, though she had gone where his thoughts could not follow. He said nothing, revealed nothing. His reluctance to read them puzzled me, though I understood his grief. It was a closed coffin that no sympathy could penetrate.*

A week of fierce riding found us traveling down the Sea of Skulls, where I had first met the bone witch. Farther south, a ship lay in wait to take us from southeastern Daanoris to the familiar pastures of Odalia, and then to Kion. But here, in this land of roaring waves and broken monsters, Lord Fox's urgency disappeared. He was reluctant to leave these dead shores, content to wander the coarse sands his sister had once made her home.

He explored the cave she had appropriated for her shelter. "We searched for her in every city we knew. I never expected she would have been here." He touched the various vials and knickknacks she had left behind. "Still so vain, even in exile," he said, and a small, sad smile crept over his face.

Lord Khalad, the Odalian Heartforger, conducted a more thorough investigation. "Not all of them are for vanity, Fox," he responded soberly, seemingly unsurprised by his findings. "There are enchantments in every bottle to anoint her hua with battle spells. She planned her revenge down to every rune."

"Did you know what she intended to do, Khalad?" Lord Fox asked. "You were missing for so long that we feared we had lost you as well."

The Heartforger met Lord Fox's gaze without flinching. "I was an able helper and a willing hand." His voice was calm. "But these were her plans, her decisions. I was another cog in her wheel, but I do not know what other levers she pulled."

"She confided in you, at least." Lord Fox turned away, more regretful than angry.

"Can we find her?" I asked, still stinging at my dismissal from her side. The bone witch had forbidden me a place in her monstrous entourage of daeva, though she had promised me her story to sing. "What good is it for us to lead this chase if a week's ride is to her a mere day's flight?"

"Only the azi flies, Bard," the Kion princess, Inessa, reminded me. "And the indar, to a limited extent. The other daeva walk the lands with one foot in front of the other, as we do. The azi cannot carry them, and she will not leave any of her beasts behind."

Over the course of our seven-day journey, Empress Alyx's daughter had made little protest at our speed, eating soldier's rations and sleeping without the comforts most traveling royalty demanded. We had left the rest of the army behind, knowing the importance of a swift return to Kion. We rode only two horses—the princess and Lord Fox on one, and Lord Khalad and I on the other. They were magnificent steeds and powerfully built, and it was a shock when Lord Fox told me they were Kismet and Chief, Lady Mykaela and the bone witch's horses.

"When Mykaela…" Lord Fox's features grew anguished. They all still grieved the loss of the beautiful asha. "Kismet fell dead when she died. It was how Mistress Parmina knew what had happened to Mykaela before the rest of us learned the news. Tea resurrected Mykkie's horse, yoked it to herself." He closed his eyes and pressed his head against Kismet's. The horse nickered and snorted, showing no signs of its previous death.

"Fox." Princess Inessa's arms encircled his waist. She leaned her head lightly against his back. Her voice soft, she said, "We're going to find Tea, and we're going to save her. Let us talk to my mother and the rest of the asha, and to Kance as well. There's always a way."

Lord Fox took one of her hands, then bent to kiss the inside of her wrist. "I didn't die when I lost contact with Tea. But I spend every day expecting it to be my last. I can't go on like this, Inessa. I can't be alive and dead all at once." He shifted so that he was holding her, hands light and familiar against her hips. "She intends to save me. She knows a spell to bring me back to life, so that my heart beats as real as yours. But she requires the First Harvest, the same ingredient she needs for shadowglass. And she'll sacrifice herself—and anyone else—to find it."

His anger now flared. "Tea's changed. Sometimes I'm afraid I no longer recognize my sister."

"Then read what she left behind for you," Princess Inessa suggested gently. "It may offer an explanation of her motivations, though her words will not change what's been done."

Lord Fox looked at the princess, and I saw the similarities he shared with the bone witch. The brother and sister had the same dark eyes, the same stubborn chin, and Fox gave Princess Inessa the same expression as when Tea looked at Lord Kalen. "I'm afraid," he said, unashamed.

"I am not." The princess smiled. "You wanted to know why Tea left Kion. You've carried the answer for nearly a week now. You cannot chase after her yet hide from her own words."

Still, the man made no move to retrieve the letters.

"She is weaker," I interjected, and his attention swung back to me. "Every time she uses her runes, it drains her. She told me once that darksglass was not meant to last for very long."

Lord Fox took out the thick sheaf of papers and stared at them. He looked tired and worn; his love for his sister has aged him, I realized, even if time had not.

Finally, he inhaled a long, shuddering breath. He handed the letters to me. "You were there when she began telling her story. Tell me how she ends it."

I accepted. My fingers touched the soft parchment, noting the faint smears in her otherwise-elegant writing. With my practiced eyes, I knew these stains were not caused by faulty ink, but rather tears.

Above us, the pomegranate-colored sky gave way to darker clouds, suggesting only a few hours of brief, portentous respite before the storm.

I

I HAVE ALWAYS KNOWN DARKNESS.

It has been my friend. Yet it has also been my enemy. Some days, it is a mist over my eyes, leaving me blind to what should be obvious. But some days, I wipe away that fog and see more clearly in its aftermath than I ever have before it.

The darkness was inside me, I think, long before I raised my brother from the dead. My silver heartsglass merely gave it a mouth, made the darkness realize that it too can hunger...

This is not Fox's fault. This is not Lady Mykaela's fault.

I have told the bard much of my story—all but its end. Once we leave Daanoris, it will be far too dangerous for him to travel with Kalen and me. And so I write the rest of it now, with the clarity it deserves. I write while the fog is lifted. While I can see.

I am sorry about many things, but I am not sorry about this.

I start with a happy memory. They are so few nowadays. As I write, Kalen patrols the city with my *azi*, and Khalad is hard at work with his forging. It is a lonely vigil tonight in the Santiang Palace, with none but my own thoughts for company.

My brother always asks me to be candid, though I know it sometimes makes him uncomfortable.

Let me be candid now.

.. ⟍⟋⟍ ..

On the day we were to leave for Istera, I woke up later than I intended and with every desire of prolonging the hour. With a low grunt, I rolled onto my stomach and pressed my face against the sheets, content to breathe into the mattress. The bed was harder than its downy counterpart at the Valerian, but I preferred this. The bed in my asha-ka didn't have his scent on the covers, and his warmth was better than any blanket. He was the only place I could rest my head and dream without nightmares plaguing me, as they had for the last three months.

I felt the bed dip beside me, felt his lips ghost over my skin. "You need to get up," Kalen murmured, his voice husky from sleep, but the rough fabric against my shin told me he'd already dressed. I squinted in the direction of the windows. It was a little past dawn. Of the two of us, he was the morning person. I no longer needed to attend classes in the Willows, but with many mandatory nights spent entertaining visitors at the asha-ka, I frequently crawled into his bed a couple of hours past midnight.

I muttered something inconsequential and burrowed my head underneath the pillow. "Go away."

I heard him chuckle, and the mattress dipped farther. "Tea."

"A few minutes."

Kalen nudged the pillow out of the way. "I know you're tired, but as generous as Zahid has been regarding our room accommodations, I don't think sleeping in would be a good plan for today."

That was true enough. Asha were offered some leeway when it came to pursuing personal relationships, as long as those relationships didn't conflict with their duties. Lord Zahid, the Deathseekers' master-at-arms, had been understanding of Kalen and me; Kalen's fellow soldiers were not above some friendly ribbing. Faced with the choice between losing my visiting hours with Kalen or embarrassment from his mostly good-natured comrades, I had quickly learned to live with the latter.

"Five more minutes..."

His breath warmed the spot behind my neck, the part that never fails to break into goose bumps from his touch. His tongue flicked out, and within a few seconds, I was both wide eyed and wide awake.

"Kalen! You cheater!"

He laughed and dodged my attempts to flail at him. "Don't make me kick you out."

He was wearing a maroon *jobba* instead of the dark coat and pants he preferred. Deathseeker or not, Kalen was nobility, and any visits he made to allied countries required formal dress.

Remembering that I too needed to hurry home and change given the crumpled state of my *hua*, I sat up and turned toward the mirror. With common cosmetics, I would have resembled a raccoon. With apothecary spells mixed in, my rouge and liner managed to look only slightly marred. "This is all your fault."

"I know," he agreed, unrepentant.

"It's rare enough for Parmina to give me the night off. I should have been resting. You said you were going to walk me home."

"We *are* home."

"I meant to the Valerian, you lout."

"I can walk you home now."

I glared at him. He walked me home in the mornings, regardless of where we ended up the night before.

He smiled back. Gruff as he usually was, Kalen could look insidiously innocent if he wished. "And I will. Councilor Ludvig isn't expecting us for another hour."

"An *hour*?" I swore loudly and hopped out of bed, pulling on my *hua* haphazardly. "You never mentioned how late it was!"

"Yes. My trying to get you out of bed had nothing to do with that."

I tugged my waist wrap into place around me and glared at him again. "This is all your fault."

"I know."

I reached up and kissed him. "Take me home," I commanded, "and if we're late, you get to explain why to Parmina."

"I would much rather face another daeva."

I paused. "I need one stop," I amended quietly.

Kalen squeezed my hand. He knew what I wanted. I always asked for the same detour. "Of course."

.. ∖⁄∠ ..

The graveyard was not far from the Willows. As was the custom, a generous portion of it had been set aside for ashas' and Deathseekers' graves, a row of daffodils planted in a line to demarcate their headstones from the rest of the populace. *Even in death, the great equalizer, important people pushed up better shrubbery than the rest*, I thought.

A small monument stood at the graveyard's center. It was a statue of Vernasha of the Roses, the founder of Kion, as well as its first asha. A single line was set in bronze at the foot of the statue, a tribute to all those who had served and given their lives to protect the kingdom. My fingers traced over the words:

A life worth dying for is a life worth living.

We stood among the Deathseekers' tombs first, where Kalen honored in silence all the brothers he had lost. Then we moved toward the ashas' side, to one grave in particular.

"Good morning, Polaire," I said, greeting her softly, sinking to my knees. Hers was a shiny, gray slab, free of the moss that claimed those around hers. It grated at my heart that she was here at all. Today, a bouquet of fresh lilies had been carefully placed over the grave—Althy's doing, I surmised.

These daily pilgrimages did nothing to lighten my guilt.

Three months wasn't long enough. Thirty years wouldn't be long enough either.

"I've been having visions," I told her softly. "But are they bad dreams or something worse? Sometimes I dream you are alive only to see Aenah use the daeva to kill you again and again. Sometimes the victim changes, and it's Mykaela or Althy or Likh or Zoya. Sometimes I dream that the Valerian is on fire. The vision is so real that I can feel the heat on my skin and the sun burning in my hair. Only Kalen helps chase those nightmares away. Is this my penance for not saving you?"

Kalen was quiet. He wrapped his arms around me as I tried in vain to slough off my sins like old skin.

I wove a tiny rune before Polaire's stone, allowed the magic to flow out of my fingers, burrowing into the ground below me. I probed the dirt for any spark that I could channel, any suggestion of life I could steal from her bones and multiply so she could rise from the earth, smile, and tell me how much of an idiot I had been while she'd been gone.

But I sensed nothing. Whatever powers bone witches could wield, they cannot bring back silver heartsglass.

"Tea." Kalen knew the futility of my attempts but allowed me my self-flagellation. I wondered if he thought it would exorcise the demons inside me. I wondered if he would ask me to stop if he knew it did not. "We have to go."

I looked down at my own heartsglass, inspecting it closely for any signs of the black that had manifested on the cruel day of Polaire's death. In the last few weeks, the dark flecks had lessened. The more time that passed since the horrific night I killed Aenah, one of the Faceless, and drove the traitorous King Telemaine of Odalia insane, the less the darkness showed itself there. Small spells masked its discoloration—Kalen was my sole accomplice in and confidant to this fact. Fox had far too much on his plate nowadays, and this was not a guilt I could advertise to friends—bone witches have been killed for lesser transgressions.

A black heartsglass was made from rage and murder. Only the Faceless bore such darkness, and the Willows would have my head should it manifest in mine. Even now, I hold no regrets for killing Aenah, though I wished I had turned King Telemaine over to his son, instead of destroying his mind. Prince Kance didn't deserve to lose his father that way, and his anger at me, his decision to exile me from Odalia, was the direct result of my recklessness.

There was no black in my heartsglass today. *But it is like droplets of blood, dripping into a bowl of fresh spring water,* I thought. *Mix it well enough, and you can't see the blood. But would you drink it? Let the taste run down your throat? How can one know liquid so clear could also bear such a taint?*

I bent my head and, briefly, allowed myself to wash her grave with a few more tears.

Kalen helped me to my feet. His warm brown eyes studied me before he placed a gentle kiss on my forehead. Faint wisps of rune surrounded us—*Heartshare* was a near-permanent runic spell that allowed two people to share strength. Kalen had saved my life with it. It was not as strong a bond as I shared with my brother, but I was connected to Kalen through it nonetheless. He knew my heart's pain and understood, and I could not have loved him more for it.

·· ∖∣∕ ··

We rode outside the city of Ankyo for a mile, to where the others waited. By asha standards, this was an unusual rendezvous point. We also had an unusual means of transport.

Those of us who formed the delegation wore woolen cloaks despite the hot day. Councilor Ludvig, the previous adviser to Istera's King Rendorvik, was garbed in Isteran colors—blue and silver, in a deftly embroidered long coat he called a *gákti*. Likh, lovely as ever, was in an eye-catching cerulean *hua*, tasteful crewels skimming up his sleeves. Althy's garb was plainer, with white doves sewn over a sky-blue fabric. Rahim, as always, was dressed to kill. His sherwani was a magnificent display of beadwork waves stitched along the edges of his shirt, with a collar of pewter threads surrounding his thick neck, which was half-hidden by his long, angularly trimmed beard. He wore no cloak himself—the man claimed to have shrugged off Tresean winters and was as invulnerable to the Isteran cold. In contrast, Khalad looked like a merchant in his rough, brown *čūqā*.

At Rahim's insistence, I had worn his latest creation—a beautiful mahogany *hua*, stitched with a jewel-eyed, three-headed dragon, which was partly concealed by my waist wrap. My mastery of the *azi* was no secret, he pointed out, and it was important for me to command such narratives in subtle ways. I slipped a small knife into my sleeve, a growing habit of mine.

My brother wore a huge grin on his face when we approached. "Have a good rest?" His voice was mild enough, but I knew Fox. We had perfected our *Veiling* rune and rarely stumbled into each other's minds whenever one of us wanted privacy—but we *knew* anyway.

"As if you spent the night alone," I grumbled at him with a sideways glance at Inessa. As usual, the princess looked stunning. The way they snuck adoring glances at each other was almost oversweet. Three months ago, Inessa had been engaged to both Prince Kance of Odalia *and* Emperor Shifang of Daanoris. My brother had fought her and both engagements nearly every step of the way.

How much things change in a short time, I thought with another pang of sadness.

"You're late." Zoya's presence was suspicious. Mykaela, Inessa, and Fox were there to see us off, but Zoya wasn't the type for such sentiments.

"What are you doing here?" I demanded.

She shrugged. "Mistress Parmina sold tickets for an *azi* viewing. They are to be summoned by none other than Lady Tea of the Embers herself."

I groaned. That particular moniker had spread quickly, a not-so-subtle reference to my connection with the daeva.

"She's dispatched me here," Zoya continued, "to ensure your pet dragon actually arrives and her guests receive their money's worth."

"An *azi* viewing?"

"Rather like a cherry blossom viewing, but with daeva. They're at the fourth floor of the Falling Snow *cha-khana*, which has a very good view of this particular terrain. Why did you think she suggested this meeting place? Because she was concerned about her safety or yours? You don't know your mistress very well."

"Did she promise you access to my room for your part in this? My room, which happens to be right next to Shadi's?"

Zoya's smile was so bright it was blinding.

"I wish Fox and I could come with you," the princess murmured to me with a sigh.

"But there are no emperors in Istera to be accidentally engaged to, Your Highness," said Zoya.

"You have a very lovely mouth, Zoya. It would look even lovelier if it remained shut for the rest of the day."

"As you wish, Your Highness."

"How is the old Heartforger?" I asked Khalad.

He smiled sadly. "Feeling his age. His own heartsglass is weakening. The exertions at Daanoris finally caught up to him, and I'm not sure he can shake it off. We brought him to Holsrath for treatment. They have better facilities to help him there. We both knew that day was coming, but…"

"I'm so sorry, Khalad."

"Kalen was a lot of help."

Kalen was the new Duke of Holsrath, a title he hated for how he came to it. His father's death at the hands of King Telemaine and Aenah was a painful subject, and not one he liked to talk about. "It was nothing," my love murmured, looking a bit abashed. "Just glad I could be of service to Khalad."

It felt odd to not be traveling with my brother. As the Kion princess's official consort, Fox grew more involved in the politics and day-to-day administration of the kingdom Inessa would one day rule. They were frequent visitors to the city, overseeing new constructions to the marketplace and tending to those in the poorer slums, often with Khalad and me in tow.

As if sharing the same thoughts, Fox smiled sheepishly. "I'm half-tempted to jump onto the *azi*'s back with the rest of you when it arrives."

"And I'm whole-tempted to drag you back to Ankyo on your ear," Inessa said tartly. "I'm not going to spend the next two days alone with the Drychta and Yadoshan ambassadors talking about trade deals. They're more likely to murder each other than reach an agreement."

"You have your own responsibilities now, Fox," I said. My feelings were strangely contradictory. I had only ever wanted Fox to have a life of his own, to be happy. But I could not stamp down the spark of resentment that he was no longer at the forefront of my life, nor I at his.

"It's strange to be away from you," my brother admitted, rueful.

"We don't have much time, you know." Zoya scanned the sky. "Are you certain the *azi* will come when you're not lodged inside its head? I'd rather not have the asha elders hear of our plans early enough to stop you."

"You didn't need to come and see us off, Zoya," Althy reminded her gently. "And don't use Parmina as an excuse."

"And not get the chance to complain?" she chided.

"We still have room for one more," I encouraged Mykaela. Physically, my mentor was in peak health. Her bright-silver heartsglass, lost for so many years, now hung around her neck where it belonged. But Polaire's death had hit her the hardest. It would not do, I had argued, to have her spending the rest of her life in vigils by Polaire's gravesite when Polaire had sacrificed so much for Mykaela to keep living. Still, the older asha split her time between her friend's tomb and her old lover King Vanor's crypt. I had often wondered about the conversations she had with the latter but didn't want to pry.

Mykaela shook her head. "We still have much work to do, Tea. It's hard enough for the asha association to relinquish one bone witch, much less two." She smiled at me and took my hand. "There are other battles to be fought here. And I expect you to bring back valuable information when you return."

I nodded. The asha association and I were not on the best of terms. I believed they were at least partly responsible for losing Mykaela's heartsglass, to prevent her from becoming too powerful for their interests. But Mykaela and the others didn't think they would go so far. They believed the association hoarded their influence while still adhering to the asha codes. I had little evidence to change their minds.

Recently, we'd received word about strange creatures prowling near Istera—creatures that resembled smaller daeva. Officially, we were to head to the ice kingdom to investigate the sightings. Unofficially, we were following up on the only lead we had: Aenah's cryptic words before she died.

In her last moments, the Faceless had shared how the legend of the Blade that Soars and Dancing Wind were corrupted sources, and that only the true version held the answers to the mysterious and powerful shadowglass that Aenah and the elder asha were keen on possessing. We hoped that Istera, which was home to the world's oldest library and largest collection of books on runic magic and asha history, would provide clues.

"I've never ridden dragons before," Rahim said to me, rubbing his hands excitedly. "But ah, my *uchenik*, I always wanted to."

"Always wanted to?" echoed Likh, who had ridden the *azi* before and did not feel the same way.

"It must feel good to be up so high, looking down at the world below." Rahim combed at his beard with thick fingers. "Good to think about how little one's problems can be when everything is small in the grand scheme of things, no? Was that not how you felt when you rode the *azi*, dear Likh?"

"I was mostly thinking about not throwing up," my new asha-brother admitted, the latest recruit to House Valerian. The asha association had initially opposed his candidacy, but after his part in fighting the Faceless in Daanoris had been revealed, support for him among the other asha had been too overwhelming for the association not to concede.

"We'd best be going, Tea," Khalad reminded me with a small smile. "Let's not keep Mistress Parmina waiting."

I laughed at that, then cast my mind out, searching—and finding—my target as its familiar presence seeped into my thoughts like molasses over scones. The asha association had wanted me to kill the *azi*. With both Mykaela and Empress Alyx's blessing, I had refused. Controlling the *azi* made the association wary to plot directly against me. And a docile *azi*, much to my surprise, had brought even more tourists to Ankyo. Where my attempts at invoking empathy in the asha leaders had failed, greed had prevailed. "It's here," I confirmed.

The words were barely out of my mouth when the *azi* landed, not ungracefully, several meters away. The sight of the three-headed dragon was familiar to many of us in our gathering, but Councilor Ludvig and Rahim swore in unison, staring at the large daeva. Likh gripped Khalad's arm.

"Good luck," Zoya said, as the Heartforger began clambering up the beast's back, assisting a nervous Likh once he found steadier footing. "Just so it's official, Tea, I *will* be crashing in your room while you're away."

I rolled my eyes. "Everyone knows you'll be in Shadi's room, Zoya, no matter what Mistress Parmina promised you."

The asha grinned as the others dragged personal trunks up the *azi*, the creature sitting quietly with minimal fuss.

"Be careful," Mykkie told me. "None of those reports we've received from Istera match what we know of daeva. Keep an eye out, and you and Althy watch over Likh. This is only his second trip outside of Ankyo."

"I will." I hugged her. "Don't overwork yourself."

"I will try. I shall let Fox know of new developments here, so he can relay them to you." She stepped back and looked up at the *azi*. It crooned and bowed its head respectfully at her.

"You better not get into trouble in Istera without me around," Fox said.

"You better not get into trouble in Kion without *me* around," I shot back, and nearly knocked him over with the force of my embrace.

"Quit dillydallying," Althy said from atop the dragon. "Or we'll be all day trading good-byes."

I hugged Fox one last time, did the same to Inessa, and accepted Kalen's help climbing up the *azi*. Once we were all settled, the daeva made a soft keening noise and flapped its magnificent wings. It leaped into the air, and I watched as my friends grew smaller as the *azi* ascended. The creature sang out. Rahim swore again.

Smiling, I glanced down for one last look at Ankyo—and startled, mouth agape.

The city was on fire. Balls of flame fanned against the gates, and I watched in horror as buildings and houses collapsed, thick clouds of dark smoke rising to obscure my view. Everything burned—

"Tea?"

I jumped when a hand touched my shoulder.

Kalen looked at me quizzically. "Is something the matter?"

"I..." The city of Ankyo gleamed back at me from below, pristine and unchanged. Soon, even that view disappeared, as the *azi* barreled through the sky, the Swiftsea soon replacing the land below us.

"It's nothing," I said shakily, but I kept glancing behind us, struggling to see any telltale trace of smoke and finding none.

A YOUNG WOMAN MET US AS *we boarded the ship that would take us to Kion. She was dressed in brilliant gold, her* hua *a symphony of vines and roses. Jewels glittered in her black hair. Several other asha stood beside her, their expressions strange combinations of worry and grimness.*

"Took you long enough," the woman in gold groused. "You were supposed to be here a day ago."

"We rode as fast as we could, Zoya," Lord Fox told the woman shortly. "What are you doing here?"

"Empress Alyx sent me, of course. We heard word of what happened." The woman took a long breath, a catch in her voice. "I am so sorry. I should have been there. Maybe I could have—"

"You had your own duties," Princess Inessa interrupted her firmly. "I took charge of this expedition. If there is anyone to blame, then I bear that burden."

"Your Highness—"

"How are the others?"

The asha exhaled again. "Awaiting orders in Kion. It would ease Zahid to know if the rest of the Deathseekers will be returning quickly. It's not easy defending Kion with only a handful of us present. The asha are spread thin as it is."

"And Aadil?"

"Sighted in the south."

The princess swore.

"A cadre of our soldiers were ambushed. No missing limbs or insanity—they were simply put to sleep. Druj must be getting soft. Kance tells us Druj's army is making for the Hollows next, that they've seen Drychta camped there. That's about all the information he sent. Frankly, I'm surprised Kance's even given us that much. They're to leave next week, and he asks if we could spare some soldiers. We'll talk more about this on the ship."

"What's that for?" Lord Khalad asked, gesturing toward the mast.

I saw nothing where he pointed.

"I'm sure you've seen runes before, Khalad." Lady Zoya shrugged. "Speed is our priority, or so Empress Alyx told me. With my help, I can get you across the sea and back to Kion in under two days. It's not as quick as a daeva perhaps, but we're not paid enough for all this tomfoolery."

"Two days?" I blurted before I could help myself. "A ship's journey from here to Kion takes three times that long."

"What can I say? We're women of many talents." She stared hard at me. "And who in the seven hells are you?"

"Tea found a scribe," Lord Khalad said, watching the men cast off the lines and hoist the anchor.

"A scribe? All the havoc she's wreaked in the kingdoms, and she wishes to have that immortalized on paper? She needs a good thrashing."

"Her story needed telling!" Perhaps traces of her compulsion *still lingered inside me, goading me into defending a woman I still sometimes feared.*

"Her side of the story?" The asha shot an arm out toward the horizon as the sails unfurled behind her. "Take a long, hard look, you idiotic man. Tell me what defense you can make of that."

I saw faint wisps of gray smoke wafting from a long way off. "What is that?" I asked, horrified.

"The smoke is from Kion, you little simperseed. Her azi attacked Ankyo five days ago. I don't know where the rest of her daeva are, but one was more than enough to destroy Ankyo. You may not know what she intends, Fox, but I do. She's calling for war, and damnation to anyone who stands in her path."

2

I T TAKES GREAT INNER STRENGTH and perseverance to survive
in the coldest place in the world, but the Isterans have always
done so with style. Brass fanfare greeted us as we landed at the edge
of the Runeswood. While I was certain most of those waiting had
never seen the *azi* before, to their credit, they stood their ground
when the dragon turned its three heads toward them, rumbling
noisily. There was, however, a faint clatter of metal hitting metal
as more than a few swords slid out of scabbards. The Isterans were
a friendly people, but they were also pragmatic.

The cold bit through my cloak. The ground was caked in
snow, crunching beneath our boots as we walked. Likh shivered.
Wordlessly, Khalad shook off his thick cape and draped it around
Likh's shoulders. The younger boy smiled his gratitude, white teeth
chattering even as his cheeks turned pink from more than the frost.
The younger boy's crush on the Heartforger grew every day.

King Rendorvik stepped forward, bowing low to his old mentor, Ludvig. His wife, Daeri, an attractive brunette with deep-set blue eyes, took her welcome further, hugging and kissing the cheeks of the women in the group, including Likh, in friendly fashion. "It's been quite some time since you've honored us with a visit, Ludvig. You've been sorely missed."

Councilor Ludvig snorted. "I'm surprised Scalzieg and the others haven't burned the place down without me around, Rendor," he said.

I started, the words calling to mind my horrific vision of Ankyo in flames from only a few hours ago.

Ludvig continued, "The lack of visible wreckage tells me they might be more competent than I first thought when they started their training under me."

The Isteran king laughed. "We stand in winter all year, my old friend. You know better than any of us how fires fear our kind of cold." He turned curious eyes toward the *azi*. At my silent command, it had lowered its three snouts to prostrate itself on the ground, a sign of its submission. "I am afraid I do not have a large enough stable to house your daeva friend here."

"We would much rather not keep him inside the city, Your Majesty," I said. "The *azi* prefers the open air."

"You must be the Lady Tea. We've heard much about you, far away as we are from most." The king reached out his hand, and I shook it. "Call me Rendor. We share the same teacher, and I would like to think that makes us kinsmen almost."

Councilor Ludvig snorted again but looked faintly approving.

King Rendorvik was a courteous man, greeting the rest of the group with an informality that was not characteristic of royalty. Kalen and Khalad, he recognized with pleasure. "It's been a while since you've visited Farsun, Your Grace." He sobered. "And how is your cousin Kance?"

At the mention of Kance, I felt my heartsglass color blue, and Kalen couldn't hide his wince. "As good as anyone can expect, your Majesty, considering the circumstances."

"I am so very sorry to hear of your uncle's malady. I hope His Majesty recovers with all speed."

It was my turn to try not to flinch. The cause of the Odalian king's sickness was a mystery to most, and I wasn't sure how the friendly royal would react if he knew that the reason for Telemaine's insanity was standing before him, accepting his hospitality.

Khalad was more forthcoming. "Whatever malaise he suffers is his own doing," he said with no trace of rancor. Khalad had more reason to hate his father than any of us. "Kance would make a more fitting king in his stead."

"Khalad," King Rendorvik said reverently. "I did not know the old king's eldest son was a heartforger until recently, but we hold both your titles in high esteem. Surely your father didn't deserve this, despite the crimes he committed?"

Khalad bowed. "I speak as a heartforger, Your Majesty, when I say that Kance is a hundred times the king our father had ever hoped to be."

The king inclined his head as well. "I trust your judgment. As badly as he treated his people and his own sons, I nonetheless hope he finds his peace. May they both find peace." *And you as well*, his heartsglass seemed to suggest.

A good-looking boy, only a few years older than Khalad, stepped forward. "My name is Cyran," he said, clasping his hands around the startled forger's. Likh was stationed behind me, but I swore I could feel the heat blistering out of his heartsglass without turning around. "The old Heartforger, Master Narel, healed me from the same long illness that His Majesty King Kance suffered from. I am told you were instrumental in the cure as well. I owe you my life. Please tell me how I can repay your kindness."

"No thanks are needed, milord," Khalad said politely. "It's all part of my work."

"At least permit me to give you a tour around Farsun?"

The blaze Likh was generating behind my back threatened to explode into the fire of a full-fledged sun.

"Perhaps next time? I'm afraid we have pressing duties that we cannot delay."

"I will hold you to that, milord."

The *azi* followed us until we were at Farsun's gates before taking to the air with one last whoop of farewell. It brushed against my mind, friendly and affectionate, and then was gone.

"Isterans are rather blasé when it comes to daeva, it seems," Althy noted.

"We have a different way of dealing with them than you Kions, I imagine."

Despite the trumpets, the procession toward the city lacked

the pomp and circumstance I was used to in Kion. There were no crowds cheering us on as we headed to the royal palace. Many citizens bowed to the king and then continued with their work, greeting us briefly and with the same casualness as we passed.

It felt strange to be relatively ignored, but after everything I'd experienced in Daanoris, the Isteran ability to treat their kings like any other Isteran for the most part came as a welcome relief.

"The daeva *zarich*'s burial mound lies within the Runeswood," the king said as we walked, "far too close to our city for comfort. But our Dark asha, Sakmeet, tamed it rather well."

"Tamed it?" Likh echoed from behind us, his emotions more tempered now that Lord Cyran had gone ahead.

"I understand that Dark asha put daeva back into the ground as quickly as possible, aye? Takes quite a toll on them, as I'm sure you know. We don't have as many asha here in Farsun as you do in Ankyo, and a few of our brilliant asha thought it would be better to prioritize their quality of life rather than ask the Willows for a new Dark asha every twenty or so years when she burns herself out. It was easier on Sakmeet to control the *zarich* and keep it away from the city than to resurrect it every few years and completely sap her strength while she's at it. We have found that daeva—our *zarich*, at least, and your *azi* too, apparently—prefer their solitude unless threatened. In the Runeswood, the *zarich* has all the privacy it desires."

I was stunned. "I didn't know," I said. Why would the Willows allow Mykaela to waste her life away with every resurrection when she could have conserved her strength this way?

"It's because of a policy of the asha association," Althy said quietly, answering my question. "They decided it was too risky to put one person in charge of all daeva. There is still the threat of darkrot from controlling many daeva at once. The Isterans had their own Dark asha and only one beast to manage within their borders. We have far more daeva to command in our territory."

"You mean it would be riskier to put one person in charge of daeva if that bone witch hadn't pledged absolute loyalty to the elders," I corrected bitterly.

"There are precedents, Tea. There have been Dark asha in the past who'd given in to temptation."

Still, if Isterans could treat Sakmeet well despite her abilities, then why couldn't Kion treat Mykaela or me the same way? "Who was she?" I asked.

"Who?"

"The Dark asha Mykaela had to kill. The one who took in too much power and succumbed to the darkrot. Polaire told me about her once, but not in much detail."

The matronly asha sighed. "It's not something we like to talk about, child. And now is not the best time for *these* questions."

I fell silent as we passed another crowd of people, some stopping to have a brief word with their liege before we moved on. Farsun was a city tucked under a constant blanket of ice, but business thrived. Brightly lit shops were adorned with signs inviting entry, and smoke spiraled out of chimneys, suggesting warmth within. Unlike Kion, there were no displays of opulence here;

people chose comfort over luxury. Caps and cloaks were more commonplace than jewelry and spells. Rahim stood out among our lot, flaunting his bright, lavishly embroidered clothes without a care for frostbite.

"What happened to Sakmeet?" Kalen asked as we entered the great hall. From the outside, the royal palace was a forbidding stone fortress. Inside, fireplaces burned warmly, and long, complicated wall tapestries added touches of color amid the gray stone and cemented bricks. "The details of her death were hazy."

King Rendorvik shook his head sadly. "We found her out in the snow, frozen to death. There was no mark of the daeva on her body, that much we could ascertain. She was prone to journeying on her own for weeks at a time, though we warned her it would grow more difficult in her old age. But she was quite a tenacious, if stubborn, lady. She would not permit us to assist her and insisted on her own independence despite the dangers. We mourned her loss and feared that the *zarich* might attack now that her hold on it was gone, but we have not heard word from it for the last two years. We have patrols stationed around the area, but the creature does not approach them."

"I do not understand," Rahim said. "What Tea has recently started with the *azi*, Sakmeet had been doing all this time? Why did we not know this?"

"Oh, you did know about it," Councilor Ludvig said wryly. "I recommended that the Willows follow the same training Sakmeet experimented with long before Mykaela ever became asha. I was shot down every time. As Althy pointed out, there are dangers to controlling multiple daeva, and as it is, there aren't enough Dark asha around to handle them all."

"We're not as luxurious as Kion," King Rendor said, guiding us to our rooms. "But we claim the softest beds in all the eight kingdoms. Stay for as long as you wish. We rarely have the opportunity to entertain visitors this far north. Would there be anything else you require?"

I cleared my throat. "I was hoping to take a look at your library, Your Majes—Rendor."

The king chuckled. "Ludvig told us that you were interested in our collection of books, but wouldn't you rather relax first? It's a long journey, even on daevaback."

"I'm afraid our research is that important," Khalad admitted. "I'm sure you know of the strange creatures sighted along your borders?"

Queen Daeria's eyes widened, and husband and wife looked at each other. "So you've heard," the king said finally. "Our soldiers have encountered three so far, but it's three more than we desire. They're unusual breeds, very unlike any daeva I've studied and hard, though not impossible, to kill. If we had encountered them in groups instead of on their own and had we not had at least thirty men in each case, we would have suffered more casualties. We do not know where the creatures came from, much less what they are or why they have been attacking us."

"We've heard similar rumors from Tresea," the queen chimed in, "though they've been tight-lipped about their own troubles. But what do our books have to do with any of this?"

"Your kingdom has the oldest known collection on runic magic, Your Highness," Althy explained. "Our collection in Kion is severely limited. At this point, any knowledge would be beneficial, no matter how far-fetched."

"I've found that old remedies are still the most effective," the queen agreed. "Our library is open for your perusal whenever you wish."

"I do not understand," Rahim rumbled after we had unpacked and regrouped. "What breed of monster are we talking about?"

"It's not something the asha elders want public," Likh explained. "We've been hearing reports of odd monsters along the upper kingdoms. There've been some rumors in Odalia about similar demons. Except it's not daeva—they're far too small. And we can't investigate in more detail or get support from Prince Kance in Kneave because…um…" The boy turned pale and cast an apologetic glance my way.

"Because Prince Kance doesn't want anything to do with me right now," I finished for him. It still hurt to say it, but I had burned my bridges to Odalia the instant I killed Aenah and destroyed Telemaine.

Rahim softened almost immediately, eyes growing bright with tears of sympathy. I saw the signs and was already bracing myself when he engulfed me with arms, twice the size of even Kalen's. "My *uchenik*, this is not your doing. You are good person, and the prince will see it. That his father suffered under thrall of Faceless trash is not your doing. He will see in time, little one."

"Unffgh," I managed to say from somewhere underneath his beard.

"And why are *you* here, Rahim?" Kalen asked, trying his best not to look amused.

"The Isterans, underneath their wool and fur, hold fashion in the highest esteem. The Queen Deira, she is kind enough to ask this humble Tresean to come to Farsun and design gowns for her girls. The Queen of Istera asking a Tresean! Back in my youth, it would be treasonous to imagine peace between our two kingdoms. It is like asking pink not to clash with the red! But I am honored, and I am determined." He swept his burly arms out, briefly forgetting that I was still clinging to them. "To keep the style yet keep out the cold at same time! It is the undertaking of my career!"

"You're doing good work, Rahim," Kalen said calmly with a straight face. "You're doing good work."

The Isterans were avid readers and collectors of literature, and I was expecting an impressive library. What I wasn't expecting was for it to take up a full wing of the castle. What the rest of the Farsun palace lacked in opulence, King Rendrovik's manuscript collection made up for with decadence. Marble floors shone and vaulted ceilings were decorated in vividly colored frescoes by, no doubt, illustrious painters. Golden motifs and busts lined the bookcases. The shelves were of cured mahogany, specially treated to last and polished to shine.

"It's not much," said the Isteran king with quiet pride, "but it's the most important place in all of Istera, and we try to present it as such."

"Uhh…" I said in awe.

"This the most magnificent room I have ever been in," Likh whispered.

"We boast some first-century manuscripts," Queen Deira cautioned. "There will be assistants to help you with your work, so you would do well to follow their instructions. Some of these volumes are quite old, and we ask you take great care while browsing them."

"Uhh…" I repeated.

"You're going to catch flies if you keep your mouth open like that." Kalen's attempt at teasing was lost on me. I wandered past bookshelves lined with rare manuscripts and incunabula. Though my fingers flexed and trembled, I was too afraid to touch them for fear they might disintegrate. I could spend the rest of my life in this library; even if I read quickly, I knew I would never finish the texts in my lifetime—or a second lifetime.

"We were told you had the oldest accounts of the Blade that Soars legends," Khalad said. "And some on runic magic. Tea and I would be very interested in… Tea? Are you okay?"

"Forget it, Khalad," Kalen said. "She's gone. Give her time."

"In that case," Rahim said, "I will go to consult with Queen Deira. Do not let books eat your *lyubimaya*, Kalen, and do not let her eat them."

"H-how many books do you even *have*?" I finally stammered, trying to take it all in.

"Almost a million at last count." King Rendorvik laughed, as we were led deeper into the library. "Our head librarian would know the exact number. It takes a lot of effort to keep the volumes in good condition, considering our perpetual winters."

"Tea," Althy said, "focus. Remember that we have a purpose in coming here."

"Yes," I found myself saying, "to read everything we can get our hands on."

"Oh dear," murmured my asha-sister. "We've lost her."

•• ⟍╲⁄⁄ ••

Kalen volunteered to consult with some of the Isteran generals about the alleged daeva sightings, and Khalad went with him. That left the rest of us free to raid King Rendorvik's library. There were nearly a million reasons to be distracted, and it took physical effort on Althy's part to prevent me from wandering to new piles of books instead of sticking to the research we came to do.

The legend of the Blade that Soars and Dancing Wind was an interesting piece of mythology. The problem was that multiple retellings had been collected, chronicling cultures and politics of multiple kingdoms, each using the narrative as a source. It was easy for me to drift into other unrelated stories before realizing my mistake—and I was making a lot of mistakes.

"But they have a complete history of asha here," I whined. "Vernasha of the Roses kept a diary that was *preserved*!" How could Althy be so flippant surrounded by so much knowledge? Vernasha was the famous asha who *founded* Kion, so surely she would understand my interest. "There's also a complete manuscript listing the adventures of the Five Great Heroes' epic in greater detail than anything I've read, and it's more than two thousand pages! Look, this is Rashnu's final journal, recounting his life after the other Great Heroes perished at the Ring of Worship—"

"Tea."

"Did you know that Aadil wasn't actually the rightful ruler of Drycht? He was a distant relation to King Adhitaya and revolted against him fifteen years ago when heavy taxation turned the people against the monarch. There are even colored paintings of Adhitaya and his sons—"

"Read them all *after* we have our answers."

Clearly, Althy had more willpower than I. She hefted a solid volume bound in thick, black leather with gold lettering. "This is the earliest retelling I can find, said to be written by the Great Hero Ashi the Swift herself. The librarians believe this to be the earliest source on Blade that Soars, so I'd like us to focus there." She raised an eyebrow at Likh, who was paging through a large tome on ancient Kion culture. "Find something interesting?"

The boy blushed and laid down the book. "All the books here are fascinating," he squeaked.

"Think about the possibilities!" It was hard to dampen my excitement, even with Althy's sensibility. "There could be runes here that we've never even heard of. Imagine a rune for every kind of spell you could imagine. Isteran librarians have been studying these books all their lives, and even they say they haven't begun to understand half of what is written here!"

"While I always make it a habit to support enthusiasm for

learning," Althy said, "today is not that day. Tea, might I remind you that this trip to Istera was *your* prerogative."

"Sorry." Chastened, I focused on the book she indicated. "*In the beginning, Blade that Soars,*" I read. "*In the beginning, Dancing Wind. They ruled the sky as the land took breath, the lands as wide as the ground held sand and soil...*" I trailed off. "So far, this doesn't sound all that different from what we sing for the *darashi oyun.*"

"The *darashi oyun* prides itself on its authenticity." The older asha frowned at the page. "We both knew coming here that discovering new source material was a long shot, Tea. The elder asha may have their secrets, but it doesn't necessarily mean they have anything to do with keeping Mykaela's heartsglass or colluding with Aenah."

"I'm positive about this." I saw their treachery in Aenah's head as easily as I could see my own reflection in the mirror. But it was my word against theirs—and I was a bone witch, tolerated and feared but never truly welcomed, while they defined what it was to be asha. All I had to go by was Aenah's claim that there was more to the story, and the Faceless wasn't known for her truthfulness either.

The woman sighed. "The librarians were kind enough to collect all known books that talk about the legend in some way—three dozen at last check."

"Thank you, Althy." There weren't a lot of people who believed me, but Althy, at least, was willing to give me the benefit of the doubt.

The next few hours passed in silence. I pored through an

unnamed collection of first-century manuscripts allegedly passed down from the first age, and a few passages struck me as odd. The feeling grew worse the longer I continued reading.

"I think I might have found something."

Likh and Althy came to peer over my shoulder as I pointed at the text and read aloud. *"Blade that Soars cloaked his lover in moonlight and wove stars into her hair. He gave Dancing Wind the brightest and most beautiful of gemstones to wear on her graceful neck. But his love came at a price. He reserved the best of creation for her, and so the lands faltered. Trees and plants failed to take root, and the people cried out for sustenance. Many rose in revolt against the god they once loved, but Blade that Soars was a cruel tyrant, twisted by his passions. At his command, unseemly creatures rose from the ground, seven in number, and suppressed the people's uprisings."*

"Wait," Likh said. "That's not right. It was Hollow Knife who conspired to taint the land because he lusted after his brother's power, right?"

I continued reading. *"Blade that Soars feared he would be overcome when he was unaware and sought to entrust his being to the one he cherished above all. At his behest, Dancing Wind carried a part of his heart within hers, and a greater part of her heart dwelled within his. She would never betray him, he believed, if he commanded a portion of her soul as well."*

"Romantic guy," Likh grunted.

"According to this, Blade that Soar's brother, Hollow Knife, ferreted out the whereabouts of that heartsglass in an effort to save the people. *'Help me, Dancing Wind,' Hollow Knife implored the* goddess. 'Help me take Blade that Soars' heart, and we can make the world whole again.'"

Althy frowned. "From what we've been taught, Dancing Wind speaks those lines, not Hollow Knife."

That was true. In the legend as I knew it, a power-hungry Hollow Knife convinced Dancing Wind's envious sister, Little Tears, to steal Blade that Soars' heartsglass to merge with his own and create godsheart. He then tried to bend the world into his own making, creating the daeva to carry out his plans. But Hollow Knife was defeated when Dancing Wind merged *her* heartsglass with Blade that Soars', bringing the god back to life to vanquish his cruel brother and exile Little Tears, who became the first bone witch.

"There is no other mention of Dancing Wind after this point," I said, scanning the rest of the pages. "In the tale we know, Blade that Soars broke his heart into three parts and sacrificed two of them to heal the land. There's none of that in this text. Listen to this: *But before he could use his brother's heartsglass, Hollow Knife found himself betrayed. For Little Tears still harbored feelings for Blade that Soars and sought to save his life by fusing half her heartsglass with his. And in doing so, she revived him and acquired part of his Darkened magic.*

"*Blade that Soars struck Hollow Knife and tried to take the shadowglass. Caught unawares and knowing his brother would succeed, Hollow Knife halted the spell before it reached completion. He was overpowered by his sibling.*

"*But the unmanning of Blade that Soars' heart made him*

weak. He could only banish Hollow Knife to the underworld, where he was to wander among the ruins of the dead for all eternity. At the moment of his exile, Hollow Knife turned his anger and the last of his strength toward Little Tears, who had deserted his cause for her love of his brother.

"'No longer will you be able to use life's magic for your own' was his curse. 'Your influence shall be limited to the ways of the Dark and of the dead. You will never be able to give away your heart again, for you shall be alone until the day you unmake your treachery and see my will done.

"And so Little Tears, the first of the Dark, fled. Hollow Knife's final blow severed her connection with Blade that Soars. Part of Blade that Soars' angry spirit dwells forever within the lands as an undying wraith, fueling the continual death and rebirth of his seven demon spawn. And so both brothers died, and a mountain grew in their place."

"That definitely isn't a *darashi oyun* I've ever seen performed," Althy admitted.

"But that's impossible!" Likh burst out. "Are you saying Hollow Knife wasn't the villain, and that Blade that Soars—"

"Was," I finished grimly. If this was true, then it meant Aenah had been right all along.

*T*HEY MADE ELEGANT WEAPONS, THE *Lady Zoya's* asha. They lined the ship's stern, their backs like jeweled cannons, arms raised like exquisitely drawn arrows. They were danger wearing lipstick and rouge, and their fierceness shone even greater than their beauty.

I could not see the runes they fashioned around themselves— not at first. The brooch the Dark asha gave me grew hot against my breast, and then I saw their hands shape thread and needle out of air, crank and wheel from ether, weaving soft, invisible silks that danced across the edges of my periphery.

Their results were undeniable. The billowing winds behind us were a testament to the ashas' power, and our ship sped faster than any I had been on. It sang across the water, our bow barreling through the foamy barricades of the sea. The sailors cried and prayed and cursed, but by the second hour, they had fallen silent, content to cling desperately to anything that was bolted down. They stared, awed and fearing, at the women in their flowing hua, with glinting suns and stars twisted into their hair, as the ship raced across the Swiftsea through no power of their own.

I could not study the bone witch's letters as often as I wanted, for the swaying ship and fierce waves gave me little time for balance, much less scrutiny. Already some of what she wrote had disquieted me, *and not for the first time, I wondered if she had summoned me for my expertise in songs or for some other purpose entirely.*

Lord Fox and Princess Inessa talked quietly with the captain, assessing the damages to expect upon arrival at Kion. Lady Zoya had provided a list of casualties and confirmed no acquaintances on that list.

"It was deliberate, then," Lord Fox said hoarsely. "There's something in Kion she's looking for. But what? Most of the elder asha died in Daanoris." He turned to the Heartforger. "What do you think?"

Lord Khalad's gaze was trained on the setting sun as the ship flew toward it. The vessel's hull hit a large wave and leaped into the air, but at Zoya's orders, the ship settled smoothly to skim the currents without slowing. "She never told me about returning to Kion," he said. "I am as much in the dark as you are. Perhaps—" His voice hitched, the rest of his words lost amid the spray splattering the deck.

"Zoya," Lord Fox asked, "did anyone see my sister leaving the city afterward?"

"No. She swooped in with only the azi. As I said, we saw no other daeva."

The man slammed his fist against the railing in frustration. "What is she up to? If she harms anyone again, I…I…"

He leaned over the edge, breathing heavily, but when he righted himself, the agony was gone. His dark gaze was focused on the water, as if seeking his reflection in every turbulent crest and tide.

"Send a pigeon to Parmina if the army has not yet left Daanorian borders," he said, voice like hammered steel. "And send another to Odalia, to Kance. If the daeva aren't with her, then Ankyo

may not have been her true target. She could be planning another attack elsewhere."

"Zahid couldn't find out where she and the azi *disappeared to."*

"Because she's still in Ankyo." Lord Fox said grimly. "Despite everything between us, I know how she thinks, know what she would do in my place and what I would do in hers. She wouldn't come to Ankyo, to the Willows, and have her azi *blow its three-headed fires only to leave again without explanation. Not after what she said in Daanoris. She's in Kion. She's waiting for us. I'll stake my life on it."*

3

THERE WAS NO AUTHOR'S NAME on the volume I read aloud
from, no title to distinguish it from the rest. An inter-
view with Istera's head librarian revealed that it was the oldest
manuscript they had, preceding the next version of the Blade that
Soars legend by many years and dispelling any theories that it
was a corruption of a previous text. The manuscript talked about
other beloved stories—the lives of the Five Great Heroes, early
battles between Tresean and Daanorian epics—but with barely a
word changed.

"Vernasha of the Roses wrote the version of the narrative we
know today," Althy mused thoughtfully.

"Are you suggesting she changed it deliberately?" Kalen
asked, and Likh gasped at the implication. "But why?"

"She may have had access to other documents since lost to
time. She ruled Ankyo, after all. And as the city's first asha, she would

have vetted most of its books." Althy turned to Councilor Ludvig. "Are there any experts in ancient legends still living in Istera?"

The man thought for a few moments, stroking at his beard. "I can think of one, yes. Garindor Sverrthiya lives in Farsun and is the preeminent historian when it comes to asha mythology."

"Garindor? That's not an Isteran name," said Kalen.

"It isn't. Garindor originally came from Drycht. He sought refuge here many years ago."

"That's some refuge," Likh said. "Istera is about the farthest kingdom from Drycht as one can get."

"It is a disgrace that Drycht do not honor their intellectuals the same way we do in Kion," Councilor Ludvig agreed. "Drycht has always been a paradise for despots. When King Aadil wrested power from King Adhitaya and the royal house of Narsethi, politics changed drastically. King Adhitaya was not himself a good man, as you might know. When the revolution happened, he was killed, and his son Omid went missing. In his first few years of rule, Aadil showed signs of intelligence, of enlightenment. The kingdom enjoyed a golden age of song and stories. Though that changed soon enough. I shall talk to Rendor and see what he can do to assist us in making contact with Garindor."

"Your hunch was right all along, little *uchenik*," Rahim remarked with a nod toward me, as the Isteran adviser left us. "Even in Tresea, I grew up on tales of Blade that Soars and the villainy of Hollow Knife. It seems inconceivable that this was a lie."

"But why?" Likh was still shaken. "Why would Vernasha change her story?"

"We don't know yet, Likh," Althy said gently. "Let us see what Lord Garindor has to say before passing judgment."

Likh's shoulders slumped. "Vernasha of the Roses was a peerless warrior! She was Kion's first asha!"

"Did you know her well enough to say that, little one?" Rahim asked. "Did she tell you her favorite colors, her favorite dress? It's easy to look at a hero and deny their human flaws. Many heroes in my childhood were blackguards in their own right, and the only reason they are lauded still is because they are but Tresean." The large man frowned. "But this too is a question I would like answered."

"And that doesn't change what being an asha is all about." Khalad's voice was soft, hushed by the cold and tempered in the presence of old books. He put his hand on Likh's shoulder. "You can't honor the past if you don't know what that past is. I would much rather know the truth than live in ignorant bliss, even if it destroys all I've come to believe. Tradition isn't always honorable. If it was, then you'd have been an asha for years, without opposition."

Likh stared at him. The colors in his heartsglass swirled rapidly, and I thought he would speak. But Khalad's hand was only a friendly gesture, and the oblivious Heartforger could not hear the wanting in Likh's silence, his unspoken confession.

The young boy-asha only nodded, bidding his heart to be silent. I exhaled, releasing a quiet breath I had not realized I was holding. It required everything not to intervene. It took Kalen and I years to breathe in the same rhythm. They would find their own pace.

"How are you feeling?" Kalen asked me quietly, so no others could hear.

I closed my eyes briefly. "If Aenah was right about this story, then what if she was right about everything?" The book of powerful runes the Faceless had given me remained in Mykaela's possession, but I already knew the spells within by heart. The elders knew them too, Aenah had claimed, but had hidden their knowledge. *The elders teach you the necessary runes to put down daeva and risk your life for their cause.* The woman was long-since dead, but the words she taunted me with remained. *Why would they teach you the very runes that would allow you to rise above them?*

My heartsglass was silver. How long before Aenah's other prediction came to pass? When would my heart fade to black and gives itself to darkness?

Kalen smiled. "Whatever the truth, we will find it," he said simply, confidently, and I believed him.

·· 〜 ··

That Garindor Sverrthiya lived in Farsun was not entirely accurate; he lived in a small house on the outskirts of the city, bordering the Runeswoods. It was at his insistence, Councilor Ludvig explained, and not because of any Isteran enmity.

A pale-faced, sickly-looking lad of about twenty answered our knock. Althy glanced at his heartsglass and rolled up her sleeves. "Off to bed you go, young man."

The boy stared. "I...I don't..."

"No back talk. You're ill with fever, and you shouldn't be up. Where's your master?"

"Right here." A white-haired Drychta came into view, looking fitter and healthier than his assistant. His heartsglass hung from a plain leather cord, pulsing a soft purple. He looked surprised to see us, then focused on Councilor Ludvig. "What is going on, milord?"

"My apologies for the intrusion, Garindor. We have visitors from Kion who require your expertise, and it is a matter of urgency."

"A matter of urgency, eh?" The man adjusted his spectacles. "And asha too, by the look of some of you. As my expertise lies in the past, which requires no hurrying, it's a strange petition indeed. I am sorry for my assistant, Yarrod. He has been ill the last few days and should've been resting."

"I will see to that immediately, Lord Garindor," Althy promised. "You all go ahead while I tend to him."

Garindor led us deeper into the house, which was filled with the oddest assortment of contraptions and bric-a-brac. Three-headed statues stared coldly down at us from high shelves, and small paintings depicted scenes of both cruel and unusual beauty—a magnificent giant of a deity stomping on an army of dying soldiers, seven-tusked elephants burst from the ground to destroy crops and livestock—all painted in bright, almost garish colors. Cruel-looking weapons of old decorated the walls.

Garindor smiled at our reactions. "This was why I chose to sequester myself from the rest of the city. Isterans are a kind and noble people, but they do not understand why I keep these instruments of destruction, even if only for study." He sighed. "I abhor Drychta policy as much as they, having lived through many of them myself. But it is difficult to rid yourself of a festering that has been ingrained into your very bones. It is not a contradiction to try to make sense of a culture that you criticize with all your being. Would you mind if I smoke? I have some very good Adra-al cigars."

None of us minded, and Ludvig even accepted one. "We were told you know much of asha mythology," he began, puffing at his cheroot.

"Ah, that I did. It was one of the reasons I was chased out of Drycht. To venerate women, they said, is to diminish men. How one can lead to the other is a question they have not yet answered, if you discount the threats on my life when they had nothing else to say." Garindor settled himself on one of the ratty chairs in the room, toeing a few parchments out of the way, and indicated that we should do the same. "What can I do for you?"

"My name is Tea."

"Tea?" Garindor leaned forward, his eyes wide. "Begging any offense, milady, but I have heard of you. You are the Dark asha who tames daeva, as Sakmeet had...but you tame the fiercest daeva. They call you Tea of the Embers—a sign of respect, of course. Your *azi* is mostly responsible for such a title, being quite a striking creature. It is an honor to meet you. Lords Kalen and Khalad I know of, and the famous Rahim Arrankan! Queen Deira has been looking forward to your arrival."

The Tresean beamed.

"Altaecia is well known here; I know many doctors who can

attest to her healing arts. And it is rare to have two more beautiful girls in my household, much less asha of such distinction."

Likh squirmed. "I am an asha, but I am not a girl, milord."

Surprised, Garindor regarded him more closely. "I was not always a good man in Drycht, my dear," he said, his voice kind and honest. "I can only profess to be better now than I once was. Had you been born in Adra-al or Rasha you would not have had an easy time, but I am glad Kion thinks differently. You are very beautiful, either way."

Likh blushed. "Th-thank you."

I continued with purpose, "We've found a book in the Isteran library contradicting what we know of Blade that Soars' and Dancing Wind's origin."

"Was that your concern?" Garindor chuckled. "Few people know of it. The original is not quite as compelling and romantic as the famous one penned by Vernasha."

"You mean it's true?" Kalen asked. "That's the oldest incarnation of the legend?"

Garindor nodded. "The volume in the Isteran library has no known author, but we believe it was written by Rashnu the Just himself."

"Rashnu of the Five Great Heroes?" Rahim exclaimed.

"Rashnu was the budding historian of the five and served as their chronicler. Samples of his writing exist in other works, and they were easy enough to compare to determine authenticity."

"But why would Vernasha write a different version?" Khalad asked.

"It is difficult to understand someone's motivations with so little of their text available." Garindor spread his hands. "We have even less of Vernasha's writings than we do of Rashnu's. She only kept one diary, and it was not a personal journal. It dealt with the problems of founding a city. She may have intended to use the legend as the basis for the *darashi oyun* and knew that her version would make for a more interesting performance."

"The original version mentions a First Harvest," Kalen said. "What does that mean?"

"That too is a question every scholar would dearly like to know. Rashnu was Drychta—an enlightened man who would have railed at the behavior of his descendants today, I might add—and his writings were in his mother tongue. Old Drychta was hieroglyphic, and this 'First Harvest' is in a similar syntax as one might write 'runeberries.' From context, this 'First Harvest' is the only plant of its kind, immortal until plucked."

Tucking the cigar between his teeth, Garindor selected a book from one of his shelves. "Rashnu refers to the First Harvest in one other document. Here: *I have seen those strange blooms with my own eyes. Its name does not accord with its appearance. I have seen lovelier roses flowered, seen taller, prouder sycamore trees. But when brave Ashi reached for the sapling in curiosity, I felt its magic flow through the air, cracking like a whip. We were not worthy.*

"*'It is not ours to take!' I screamed, but too late. For an instant, I saw the tree, a Sacred Tree, beckoning me into light. Then it blinded me, sent me to my knees, threw me through the air.*

"*When I recovered my wits, my companions were gone. Where*

they once stood, the First Harvest remained—small and unimposing, deceiver, murderer. The best men and women I knew, who with me had survived countless wars and hardships, were felled by an incongruous sapling. May the light save their souls, and may the light save me."

Khalad leaned forward. "That was Rashnu's account of the death of his fellow Great Heroes, is it not? At the Ring of Worship in Drycht? But what's a Sacred Tree?"

"Yes, Rashnu was never the same after that. They say the Ring of Worship is where the Great Creator first breathed life into the world, and that his sons' sins corrupted the area. None has ever returned from it, aside from Rashnu. Even Vernasha made her final journey there, then passed from men's sight forever. Others have made the expedition never to be heard from again. If the dry, desert heat didn't wring those poor adventurers dry, perhaps they too were victims of this strange *Sacred Tree*. Daeva refuse to enter the area, it is said. If the First Harvest is within, then there is something that not only prevents its fruit from being plucked, but also kills anyone who—"

A scream rang through the air. It came from the other room. Kalen was quick on his feet, and we all hurried behind.

Althy was sprawled on the floor. Garindor's young assistant hunched over his bed, horrible noises emanating from his throat. His eyes were wide and bloodshot.

As we looked on, horrified, his face twisted. Clumps of hair dropped from his head as his skull flattened and shrank, but his scarlet gaze grew as his eyelids and brows disappeared and a snout sprouted from the remains of his nose. His fingers fused together, the tips turning razor-sharp, until he was no longer recognizable as human. Instead, what stood before us was a grayish-green creature that resembled a praying mantis, taller than Rahim, with several rows of teeth along its mandible. It screeched, a horrible, air-ripping sound, and reached for Althy.

My fingers flew, the *Compulsion* rune flaring bright before me. "Stop!" I commanded, but the magic ricocheted off the creature's scales. Stunned by my failure, I attempted the *Resurrecting* rune, which I used to control daeva. It had the same effect.

Kalen's sword barred the creature from striking Althy. He made a quick movement with his other hand, and his blade burst into flame. Hissing, the creature stepped back. Likh was quick to braid a series of *Wind* around it, pinning it in place.

Garindor gasped. "What happened to him?"

"I don't know," Althy said. It was rare to see her so frightened. "I've never seen anything like this before."

Kalen added his strength to Likh's, reinforcing their grip on the monster. Still, Kalen held his burning sword aloft should the monster shake itself free. "What do we do?" Kalen asked me.

"I can't do anything. Dark runes won't work on it." Fear swirled at the center of my heartsglass. An *azi* responded to my beck and call, but it meant nothing to this historian's assistant. With this new form of daeva, I was helpless. "Khalad?"

The Heartforger was just as stumped. When I looked at his face, I found my own emotions mirrored. "I don't know what it is, but it's not a daeva."

"I'll send for Rendor immediately," Councilor Ludvig said

brusquely. "We'll have as many men as he can spare to contain it. I am sorry, Garindor, but we have no other choice."

"I understand," the Drychta said weakly, sinking into a nearby chair. "Not daeva. These—these are foul, Blighted creatures. Yarrod, my poor boy…"

Tea? Are you all right? Tea!

Fox. I counted my heartbeats and rearranged my emotions, trotting calm and assurance to the forefront so they were the first emotions he read off me. *I'm okay. We just had an incident.*

An incident my foot. I saw that thing!

We have the situation under control, Fox. How's Inessa?

Probably wondering why I marched out of the room. Are you sure you're okay?

I promise.

There's something… I can't explain it, but there's a strange emptiness between us. It wasn't there before.

I stiffened, taking care not to think too deeply about my heartsglass to avert suspicion. *Must be because we're so far away. We've never been separated by kingdoms before.*

I suppose so. I felt him relax, though not completely, because that wouldn't be Fox. He pressed me. *What in the seven hells is going on there?*

I don't know. It's not daeva, Fox. I can't control it.

Then what is it?

I wish I knew, I thought grimly, staring at the snapping face, the wriggling limbs of the abomination before me. *I wish I knew.*

*T*HOUGHT IT SILLY, THE FIRST *time I heard it," Lady Zoya said, long hair streaming behind her as she scanned the sea with a practiced eye. Under her command, the ship purred like a cat, keel pointed unerringly toward the future. "It's an old legend. Myth. Who cares what some senile old fool wrote centuries ago? We don't deal in ancient stories and potters' tales. What does that have to do with the here and now? Blade that Soars can't help us. Hollow Knife can't help us. There's nothing more useless than the devout follower of a dead god, unless it's the dead god himself."*

She tore her gaze away long enough to survey me head to foot, as if I were an unknown specimen, and turned away again. "I'm not as big on tales as Tea was," she said, her flinty, gray eyes once more marking the horizon before her. "Old tales aren't going to change the world. I've performed the darashi oyun for a few years now, and I'd never once believed in the words, only in the dance. That's what's important, isn't it? The things you do. But lately, I don't know. I never knew about the Blight rune. Never realized there were blighted creatures until I disemboweled one myself. What else didn't the elder asha tell us? What else hadn't Tea told us?" Her hands clenched the ship's bow. "Why would she attack Ankyo?"

I had no answer. All that I knew of the Lady Zoya, I learned from the Dark asha. They were former enemies, rivals and friends, confidants and close companions. And now Lady Zoya directed her anger against the bone witch into the whirling winds that jettisoned salt and other furies into the air.

"We had a bad run of blighted a month ago," she continued. "Fox saved us. He fought off a couple single-handedly, saved Inessa and Her Majesty's life. Even had time to rescue Hestia of all people, that ungrateful derriere, as Polaire often liked to say. She would have been blight fodder if I had the choice. I'm the worse of us two, but even I draw the line at what Tea's done. I could understand why she hated them, but not why she would allow her hatred to harm everyone else.

"Maybe Tea was right to tell you her story. It's no use keeping emotions bottled up inside. Sooner or later, you burst with all you want to say. Shadi would always listen, but Shadi's in Ankyo and I'm still here." She stared at me. "Well, go on. You said you had a song to tell, didn't you? The crew is clinging to one another, but here you are, holding on to those papers like they're your lifeline. What do you want to know, while I'm in a mood to talk?"

I looked down at the letters. I had been tempted many, many times to skip forward, to read the end of those pages first—but something held me back. It was not the right way to read a story. "Do you miss her?"

She seemed taken aback by the question, her slate eyes meeting mine again. "Yes," she said. After another pause: "And no. I miss what we used to be. Did she ever tell you how I used to push her around? I never gave her an apology, and she never asked for one. We just kept on until the moment for it had passed. I wish all were as it used to be."

Her fingers fluttered, and the ship picked up speed. "But those days are over. She harmed my friends, Bard. I lost so many good people these last few months."

"So did she."

Lady Zoya smiled with lips a shade of cruel. "It's not considered 'losing them' if you're responsible for their deaths, Bard. She torched my city. What kind of hatred runs that deep? That's the quandary, isn't it? Besides, if she goes down, we lose Fox. Why take you into her confidence? What does she have left to say?"

She stopped speaking as more heavy gusts of wind roared by.

"What does she have left to say?" she asked quietly. Her gaze turned to the letters I held, and I realized it was not a rhetorical question. "Tell me."

4

NONE OF ISTERA'S HISTORIANS KNEW much of runic magic, despite the wealth of research on hand. Having red heartsglass prevented them from seeing its effects. Sakmeet's silver made her the foremost expert, but her notes were all we had left to go by.

Lord Garindor was the next best thing, but even he admitted his limitations. "Those of us with purple heartsglass see magic on a very different spectrum than those with silver," he explained. "We simply cannot observe some weaves that are obvious to all asha."

We had returned to the library while the king and his councilors debated the fate of the historian's assistant-turned-creature. That this daeva-like being had started as a human, not an unnatural aberration, had shaken the Isterans. If there was a rune capable of turning people into monsters, King Rendorvik argued, then perhaps there was a way to change them back.

But the librarians—bless their staunchly patient hearts, as they worked to supply us with information—spent their lives dedicated to these books and still had little idea of the runes we sought. It was not likely that we would succeed, our experiences as asha notwithstanding.

Still, Althy threw herself into the ongoing inquiry. Likh appeared distracted. He kept abandoning the volume he was perusing to prowl the room, lost in thought. Kalen and Khalad were helping guard the strange creature that had once been Yarrod. Lord Garindor, though rattled, had insisted on accompanying us, determined to help.

"I can do little for my assistant's condition," he pointed out, "but what expertise I can offer lies here, among these old books. Permit me to assist you in any way I can."

"You are very kind, milord," Althy told him gently. "But I'm afraid we don't know what questions to ask, knowing very little of this ourselves."

"Are there any generalities regarding your research that you can tell me? Perhaps I can narrow the field."

"We seek information on any runic spells that could cause this transformation. We have never encountered anything like this in the Willows before."

The man thought about it. "No, I cannot say that I am acquainted with such a spell. I have looked through many manuscripts on runes, but our experiments were restricted without a silver heart to guide us. As such, we thought it best to turn over our research to the Isteran asha in the hopes they would make better sense of them, though they also found little. Sakmeet was always very private about her own findings."

"If she knew anything about these runes, she didn't write about them." Likh was going through Sakmeet's old notes, and he sounded frustrated. "Her handwriting is difficult to read."

"What else can you tell us about Blade that Soars' and Dancing Wind's origins?" Althy asked Lord Garindor. "Perhaps we can find another connection there."

"Ah. Unlike its popular version, the legend says little about Dancing Wind, for she had almost no agency in the story. Her role was simply that of Blade that Soars' lover. A few colleagues have even gone so far as to theorize that her abrupt disappearance suggests she died long before Hollow Knife stole his brother's heart—that her death may have triggered Blade that Soars' war against the world.

"In the *darashi oyun*, which Vernasha penned, Dancing Wind takes on Hollow Knife's role, and the latter is cast as its main villain. We scholars thought it was nothing more than a romanticized version of the legend. Scholars look down on embellishments, but we never thought Vernasha had another motive."

"That Dancing Wind and Blade that Soars shared two halves of the same soul?" Rahim asked.

"I am afraid you are mistaken, Lord Arrakan." The scholar took off his spectacles, wiping them vigorously. "Blade that Soars and Hollow Knife are two halves of the same whole. They are brothers. For Blade that Soars to gain power, he would have to take Hollow Knife's heartsglass, not that of his lover.

"It was not Blade that Soars who formed the world. Older texts indicate a Great Creator shaped the world and begot a son for its stewardship. But then he split his child into two brothers, so their abilities were also halved. There are enough similarities between that ancient document and the Blade that Soars legend for us to say with certainty that this Great Creator was their father.

"Blade that Soars resented his father's decision to make them two, however, for it greatly diminished his strength. He had wished for a perfect world, free from pain and suffering, and to do so, he strove to be his sire's equal in power. It was he, not the Creator, who taught magic to his subjects. Hollow Knife criticized his brother's actions, fearing the chaos that could come from the spells of imperfect creatures."

"Aenah always said Hollow Knife was the true hero," I murmured, remembering what Aenah had told me while she languished in the Odalian dungeons, pretending she had had no relationship with Telemaine. "It was why the Faceless worshipped him."

"But isn't that good?" Likh asked. "To want a perfect world?"

"To be perfect without suffering means no change. If you know neither hurt nor hardship, then you will not know the strength they can summon within a person. What is life's meaning if you cannot distinguish between happiness and sorrow?"

"It would have been nice for the Great Creator to make the world with a little less suffering though," Likh said sadly.

Garindor smiled briefly. "Blade that Soars certainly agreed with you. He believed that the world would be destroyed by its flaws. So he offered magic as a means to address those ills, for his people to forge a better life. But even he abused this power, giving the best of it to Dancing Wind and subjugating his dissidents.

"Hollow Knife determined the only way to stop his brother was to take his heartsglass and merge it with his own, to double his strength and restore the world in the image his father had originally intended—one without magic—even if it meant forfeiting his own life. And because Blade that Soars gave the core of his heartsglass to Dancing Wind, Hollow Knife had to take hers."

He shifted some books off a heavy pile and selected one volume, opening it to reveal Drychta writing. "The unnamed book you referenced is only a piece of the puzzle. It is the oldest book written in the common tongue that talks of the legend, but *this* Drychta book—*this* precedes it by at least a year. Few people study Drychta, so it tends to be overlooked by even the best Isteran scholars. But I know this manuscript's value; it was discovered twenty years ago, hidden within one of Drycht's numerous mountains. It lay in a strange cave filled with unnatural flora, unearthed only because of a sudden rock slide. King Aadil decreed its contents heretical because it criticized the absolute rule of kings, and many of my colleagues were killed for defending the tome. This book is more important than my life, and I barely escaped with both intact. I came to Istera because they treasured and honored knowledge in all its forms—Aadil did not."

"What does it say?" Althy asked. "I can speak a little Drychta, but not to read."

"Let me translate. *'Help me, Little Tears,'* Hollow Knife

implored the other goddess. 'Help me take Blade that Soars' heart, so that I can make the world whole again.'"

He paused. "Until this point, the text is the same as in the other book, but there are passages in this Drychta book that the former did not have: *And upon taking his brother's heartsglass, still stained with his lover's blood, did Hollow Knife turn to slaughter the seven creatures of Blade that Soars. From each, he drew a shining stone, a different color for each carcass. He took these gems into his own heartsglass with much suffering, but his will was true, and all seven beasts were revived under his bidding. No longer were they ravening beasts that terrorized the people. They became docile and obedient. And with them, his heartsglass shone as black as Blade that Soars' shone bright. Then he reached for the First Harvest, to join dark and light to create shadowglass.*

"The text here then follows the other book's. *But before he could use his brother's—*Lady Tea?"

I rose from my chair, hands clenched. I stared down at Sakmeet's notes, the letters blurring together. "Dark into light," I said hoarsely. "Shadowglass. Althy, this is all in Aenah's book. *To you, seeking Hollow Knife's path: present yourself to the mountain for judgment. If proven worthy, arm yourself with a heartsglass of black, where love's blood had shed over. Boil seven daeva's bezoars separately, and drink a vial's worth of their waters. Weave Compulsion in the air; its heart shall reveal itself to you. Take it into your heartsglass, and be born anew.*"

I knew that shadowglass spell; I had committed it to memory nearly two years ago, and it was now a mantra, buried so deep within my psyche that nothing could pull it loose. I had pored over those words for so long that sometimes they came easier to me than my own name. Shadowglass was the reason the Faceless had tried to take Kance's heartsglass. Aenah had died for the chance. She had tried to kill me for it.

Polaire had paid the price instead.

And what was the next part of that spell? *The unity of seven into darksglass and Five into lightsglass is the key. Merge both with the First Harvest and be born anew, with shadowglass to do as you see fit.*

"The last place I would have looked to find confirmation is with that Faceless's book," Althy said grimly. "But you're right."

"I'm sorry," Lord Garindor said. "I don't quite follow."

"We're in trouble," Kalen interrupted grimly as he strode in, Khalad trailing after him. "Tea, soldiers have reported sightings of the *zarich*. It's left the Runeswood."

Likh paled.

I gritted my teeth. "Has it attacked anyone?" The Isterans hadn't seen the creature since Sakmeet died. For what reason would it leave the safety of its home?

Kalen shook his head. "The Isteran soldiers have been briefed for occasions like this. They're keeping their distance but tracking its movements as best as they can."

"How is Yarrod?" Garindor asked.

"Dark magic might not do much, but runic wards still work on him," Khalad responded. "Kalen made sure of that. He's in no danger to himself or others—for now."

Althy stood, but I shook my head. "It would be better for

one of us to stay here. The wards might hold Yarrod in place, but we'll need someone close to make sure he doesn't break free. My magic is useless, but yours isn't."

The older asha paused, then nodded, still frowning. "Take care, Tea. We've never confronted the *zarich* before. That had always been Sakmeet's duty and that of her Isteran predecessors."

"I will." I started for the door and Likh followed. "What are you doing?" I asked. The boy asha shrugged. "You might need help. I'm pretty good at this now."

"Promise me you'll stay at a reasonable distance."

I marched toward the palace entrance. Already soldiers were running back and forth, as orders were called out over the din.

What's happening, Tea?

Fox. *Tell Mykaela that a* zarich *has been sighted near Farsun. I'm off to take care of it.*

Be careful. I could feel his worry, his frustration. That he wasn't here with me was eating him up.

I will. Kalen's here. You know he has my back. Anything happening in your neck of the woods?

The elders are up to something, but they haven't made any moves yet. From what Zoya and Shadi could gather, they've been recalling some of the asha who'd been contracted out to other kingdoms. I'll tell you more when we get back. Don't make any rash decisions.

Have I ever?

Wordlessly, I called for Chief, and soon my Gorvekan horse came cantering. Kalen was already astride his own stallion, Likh and Khalad scrambling up their own steeds.

It was easy enough to pinpoint the *zarich*'s location. We only had to follow the reports the soldiers provided and investigate its fresh tracks leading from the Runeswood.

The beast hadn't wandered too far from its home. We found it settled by a frozen stream on the edge of the forest leading toward the River of Peace, which marked the boundary between Istera and Tresea.

The *zarich* was a disconcerting creature to behold at first. It resembled an upright goat but was the size of a small barn. The five horns growing around its head glistened from the snow, and its face was overrun by a mass of eyes that never closed all at once. Despite its mammalian appearance and its cloven hooves, the *zarich* was overtly reptilian, with scaled skin and a long snout protruding from its crowd of eyes, reminding me of illustrations I'd seen of long-snouted swamp creatures that inhabited parts of northern Yadosha.

The creature let out a soft, slithering hiss as we approached, but it did not attack. It was not like any daeva behavior I had encountered before.

"What's it doing?" Likh asked nervously.

"I'm not sure." I drew the *Raising* rune and, carefully, entered the creature's mind. What I found was not so much thoughts as impulses, strange yet familiar, repulsive and enticing. As I probed deeper, the *zarich* put up little resistance.

Somewhere in another corner of my mind, I could feel Fox's thoughts drift toward me, tensed like he could ride into battle in an instant to aid me.

The *azi* responded too. It uttered a soft, plaintive sound. The *azi* was not angry, nor was it combative. I could feel its presence slide through my mind, reaching out to the *zarich*.

The *zarich* blinked its eyes at us and then turned. It padded deeper into the forest. The beasts' emotions tumbled into and against each other until one stood out.

Follow.

"Are you serious?" Kalen asked as I adopted its suggestion, moving deeper into the woods after it.

"It doesn't want to fight. The least I can do is see what it wants to show me."

"And you find nothing wrong with that?" he muttered, but he and Likh followed me anyway.

At a small clearing, at the foot of a magnificent pine tree, the *zarich* began to dig. Its massive hooves kicked up ice and frozen dirt with little effort. For five minutes, it pawed at the ground until it dug a considerable hole. Then it turned to look at me and bleated.

I sensed it. There was another presence within the *zarich*'s mind. I could feel it gathering as if to take control. I remembered my time in Daanoris—of the Faceless, Usij, and his past attempts to entrap me in this manner with the *savul*. I recoiled at the memory and reacted on instinct, putting everything I had into one word.

"Die!"

The *zarich* didn't fight me. Its head lowered, as its many eyes drifted closed, its limbs settling against the ground. It let one last cry, melancholy and regretful, and ceased to move. Still braced for an unexpected attack, I waited, probing its head once more, but its mind was gone, and so was the other presence along with it. I felt Fox's relieved sigh, felt the *azi* turn away with an unhappy wail.

"Was that supposed to happen?" Likh asked shakily. "Not that I'm complaining, but that was easier than I hoped. I wish they were all like that."

"It wasn't intending to fight." I moved to the daeva's prone body and fished out my knife. With its blade, I searched at the base of its skull, where all five horns circled around. Likh turned pale as I slid past the brains and the black blood, finally locating and bringing out another bezoar, its bright surface shining despite the gore.

"I'm sorry," I told the beast quietly. I couldn't risk anyone entering my mind again, however friendly the *zarich* appeared to be.

Kalen lowered himself down the hole. "This is all that's in here," he reported, lifting out a small sack. Deftly, he undid the knots.

"It's paper!" Likh burst out.

"It's more than that," Kalen said grimly, scanning the contents. "One is signed by Sakmeet herself. The other…is in Vernasha's handwriting."

"So the *zarich* remembered Sakmeet's instructions, even after she'd died?"

"She must have had a strong bond with the daeva, similar to Tea's bond with the *azi*." Kalen handed me Sakmeet's letter to read. There was a strange symbol drawn across the page—a kind of mountain, by the looks of it.

If you are reading this, then I am gone. For the love of Anahita, say nothing of these findings to the elders of Kion.

I have lived longer than most bone witches, long by even asha standards. But the elders will reject what we Isteran witches have discovered. They will destroy my books should they learn what I have recorded.

My predecessor, Parika, told me a story passed down to her by the previous bone witches of Istera. It is the story of how the elders of Kion came to Farsun under the pretense of diplomacy but sought in secret to destroy certain volumes in Istera's library. A Dark asha, Talyri, knew that hiding the books would be impossible; the elders had demanded a complete list from the Isteran king. But one book was unnamed and escaped the librarians' notice. Only that text was she able to save.

As she watched, horrified, the elders destroyed the other books, and the old king did nothing to stop them. Talyri managed to steal a letter written by Vernasha herself, which one of the elders had possessed. She—and I—stand by its truth. She guarded the unnamed book for the rest of her life, as did her successors. As did I.

It is a terrible thing, to force a witch to hide from her fellow sisters. It is a terrible thing to destroy a book in order to better live a lie.

The Kion oracle once told me that my writings would one day change the world. I wished I had asked her if I would change it for the better or for the worse…

I leave you with a symbol I found in my research: the mark of the People of the Shadow. My predecessor told me it marks those who guard the secrets to shadowglass. Perhaps it can be of use to you, my dear reader.

I wish I had the strength to denounce Kion's lies. But I am too old, too tired. Safe within Istera's tolerance, I have neglected my duties to my sisters in the southern kingdoms. I am sorry. May this redeem me.

Shaking, I gently laid Sakmeet's letter aside, and picked up the other page.

"What does it say?" Kalen asked.

"Beware the Dark asha," I read in Vernasha's flowing hand, "for the only good bone witch is one deprived of heartsglass. Temper them, weaken them, collar them if you must. They are Little Tears's seed, none of whom must come to pass."

*T*HE VERITABLE ASHA LADY ALTAECIA *waited as the last of the winds deposited us at Ankyo's port. On any other day, the harbor would be alive with the sound of merchant ships and merchant greed, a jarring cacophony of language and dialects that had everyone from Gorvekai hunters from the Srevny Fjord down to the camel eaters of Karinsha haggling and bargaining for precious cargo. But a blockade was in progress, with soldiers outnumbering the traders fifty to one. We were one of only three docked ships, and for good reason.*

Smoke curled out of the city of Ankyo, twisting against the evening heat. From the pier, I could see fallen houses, the pristine, white walls common in Kion architecture reduced to rubble and dust. Teams of masons labored to clear the streets, but many citizens, stricken and shocked, huddled underneath the curved roofs of other surviving buildings, still clad in their weekday finest. The jewels in their hair were a discordant note among the wreckage. They were not people used to poor defenses.

Even among the wreckage and the slag, the city remained a stunning sight. Not all the structures were damaged, and many had escaped the daeva's three-headed fury unscathed. Scrub off the soot and clear away the broken timbers, and the aesthetics were intact, the way layers of dirt do not hide a girl's beauty. Ankyo always carried about it an air of perfumed danger, like elegantly dressed women with a secret—a coquettish smile behind every painted fan and a knife hidden up every silken sleeve. Their asha—epically, socially, traditionally—had always danced too close to the fires of history, tempting its flames. A burning seemed inevitable.

I had never felt comfortable in Ankyo. At least Drycht never hid its contempt of me.

The night smelled of lingering wildfire. The scent of incense was gone, but something else lay scorching in its stead. Every now and then, one of Kion's soldiers cast a wary gaze at the dark sky above, dreading an attack.

The Dark asha's description of her mentor was accurate; Lady Altaecia could have been a fishwife, if fishwives were accustomed to gravity and elegance. Her hua *was a silvery moon peeking through wisps of clouds, and it did nothing to hide her round, pleasant figure. But I could feel the power emanating from her person, knew she was a woman of importance despite her drawn face and eyes that had not known sleep for many nights.*

With her was another strange figure—a fellow Drychta, white-haired from age, with stooping shoulders and a drooping beard. But his eyes were alert and ever vigilant, making note of those who disembarked before settling curiously on me. My discomfort grew at his silent inspection.

"Got them all back safe and sound, Althy," Zoya said, "and with a couple of hours to spare." Barely were the words out of her mouth when a beautiful woman with golden skin and long braids dashed forward, enveloping her in a warm hug.

"You overexerted yourself again, Zoya," she scolded, peppering the other woman's face with kisses. *"I could tell. I told you not to."*

Zoya blushed, her sardonic expression softening. *"We wanted to return as soon as we could. No telling if Tea intends to mount another offensive in the interim."*

"What has happened while we were away?" Lord Fox asked tersely. Lord Khalad appeared preoccupied, nodding distractedly at the others before walking ahead, too occupied to even greet Lady Altaecia.

Lady Altaecia sighed, watching him leave. *"This trip will be hard on him. No word yet of where Tea has disappeared to. Her azi is nowhere in sight. But…"*

"But what, Althy?" Inessa prompted.

The older asha schooled her features, though her jaw remained set and square. *"She lurks nearby. I can almost feel her in the air, crackling with magic so subversive that not even I can see. And who is this?"*

"Only a bard, milady," I offered.

She frowned. *"Ah. The chronicler Tea dragged into this mess."* She extended a hand, but not to grip mine. *"Her letters. Where are they?"*

I paused, tightening my hold, the pages crumpling in my obstinacy. This was the only task she had given me. Venerable as Lady Altaecia was, I could not comply. The Dark asha had given them to me.

She sighed. *"We are wasting time."*

"We have had little chance to read them, given Zoya's enthusiasm for speed," Lord Fox said. *"Tea entrusted her papers to him, and he feels compelled to watch over her words. We can read the rest of them once we return."*

Lady Altaecia pursed her lips. "Very well. We must make haste for the Valerian. The Willows was the hardest hit, but whether by coincidence or from a belated sense of obligation, Tea left the Valerian untouched."

She winced. "The oracle…she forewarned us, saved us. She had been refusing visitors the last few months. We thought she was ill or worse until she reemerged a week ago and spoke of fire raining down on Ankyo, and by the time the azi arrived, we had taken the bulk of the citizens to safer ground. We would have suffered worse without her warnings."

"I hope," said the elderly Drychta beside her, "that you would give me the chance to study her letters as well, milord. I promise to treat them like I would one of my rare books and give her the due honor she deserves."

"Tea brought about Mykkie's death, however indirectly," Althy said, though the look on her face was in contrast to the harsh words. "The time to honor her has long elapsed."

A spasm of grief passed through Lord Fox's expression, though he steeled himself quickly enough. "We'll talk more at the Valerian."

"I am glad to see a fellow Drychta, even if I'd hoped the current state of affairs would be different," I said. "But how do you know the Dark asha?"

"We knew each other only briefly, kinsman, but it was enough to know her friendship. My name is Garindor Sverrthiya. I know nothing of fighting, but perhaps I can be useful elsewhere."

*T*HE LEGEND OF *B*LADE THAT *Soars poses too many questions,* Vernasha wrote. *Bone witches will demand answers we should not be at liberty to divulge. The tale tells us to use our magic to set the world right, but at the cost of magic's possession. I reject such sentiments. We can do far more by retaining what the Creator graciously bestowed upon us. To sacrifice such power holds neither merit nor results. The People of the Shadow may think to stop us, but they are few in number, and we are many.*

I intend to reframe the legend to suit our purposes. A harmless lie is better than a harmful truth. Better to wield strength in an imperfect land than to be powerless in a perfect one.

"Wow," Likh commented. "Vernasha of the Roses was kind of a bitch."

"Likh!" Rahim exclaimed, unsuccessfully curbing his laughter.

Althy had nearly drove the librarians insane, having them

pull every conceivable book Istera had about rune magic. But despite our efforts, there was nothing much to find.

They are Little Tears's seed, none of whom must come to pass. Vernasha had meant Dark asha. That was why Dark asha could command the daeva—only those who commanded the Dark could bring about shadowglass.

"Likh may have a point, Rahim," Kalen said wryly. "It seems that Kion was built on a lie."

"Nobody's going to believe us," Khalad pointed out. "The legend according to Vernasha has been too ingrained in people's beliefs. They would cling to their faith rather than see it shattered. I suspect that was what Vernasha intended all along."

"I can't believe it." Likh sounded disheartened. We had compared the letter Sakmeet had hidden to a collection of Vernasha's other works, and the writing matched perfectly. "This isn't why I wanted to be an asha."

"This shouldn't stop you from being proud to be one," Althy said firmly.

Likh stared down at his lap, downcast. Khalad cast a worried glance at him.

"It's late," the older asha went on. "A day changes nothing, and we will be back at Kion tomorrow. We'd all best get some rest."

"Althy," I said, after the others had left, "how did Mykkie kill the last Dark asha before me?" Now that the urgency had passed, I wanted my answer.

"You are persistent," my mentor said. "But I did promise

you the story in our freer moments. Her name was Illara. She
was a strong-willed novice in her own right. You remind me
a bit of her, in fact. But unlike you, she was too free with
drawing in the Dark, and she took on more than she could
handle. She grew reckless and intractable. Her heartsglass had
not even darkened yet when she botched a daeva raising and,
in a moment of madness, tried to use it to attack Arhen-Kosho.
She assaulted a small fishing community, swept it out to sea. And
while Mykkie grieved, she never faltered. She killed her charge.
It was the only way. Don't think much of it, Tea. You're different
than she was."

Althy excused herself after sharing the story, and I stared at
the paper in my hand, as if I could rearrange the words if I willed
it long enough. There was more to Vernasha's letter beyond her
admission of guilt.

The Blight *is a terrible rune,* Vernasha had instructed. *At
its command, you can twist someone beyond recognition, allow him
the form and shape of a terrible daeva—a lesser size, but as rabid.
You can perform this blight on any unsuspecting person, letting it
incubate within him for days and weeks with no one the wiser. The
result is a monster of your own making, a daeva that not even a
Dark asha can command. Any asha can create the necessary poison
to introduce into her victim's food and drink, but a bone witch must
cast the final spell. For this reason, we must deny those accursed
women this rune.*

*Still, the casting is long and complicated. The rune must be
woven into food and drink at least three times in two days, then at*

least once every three days following. Take too long and the spell will be rendered irrelevant, and you must repeat the process all over again. Once done, perform the rune one final time over the person to awaken his demons. The only known cure is a merciful death—of either the target or its summoner.

The Blight rune is a secret our elders must uphold under penalty of death. Vigilance is key.

Vernasha had scratched a strange rune on the paper that resembled a floating eye. This Delving rune glows red, she had written, should the Blight rune fester within us.

We were quick to take her advice and relieved to find that none of us had symptoms of the blight.

Kalen then tested it on poor Yarrod. The rune glowed red.

I'm surprised you're letting me in on all this, Fox murmured in my head. Not that I'm complaining.

I don't want to keep secrets from you, I responded, trying not to think about my black heartsglass, other details I hadn't told him.

What do you want me to do?

Inform Empress Alyx about this new development but ask her not to act until we return.

What about Inessa?

You'll tell her regardless of what I say.

I felt his grin. I wouldn't if you asked me to. She'll understand.

I don't want to put you in a spot where you have to choose between us. I'm gonna turn in; it's late.

Take care, Tea. Love you.

Love you too, Big Brother.

"You cannot keep punishing yourself, Tea," Kalen said quietly, coming to sit beside me.

"Are we seriously going to kill the boy tomorrow?"

He sighed. "They cannot keep him indefinitely. He's already injured a few soldiers. King Rendorvik understands the situation. I'll wield the sword myself if I have to. I'd take the burden from you if I could."

"I know." I turned to kiss him. Waking up in Kion beside him felt like an eternity ago. "But there are still so many questions. Who used the *Blight* on Garindor's assistant? Was our presence the trigger? Vernasha gave no hints as to what the rune itself looks like, only the *Delving* to find it on someone else!"

"I think you'll agree with me when I say we should prepare our own food and drinks from now on. I make excellent baba ghanoush."

"I'm serious, Kalen."

"So am I." He gathered my face in his hands. "What can I do to help you?" He pressed his forehead against mine. "Are you still having nightmares?"

"I had one when we left Kion," I admitted. "A waking nightmare, on the *azi*. I turned and saw the city in flames."

He frowned. "Has it happened again?"

"Not since arriving here, no. And my heartsglass has been clean for nearly two weeks. I've seen no specks of black. Do you think…perhaps I've…?"

"It's possible. You've been taking better care of yourself and drawing in less of the Dark might have been the simplest solution all along." He kissed me again, long and sweet. "Trust yourself a little more than you trust me, Tea."

"That would be impossible, love," I whispered back.

•• ⇜ ••

I burned.

I was flames and carnage. Howling, all the more terrible for how human it sounded, emanated from the thick of smoke. Fires sprouted around me, the air and screaming all the nourishment they needed.

But I felt no heat. The searing pyres bowed their pointed heads at me, a grotesque parody of genuflecting, and crackled their names. I expected them to pirouette out of my way like loyal dogs, but they brushed against my *hua* and lingered, ringing fire across my back like wings. There were silhouettes against the bonfires, figures in the ember. I approached.

Althy lay on the ground before me, dead. Her face was smeared with blood, and a knife pinned her to the ground, the hilt buried in her stomach. Likh was beside her, his legs folded unnaturally beneath him like a broken marionette, his graceful face upturned for a kiss that would never come. I saw the unmoving figures of other corpses in shadowed relief. Bodies lay atop each other, eviscerated and sharing the same shadow. Empty heartsglass watched me pass.

A figure staggered out of the darkness and tangled itself in my dress. My sister, Daisy. Her blood-soaked face stared back at me. "Why?" she whispered. I looked down and saw that my hand was buried inside her chest, staining my *hua* red.

No, I thought. Despite the smells of death, enough light filtered through the darkness to shine on my senses. This isn't real. *This isn't real.*

"No!" I cried, but the knife wouldn't drop from my hand. It dug into my palm, and I felt its blade slide through flesh. "No, no, no, no—"

"Tea."

The fire wavered, faded, and I stood, rooted in complete darkness. The voice was familiar but odd to my ears. It held a note of fear, which I didn't associate it with.

"Tea. Listen to me. I'm here, Tea."

I opened my eyes—and nearly toppled off the ledge when I saw the hundred-foot drop before me. *Why am I standing in an open windowsill?* I thought, dazed. Why was I here? I could feel every breeze that sang through the palace, striving to upset my precarious balance.

"Tea. Take my hand."

I turned slowly and saw Kalen, arm outstretched, ready to interfere should the winds have their way. "What happened?" Hadn't I been asleep?

"Let's talk after you get down from there."

I took his hand. All gentleness disappeared. He dragged me inside in the space of an exhale, wrapping me in arms that threatened to squeeze the breath out of me, his heartsglass digging into my rib cage.

"What were you doing?" he choked out. Only then did I see Likh standing behind him, petrified.

We were in the castle library. I stood before an open window, staring down at what would have been a fatal fall. Clad in only a thin nightgown, my skin was chilled at the cold. "What happened?" I repeated.

"You walked in," Likh gasped. "You opened the window and tried to climb out! I tried to stop you using runes, but they didn't work!"

Kalen added grimly, "When I woke and you weren't in bed, I thought you were sneaking off to do more research. Then I heard Likh call out. My runes didn't work on you either."

"I don't—I don't remember anything except for a nightmare." I'd never sleepwalked before. My gaze traveled down. Even in the gloom, I could see the fading swirls of black in my heartsglass. I trembled.

"You scared me." Kalen's lips were on my hair. "I thought you were negating our runes somehow, that you wanted to—"

His voice broke. I began to cry, apologies pouring out of me in hiccups and tears. I clung to him, letting out all the frustration I'd tried to keep bottled in since Polaire had died, since my heartsglass had turned black, since the nightmares had begun. I heard Kalen saying something to Likh, promising to explain everything in the morning, then he rose with me in his arms and carried me back to our room.

"You need watching," he murmured, his hands trailing down my back, willing me to stay with him—here, in bed with the twisted sheets and the familiar heat of his skin, not in the hellscape of my mind where my body attempted to step off towers with neither my cognizance nor my permission.

"Will you watch me?" I had never been so afraid before. Not even when Aenah or Usij controlled my thoughts, not when facing down daeva. There was no outside influence to blame, only a traitorous heartsglass that tainted the rest of me with secret plagues. Kalen had given me the best of him, but the best of me lay in pieces. Hardly a fair trade.

I'm no different than Illara. I'm no different.

But the words froze in my throat, refusing to give the thoughts a voice. I was selfish and frightened, and did not want to let him go.

Kalen pressed his lips against mine, and I held on for dear life. "Always."

No other dreams haunted me for the rest of the night.

.. ⭒ ..

"Hold still," Kalen told me the next morning as he wove *Calm* on me.

Given the power asha had at their disposal, it was easy to overlook the passive runes. I often did, and somewhere in the back of my mind, I could hear my old fighting instructor, Lady Hami, berating me.

I closed my eyes as he centered the rune around my heartsglass, working it into complicated weaves so the effects would last longer. Almost immediately, I felt lighter, stress leaching out of my pores. The rune didn't mean freedom from *all* my burdens, but the load grew more tolerable.

I was a reluctant recipient. *Calm* took strength away from its caster, though Kalen, true to form, showed no signs of exhaustion. "Only for now," I told him. "You can't do this all the time."

"I'll pace myself. How are you feeling?"

"A lot better than last night." Bathed in the sanity of daylight, it felt like my emotions had been organized into neat catalogs, tucked away into the bookcases of my mind. "Kalen, why didn't your or Likh's runes work on me last night? Was it something I did?"

Kalen frowned. "Dark asha aren't generally able to deflect runes without raising some protection to take the blow. Althy can check you over once we return, and I'm sure Mykaela can figure out something."

"I'm scared. Mykaela never had this problem."

He sighed. "There're a few things you can do that Mykaela can't, Tea. And I suspect that might be one of the reasons for your differences."

It hit me then, what he was trying to say. "Is it the *azi*? You think my connection with the *azi* is making me crazy?"

"You're not crazy," Kalen was firm. "But I don't think asha are supposed to be in contact with those creatures for prolonged durations, especially when they're in your head. I don't know how Sakmeet managed it. It seemed to prolong her life, but given the manner in which she died, out there in the snow with no protection...it worries me. I don't know what Althy or Mykaela are going to decide, but I think they're going to ask you to disengage from the daeva, Tea, no matter how fond it is of you or you of it. It's too risky, and this is still unknown territory."

"I'm not going to kill it," I was quick to argue, though he made sense. "The *azi* has hidden itself from us all these years, and the only reason it started attacking Kion was because of Aenah's control. I know it won't harm anyone else, even without me in charge."

"But what if someone else gets ahold of it? Druj is still out there, and I don't know how many more followers Aenah and Usij have left."

"I hate it when you're right." I paused, surprised at how sad I felt. The *azi* had stopped feeling like a weapon to wield a long time ago. I knew it was inevitable, but... "If you think it's for the best."

He smiled at me. "In another life, you would be fighting me tooth and nail."

"I'm blaming you and this blasted rune." My heartsglass was clear again this morning, but I no longer trusted its hue. "And I'm going to tell Fox too. About the black in my heartsglass."

He nodded. "I was wondering when you would."

"He's with Inessa. I didn't want to put him in the middle." I took a deep breath. "But that doesn't mean I shouldn't tell him when we return."

"I should cast this spell more often," he teased. "You're adorable when you're mad, but you're even more so when you agree with me."

I took his hand and pressed it against my lips. "What if that's not enough?" I whispered. "What if something else is making me do this?"

"Then we'll push it out, eradicate it. There are many people back home wanting to help you." He smiled. "And I won't make the same mistake I did last night. I'm sticking close to you for the long term."

"How awful," I said, tugging his head down into a kiss.

••• ⁍⃝ •••

The *Calming* rune was enough to keep me placid when it came time to kill poor Garindor's assistant. King Rendorvik had tried to convince the old man not to attend, but the latter was adamant. "Yarrod's a good lad and a hard worker. The least I can do is to be there for him till the very end."

Kalen had volunteered to do the deed, arguing it would be too dangerous for the king to carry out the execution, given the prisoner's condition. His blade was quick and sharp, and the grotesque mantis-like daeva died instantly and without further pain.

King Rendorvik ordered full honors for his burial. "You would not have come all the way here if your work wasn't important," he said, "I appreciate your offer to stay for the funeral, but it will take time that you don't have."

"Thank you, Your Majesty," Althy said, grateful. "I only wish we could do more."

"You can help by finding the madman responsible, Lady Altaecia."

"I'll stay behind to help Rendor," Councilor Ludvig informed me. "A full investigation must be carried out, and he's asked me to take charge. Let me do what I can here while you do what you can in Kion. Perhaps we can find the answer coming at both ends."

"I will miss you," I told him tearfully, hugging him tight.

He snorted. "I'll see you in a few months, child. Let's not be too dramatic about this." But I thought his eyes were misty as he said it.

King Rendorvik presented me with Sakmeet's journal before we left. "She had no living relatives here, and her writings should be appreciated by one who understands her work." I was touched and thanked him warmly.

Lord Garindor promised to hide both of the rare books should any other asha come from the Willows. Lord Cyran seized Khalad's hand, promising to help the Drychta protect the tomes with his own life if necessary, oblivious to Likh's displeasure.

All good-byes said, I reached out toward the *azi* again, knowing full well it might be the last time. The daeva understood; I found sorrow instead of anger, but the thoughts reaching out to me were those of comfort. This time, there were no visions of Istera in flames to torture me as we climbed up into the sky and became lost among the clouds.

As before, we landed a good distance from the city, where we had departed. To our surprise, soldiers arrived as we were disembarking. At their head was the elder asha, Hestia, smugly in the lead. With her was the Deathseekers' leader, Zahid, and Kalen's friends Ostry and Levi, both unable to hide their discomfort.

The *azi* was quick. As soon as we had disembarked, it launched itself into the air and vanished from view, heedless of Hestia's stuttered ultimatums. Seething, she turned to me instead.

"Tea of House Valerian." Even under the spell of the *Calm* rune, I had to resist the urge to smack the smirk off of the elder's face. "On behalf of the Willows, I am arresting you for the murder of Sancha al-Sarim."

"Who's that?" Likh asked, confused.

Kalen planted himself in front of me, and Althy stalked toward the other asha. "What evidence do you have?" she demanded.

"The evidence of Dark magic. Witnesses report a girl transforming into some foul creature—one much like a daeva, which only a bone witch is capable of. Mykaela has been cleared of the crime, leaving only one other bone witch."

There was some movement among the Deathseekers. I looked past them and saw, much to my shock, my family in attendance. My mother and sisters were weeping, and Daisy was pale. My brothers stood silently beside my father, though they cast frequent glares at the elders.

It was the first time Councilor Ludvig broke a promise to me; our good-bye at Istera was the last I would ever see him.

Y ES," COUNCILOR LUDVIG ADMITTED. "*I never saw her after that.
Hindsight is quite the bastard, isn't it? I should have accompanied her back to Kion. I did good by Rendor and his father for decades. Could have done good by her…*" His voice trailed off, and he coughed. "*What good is half a century of experience when I've got nothing to show for it but an old man's regret?*"

The Valerian survived the fires that had engulfed many parts of Kion, a miracle given the ruination of the Willows. Cha-khana stood smoldering, stripped down to their foundations, and other asha-ka fared no better. Their noted botanical gardens lay in ruins, centuries of landscaping and meticulous tending eradicated in the space of minutes. In between the dawn and the dead, very little remained. The destruction here was worse than the rest of Ankyo.

Now it served as a base of operations for its surviving leaders. Mistress Parmina granted Councilor Ludvig temporary rule of her asha-ka while she was away, and until she crossed the Swiftsea with the rest of the Kion army, the Isteran made the most of his duties, overseeing both the repairs for other asha-ka who were not as lucky and negotiating safe havens and supplies for the rest of the newly homeless.

A quick word passed between Khalad and Kalen, but the Heartforger did not follow us into the Valerian. His face was drawn, an invisible weight pressing down on his shoulders that made him *bend, an old man despite being in his prime. But he walked with a steady, inexorable pace, quickened by some intangible motivation. He strode past the Valerian asha-ka toward some destination I could not fathom. I paused, unsure if I should follow, but Lord Fox made the decision for me.*

"Leave him be." He sounded harsher than usual. "It's been a while since he's set foot in the Willows, and there's someone waiting for him. This is not the time nor the place for an audience."

"Is it family, milord? Or the old Heartforger?"

"No. Old Narel passed away some months ago. Khalad left Kion shortly after that. I always thought that grief from his master's death motivated his wanderlust. Khalad would not have chosen to leave her here in Kion otherwise."

Her?

Fox continued, "But his alliance with my sister puts his reasons for leaving in a different context entirely."

"Was someone he knew injured by the fire?"

The man smiled briefly. "You will get nothing else out of me, Bard. Tea may have granted you permission to her story, but Khalad's is not open to discussion until he says otherwise."

"They might come after him next, Fox," Lady Altaecia cautioned. "The elders' numbers have greatly dwindled, following Hestia and the others' deaths. They may suspect him to be Tea's accomplice."

"We'll look after Khalad," Zoya promised. She'd entered the room long enough to catch the tail end of our conversation. "Where is he now?"

"With her," Princess Inessa said gently. "Give them as much

solitude as he desires but remain ever on alert. Notify us if any other problems arise."

Zoya's face fell, adopting the same melancholic expression the Heartforger had worn. Shadi sighed heavily and linked her arm to her sweetheart's. "We understand, milady. We've been staying with her while he was away. It would be good to tell him what happened in his absence."

"It would be best if you moved into Parmina's room," Councilor Ludvig suggested. "It's the largest in the asha-ka. I have soldiers and volunteers trooping in and out of here at all hours, and it would be best if you talk in more sequestered quarters, where there are fewer strangers to overhear."

"I'll help you sort out the logistics, Lord Ludvig," Fox offered. "There's enough work here for twice our numbers."

"As will I," Princess Inessa interjected, a stubborn tilt to her chin. "Morale ought to increase when the people see me here. I've already sent word of our arrival to my mother. She'll send for me if she needs. What do the current reports say?"

"There was damage to many properties in the business district, but the worst hit was the Willows, Your Majesty," the old man reported. "Tea, at least, had very good aim. She hit the council house hard— not even a post remains. Many of the asha who'd been inside reported extreme lethargy. It appears they'd been compelled and herded out of the building before the first of the dragonfire hit. Those in nearby asha-ka and cha-khana mention the same experiences. All the runic wards around Kion still stand though. It does little to prevent the azi, but if Tea is still within the city, she would not be able to draw in the Dark and cause more mayhem."

"*She minimized our casualties, at least,*" Lord Fox muttered, and I remembered the steps she had taken to prevent the Daanorian soldiers from engaging the Kion army in battle back in Daanoris, the aid to the civilians affected by her invasion.

"*Not quite. At the temple of—*"

The rest of the conversation was lost as Lady Altaecia guided us into the next room. "*Now that we're all nice and settled,*" Lady Altaecia said, "*tell me more about her letters. Whatever possessed her to take in a bard, of all people?*"

I was wary of relinquishing Lady Tea's writings, but Lady Altaecia was every inch the authoritarian that the Dark asha had recounted. I handed them over reluctantly, my eyes on her fingers as she rifled through the pages. I was tempted, again, to ask her to skip to the last page, wanting to know the Dark asha's true ending—but refrained.

Lady Altaecia looked up and chuckled. "*I don't intend to eat them, good sir. Surely you know why I am invested in what she has to say. You may be wondering where the rest of us are. You've met Zoya and Shadi. Likh is away, fighting another battle outside of Kion, with all our support. Parmina is expected to arrive in another week. Rahim is somewhere in the city, rallying the people with Chesh. He and the other shopkeepers are coordinating with Alyx's troops and offering aid to the hardest hit. Have you finished reading these pages?*"

"*Not all of them, no. Lady Zoya's control of the ship made it difficult for study. But I read about her meeting with Lord Garindor*"—the Drychta nodded in confirmation—"*and about your findings in Istera.*"

"*My king asked her to avenge poor Yarrod's death,*" the old man added dolefully, "little had we known then that it would be many months in the making, with the end still nowhere in sight."

Lady Altaecia leafed through the sheets. "I didn't believe her at first," she murmured. "It was such a fantastic, unvalidated theory, to believe that the elders kept secrets of this magnitude from the rest of us. But Tea proved me wrong, made me trust her. For a time, I even held out hope that she had a motive for this madness. That she had a reason to raise all seven daeva and bind them to her. That she had a reason to travel to Daanoris and upset the kingdom for the price of a Faceless's heartsglass. She intended to raise shadowglass and take magic from the lands. The elders oppose it for good reason. It is a hard pill to swallow, to go from vaunted silver hearts to the common red, and all their influence gone with it."

"But why did you believe their words over hers? Did you not consider them your enemies, even then?" I asked. Lady Altaecia had accompanied the Dark asha, had seen all she had. Surely she knew of the elders' culpability. What could estrange a trusted mentor, cause her to abandon her ward in her hour of need?

The woman turned to me, the grief in her eyes genuine. Pain puckered the skin alongside her crow's-feet. "Because Tea killed an innocent, my boy." She spoke softly but with authority. "The darkrot took control, and she slew an innocent, and her brother was there to see it all with his own eyes. I cannot trust a Dark asha on the cusp of darkrot, no matter how deeply I love her. The black has taken hold of her heartsglass, and it is only a matter of time before it corrupts Tea completely, bringing us all down with her. Was not the destruction of Kion—for no other reason than petty vengeance—enough proof?"

6

T HE CHARGES ARE RIDICULOUS," ZOYA complained as we sat down to lunch.

The cell I was provided was the cleanest in the Kion dungeons. Kalen had put two soldiers to work scouring and scrubbing. It was bare of furniture and essentials but comfortable enough to while away time. Zoya had solved the former issue by dragging in tables, pillows, and a softer, wide feather cot ("Needs to be big enough for two people, I reckon," she quipped wickedly, and I blushed), glaring at the guards, daring them to protest. They did not.

Althy and Kalen were still conducting daily *Delvings*, and our food was carefully monitored, prepared by either Althy or my mother, the latter soon taking over the kitchens in the Valerian asha-ka and shooing the Valerian's suspicious maid, Farhi, away.

To ensure my good behavior, the association had uprooted my family from Knightscross while my case was pending. My connection to the *azi* remained intact, however—a secret I kept. More than once, I was tempted to sic it on the elders for the condescending way they had treated my parents and siblings.

"Bone witches aren't the only suspects. Druj is still running amok." Zoya slurped her tea and slammed the cup down on the table. "They have little to stand on, and they know it."

"The elders are doing everything in their power to restrain Tea's movements," Shadi reminded her, setting down her own empty cup. "And despite the flimsiness of the evidence, they remain in charge. They've successfully argued to withhold their findings until the trial commences."

"A witch hunt, then," her lover grunted.

"They want to humiliate me," I said shortly. "To have my family on hand to watch."

"Well, they thought wrong," my mother butted in, adding a plate of eggplant *tahdig* to the table. My father and brothers had accompanied Kalen to the barracks and weren't expected back for the rest of the day. "We already know that they're bullying you for being a bone—a Dark asha. And we won't let them."

"Of course not!" Daisy chimed in cheerfully, following with some grilled *jujeh*. "Buck up and eat something to keep up your strength, Tea bunny. You're skinny enough as it is."

Mistress Parmina had been kind to house my family. She and Mykkie went to the association daily to argue my defense. I scowled at my sister, then transferred my grimace to the plate she had set down. Daisy was not known for her cooking talents, and I doubted that my years away from home had improved her skills. "I'm not skinny."

"Yes, you are. All this magic takes energy." She smiled brightly at Khalad, who sat beside me. "They say you're the Heartforger. My sister's told me stories, though I've never quite understood the intricacies of the work you do. It sounds rather noble."

Khalad blinked, looking up from some complicated work involving vials. "Pardon, Lady Daisy?"

"Don't bother the man, Daisy." I was in no hurry to inform her about Khalad's orientation—she'd learn it soon enough, and there were other things to worry about. Mykkie, Zoya, and Althy had been running themselves ragged investigating Sancha al-Sarim's murder, and I still didn't know who she was or why I had allegedly killed her.

"And Fox is with a princess now. Fox!" Mentions of royalty had always rendered my sister awestruck. "I wasn't expecting— well, I assumed being *technically* dead would close some doors when it came to relationships, but sweet Anahita of Koshti, the *princess of Kion* herself—"

"You don't understand the gravity of the situation, Daisy," I interrupted. As I expected, the *jujeh* tasted horrible, but I chewed on valiantly.

"Of course I do." Daisy refilled our bowls of tea. "I was there when you raised him from the dead, remember? I don't claim to know anything about asha politics, but this isn't all that hard to understand. You're a powerful asha, more powerful than they are, and the Willows don't want that. I'm happy for Fox, and I'm happy for you. Father has already given his blessing."

I almost choked on the *jujeh*. "What?"

"Sir Kalen didn't ask Father to the barracks just to show him around. Father already suspected he would ask permission to court you." She waggled her eyebrows. "Though I figured that's putting the cart before the horse at this point."

I looked down, a warm glow spreading across my cheeks.

"Ah, I wish I had more of both your luck! My interests have dried up in Knightscross, so to speak."

"Did they blame you?" I found myself asking before I could stop myself. "Or Mom and Dad?"

Daisy stilled. "For what?"

"The people back home. Did they blame you for me?"

My mother sighed. "There were many who thought bone witches the spawns of the seven hells. But more were afraid than they were hateful. They feared retaliation should Lady Mykaela—or you, for that matter—hear of any mistreatment, and they relied too much on Rose's and Lily's services as forest and water witches to be too hypocritical. We knew the towns-people had resentment, but they left us alone and bought from your father's forge as they always had."

Daisy grinned. Her heartsglass shone a healthy, cherry red. "You being Dark asha actually elevated us in the community, albeit not in the usual manner. People go out of their way to give due deference, strain their backs as they bend over. Whatever they may personally think of us, they are outwardly respectful."

"I'm sorry." I didn't want that. Knowing they were disliked was worse than receiving false courtesies, polite or not.

My sister shrugged. "We're a hardy breed, and it'll take more than a cold shoulder to take us down. I miss talking to you, Tea bunny. It's been a while since we've had any sisterly heart-to-hearts." Daisy clasped my hand to hers. "We all miss you," she said earnestly. "Mama wouldn't stop crying for weeks after you two left, and the only comfort she had was knowing two of her children were leaving, instead of one remaining in the ground."

"Oh, Daisy." My mother sighed.

It had been hard growing up these last years without them. In many ways, my family members were almost strangers to me now. The more years standing in between their lives and mine, the fewer chances there were for them to intersect. "It wasn't smooth sailing for me either, as you can tell. I had to learn to be something I knew nothing about. And Fox had it even worse."

"But you both made so much of yourselves," Daisy argued. "More than the rest of us could in Knightscross."

"I'm in prison, Daisy. That's not exactly an upgrade."

"Not for long, I'm sure. You have friends in Princess Inessa and Empress Alyx! I figured occasional arrests came with the territory. Dark asha frequently clash with people in power, just like in the books you used to read. You used to love all those volumes on asha."

"I was sillier then. Reading about asha was very different from becoming one myself."

"I knew you'd leave the village sooner or later. Mama's

looking a bit teary eyed again, but it's true. When Lady Mykaela first arrived and told us you were going to be a novice, it seemed like you were simply fulfilling your purpose." She smiled. "I was jealous. I thought about leaving Knightscross myself, but it's hard to give up the safety and comfort of family for the unknown. I don't have a silver or a purple heartsglass, but do you fancy one of the zivar or dress shops here would be willing to take me on?"

"You want to stay in Kion and work?" I was delighted. "Mama?"

"We talked about it, Tea." My mother sounded rueful, proud. "Your father and I agreed it was Daisy's decision to make."

Daisy made a face. "As I said, I've exhausted all my options in Knightscross. Hawk and Wolf can run the forge just fine."

Khalad looked up, briefly distracted. "Was all that previous talk intended to butter up Tea into giving you a job at the Willows?"

I burst into laughter. "I don't mind. I really don't." The idea that I would have one more sibling in Ankyo with me was marvelous. And whatever flaws Daisy had, this was her way of asking me for my blessing. I responded with a hug. "Chesh's is the best zivar shop in the city. I accidentally filched one of her assistants, and I can ask her if you can replace him. Or you can work with Rahim Arrakan."

"*Rahim Arrakan?*" Daisy was wide eyed. "You know *the* Rahim Arrakan?"

I had no idea Rahim was popular in Knightscross.

"I'd love that! I appreciate all the money you and Fox send back home, but I'd like to earn one of his dresses with my own money. Besides," Daisy sighed. "He's rather handsome in a rough, burly sort of way, don't you think?"

Khalad and I looked at each other and decided, without needing to voice it aloud, that Daisy should find *that* out in her own time too.

"And where is our brother anyway, Mr. Heartforger?"

"Sneaking into Hestia's quarters with Zoya and Shadi."

"What?" I cried.

"Oh, right." The Heartforger looked abashed. "I wasn't supposed to—"

But I had already sent out my mind, touching on the edges of Fox's as he rummaged through the elder's study. The wards couldn't stop that.

What are you doing? I seethed, and he straightened up.

Damn it, Khalad!

Don't you damn it, Khalad *me. Why are you at the Imperial asha-ka?*

What does it look like? We're looking for anything that resembles a Blight *rune.*

You don't even know what the Blight *rune looks like! And you're not doing much to hide yourselves!*

"Are you talking to Tea?" Zoya asked Fox while she snooped around a heavy stack of papers lying on a table.

"How did you know?"

"Your nose always scrunches when she's in your head, especially when she's about to lose her mind."

I am not losing my mind!

"She is definitely losing her mind," Fox confirmed.

"Well, tell her not to worry. Shadi's keeping a lookout, and Mykkie's keeping nearby asha distracted."

You brought Mykkie into this?!

"She volunteered, actually," Fox said, defending them. "This isn't as harebrained a scheme as you might think, even if Zoya thought it up."

"Oh, ha. Ha-ha. You're going to regret that." Zoya held a book aloft, triumphant. "I take apologies as payment in *paloodeh.* With extra cantaloupe."

The Blight *rune?*

"Well, not exactly," she admitted when Fox asked, "but we found the next best thing." She turned the volume over to my brother, and in his mind, I gasped.

"It's the same unnamed book we found in Istera," Zoya said. "Not as decrepit as the one there, so I'm guessing this is a later copy. But it's an unaltered version, with the foreword written by Vernasha of the Roses intact. Hestia can no longer claim ignorance about shadowglass—not only does she have the original legend here, but it also contains Vernasha's letter in all its bigoted glory."

•• ⁣≥⁣∕⁣≤ ••

It was evening by the time Lady Mykaela and Mistress Parmina arrived at the dungeons. Neither looked happy. They received Zoya's revelation with grim satisfaction but, as Althy put it, "it's enough proof for us to realize their meddling, though not enough for the public to believe the same." She rubbed at the bridge of her nose. "It's not enough to accuse the elders of conspiring to steal Mykkie's heartsglass. The best we can do is obstruction, perhaps, but they can always claim they were withholding information in good faith. Whether or not they were responsible for the blighted is another thing entirely. We can't accuse them without more objective evidence."

"They accused Tea without evidence," Zoya grumbled. "Why can't we do the same?"

"Because people tend to believe those who are in charge, no matter how ridiculous or corrupt they may be," Mykaela told her gently. "Who would you believe—an asha council with centuries-old roots in the kingdom and a reputation for justice and order or a bone witch you've been taught to fear all your life?"

"I—I would think I'd know the difference." Zoya looked troubled.

"Most people would like to believe that about themselves, yes." Mykaela sank wearily into a chair. "But we have been conditioned to obey authority in subtle manners, Zoya. You would be surprised at how very few actually speak up in the face of injustice."

After a pause, she continued, "We've discovered who Sancha al-Sarim is. She was a runeberry picker from Murkwick village."

"I've only been to Murkwick once," I protested. "Several years ago. You'd taken us there from Knightscross after I'd raised Fox."

"It only took that one time." At Mistress Parmina's imperious gesture, Shadi trotted off to find a cushion. "A few witnesses recounted her slapping you."

My mouth fell open as I remembered. "I called Mykaela a bone witch, and the girl took offense. But I never knew her name."

"Well, you know it now. Hestia claims this as your motive for killing her. Though I wonder what possessed you to wait years to exact your revenge after having met her only the once. The Willows haven't been able to adequately explain that yet. Foul magic transformed the girl. The Deathseekers were forced to kill her before she harmed anyone else. Althy believes it to be the work of this *Blight* rune you uncovered in Istera. She and Likh are still in Murkwick, drawing *Delving* runes to ensure none of the other villagers have been compromised."

Knots formed in my stomach. "I'm sorry," I said, and Kalen's hand found mine.

The Valerian mistress dismissed my guilt with a wave, settling against the pillow. "Oh, posh, Tea. You've earned me quite a lot of money since you've arrived, and it's only fair that I protect my best investment. Besides, I shall enjoy any chance to tweak Hestia's nose. But theirs is a heavy accusation nonetheless, even with scant circumstantial evidence."

"For now, the elders' main goal is to keep you stationary," Mykaela noted dryly. "The wards make sure of that."

"Do they know about what we found in Istera, Mykkie?" Kalen asked.

She shook her head. "As their predecessors believe they destroyed all the compromised books, they might think themselves safe. Quite foolish for Hestia to keep another one in her study. It was good of you to entrust the original book to Lord Garindor.

I suspect the elders may pay the Isterans a visit themselves, so at least King Rendorvik has been forewarned."

Fox smiled briefly at me. "Alyx has granted you leave to go to the oracle, if you'd like. Asha are allowed to present themselves to her for counseling apparently."

"*Alyx?*" Shadi drawled. "Are you on a first-name basis with the empress now?"

My brother reddened. "She doesn't like to be referred to by her title when not in a royal capacity…"

The young asha smiled. "I trust that your relationship is going well, then?"

"It is." Fox's face glowed. I didn't need for him to speak to know why; images trickled through our shared link, the *Veiling* rune briefly lifting for me to glimpse happy thoughts of him and Inessa.

Mistress Parmina snapped her fan. "You're a terror, Tea. You're impulsive and disobedient, and you have a habit of dragging other people into your fights. But you've grown on me, and those hags deserve what is coming to them. It's about time we find better representation in our association. Perhaps I will decide to run for council myself."

"Wouldn't you worry that, by joining those hags, you'd become a hag yourself?" Zoya asked.

"Zoya!" Shadi scolded.

"Well, shouldn't the rules be changed, rather than the enforcer of those rules?"

"What do we do next?" I asked Mykaela, as Zoya and Mistress Parmina fell into a spirited argument.

"I don't know yet. The Willows are waiting for something." Mykaela frowned. "And that's what's been nagging at me—I don't know *what* they're waiting for. But whatever they have in mind, we'll fight them. What do *you* wish to do now?"

"I think," I said, "that I'd like to take Empress Alyx up on her offer and pay the oracle a visit tomorrow."

"Good." Mykkie sighed. "I miss Polaire. She always had a plan."

"I wish she were here too," I whispered. Polaire and Mykaela had performed the *Heartshare* as well, and Mykkie had been with her in her final moments. I couldn't even begin to know what that loss must have felt like.

"I swear I can still feel her sometimes, at the oddest moments. *Heartshare* is both a blessing and a curse. I haven't had my heart back long, but I struggle to know whether this is my heart, whole and true, or if there remains in it parts of her that she left behind." Mykkie smiled sadly. "Somehow, that brings me much comfort."

The conversation turned to other matters, and soon it was time for the others to leave, Fox opting to remain behind. "Is Kalen staying with you tonight?"

I nodded. "I told him it wasn't necessary."

"Of course it is. I doubt he'd choose a warm bed in the barracks while you're here." He paused. "But I can tell you're worried, and it's not about that."

"There is something you need to know about me," I whispered, dreading my confession.

Fox's puzzled expression cleared, giving way to worry as I

told him about the black specks on my heartsglass, the spells and zivars I'd used to hide my desperation.

"Darkrot?" he asked, giving voice to my own fears.

"I...I don't know. I mean to tell Mykkie soon, once this is over."

"Letting her know now would only give credence to the elder ashas' accusations, will it?"

"Undoubtedly."

"But you can't keep this secret. Surely Mykkie would keep quiet, as would Althy."

I thought about Illara, the girl before me consumed by darkrot, the Dark asha Mykkie had slain. "She would give me over to the association without a thought, Fox, if she didn't kill me first. She loves me, I know that—but her views on darkrot are uncompromising." *Mykkie killed her charge long before the black showed in her heartsglass*, Althy told me. *It was the only way.*

He was angry, as I had feared. "This is your life we're talking about. The strange emptiness between us back when you were in Istera—it was your heartsglass and not our distance, wasn't it?"

"I...don't know."

"Something happened in Istera, didn't it? I know it did."

"I might have nearly jumped off a tower without realizing it," I whispered. "And I...saw Kion on fire, in a vision."

"Tea!" I could feel his panic. "You know what happens with darkrot! Do you seriously want to allow yourself to get worse before you get better?"

"Give me a few more days to sort myself out. Just give me that long. Please?"

My brother closed his eyes, still mad, but willing to compromise as I'd offered a deadline. I could feel the fear he was trying to hide from me; he'd heard Mykkie's stories of darkrot and madness, and knew all too well what would happen should I fall under the same curse. "Fine. I'll give you three days, Tea, and then I'll help you make them see reason. No more delays."

·· ⩊ ··

Fitful dreams plagued me later that night. I dreamed that I was inside the Ankyo cemetery, the moon staring down at me with all of its judgment and none of the sympathy. Polaire's grave stood before me in the quiet. I was barefoot and dressed only in my nightclothes. The cold was a cutting knife, its blade skimming against my skin.

A harsh, grating sound broke the silence. The ground underneath me moved. Something had been disturbed in its sleep and now struggled for a way out.

I tried to leave, but my feet refused to obey. The noises grew louder until the earth before me broke apart, freeing its prisoner. The corpse that crawled out looked worse than human. Bits of brown hair clung to the base of its head, but its hollow sockets and yawning mouth gaped back at me from a grotesque skull in the final stages of a great and terrible decomposition. Strips of decay that were once skin dripped from its bony fingers, and remains of yellowed teeth that looked unnaturally bleached against the darkness dotted the remains of a jawline. Ironically, her dress survived when the rest of her had not—a white *hua*, tattered and stained from dirt and death, the embroidered crest of House Hawkweed still visible on her breast.

The corpse staggered toward me, and I could do nothing but wait, petrified, as it brushed its rotting face against mine.

"Your heart is the key," it whispered in Polaire's voice. "Love's blood soaked through, in a tinsel of sparkled black. Do not let them take your heart."

"I don't know what you mean," I cried, terrified. The winds around us picked up, my hair whipping around as we stood in the center of a forming tornado, us at its eye.

The corpse took my heartsglass in a skeletal hand. I looked down to see a swirling miasma of black instead of silver. "No," I choked out.

"You cannot hide who you are, Tea, my poppet. There is black in all our hearts. We hide it well enough and bring it out on harder nights, when we think no one sees."

"I don't want it!"

"There are worse things than black heartsglass, Tea. Silver is just as capable of hate." She leaned closer then, dead lips against my ear. "Trust your enemies little," it whispered, "and trust your friends even less."

I came awake, sweating profusely despite the mild breeze coming in through the half-open window. It was dawn, and the space beside me was empty of Kalen. I twisted and saw him putting on his Deathseekers' armor.

"Kalen?"

He glanced at me and tried to smile, but his face was grim. "I was hoping to let you rest longer," he said.

"What do you mean? What happened?"

"There was another suspected *Blight* attack. This time, it happened in Knightscross."

*L*ADY ALTAECIA WAS IN ERROR," *Lord Garindor told me.* "*Black heartsglass is not proof of darkrot.*"

We stood in the room that once belonged to the bone witch, and it struck me how ordinary it was. The closet was heavy with hua of different kingdom styles and colors, and the dresser overflowed with an alarming assortment of cosmetics and perfumes. Books filled the shelves of one wall, and other paraphernalia lay neatly stacked in piles at one corner: silk handkerchiefs with Arhen-Kosho motifs, jade from Daanoris fashioned into plain rings, even an ancient gor-fa knife from Drycht—no doubt presents collected from clients she entertained at the cha-khana. A black armband, similar to what most Deathseekers wore, lay carefully folded on her nightstand. It was a room befitting a teenage asha, untouched at Mistress Parmina's orders.

"*The darkrot is a subversive magic,*" *my kinsman continued. He had, quite unfortunately, volunteered to accompany me, but now idled in the doorway, uncomfortable at stepping into the room of a woman not in his family, even after all his time in Istera.* "*That subversive magic corrupts Dark asha with no outward sign of its taint. History shows that most Dark asha bore no black heartsglass when they succumbed to it.*"

"*Black heartsglass,*" *I said,* "*is more in keeping with the Faceless.*"

"*That is true. But that is not a sign of darkrot either. If you* remember, from Tea's own telling, Hollow Knife had to achieve the black before he could create shadowglass, as they call it. Many associate this with evil, for most Faceless bear that stigma. But black heartsglass only means that a practitioner of the Dark has survived some traumatic experience, often the death of a loved one.

He recounted, "And upon taking his brother's heartsglass, still stained with his lover's blood, did Hollow Knife turn to slaughter the seven creatures of Blade that Soars. That was part of the original legend. Stained with his lover's blood—even gods, I assume, suffer trauma. It's why I believe Dancing Wind died. Whether her death was by design or by accident, that is the true question."

"I can see how that might have made her eligible," I murmured. "But the Dark asha's letters also talk of needing to present herself to a mountain to be judged worthy."

"I confess I know little about that." Lord Garindor sidled as close to me as he dared. "Incidentally, old runic magic and legends are not my only métier. I am a historian first and foremost, and have devoted my life to researching and compiling the genealogies and bloodlines that shape Drychta royalty, from the early days of Mithra and Rashnu down to Aadil. The mad king is an unusual study. He was not the direct successor to the crown—he usurped the rightful ruler, Adhitaya, and slew all his known family. I wager the people would prefer King Adhitaya to the warlord ruling in his place."

"Maybe so."

"Drycht has a long history of pain. Adhitaya was not as cruel as Aadil, but people often think the olden days are better than the ones they have to live through. Drycht nobility has always had a cruel streak. I remember how Princess Esther of House Ordith tried to elope with a struggling craftsman, how both were put to death for their efforts. How a poor boy accidentally stumbled in Adhitaya's presence, his legs cut off for his impertinence. How the noble House of Hazirat massacred the Parenka district because their farmers asked for more rice. But sometimes—sometimes—some rare few are capable of benevolence. Adhitaya's son, the young Omid, was said to have been a kind man, unlike his father. King Walid ushered in fifty years of peace. Queen Thana often opened her coffers to the poor."

I closed my eyes, struggling against tears. Lord Garindor was too observant for my taste. "I am not interested in the past of a kingdom that rejected me, milord."

"Sometimes the past is all we know." He paused. "Milord."

A commotion rose outside. I dashed to the window and so did my kinsman, briefly forgetting his Drychta decorum.

A circle of elder asha gathered outside the Valerian, facing a small group of soldiers. At the latter's helm was a beautiful woman clad in royal red. Her face resembled Inessa's, though the princess stood on the woman's left. Lord Fox emerged from inside the asha-ka, Lady Altaecia and Councilor Ludvig beside him.

"She killed Hestia!" one of the asha sputtered. "And still you protect her! Still you defend her!"

"I defend no one but my family." Empress Alyx was cold ice and hot passion all at once. "It is because of Hestia that Ankyo lies in ruins. Did you think I would not suspect? I know that Hestia frequently leaves Kion for her own private matters—she had done so in the weeks leading to Tea's disappearance. What other information *did you all keep from me, the sovereign you have sworn to defend and obey? The secrets you hide from us have long outlived Hestia, and it is time they be cast out into the sunshine for all to see. How long have you known about the* Blight *rune?"*

The older woman faltered. "I... Hestia has always been in charge of—"

"Hestia is no longer here. You have lost half your allies, transformed into the very creatures whose existence you sought to hide from the rest of us. Inessa herself was present when they were slain, and not all by the Dark asha's hand. Were you so desperate that you were willing to sacrifice your own? We lost Lady Mykaela for your treachery!"

The asha wrung her hands. "We had nothing to do with that! We hid the rune, but never did we dare invoke Blight *for our own means! Only bone witches and Faceless can strike its killing blow! Even Hestia wouldn't dare taint herself with such vile magic! We wanted neither her nor Mykaela dead!"*

"They speak the truth," Lady Altaecia observed. "Their heartsglass is as clear as day. Whatever crimes they committed, the murder of the other elder asha cannot be laid at their door."

"It's that foul bone witch's curse!" another of the elders spat out. "Even now you keep her familiar as a pet!"

Lord Fox said nothing, but Princess Inessa was not as kind. She lunged forward, a sword drawn from a belt on her hip, and the elder found herself staring down its pointed tip. "Retract those words," Princess Inessa stated coldly, "or lose an eye. Lord Fox Pahlavi has proven his loyalty time and time again. When given the choice between his sister and Kion, he chose my kingdom every time. If the

Dark asha received assistance, it was not through him. Even Hestia herself admitted his innocence. When the blight pestilence came upon this city months ago, he saved her. Or has dementia robbed you of your memory?"

"We are innocent, Your Highness! We only hid the forbidden runes for fear they could be exploited by others. We'd never—"

"As the council house has been decimated, you are all to return to your own respective asha-ka until further notice," Empress Alyx ordered. "My men will guard you for your own safety until I have salvaged what I can of my kingdom. Remain there until I send for you again."

Once the asha had departed, Lord Fox kneeled before the empress with his head bowed. "Your Majesty. I am sorry." His voice cracked.

"Rise, Fox," Empress Alyx said, as gentle as she had just been harsh. "If you had not been by my daughter's side all this time, I would have had reason to suspect you. But you have comported yourself with the loyalty and diligence I would wish for from my most trusted generals. You saved Hestia's life, even while she fought for the end of yours."

"I could have brought in my sister. I had the chance."

"He is a good man, this Lord Fox," Lord Garindor murmured beside me. "Guilt feels heavier on good men's shoulders."

"Ridiculous," the princess argued. "Tea was surrounded by daeva. You could not have dragged her, kicking and screaming, back to Kion, whatever you might claim."

"You saved my life," Empress Alyx reminded him, "and my daughter's. I am only sorry that you cannot protect Tea like you do us."

"She made her bed, built it with nails and needles. Now she

must lie in it." Lord Fox rose to his feet, his expression resolute. "There is still the matter of the oracle, Your Majesty."

"What of the oracle?"

"Her temple has been destroyed. There is no sign of her body among the wreckage, nor of any of her attendants. I am heading there now to investigate further."

"For what?"

"For Tea." There was a leanness to him, eyes narrowing and jaws shifting into an expression I recognized whenever he thought about his sister or when he believed her near. "I felt her. Briefly. I felt her satisfaction when you dressed down the elder asha. She is somewhere in the city. And I intend to find her."

I didn't wait. I spun away from the window and dashed downstairs, shouting half-sentences to Lord Garindor about my intentions, stopping only to snatch the letters I had set aside for Lady Altaecia to read.

The bone witch may have abandoned me, but I knew my duty.

7

T HE TEMPLE OF THE ORACLE stood out like an overgrown
weed amid the lush greens and roses of traditional Kion
aesthetics, but it was all the more remarkable for it. There was
an honesty and earnestness about that domed shrine—unlike the
asha-ka, which was arrayed on all sides. It made no attempt to
impress with its simple, white walls and modest greenery. The
only feature of note was the bell that hung over its main doors for
visitors to ring, announcing their entry.

I was here alone, as was the custom. Fox and Kalen had gone
to Knightscross. That my family was in Ankyo and not in our
village brought me selfish relief, but the thought of another blight
assault was worrying. I had promised to contact Fox as soon as I
was done. Communing with the oracle was a private affair, not to
be shared even among the closest of siblings.

The winding corridors were the same as I remembered. I

had visited these sacred halls more times than any other asha, and I could have walked its silent paths blindfolded. It was unusual for a full asha to visit the temple of the oracle more than half a dozen times in her lifetime, and yet here I was, making my twenty-seventh visit. It's been said that an asha confided in only two people in her life: her hairdresser and her confessor. I had no deep ties to any of the gods worshipped within the Willows, but the oracle was the closest thing I had to a confessor.

The last several visits, however, had been failures. I sought the oracle many times for counsel on shadowglass and my own black heartsglass, only to be rebuffed. No number of zivars thrown into her fires as offerings could change her mind. I had not expected this visit to be any different than the last.

I did not know how old the oracle was, only that she had presided over this temple when Mistress Parmina had been but a baby. The mysteries of her shrine were a puzzle; no one in the Willows claimed to know the process of selecting and training temple candidates. Some believe that the oracle was a title passed down from mother to daughter, that both come from an unbroken line of revered seers since the time of Vernasha. Still others were convinced the oracle was immortal, though no such spells or runes exist.

All I knew, as did everyone else, was that the oracle was a permanent fixture of the Willows. She—or perhaps more accurately, one of her ancestors—had been present when Vernasha first founded Ankyo, and she will be there when the last asha-ka closes its doors.

The flames burned lower than they had on my last visit. The oracle was unchanged, or perhaps no one had lived long enough to see the variations between successors. A veil was drawn across her face to mask her features, though at times it would shift to reveal a soft, generous mouth. She was dressed from head to toe in a flimsy, silver gauze that revealed nothing and suggested everything.

As before, no servants tended her fires, none available to offer sustenance amid the heat of the hearth. The oracle seemed to survive without the need for food or drink or sleep. Worship was her nourishment.

I knelt before her and shook my crescent-and-stars pin out of my hair, one I had worn since my days as a novice.

"That is not necessary."

I paused, shocked. This was different. It was customary to offer a zivar to the oracle's pyre; in exchange, she might dispense advice or predict one's future. "Are you turning me away?" I asked, my voice small and insignificant in the expanse of that bare chamber.

The oracle was silent. I could feel her eyes studying me from behind her veil. "Only those who call themselves asha are granted passage within these sacred halls," she finally replied.

"I am an asha."

"Asha serve the Willows and abide by the laws dictated by its elders. You no longer believe in those precepts."

Her assumptions angered me. "You're wrong. I am an asha regardless of what laws of the Willows I disagree with. I am an asha even as I go against the elders' will. Obedience to a decree I had no say in does not make me an asha. My service to the people, performed to the best of my ability and to the best of my belief, is what makes me an asha. Protecting my fellow sisters and brothers makes me an asha. And that includes searching for truth. If the Willows' rule is all that matters here, then maybe you're right. Maybe I'm not an asha."

I stood, but the oracle's voice, stern and demanding, stopped me. "I gave you no permission to leave."

I had never seen her like this before. The oracle had always maintained neutrality. And now this mysterious woman, this seeress who had prophesied that I would one day take control of the *azi* and kill a Faceless sounded almost afraid.

"Shadowglass," she said simply, and I froze. "You seek it."

"I do not want it for myself. I only wish to prevent Druj and any other surviving Faceless from possessing it. It was not fair for the asha elders to hide this secret from the rest of us. We had the right to know Blade that Soars' true origins."

"That magic is a deviancy and must be rid from the world?" The oracle's voice had softened into velvet. "Do you understand the consequences of such knowledge?"

"It isn't right for them to keep us in the dark."

"And what would you do should you get your hands on shadowglass? What would you do, if you were able to keep the Faceless at bay, if you were able to convince the elders to impart this knowledge onto the lands? What will you do, my daughter?"

I had never wanted this power for myself. Shadowglass offered two options, it was said; immortality was one. And unlike Aenah, I had no plans of living forever.

The other was to rid the world of magic. But even I, who had relied on magic for so long, could smell my own hypocrisy. I balked at the idea.

How could we live without magic? I could not fathom the idea of a world without heartsglass, without the familiar glows of red and purple and silver to tell us the healthy from the sick, the deceiver from the truthful. Without magic, the asha would lose their luster, would no longer wield the influence and power we enjoyed. They would become nothing beyond glorified entertainers, diminished in stature in everyone's eyes.

I could understand why the elder asha would keep the shadowglass spell their secret, to go so far as to burn books and deny knowledge. It is frightening to lose the power that you and your sisters have known for thousands of years.

But...

"I want to live." The words came easily. Despite all the nightmares I'd suffered in the last few months, it was this admission that shook me to my core. It was my one constant fear since leaving Knightscross for a new, uncertain life in Kion, worse than slaying daeva or facing down Faceless and their minions. "As did the bone witches who have come before me and the bone witches who will follow after. We shorten our life spans every time we face the Dark and receive little applause for it. Instead, we are given derision and anger. All we want is the chance to live a full life.

"I have seen what the Willows did to Mykaela. I've seen them turn away after her heartsglass was taken from her. I have seen her fight hard to live. She gives so much of herself and has suffered greatly in return. I no longer want to see her in pain. I want her to live the rest of her natural life in comfort, without the threat of the Dark sapping away at her soul. And as selfish as it may seem, I do not want to share the same fate she has already endured for so long."

"You would not use shadowglass for yourself," the oracle said, shaping her words with deliberate languidness, "but as a threat against the elders should they fall out of line. You would force the elders to relax their laws, to institute regulations that would lengthen your life spans. Blackmail."

"Yes."

The oracle bowed her head. Silence crackled between us for several seconds. The flames dipped lower, as if as troubled by my pronouncement as their mistress.

"It would be easy to carry out what shadowglass was intended for," she said. "No magic, no asha. You can resume the life you led before you were conscripted to the cause, and your mentor could live and thrive. The elders you so despise would be deprived of their status and would no longer harm you or your loved ones. And yet you seek a middle ground, still unwilling to give up magic in its entirety.

"The elder asha refuse shadowglass—they crave magic for the dominance they exert on the kingdoms, and fear to lose what Vernasha of the Roses accomplished by cunning. The Faceless are willing, but they too will use shadowglass as Blade that Soars had and not as Hollow Knife desired, no matter their claims of worshipping Hollow Knife. But why do *you* hesitate?"

I closed my eyes. "Because without magic, I will lose my brother. Let the elders have their magic and their power plays. All I desire is my brother, here with me."

"He is dead."

"He's the closest he will ever be to living."

The oracle sighed, and from somewhere unseen came the sound of a chorus echoing her soft lament. "When shadowglass is created, with lightsglass and darksglass fused together, on the day you pluck the First Harvest from its sacred tree, your world as you know it shall end."

"But I have no intention of using its—"

"What you intend does not matter. The Faceless have long hungered for shadowglass; they have cannibalized Hollow Knife's words, bent and shifted them into their own making, so that his teachings matched their greed. Like Blade that Soars, they will take the magic left by the Creator and gift it onto themselves without thought. What they do not understand is that wearing seven daeva in their hearts will be worse than darkrot, and they will die from too much of the Dark before the year is out.

"The elders only seek to control, to incite fear in the hearts of those who wish to seek it out. The very thought of a world after shadowglass sends fear down their spines; it curdles their blood as it once did Vernasha's. They were content to let the Faceless squabble over their share for as long as they retain hold of its secrets. You tread on dangerous ground between both, Tea."

She had never called me by name before. "Are you telling me not to seek it out?"

"Use shadowglass to become like Blade that Soars—or follow Hollow Knife's path. There is no middle ground, Tea. There is only a choice, and not even I know the right path to take."

"I cannot live like this." It was hard not to sound desperate. "I cannot live a life like Mykaela's, forever sacrificing herself for a world that would not have blinked an eye at her death. I am selfish. I am not the compassionate woman she is. Sometimes I feel she is far too kind for her own good. I will serve the kingdoms, but not at the cost of my health. I do not want to wait until I am feeble and weak, able to do nothing but wait as the magic eventually takes its toll. I want the right to enjoy my old age as much as I do my youth. I want Mykaela to have that right. It is not fair."

"When she was a young girl your age, Sakmeet came to me, just as distraught. She shared your fears, your hurt. I saw the same visions of her as I had of you. But while you control the *azi*, I saw her harnessing the *zarich*. Daeva can be gentled with lesser consequences to your heartsglass."

"Why didn't you tell me all this before?"

"Twenty-seven visits to my chamber and still ignorant of why you come. For me to answer, you must first ask the question. Mykaela never did. As you said, she is far too compassionate for her own good. One daeva is adequate, but to command them all invites the same darkrot you fear. It is the same with shadowglass."

"Then what else have you not told me?"

"There is nothing else to tell you." The oracle turned away.

"Wait! What of my heartsglass? If you can see into the future, then surely you've seen what happens to it."

"There is little to do. Black heartsglass is as much of you as it was when it had been silver. It is what you choose to do with it that matters most." For the first time, I detected a trace of fatigue on her person, a faint tremble of her shoulders. "Now I am tired and wish to rest."

I knew no amount of zivars or entreaties would move her at that point. So I stood and watched as the oracle departed to some unseen inner chamber, her head bowed as the flames sprung back to life, kicking up such a storm that it obscured her from my view. When the fire settled, she was gone, and with it, my last hope.

*T*HE BRASS BELL HUNG, SILENT *and broken, over scaffolding once
a part of the oracle's temple. This was the worst casualty within
the Willows, and the roads leading to it were paved with detritus and
the smell of burnt jasmine. A sense of mystery had always permeated
the bone witch's recountings of this sacred place, and it almost came as
a disappointment to me to realize that, when stripped down to its bare
bones, it was not so different than the other asha-ka and* cha-khana
*that gilded its borders. There was no magic here, and the zivar on my
breast remained dull and dormant.*

*The winding corridors that weaved through the shrine's inner
maze were gone. The high ceilings and heady incense spiraling out of
its slender chimney were gone. Even the domestic fires that had once
burned with care within the sanctuary, the holy flames that had borne
witness to asha professing desires under the guise of confessions—
even their hearthstones were blackened beyond recognition. They lay
collapsed under the weight of the building's domed roof, destroying an
institution that had served Kion faithfully for centuries.*

*There is an epic of the semi-mythic warrior-czarina Agafya the
Good, a favorite tale of the Isteran-Tresean war saga. She had laid
claim to Grezel, consequently sacking that Isteran city. She took great
pains to destroy the temple of the Great Hero Anahita, the Isterans'
pride and joy.*

Were not the walls built to keep all pillagers at bay? the poems sang. What foul manner of beast could tear down the dwelling of Anahita, that blessed temple upon temples? No man alive can equal its defenses, and for as long as it stands tall and proud, brilliant and ivory polished, Istera shall rule.

But sleek-eyed Agafya looked and saw the crumbling walls and aging remnants of an old order, not the vaulted shrine boasted of in ancient ballads. And so she raised her spear and cried aloud: "I am she who was born in the mouth of a mountain, nursed by warriors of the spring and reared by the wildness of winter. I am the new and the strong, while you cower behind artifacts of bygone eras. If this paltry shrine is all that speaks to Istera's strength, then let it come tumbling down. I am no foul beast—I am only Agfaya." And so did the czarina break Istera's stronghold and chain them to her reign. And all that remained of Anahita's temple were the shadows of better days.

Anahita's temple had been a symbol of Grezel's power, as the oracle's temple had been of the Willows'. Had not the Dark asha admitted to me her fondness for old stories?

"There are no bodies," Lord Fox reported, "and there are no signs of violence beyond the flames."

"The oracle has survived for millennia, Fox." Lady Altaecia stooped down to pick up something that glittered in the moonlight. It was a half-melted zivar, its jewels shattered from the heat. "I do not believe she would perish so easily. She told me once that I would raise a girl who will one day change the world. Mykaela told me she was given the same prophecy once. Perhaps the seeress knew about Tea all along."

The man gazed at the rubble. "She was the first to tell Tea her future. She warned us that Tea would come to burn the city. Tea must have known and resented her for both."

"It would appear that there are many things that Tea resents," Zoya noted dryly. "But I would not have believed her to be this petty."

Altaecia scoffed. "An innocent city laid to waste, Zoya, and you don't find her petty?" The round asha challenged.

"Not like this. I can understand her rage against the Willows, but the oracle was not to blame for speaking the truth." The pretty woman laughed. "Look at me, defending the oracle! She rejected me when I first presented myself as an asha novitiate, Bard. I had not come to her hallowed halls to be an asha, she said, but to win the heart of one. She was right, but I hated her for years. It was a blow to my pride. But I expected Tea to have a firmer hold on her temper than this."

"Unless the darkrot has already began to infect her senses."

A small blast erupted from nearby; one of the houses had caved in, sending fresh waves of fire spreading onto nearby asha-ka.

"Stay here, Fox," Lady Altaecia ordered. "I will attend to this. Zoya, come with me."

The women dashed off, but Lord Fox turned away. "She's here," he said, as if the words were rigid on his tongue. "She is—" He spun in a circle, gaze searching the smoke and the soot. His eyes narrowed, and for a brief moment, he was as still.

"The graveyard," he finally growled. "She's in the graveyard."

8

*F*IRST THINGS FIRST, FOX SAID, speaking directly into my mind. *There was some damage to the forge, but Wolf says it's nothing they won't be able to fix.*

My brother, Khalad, Althy, and Kalen had ridden out to Knightscross with a handful of Deathseekers to assess the damage and hunt for the blighted victim, who had not yet been captured. Daisy accompanied them, volunteering her assistance to coordinate with the rest of the villagers. Inessa was also of the same mind, which meant she and Fox had spent a good half hour in the palace arguing about the necessity of her presence. I sat and stewed quietly in a corner of Fox's head, resisting the urge to yell at them to hurry up because the princess was going to win anyway, as she often did. Fighting and making up were integral parts of their relationship—which was unfortunate, as I was privy to both whenever my brother or I forgot to keep up our barriers.

The *Veiling* rune had been dropped for the time being, for me to see the village through my brother's eyes. A great number of houses had been destroyed, a host of injuries reported. Althy had her hands full attending to the victims, and Khalad helped her.

Who's been hurt? I demanded. I was sitting on a fluffy cushion in the Valerian asha-ka with my legs folded underneath me, but I could also feel myself walking across the ground, the sun's heat beating down on my head at the same time. It was a dizzying sensation, and I had to remind myself not to step forward using Fox's feet instead of mine.

Sadness touched Fox's thoughts. "Old Kebble and his wife died when their roof caved in," he said aloud. "Their children were injured but are out of danger. Their aunt is attending to them. The Habbat twins were hit by some debris and they're sporting a few concussions. And Mrs. Drury has a broken leg. She was more terrified at seeing me again than at the prospect of losing a limb though."

Why am I not surprised? Mrs. Drury had been the first to turn against us after I'd resurrected Fox. *Who was blighted?*

"That's what Daisy and Kalen are trying to find out."

"No longer trying," Daisy said. She hurried toward my brother. Her face was pale. "It's Sam, Fox. Sam Fallow."

The name sounded familiar. *Wasn't that Daisy's old flame?*

"I'm not sure that's important right now, Tea."

"Who are you talking to? Is Tea in your head? Lady Zoya tried explaining, but she lost me in the middle of it." Daisy placed her hand against Fox's forehead. "Tea? Can you hear me?"

"That's not how this works," my brother growled. "She can hear you the same way I can. Has Kalen tracked down Fallow?"

"He and his Deathseeker friends are saddling the horses as we speak. They think he's fled to the Kingswood." Daisy shuddered, tears filling her eyes. "They said he had antennae and bulging eyes like an insect. Why would anyone do this? Can you save him, Fox?"

"I'll try, Daisy," Fox told her, skirting away from an actual answer. "I want you to stay here and help Khalad and Althy. Do whatever they tell you to do and don't stray too far from them until we return."

"I'm coming with you," Inessa said firmly, emerging from the forge. "You've been training me for more than a year. You said I was good at it."

"Not that good yet. I want you to stay and protect Daisy and Khalad. Don't fight me on this, Inessa."

The princess glared but, sensing his urgency, relented. Fox had borrowed Chief for the journey and lost no time vaulting on my horse and cantering off in the direction of the forest.

He quickly caught up with Kalen and the others along the edges of the Kingswood. "I'm surprised Inessa isn't with you," Kalen remarked.

"Not for want of trying. Any luck?"

"Ostry's found signs it passed through this way. Is Tea with you?"

What can I do to help?

Fox relayed my message.

"Can she locate the creature the way she can locate daeva?"

I cast the *Scrying* rune and focused, but all I could find were faint thoughts coming from the other Deathseekers. Fox shook his head.

"Worth a shot. We're trying to corral the borders and see if we can close in on it from—"

A yell rose up nearby. I recognized Levi's voice.

"Over there!" Kalen wheeled his horse around, riding hard toward the sound.

Fox followed suit, Chief beating the other steed by a few yards.

Levi was on the ground. A quick check told me he was unconscious and wounded. Ostry was trying to drag him away as he struggled to put up *Shield* runes between himself and the strange creature that stood a few meters away.

There were certain similarities between this blighted beast and Garindor's assistant, but there were marked differences too. This one was insect-like and taller, seven or eight feet at the most. It had leathery, mothlike wings that beat futilely at the air behind it. Three pairs of large beaks sprouted along its chin, and its hands were like crab pincers.

Fox raced forward on Chief, drawing his sword and blocking the creature's attack, giving Ostry ample time to drag Levi away to safety. "Aim for its head!" I heard Kalen shout as more Deathseekers arrived.

The creature let out a heavy wheezing sound and tried to attack again with a pincer. Fox moved to obstruct it again, and Chief reared up to give the monster a swift, hard kick to the face.

It stumbled back, and arcs of fire—courtesy of the Deathseekers—sailed toward the creature. The blighted squealed. Its leathery wings folded around its hideous frame, and the flames burned uselessly against its hide. I felt the shift in the air when Kalen summoned cold runes instead, but they had the same effect. The ice seemed to melt even before it touched its wings.

Fox slid off Chief and moved in closer, hacking at the furred feathers with little effect. Frantic, I tried to throw myself into the creature's head and encountered resistance.

In the past, that meant another mind was in charge. Faceless like Aenah and Usij were fond of such tactics. But here I could detect no other thoughts, could find no outside forces commanding its actions. Instead, I felt a roiling, red hate that drowned all cognitive thought. It was the same malevolence I'd felt when I'd tried to control Yarrod. Whatever Sam Fallow was before this transformation, he was long gone.

It's not submitting to me, Fox!

Keep an eye on Kalen and the others, and make sure they don't get too close was Fox's reply as he swung his sword the instant the creature reemerged from its grotesque cocoon. The blade bit through an extended arm, hacking it off at the elbow. The creature wailed and retreated. "Kalen, the wings might be impenetrable, but the rest of it isn't!"

"How are we gonna hit it if it keeps cheating?" Mavren demanded.

"I have an idea."

Don't you dare, Fox! I screeched.

You'll fix me up once we're back, right?

The creature's wings lifted again, but this time Fox slid nimbly into the small opening it presented, disappearing from view as the wings snapped back into place around him. Almost at the same time, I felt the *Veiling* rune between us flare to life. The wall was up before I could stop him.

Fox! I hammered at the barrier he had created. *Fox!*

There was no answer, but in his haste, the link between us had not been entirely broken. I could still feel him, despite his detaching me from his mind. I could feel him being stabbed with those hooks, yet I felt none of the pain. I could do nothing but watch as the creature's remaining pincer and beaks began to eviscerate Fox everywhere they could reach. It was a horrible violation to feel no agony even as it tried to kill my brother.

Fox angled his sword and thrust. The blade plunged straight into the creature's head, coming out the back of its skull—

—Fox was shredded from the inside out. His screams told me he could suddenly feel pain, that he had somehow became human in that split second, only to suffer a grisly death. But the blighted monster was gone, and I had taken his place, my hands winnowing through his insides. Fox's blood soaked my hands, and he collapsed, a mangled unidentifiable blob of blood and bones, and I began to scream—

The creature made one last feeble cry, and its wings retracted. The blighted monster went still on the ground, blood seeping from its head and puddling in a slippery black. Fox blinked against the bright light in full view of the others.

On anyone else, the pincers would have been fatal. One deep laceration had nearly bisected Fox, and one beak had sunk into his neck, leaving a gaping hole. He was streaked in deep cuts, one hand ripped to shreds. Some of the Deathseekers, fierce warriors who had seen their share of battles, blanched as they looked at him, their faces turning white.

I clasped my head, breathing hard. The false vision of Fox had seemed real…

"Need help?" Kalen asked my brother quietly, face guarded.

My brother shook his head. "Sorry. I know you wanted to bring him back alive if possible…"

"I don't think we had a choice. I knew it wasn't likely when I saw the full extent of its abilities." Kalen glanced down at the corpse on the ground. "We'll bring back the body. Levi's our priority."

"That was some hardcore fighting, Fox," Ostry said with admiration, despite being green around the gills. "Rather painful though?"

"For it, maybe." *Tea? Are you there? Tea?*

I couldn't reply. In my mind's eye, I still saw his fallen body, his lifeless, dissected form. *I did that. I killed him. I killed him,* echoed through my head.

Tea? Tea?

I killed you.

•• ⟩⟨ ••

"You didn't kill me," Fox said once they'd returned. I was tending to his wounds, the wards modified so I could draw on *Bloodletting* and watch his flesh slowly knit back together. Even seeing him made whole again couldn't shake the nightmare from my mind.

"Then why do I keep having these visions?" I demanded bitterly. "Am I going crazy?"

"Is it because you were in my head before I fought the blighted? You've never done that before. Not while I was being... Well." He looked pained.

"Maybe." I gulped in air. "And it's the first time you fought a daeva-like creature without me in control."

"I know. It won't happen next time. I'll boot you out of my head—"

"Next time? Fox, are you hearing yourself? Next time? Is this how you really want to live? Is this how you want to come home to Inessa, looking like you've been tortured and left for dead? What's *next time* going to look like? What body parts will you be missing? Your head? I'm sure Inessa would love that."

"You leave her out of this, Tea!" my brother fired back. "I don't have much choice!"

"Maybe you should! Maybe we should have found a better way to live instead of me putting you back together all the time!"

Fox quieted. "There isn't a better way, Tea."

"What if there was?"

"What?"

"The book we found in Istera for starters. It said that we weren't intended to have these abilities, that no one should have been an asha or a Deathseeker to begin with."

"Hollow Knife was a trickster."

"And so was Blade that Soars!"

"You know the real problem? It's that damned heartsglass of yours! It's darkrot, Tea. You're so stubborn thinking you can control it! We have to tell Mykkie, or it'll be too late!"

"You promised me more time!" I yelled back. "It's my decision! Not yours!"

"You're tired." Fox sounded exhausted, grim. "And you're obviously stressed. We'll talk about it tomorrow."

What was the point? My brother wasn't going to believe me tomorrow any more than he did today. But I nodded, because he was right about one thing: I was tired of talking.

"Are you okay?" Kalen asked, entering the cell after Fox had left.

I sniffed, looking away.

"I can go."

"No." I reached for him, and a new vision rose to meet my gaze. But unlike Fox's horrible deaths, there was warmth, love. *Another Kalen superimposed himself over the original—stubbled, face framed by long hair and a wilder look, reaching his hand out for mine.* Are you ready, love? *he asked.*

Then there was another me accepting his offer, rising to my feet, feeling strong and beautiful and happy, answering him in a voice that was mine but also wasn't. "Always."

I blinked, and both were gone. Kalen, clean-shaven Kalen, was the only one left.

"Please stay." My voice was husky, unwilling to think about what this meant, why all my visions prophesied the worst for everyone but him. "Always stay."

.. ⟍⎮⟋ ..

I was dreaming again. I held a knife and I was covered in blood, but the blood was not my own.

There was someone on the floor in front of me. I saw red pouring from her chest, and I knew she was dead. Her eyes were wide, mouth open in stunned surprise.

She looked familiar. I tried to place her face through the strange haze that obscured my view but could not.

She wasn't enough, something in my head spoke up, but it was not my voice. It felt wrong to have it there, but try as I might, I could not dislodge it. *We need another.*

"Tea," someone said from behind me.

I turned.

Fox stared back, face so pale that the moonlight drifting through the window did nothing to change his pallor. He looked past me at the fallen figure, then sank to the ground, his breathing uneven.

"Tea," he said again. "Why?"

My view widened. I was standing before the entrance of the Valerian asha-ka, not in my cell. But I was wearing the same clothing as before I had drifted off to sleep. I blinked at the knife in my hand. I knew this make, this style. I carried it with me often, only now it was stained crimson. Disgust and fear raced through me. I dropped the knife, and it clattered to the ground.

Fox cradled the dead girl in his arms, sounds of agony coming through his lips. There was more commotion behind me. "Tea," Kalen said, in a voice so gentle that I knew something was wrong.

I looked down at my heartsglass. It was the darkest black. When I looked back at the dead girl, the haze lifted. I knew why she was familiar.

Her name was Daisy. She was my sister.

The horror broke through.

This was not a dream.

*S*HE KNELT BEFORE TWO GRAVES *and wept.*

She had fractured the kingdoms. She had brought revolution to Daanoris and sent hellfire raining down on her enemies in Kion. She tamed seven daeva, fought armies, killed two Faceless. She faced blighted creatures and lived when others more experienced in years and skills had not. And yet, it was these small headstones, half-hidden among the weeds, which broke her.

"Rise up," she told one of the forlorn mounds, the words built out of panic, cobbled from hysteria. "Rise up. Rise up! RISE UP!"

Nothing moved but the ferns, bending, swaying in the breeze.

"I raised Kalen. Why can't I raise you? I broke so many rules, one more shouldn't hurt like this. Why can't I break the silver? Why can't I break the one law I would give everything to overcome?"

Beside me, Lord Fox did not attack. Lord Fox did not summon the soldiers. Instead, he slipped across the grass like a wayward shadow and stopped where she knelt. His hand hovered above her shoulder, seemingly caught between maintaining the gap and being a brother—but the distance won. He was silent as she cried until she had nothing left to give.

Uneasy, I shifted away, knowing I was an unwanted stranger during this private moment, though not before I read the plain carvings on those round stones. Daisy Pahlavi, said one. Polaire Ishina, said the other.

The Dark asha's sobs quieted, stilled. Finally, she found enough breath to speak, and when she did, she talked as if she had never left, as if she had not just grieved. "Heartshare. Parts of Kalen remained with me even when he died, because Heartshare never completely leaves. His blood is on my heart, like Dancing Wind's was on Blade that Soars'. Stained with his lover's blood. That's the answer, isn't it?"

She addressed the stones. "Is that why you refuse to return, Polaire? Or are you still angry at me?"

"Tea." *Lord Fox's low timbre broke her focus.*

She looked up at him. "You honored my request to have Daisy buried here, among the ashas' graves."

He nodded.

"A pauper's grave is my fate, or a dishonorable cremation." *She bent down and pressed her lips against the smooth rock, marking her farewells with red lipstick.* "Did Mykkie raise her after I left?"

Lord Fox nodded again, his expression unreadable. "Yes."

"I'm sorry. That must have been hard on you. On Mom and Dad, on the others. I don't think I could have borne it in your place." *She leaned back.* "Are they well?"

"They're all in Knightscross, safe."

"Good. What did—what did she say when Mykkie resurrected her?"

"Why don't you raise her yourself, so she can tell you in her own words?"

Tea's hands formed dainty fists. "I can't."

"You can't or you won't? Are you afraid of what she might tell you? Are you afraid to acknowledge that you killed her?"

"I don't remember!"

"It doesn't matter! She said you did it! I saw you! What other proof do you need?"

"What did you see?" Her voice was quiet, but the wind carried it anyway. *"You never told me what you saw."*

He looked up at the sky, then back at the city. His voice shook. *"I woke and realized something was wrong. Your mind was closed to me. Nothing I did could tear past the Veiling. I don't even remember which one of us had set it up. I knew Kalen was on patrol, that he wouldn't be back till midnight.*

"So I returned to check on you. You weren't in your cell, so I went to find Daisy—and arrived just in time to see you stab her. She…" Lord Fox's voice broke. *"She didn't know why you did it. She died never knowing why. She was our sister, Tea."*

A fresh sob swelled from the dark asha's throat. *"I don't know."*

"Does it matter?" The man sounded tired now, his anger exhaustible after all. *"I should have told them about your black heartsglass. Mykaela might have found a way to prevent this. I should have taken you in back in Daanoris. Every time I hesitate, give you the benefit of the doubt, we wind up losing people we both love—Polaire, Daisy, Mykaela… Turn yourself in now, Tea. Let's end this."*

"I can't do that. It's far too late for any of you to stop me." A grimace shaped her lips, followed by a specter of a smile. *"I told you in Daanoris that you would live, Fox. You will find your happily ever after with Inessa. Fate has different plans for me."*

"Enough, Tea!" Lord Fox stepped forward his hand outstretched, but a new figure emerged from the darkness, sword already drawn.

"Step away from her," Lord Kalen said.

Lord Fox's hand drifted to the blade on his hip. "Have you both come here only to sack Ankyo and visit Daisy's grave?"

"And to warn your army not to attack Drycht."

Lord Fox said, "Aadil is loose. The others have already agreed. We will eliminate his—"

"I will meet you in Drycht if you wish. But your army stays behind. Druj planted traps along Aadil's borders. You will wade through your comrades' blood before you reach his mountains."

"Why not bring me there now?" he challenged. "Surely your daeva will be enough to overcome Druj's traps."

"Not yet. I am hunting." Her eyes narrowed. "Druj prevents me from taking the First Harvest and hides from my thoughts. Even with my strength, the False Prince's followers still have knowledge of runes that elude me. If I am to continue, I must kill the Faceless first."

"Then maybe he does the rest of us a favor," Lord Fox rasped, "if it keeps you from shadowglass."

Then it was Lord Kalen's turn to advance on the young general. Lord Fox tensed, his hand gripping his sword's hilt.

"I will have none of that from either of you." The Dark asha rose to her feet. "I am leaving, Fox. You can strike me down if you'd like, but I will not turn myself in to anyone from Kion."

"You attacked Ankyo, Tea!"

"I spared as many of the citizens as I could. Even the elders."

"Then why…"

"You can kill me, Fox. I would forgive you. Some days it would be so much easier to close my eyes and never wake… I know I've done *little to earn back your trust. But I ask for one last chance. You will find peace, Fox. It may not be the serenity you expect, but you will be all the better for it. You will find peace, and so will Khalad, and you'll all be rid of the daeva and the blighted and everything else you feared about me. I swear that I will never raise my hand against Kion again, no matter how many armies they send after me. I will save the kingdoms, and I will save you in the process, and maybe I will save the bits and pieces of myself that need rescuing too."*

Her eyes found mine and she smiled. "I am glad to see you safe and sound, Bard. You won't have long to wait."

She walked away, Kalen gravitating to her side. Lord Fox lifted his blade again, lowered it, raised it. Finally, it slipped out of his hand, and he watched her leave us, for the third time.

"I wouldn't have forgiven myself," he said out loud to the darkness that had swallowed up Lady Tea and Lord Kalen. "She could kill a hundred more asha, and I still couldn't forgive myself for ending her. And she knows it."

9

P EOPLE TALK ABOUT THEIR MINDS shutting down in the face of hopelessness, but mine opted to travel through different sceneries in the days following Daisy's death. I couldn't recall being moved from my cell to the securest dungeon the kingdom possessed, one closer to the palace and tied with the most restrictive wards.

I had no recollection of being led to the palace, where I presumed people stood and gawked and hurled insults as I passed. I don't remember the chains encircling my wrists, though I remembered their weight. I paid no attention when Empress Alyx announced my imprisonment before her court; I only saw a vision of the Kion monarch, visibly aged from stress and worry, and I felt sorry for the inevitability of what was to come. I turned a deaf ear to Princess Inessa's fumbled explanations to me: how her mother had no choice, how they would do their best to explore another truth for my sake, how this must be a misunderstanding. In stark contrast to her mother, I saw the princess becoming fiercer, ceaseless, and more beautiful in the coming months, and I was glad for Fox.

Fox. The barrier between our thoughts was back, and it may as well have been made from the strongest steel, for I could no longer feel his mind.

I couldn't blame him.

Even Hestia and the other elders' undisguised glee did nothing for me. Maybe they were right. Maybe I deserved this.

I was confined to a true cell this time, with cobwebs and rats and no asha-ka comforts. I gave up all introspection, content to count down the days until I was tried in court, until a verdict was passed and I was sentenced for my execution. There was nothing else to do but wait to die.

Not even Kalen could reach me. He visited every day, always under the watchful supervision of soldiers and brother Deathseekers. I would close my eyes and turn away, so he wouldn't bear the shame of facing a murderess, a kinslayer.

"I still love you," I heard him say once, and my instinct was to reject those words, to relegate them to some reality where I never had to hear him say them. He couldn't. I had done far too much to justify understanding, much less forgiveness. I had lost his friendship once after meddling in his head. Surely murder was worse.

The words gave me more hope than I wanted to deserve. But I didn't want him to love me, not like this. Not in a dank prison surrounded by strangers. It was better for Kalen to distance himself from me. I didn't want him to take away my isolation. It was all I had left.

Others had tried. Likh pleaded and cried, asking for answers I couldn't give. Zoya was belligerent and demanding, yelling through the bars at me for giving up so easily. Mykaela came by every day, to talk to me in soothing tones like I had stolen another asha's *hua* and only needed to apologize to make things right. Althy said nothing when she visited but forced fresh clothing on me and better food than the standard fare provided by the prison wardens. Of all who came to visit, she understood best.

Even Rahim took part, staring at me with his puppy-dog eyes. "Whatever else you might say, little *uchenik*, I refuse to think you are what you claim."

It was hard to agree when Fox believed otherwise. While I paid little attention to anything during those terrible days, I couldn't shut out Fox's voice. Fox, telling the association how he had witnessed me murder my own sister. Fox, telling Mykaela and Mistress Parmina of my frequent blackouts and visions. Fox, telling Empress Alyx of my black heartsglass that I had kept hidden for three months.

It was ironic that the brother I had raised from the dead was providing the evidence necessary for my forthcoming execution, knowing it would kill him as well.

Would Inessa protest? Perhaps as a concession I would live, stripped of all companionship and warded for the rest of my life. I had killed Daisy. I deserved everything they did to me. I only hoped they decided Fox did not deserve it too.

Daisy.

Once, as a little girl, I was a target of the older boys and girls who ridiculed my preference for books over outside play. Their antics culminated in a book being snatched from my hands and stomped into the dirt.

I had barely started to cry when Daisy dashed into view, knocking out one boy with a punch to the face before the rest were even aware of her presence. She snatched up a fallen branch and swung at the rest, keeping them at a distance. "You want to hurt my sister?" She had snarled, "You get to go through me first."

She fended them off long enough for Fox to come running, my brother making short work of the rest. For the next two days, I followed Daisy around like a young duckling trotting after its mother, until she grew irritated and demanded I go away as payment.

I soon lost myself in memories of her. I couldn't retrieve and store memories in vials the way Khalad could, but had I access to that magic, I could've bottled them myself, so vividly I remembered her now that she was gone:

The confident way Daisy had with boys, breaking their hearts when she deemed them unworthy of her affection, and how right her assessments often were.

Her often-successful attempts to play matchmaker for other boys and girls in the village, sometimes more in love with the idea of love than being in love herself.

Her fantastically bad cooking, which did not dim her enthusiasm for it. She had no real aims in life, she used to joke, beyond finding a good man who would tolerate her meals.

The way she curled up with me and my books at bedtime after Fox left for war, asking questions about them, which I'd been so proud to know the answers to.

I wanted to collect every memory I had of Daisy, bundle it in a spell so I could keep her the same way I did Fox. But the elders wouldn't let me. I was no longer trusted. Not that Daisy wanted to be forever tethered to her killer anyway.

The days blurred with me so caught up in the past that I soon lost track of the present.

Khalad was the last to visit. He sat next to my cell, saying nothing for the longest time. I concentrated on a crack on the wall above his head and thought about the time Daisy had danced at Kingscross's *Heartsrune* ceremony. It was the last I'd attended before Fox died and I raised him from the dead. I remembered my jealousy, watching her twirl in the prettiest red dress, knowing I could never be as graceful.

"I want to see your heartsglass," Khalad said.

I made no response.

I heard him leave and engage in discussion with one of the guards. Warily, they allowed him entry to my cell. He crouched beside me and took my heart in his hands. I stared ahead as if he weren't there.

"I've known about the black in your heartsglass since Prince Kance exiled you from Odalia."

I started.

"I said nothing because you were in no danger. Very few Dark asha exhibit black heartsglass, even in darkrot. It's more often associated with the Faceless, a status symbol among themselves. Master tried to explain the misconception, but old suspicions die hard, even among asha. Black heartsglass don't indicate insanity, he said. But it could signify a greater capacity for the Dark than most, which in turn makes it susceptible to darkrot. That's all."

"Then why am I going crazy?" I whispered, hoarse from my silence.

"I don't know, but you're not going crazy because of *this*." He quieted, speaking beyond the guards' hearing. "I suspect someone could be poisoning you."

"What?"

He tapped my heartsglass. "There are fluctuations here that are unusual and have nothing to do with color. I've seen it before in people dosed over long periods of time. When I requested permission to examine you, only Kalen knew the real reason why."

"I don't understand."

Khalad was angry. He'd been angry since entering my cell, but it hadn't registered until the snarl tucked into his mouth. "Because whoever has been poisoning you must be a member of our party, Tea—either in the Valerian, or, more broadly, in the Willows. No one else could have gotten close without arousing suspicion."

My head spun. "But…that's impossible."

"Like I said, we have to make sure. Kalen's right. He's always believed you, Tea. It's killing him that you won't talk to him."

"I…I killed Daisy, Khalad."

"You know compulsion more than anyone else here, Tea.

Three months ago, we had no idea *Blight* runes even existed. What else will we discover in another three? Magic isn't the only way to poison someone."

Food and drink perhaps, the same way blighted victims were targeted. But Mykaela herself had delved me and found nothing wrong. "Is someone coming after me?"

"I can believe in one coincidence, maybe two. But a blight attack in Istera, then two more after we returned, all to shine suspicion on you, is stretching credulity a little too far. Don't give up on yourself."

"Has Fox?" I couldn't help but ask.

Khalad looked down, and that was answer enough. Strangely, I felt neither anger, nor sorrow. Khalad sounded logical, but I didn't believe him. I believed Fox. We were the only witnesses, and poor Daisy could no longer defend herself.

The Heartforger's words lay heavy on my mind long after he'd left. Part of me didn't want to care, but a greater part of me was unsettled. I didn't want to wish; I didn't want to hope. I was content to eke out the rest of my short days in prison, awaiting the blessed relief of the hangman's noose or the executioner's ax. There would be no surprises lurking there. No more daeva, no more politicking—just a short drop into forever and then peace.

I deserved it. I had killed Daisy.

Hadn't I?

I could almost hate Khalad for giving me a reason to fight my sentence, no matter how small my chances were. As a Dark novice, I was indifferent to punishment, jaded in the knowledge that I would be forgiven. It was the price I exacted—my services in exchange for my freedom and their dislike.

And Fox. That hurt me most of all, losing his trust. If he swore I'd killed Daisy, then I was guilty, no matter what Khalad said. My hand delivered the killing blow, and no holy waters could ever wash them clean.

•• ＞丨＜ ••

I had a visitor later that night.

I woke with my mind primed to fight. Someone was in the dungeon with me. I had no light to go by, and there were no other prisoners in the jail. The small barred window above my prison cell was of little help, and what little moonlight filtered through gave me shadows and shapes, but no particulars of contour or color.

"Hello?" I called out into the darkness, surprised at how weak I sounded in the echoes. "Is anyone there?"

The only response was rustling. A vague shape emerged from the shadows down the dark hallway. It jerked and unfolded itself into an upright position.

"Hello?"

It moved closer. I caught sight of Levi's familiar face in profile and relaxed. He was doubled over, clearly still in pain from his injuries. "Levi, what are you doing? You're supposed to be resting—"

The Deathseeker's mouth twisted. With sick, mounting

dread, I stared as his face literally ripped apart, a black and scaled flailing mass emerging underneath. The strange movements that I thought were from sickness were actually slithering motions, because Levi's feet were gone. In their place were the thick, mottled curves of two snake tails as he edged toward me.

I rose to my feet, screaming for someone, anyone, to come. It was almost at my cell now, hands lengthening like tentacles to glide in between the bars, reaching for the edges of my dress. I sidestepped its questing, jelly-like extremities—once, twice, thrice—but knew I could not fend off an attack as more of it slipped between the steel bars.

The flash of a sword swung in the darkness and cleaved an armlike feeler off its blob of a shoulder. The creature that had once been Levi yelped and withdrew. Kalen lopped off another. "Levi," he groaned, already grieving.

The monster showed no recognition. Fangs protruded from the now-reptilian mouth, blue vomit dribbling down its craw. The head lunged forward, an implausible cobra striking from within a collection of limbs.

Kalen's aim was true. The sword cut cleanly through the beast's neck, sending small jets of blood into the air. The headless creature fell but continued to thrash on the floor. A glint of silver caught my eye. There was the spark of a heartsglass embedded in the deceased Deathseeker's stomach. Kalen spotted it at my cry and swung his sword again, digging the stone out of the creature's abdomen. The monster groaned and finally laid still.

"Kalen," I sobbed. "How—how—"

A rune flickered to life before me, the only real light in the cell as Kalen forced through the lock that barred me from leaving. "We have to get you out of here."

"What?"

"Empress Alyx wants to speed up your trial, but Mykaela scried on the elders. They intend to drag you out tomorrow and have you executed without the queen's knowledge."

"Did they... Levi—?"

"I don't know. If they're responsible for this too, I..." His voice broke. "Now's not the time."

Without waiting for a reply, he lifted me up and swung me on his shoulder. I made no protest, still in a daze. I remembered the last time I fled in this manner, under threat of death. It was in Odalia. I was imprisoned by Kalen's own father, the Duke of Holsrath, and made to flee with the others like thieves with consciences, desperate to return to Kion and ensure both Princess Inessa's and Prince Kance's safety. It felt like I was in a series of cyclic chapters that only foretold the same endings, no matter what forks in the road I faced.

The guards who were watching over my prison were dead, no doubt at the Levi creature's hand. I recalled their bodies as Kalen ran down the corridor and out of the palace. Likh and Khalad stood by the entrance, horses saddled and ready. Mykaela and Inessa were there too, as was Fox. My heart twisted.

"Likh and Khalad will come with us." Kalen settled me atop Chief. "The others must stay behind."

"Where are we going?" I choked out through my emotion.

"The city-states of Yadosha," Mykaela said. "Seek out First Minister Stefan. He will give you sanctuary in my name. Now, hurry. You must leave before any outcry. Shadi and Althy are running interference to hide your escape from the others for as long as possible."

"They took Levi, Mykkie," Kalen said hoarsely. "They blighted him. He slaughtered the guards."

Mykaela closed her eyes. "The poor man. The gods rest his soul. He's our problem now. Yours is to take Tea safely to Yadosha."

Inessa stepped forward, reaching up to hug me tight. "I bring nothing of importance to this conversation," she said softly, "beyond shielding Mykaela from suspicion. But I wish you all the best, and I hope we can bring you back here, absolved of all guilt." She turned to my brother. "Fox?"

My brother said nothing, his head lowered. I reached out to him. The *Veiling* still stood between us, but I could sense faint stirrings of emotions—betrayal, anguish, mourning. Anger. So much anger. I trembled. He was not yet ready to forgive me. "It's all right, Inessa."

Kalen settled himself behind me; Likh and Khalad mounted their own horses.

I love you, I said softly. Something shifted on Fox's end, but he made no reply. I let Kalen wrap his cloak around me, hiding my face from view, and watched as he took the reins. Soon, all three horses were racing down the road at breakneck speed.

"We might need assistance with the guards," Khalad told me. "Are you up for it?"

I nodded and focused. I reached out with *Scrying*, letting it drift toward the city gates. I found a soldier's mind. *Ignore us*, I ordered, weaving *Compulsion* into the mix, and felt it settle. I spread out farther afield, calming the thoughts of every soldier I could find. Without anyone chasing us or sounding the alarm, it was easier to escape this time.

Open the gates, I told the last guard, and the heavy doors creaked before us. I held my breath, expecting someone to let out a warning, for the army to mobilize and surround us, for all this to be a trap, but all I could see as we headed out of the city were the gate tower fires and blinking lights of wayward lampposts as we left home for the last time.

*Y*OU LET HER GET AWAY!" *Lady Altaecia is a different person when she's angry. Her bobbed hair rises up like the inflamed comb of a rooster, and her round proportions suddenly become oddly angular. "Why didn't you call for us? What possessed you to rush to the graveyard—not with a handful of soldiers or Deathseekers, but with a bard you endangered! You knew you could not take her on your own. Any elder with enough malice could claim aiding and abetting!"*

The older asha had reason for her ire, but Fox was implacable, emotions disguised to prevent scrutiny. He had been reading part of the Dark asha's letter when the older woman barged in, and he'd smoothed the papers on the table, fingers lingering on the final words of one page, before focusing his attention on her.

"You were busy elsewhere, as you recall." By contrast, he sounded almost meditative. "I had nothing to go by beyond gut instinct. Tea set up a Veiling barrier on leaving Daanoris. I have no access to her thoughts, only assumptions. But even with all the asha in the Willows standing behind me, I doubt they could bring in Tea. She's different now, Althy. She would sacrifice more in an instant if she had to."

"Are you suggesting we do nothing?"

"No. I'm suggesting we track sightings of her azi. We need eyes and ears to tell us where the rest of her daeva have gone. Kion was a

distraction. *Where are the other six? That's where we must be.*" His eyes hardened. "*She doesn't want us in Drycht.*"

"*For once, I am tempted to agree with her. They don't call it the desert kingdom for nothing. The only way into the Dry Lands is through the Drycht cities, and we'll have our hands full there. Even if we are successful, the trek to reach the Ring of Worship will kill our soldiers. I trust you, Fox, but you will forgive me when I say few people have reason to when your sister is involved.*"

"*We'll figure that out when the time comes,*" Princess Inessa broke in. "*Our army is to meet up with Kance in the Hollow Mountains, where he believes Aadil has taken up defenses. From there, only a sea voyage separates us from Drycht. And you know as well as I that the elder asha would have let Fox languish in prison with or without the Veiling. He saved me, and he saved my mother and Hestia. That was what convinced them of his loyalty. If Tea is postponing her quest for shadowglass to hunt down Druj, we have time. We must find him before she does, and it is possible he is still with Aadil.*"

The asha scowled. "*Very well. We will send scouts for the other daeva. We have far too much to do to argue about a moment long passed. The Yadoshans offer their support, and we are running out of room to house visitors. As for Kance, the King of Odalia is not in his kingdom. The boy has gone off with his army again, and we know how that turned out last time. I am still disappointed in you, Fox. Do not presume that I would have turned down the chance to talk to Tea myself.*" Her tone grew mellower, wistful. "*I helped raise her too.*"

"*Your Highness and Empress Alyx were in danger?*" I asked the *princess quietly after Lady Altaecia had bustled away to address some new concern.*

"The Deathseeker, Levi, was not the only casualty of the Blight *runes. A sudden spate of blighted folk followed in the days and weeks after Tea and the others had fled. One of—one of my handmaids changed in front of my very eyes in the middle of the throne room, followed quickly by three more courtiers. We were clearly intended to be the targets. But Fox killed them on his own." A small smile graced her lips. "He was incredible."*

"Inessa," Lord Fox began, a touch of embarrassment about his person.

She waved him aside. "But Hestia, in a moment of madness, accused him of an assassination attempt and confined him to the dungeons. Word was quick to spread among the soldiers and Deathseekers, and they rallied to his cause. Only Dark asha can complete the Blight *spell, and Fox, while a familiar, could not draw in the Dark. Her unjust punishment of him worked to our advantage. Enough people in the city protested—I told you all our charity work was more than show, Fox—and the association was forced to release him. Several weeks ago, there was another wave of blighted, only this time Fox saved Hestia as well."*

Only for the elder to die a horrible death in Daanoris. "But was the Dark asha's name cleared?"

"In a sense, yes, but so were the elders'. They could not complete the spell on their own. They claimed withholding the forbidden runes was to prevent a wayward Dark asha from getting her hands on them. We could never prove the case for Mykkie's heartsglass, but even

Mykkie thought them innocent. Tea was out of Kion's borders and too far away to cause mischief. It was an impasse of sorts."

"But not the murder of her sister?"

The princess's smile wobbled. "No. Not that. But…Fox was the only witness. Without him, the case against Tea was weak. In the end, that's what finally convinced the elders that he wasn't on her side. It was the only charge they could lodge against her that we couldn't successfully argue against."

"I had to confess everything to Mykkie, to ensure she had all the resources she needed to defend Tea." Lord Fox was stony eyed, impassive. "I had to. But that meant informing the elders of what truly happened. In the end, it didn't matter. One of my sisters is dead. Killed by our own sister. There is no side to take." He flipped through the rest of the bone witch's pages. "We're taking too long," he snapped at his own impatience. "If there is a clue here, then surely we should see it to the end…"

He stopped and spoke my worst nightmare. "These pages are unfinished. The last page—it breaks off in the middle of a sentence."

"What?" It was my turn to stand, to rush and scan the pages myself.

He was right. We didn't have the complete story.

10

I T WILL DO YOU GOOD to eat," Likh reminded me, carefully placing perfectly grilled fish before me. Likh, I soon discovered, had packed with the intention of turning every veldt we wandered into a home, to domesticate every plain and mountain we camped on. The food he made was simple but with the same caliber of an Arhen-Kosho chef's.

In the first hours after our unexpected flight, I also learned that Likh had done my packing for me, that I had no scarcity of zivars and *hua*. He, Kalen, and Khalad had been planning our escape from the instant they learned of my impending execution. I knew I should be grateful, but part of me wanted to laugh at the insanity of it all. I had killed my own sister—clothes and trinkets were the last things on my mind.

I accepted the stew but continued to stare numbly at the horizon, fighting the urge to cry or throw up. I had never seen

Mithra's Wall this close before. I had never been to the Yadosha city-states. From my perspective, the mountain ranges were an imposing fortress, shaped like a *nanghait*'s profile. They stared back at me, almost literally—each peak a more repulsive face than the next. Nature had once been an inexperienced sculptor, and Mithra's Wall was one of its first attempts. It was not like the elegant snow cliffs of the Bayevik Mountains that skimmed Istera's Ice Knife. It was not the slim, majestic cliffs of the Hollow Mountains that guarded Odalia's south, nor was it even the bullish, armor-like mountains of Daanoris's Haitsa range. It was not a popular destination for tourists who preferred their scenery genteel and refined, but its ugliness was what most Yadoshans loved about it.

Monstrosities had monstrous legends to explain their monstrous natures, and theirs was of the Great Hero Mithra lifting the earth to impede the newly resurrected *nanghait*'s approach into Yadosha. Its burial mound was located on the other side of the range, which seemed to support the story, but I don't have much reason to believe in old tales nowadays.

At Kalen's urging, we had ridden for the rest of the night, not stopping until the darkness rewarded us with the glimmer of dawn. He wanted distance between us and the city before he would allow me to summon the *azi*, knowing the sight of it would alert others to our escape, if they hadn't discovered it already.

All talk of my killing the *azi* had faded; the daeva was our only chance of outrunning any pursuers. Kalen sold our horses at a nearby village, keeping only Chief, as no other steed, save Kismet, had ever willingly mounted the daeva.

I called for my beast familiar but remembered little of the flight until we landed a few miles away from Thanh, the closest Yadoshan city to the Wall. We took time to refresh alongside the Five Rivers, one of the many streams running through the city-states, and Khalad and Kalen caught some silver-backed trout to break our fast, which Likh had duly cleaned and cooked.

I knew they were doing their best to put me at ease, and I applauded their efforts, if not their success. All throughout the night, Daisy's lifeless countenance swam before my eyes, and nothing could shake the image of her dead in Fox's arms. The visions I had seen with uncomfortable frequency during my time in the dungeons had disappeared, and only her face remained. Not even my memories of her helped.

I stared down at my heartsglass. A beautiful swirl of black grew on silver, a cluster of stars slowly being consumed by darkness.

Likh chattered on, sketching out the rest of the details they'd worked out while I'd been imprisoned. "The plan is to lie low while Mykaela and the others fight on our behalf back in Kion. Zoya and Parmina believe we've still got a good case. All we need to do is to—"

"I killed her."

Likh paled. "You can't say that, Tea. We don't know what really happened."

"What else is there to prove? She is dead, because I had stabbed her with my own knife." And then I began to laugh. "What else do we need to know what happened? Is my testimony not enough? Was Fox's account insufficient? My knife, my hands, my blood—I killed her, and you should have let me stand at the scaffold and hang by the neck. I'm worthless, and I killed her. I killed her. I killed—"

I didn't see him raise his arm, but the blow was hard, snapping me across the cheek. I recoiled, stunned and blinking.

"They're going to find you innocent," Likh said calmly, like he had done nothing out of the ordinary, "and we're going to hide in Yadosha with their leaders' blessing. A newly resurrected *nanghait's* been skulking about, I'm told, so they're more than likely to welcome us. The asha association's reach doesn't completely extend into the city-states, so they'll have a harder time influencing people there. Yadoshans are an independent, rather stubborn folk, and they don't take to being told what to do if they don't want to do it."

"I'm sorry," I whispered.

"Don't be. I'm only sorry we couldn't figure out a better way to do this." He grinned at me. "Besides, I've never been to Yadosha before. I've always wanted to explore more of the world."

"Why are you here? Your asha training hasn't been fully… Won't they be worried about—"

Likh's face hardened. "I won't be missed in Kion. Kalen has Zahid's blessing, and Khalad pretty much goes wherever he wants to. Master Narel, the old Heartforger—his condition hit Khalad harder than he lets on, but I don't think even his master would disagree with Khalad's decision."

On any other occasion, I would have been proud of Likh. He was no longer the shy, doe-eyed assistant working in

Chesh's shop, offering pretty zivars and dreaming of dancing. But there was something wrong with Likh. There was a strange silence around him that I was still too sluggish to comprehend. "What were you doing in the Isteran library that night? I've been meaning to ask."

Likh froze. "That's—that's strange to be changing the subject so abruptly, don't you think?"

"Nothing about our situation is normal." That night had been a blur to me; I remembered the dream I had more vividly than its aftermath. But even so, finding Likh there had struck me as odd. "Were you doing more research about the blight?" *Focus on Likh. Focus on Likh. Don't think about sisters or brothers or blood. Focus on Likh.*

Likh gazed down at his stew. "Remember when you said that there could be runes for spells we haven't even thought of yet?"

"I do."

"What if—what if there was a spell no one thought existed, but you've been thinking of for the longest time, long before you were even an asha? And what if you thought maybe the rune does exist, only that no one's been looking for it?"

"I don't understand, Likh."

"I've always thought that I was *born* wrong," Likh whispered. "In the wrong body. I was wondering—I was hoping—that maybe there were other people who thought like me. People who felt different, like me. That maybe there was a rune where we could— where I could—change to be more me than I am right now. To occupy a different body more in keeping with my mind."

"Oh," I said, puzzled at first. "Oh...oh. Likh, have the other asha been giving you trouble in the Willows?"

He looked embarrassed. "There's a lot of teasing. Some are lighthearted, but others...aren't. And I haven't been getting a lot of work in the evenings. A lot of clients stop asking for me when they—when they realize I'm not a girl or after they've grown used to the novelty of—"

"Oh, Likh. Why didn't you tell me?" I wrapped my arms around his waist, pulling him closer. "You should have told me."

"You've already done so much. You've made the impossible happen for me. I still don't know how to repay you for that." Likh gulped back tears. "I wanted to figure this out on my own."

"And you thought that meant coming with me to Istera to see if there were any spells that could help you?"

"Was it too wishful a thought?" The poor asha sounded so dejected.

"No. I wished you'd told me earlier, Likh. Is that why you chose to come on this journey? To help protect me? I can't ask that of you, Likh. You're a new asha, and you have a good career waiting for you in Ankyo. Zoya and Shadi will help you find better clients, make your own—"

Likh hiccupped with laughter. "I wish that were the only reason I'm here. No, I don't have much of a choice anymore. I had to come. Otherwise, I'd probably be dead."

"What?"

"*Delve* me."

Even before I'd finished the spell, I could see the glowing

red creeping up his shoulders. My thoughts turned to ice. Now I understood the odd silence cloaking Likh. Runic wards were suppressing him from using magic—and from having magic used against him. "No. Oh no. Oh, Likh."

"I've been blighted," Likh said. His smile was both sad and beautiful. "I'm sorry, Tea. I'm not cut out to be an asha after all."

•• ☄ ••

The hasty flight from Kion had not been kind to my complexion. Languishing in dungeons for days tended to do that to a person. Khalad told us that the Yadoshans would be waiting for us once we entered Thanh territory, and I'd asked for time to bathe and make myself presentable. The Ashi river, named for the Great Hero herself and very unlike her namesake, was a wide, mellow stream perfect for that purpose.

I held my breath and dunked my head underneath the icy-cold waters. For a brief moment, I was tempted to let go, to drift until I reached the faster currents, to disappear for good. My death, I thought, would solve so many problems. Khalad would get away with aiding my escape by virtue of his position, and Kalen would likely be pardoned for letting his heart overrule his head. Likh would be spared for simply obeying his superiors. If I was being framed for the blight epidemic, then there was no one else to blame. And under closer watch, the *Blight* spell on Likh would dissipate.

But a new thought entered my head, unannounced and

unapologetic for its trespass. It was Fox, sitting in the very dungeons where I had been imprisoned. His expression was relaxed, head tilted toward the little sunlight that slipped through the bars. The *Veiling* was down, possibly because the Willows warded the prison despite Fox's lack of magic, though he was oblivious to my presence. I retreated, closing my mind quietly and sealing it shut. He'd been imprisoned in my stead, no doubt accused of helping me flee. That snapped me out of my misery. I came up for air, sputtering.

"Idiot!" Kalen, who had been keeping watch from the banks, had stripped off his cloak and his armor and stood a few feet from me, his breeches soaked and his face glowering.

"I wasn't going to drown myself," I lied.

"Don't scare me like that." He reached for me, and I let myself float into his arms. Only after I was firmly secured did his grip relax. "I told you I'd look after you, and I meant every word."

"I know." I leaned my head against his chest. "Sorry."

"We'll fight for you, Tea. I'll stake my life on yours."

"How did you know I didn't kill Daisy? Who else could it have been? And with my dagger? Fox was convinced. What other evidence do you need? Even I think I must have done it." I plunged my hands back underneath the water, frantically scrubbing, scrubbing, *scrubbing*, trying to rid myself of the blood that lingered underneath my fingernails, in the places I could feel but not see. "She's still on me, Kalen. Daisy's blood is on me, and I can't get it off. I can't. I can't—"

He grabbed my hands, stilling their movements. "I love you, and I know you didn't do it. I don't give a damn what Fox saw. We shared—*share*—heartsglass, Tea. I can sense you, and I know you didn't do it. We might not have the same bond as you have with Fox, but there is nothing in you to convince me that you willfully and deliberately killed Daisy."

"How can you be so sure?" I trembled, so filled with love for him that I was afraid my heartsglass would break. "How can you be so sure of me when not even I am?"

He looked at me like I was precious and kissed me. "I know you, and I will always know you. Tea—that night when Polaire—" His voice still broke at the mention of her name. "When Polaire died, I felt you kill Aenah, and I felt your grief. I felt the hatred you were capable of like it was my own. And in that instant, I loved the darkest part of you, because I understood, better than Fox or Mykaela could. I've known you at your worst. And even at your worst, you would never kill your sister."

I cried. He held me until I had no more tears left to shed. His heartsglass was warm against my cheek, despite the morning cold. "I don't know that I deserve you," I managed.

He kissed my fingertips. "We will find a way, Tea. Khalad told you about our suspicions, didn't he? Since when have I ever been wrong? These blackouts you suffer from—they explain your nearly jumping out the library window. There's more to this than we know, and time away from Kion should rid you of any poison in your blood."

"I...I want to believe these blackouts are because of some toxin. But my blackouts can't absolve me from murder. And oh, Likh. What happened to Likh?"

He sobered. "We're still working on that. We discovered the rune shortly after they arrested you. I don't understand it either—he ate all the same foods we had. Althy and Shadi were convinced he hadn't consumed anything they or your mother hadn't prepared. It was his idea to place himself under wards. We thought it best that he come with us, to give the rune time to dissipate on its own."

"But when we return to Kion, it won't stop someone from trying again—"

"What if we *don't* go back?" He stroked my cheek. "What if we never go back to Kion? Then you would have no need to be a bone witch. Likh has no reason or desire to return, and most other kingdoms would be glad to have a heartforger like Khalad nearby. If we hide well enough, the elders will stop seeking you out."

"I can't ask that of you."

"I know you, Tea. Your sense of responsibility is keeping you from agreeing with me. If this is the only peace we can know, then let us disappear."

"But your titles! You're a prince, a cousin to Kance—"

"Titles are worthless to me," Kalen said gently. "Tea, I rejected my father's dukedom. I have distant relations to the south and turned my titles over to them. They're decent folk and should carry the position well. I'm rarely in Holsrath, and Deathseekers are supposed to forsake all titles anyway, no matter how many times Kance or Alyx insist. There is nothing tying me anywhere, nothing tying me to anyone but you. We can talk more about this once we arrive in Thanh. In the meantime, wear this."

It was a simple, pink rose pin, set in silver but otherwise unadorned. "Likh made it for you," he said. "It will mask the black in your heartsglass until we can figure out how to get rid of it."

I knew I couldn't change his mind—for now—and sighed. "This could have waited until I was dry, Kalen."

"Well, the Grand Duke Besserly and the other Yadoshans are waiting for us at camp, and while they're not as knowledgeable about heartsglass, I thought it best to be prudent. We can—"

I nearly shot out of the water. "Lord Besserly is *here*? And you've been letting me prattle on this long?"

"The Creator himself can wait. I wanted to talk with you first. We can…we can stay in Yadosha. We can go anywhere you want. We don't have to return to Kion. Can we both promise not to make any drastic decisions until we have that conversation?"

I looked up at him, at his earnest, worried face. He was right; he knew me better than I knew myself. He had known my thoughts when I had plunged into the river, torn between reaching for the surface or sinking down. It was not quite a familiar's bond. It was more distant yet more intimate. "I swear," I whispered, "that I will never hide anything from you ever again."

•• 〰 ••

The Yadoshans were a notoriously rowdy group, but Lord Besserly was a tactful man when he wanted to be. He was also a courteous and pragmatic one, paying no attention to my wet hair or to the state of Kalen's clothes. "Lady Mykaela has briefed me on your arrival, Lady Tea. On behalf of the city-states of Yadosha, I extend our hospitality to you and your friends for as long as you see fit. Please allow us to escort you to Thanh, where we have made what I hope are ample accommodations. Is there anything your ladyship would like assistance with? Is the *azi* still around, perhaps?"

"I'm afraid the *azi* has left, milord," I told him. "I've learned from experience that it has a tendency to make people nervous with its presence."

The duke's face fell. "And I was so looking forward to seeing it."

"The next time I require its aid, you'll be the first I call, Your Excellency."

"I would like that very much. Is there anything else before we leave, milady?"

"A moment, if you will." I closed my eyes and explored my mind, coming to rest on the door between myself and Fox. Painstakingly, sorrowfully, before I could make myself change my mind, I reinforced the strength of the barrier, separating any lingering traces of my thoughts from his.

He couldn't be a part of this. Mykaela had access to the same runes I had, and it would be easier for her to verify that Fox knew nothing about what I choose to do from now on. This was the only gift I could grant him, the only way he could find some semblance of a normal life with Inessa as long as the threat of arrest and execution hung over my head.

For nearly five years, I had been connected to my brother,

and the act of separating myself from him was almost physically painful. It felt like I was saying good-bye to a part of myself that I might never get back.

But even as I disentangled the last threads between our consciences, I waited for a sign, some acknowledgment that he was aware of what I was doing. But there was no angry tirade, no desperate plea for me to stop—nothing.

And so, not wanting to erupt into another fresh wave of tears after having already spent myself earlier that day, I fortified the wall between us and opened my eyes.

"Lead the way, Your Excellency."

*E*VERYONE WHOSE FEET SO MUCH as *touched Valerian territory was thoroughly questioned about the missing pages from Lady Tea's writing. Councilor Ludvig had seen no one suspicious, nor had Lord Fox, Princess Inessa, and Lady Altaecia. Zoya disavowed any knowledge of the missing pages, though she and Lady Shadi were the last people in their vicinity before the theft was discovered. None of the elder asha were sighted near the asha-ka. The lone remaining maid, the young girl the Dark asha fondly called Farhi, took offense when I asked her.*

"Are you suggesting that I am disloyal to my mistresses?" she demanded.

"No. I didn't mean—"

"I am not! Once, in the past, I had been accused, and my innocence was proven. The Lady Tea—I do not always agree with her ideas, but she has always been good to me. She gave me sweets and food when it could have caused her trouble, and she took on chores without telling Mistress Parmina when I was sick. Even now I keep her room neat and tidy, so that when she returns, she cannot say I have been negligent in my duties." She glared fiercely at me; even this far from her motherland, she polished her Drychta pride until it shone. "I stole nothing, and you will tell the Lady Tea when you see her that I repay my debts always, that my loyalty cannot be bought for a thousand shekels or even more."

I started to doubt myself. Perhaps the bone witch had never intended to give me her full story. Perhaps the Dark asha herself had suppressed those final lines, denying everyone an ending until she could tell it on her own terms. Maybe—

No. I remembered the precise way she had summoned me, the painstaking measures she adopted, the cunning way she constructed contingencies atop contingencies. Her desire to see her story through to the end. She would not leave it half-finished.

My options depleted, I fell back to blaming myself. I could do little in battle. I was not a vaunted strategist like Lady Altaecia or the Isteran adviser. I had no resources I could offer, had nothing to my name but my prose. I was the protector of her words, and even there, in that simplest of tasks, I had failed.

It was my kinsman, Lord Garindor, who offered the most logical solution. "You know two things," he pointed out. "The first, you must find Lady Tea to learn what you have lost. It's not an easy task, but I have faith."

"And what is the second?"

"There is someone here in Ankyo who seeks to sow discord and spread chaos. Perhaps an enemy of Lady Tea, one responsible for her imprisonment—perhaps even the murderer of her sibling or a catalyst of her murder. Did not her letters say that the young Likh had been poisoned by the Blight, *despite the great pains taken to monitor their food and drink? There was a traitor among them there, and there may still be one now."*

Lord Fox and Princess Inessa took his words as seriously as I did. "We're at a disadvantage," the former muttered darkly. "We don't have a Dark asha on hand to compel people or scry into their minds. I'll talk to Zoya and Shadi and see what they can come up with."

For now, there was little else to do but welcome the Yadoshans, who had just arrived at Ankyo. A score of regiments surrounded the city, camping out on the plains, their banners of crimson and navy flapping in the wind, while their representatives rode into the city to greet Empress Alyx. Yadoshans had never been formal, and from the roll of their shoulders and raised weapons, it was clear they were eager for a fight.

"First Minister Stefan says we are yours to command, pretty queen," one of the men spoke, which was about as ceremonious as they managed. "I look forward to fighting the… Well, I'm not entirely sure if we'll be fighting Drychta or the Faceless or both, but we'll give either one as good as we got!"

The empress shot him a wan smile. "I appreciate your enthusiasm, Lord Knox. The enemy, for now, shall be the Drychta. King Kance has already left for the Hollow Mountains, and if we hurry, we can catch him before he knocks down the range."

Lord Knox whistled. "We had a tussle or two with the Drychta a few months back at Mithra's Wall, and King Kance was in the thick of it there as well. Doesn't look like he'd be at home in a fight, that king, but the lad does a good enough job in battle despite his green blood. If I may be frank, I'm relieved. We've heard stories about what little Tea has been up to these days, and we're not keen on facing her in battle—not just because she's a friend, but also because we've seen the damage she can do on her lonesome."

"I hope that day doesn't come, Lord Knox. Lady Tea's motivations are…unclear at the moment."

The man glanced around. "Not sure it could come any clearer, given what she did to your city, Your Majesty."

"We will survive, and we will rebuild. We always do. The casualties have been minimal fortunately. Let us return to the palace. My advisers would like to speak with you and your men."

The tall, muscular leader fell into step with me as we entered the palace. "Princess Inessa over there tells me you're Tea's chronicler," he remarked. "She must have lots of interesting yarns to tell."

"Did you meet her in Yadosha, milord?"

The man's face split into a wide grin. "Of course. Her and Lord Kalen and the other pretty asha and the Heartforger. Ain't every day someone hauls in a nanghait for my men to mess with. Best time of my life. Most frightening time too. But you aren't living if you've never faced danger that would give you a good, long piss in the pants, am I right?"

II

I WAS NOT PREPARED FOR THE nearly citywide ovation we received upon entering Thanh. At certain points, I feared we would be mobbed by the well-meaning folk, despite the soldiers First Minister Stefan had stationed to prevent the more enthusiastic of the citizens from drawing too close.

The Thanh roads were a series of wide streets that preferred corners and sharp turns over straight lines. Large stone houses and two-floored shops lined the main avenues, all representing dizzying arrays of architecture that drew from every conceivable culture. There were Kion-style bungalows with high, ornamental Daanorian spires, palafittes common to Arhen-Kosho held up by Odalian columns, and wide, squat tenement houses notable in Drycht.

The people were as complex as their engineering and as equally varied. Men hanging around outside taverns raised their mugs to us despite the noonday hour and called out cheerful greetings. Nobles bowed low, proper and urbane as an average Kion, but there were rowdier groups, almost all clad in armor, who broke into patriotic song as we passed. Thanh had never struck me as a military town, but many of the men—and even some of the women—were outfitted in various kinds of plate mail. I was no stranger to Yadoshans, but it is one thing to entertain a small group of garrulous, good-natured Yadoshans in Ankyo for a trade meeting, and another to be faced with a city full of them.

"We're a very affectionate group," the duke informed us, a huge grin plastered on his portly face as we finished the trek, arriving at the House of Lords, a squat building built from limestone, with high towers stationed in all four corners. "You're the first Dark asha to grace Thanh in more than ten years. Most of the asha in Yadosha were recalled last week by your asha association. Our people have been hard-pressed to find their entertainment elsewhere, and in these city-states, that usually means front seats to a tavern brawl."

That got my attention. "Were you told the reasons for the asha departure, your Lordship?"

"Ah, so you don't know either? The elder we communicated with—Lady Anastacia—said that a serious political matter had arisen in Kion, one that needed the attention of all the asha-ka mistresses. Important enough that asha with no official political standings in other kingdoms were required to report back. She even wanted the married asha and those under the patronage of our more influential nobles. Naturally, the ministers turned down the request. A contract is a contract, and I'm sure we sent back enough asha to satisfy their quota."

"Coinciding with your arrest," Khalad murmured under his breath. "Definitely not a coincidence."

"We'll make a brief stop here at the House of Lords, to await the First Minister," Lord Besserly continued. "And then we can proceed."

"I'm sorry," I said. "Proceed to what?"

"To the *nanghait*, of course."

"What?"

"I'm surprised you hadn't seen it on the way here, milady. It's usually on the other side of the mountains when it resurrects, but it's somehow made its way to our side before we had our first sighting. Surprising, no? We weren't expecting its resurrection for another four years. In our Interior Minister's defense, he's quite terrible at arithmetic."

"But…why would you elect him if you knew he wasn't good at his job?" Likh asked.

"We rolled dice for the position. Fair's fair."

"Fair enough," I echoed. "I would have appreciated some forewarning about the *nanghait*, Lord Besserly."

"My apologies. My assistants may have jumped the arrow when they communicated as much to your Lady Mykaela. They may not have stated our intentions clearly…or they might have been drunk when they sent the missive. Drunk, more likely."

"So when Lady Mykaela told them we were coming," Khalad murmured, "the Yadoshans assumed it was for hunting the *nanghait*."

"Lady Mykaela gave us rather short notice this time," Lord

Besserly went on. "It's not how she's planned these things in the past. I haven't gotten the chance to thank you for saving me, have I? They tell me it was you who uncovered the plot to kill me, that you extracted it from some imprisoned Faceless months ago. If you would believe it, I was having lunch with the would-be assassin as I received the warning! Bloody hard to keep a straight face after that, especially when I was complimenting him on the grapes he'd sent me as a gift. Made him eat a bunch of them, just to see if they were as poisonous as the soup he tried to murder me with." The Yadoshan laughed; what would have been a traumatizing incident to most was his funny anecdote. "Is that particular Faceless still around, by any chance?"

"She died, milord."

"Ah, rotten luck. Was it a clean death?"

"No, milord." I thought about Aenah's last moments without regret. "It was not a clean death."

"Well and good. I wished I could have run her through a few times with a sword myself, but I suppose you must be cautious around that lot." He sobered. "I am very sorry to hear about Lady Polaire. She was a wonderful woman. What a fantastic minister she would have made, had she been Yadoshan. Would have given Stefan a run for his money if she'd fought against him in the commons, and she could drink me under the table if she'd had a mind to. She was well respected here, admired by my men. My heartfelt condolences."

"Thank you, milord. She is—she is greatly missed."

It did not take long for First Minister Stefan to make his

appearance. The leader of the city-states was a tall man, easily several inches over six feet, and round as an ox. He was also heavily clad in chain mail, as were the assistants who accompanied him. "First Minister," Kalen greeted him, a little warily. "I'm not entirely sure chain mail will be necessary for this hunt."

"It's always best to be prepared, wouldn't you say?" Lord Stefan rubbed his hands. "I will leave the hard work to you and your friends, Lord Kalen, but the last time your Lady Mykaela put down our local daeva, she deigned to inform us only after the fact. While our army may not be up to speed when it comes to dealing with the *nanghait*, at least permit us to offer some backup, to save face if nothing else."

"Can you promise me, then, that this has nothing to do with the games regarding the *nanghait*?" Kalen asked.

"I am afraid," Minister Stefan responded, his cherubic face beaming with insincerity, "that I cannot make that claim."

"Yadoshans," Khalad sighed. "Lord Besserly, surely you can see why the practice should be discontinued?"

"Actually, good sir"—Lord Besserly drew back his cloak, revealing that he, too, was wearing armor—"I was rather looking forward to it."

"Games?" I asked Kalen. "What do they mean?"

He scowled. "The Yadoshans are some of the bravest people in the land—and also the most ridiculous. There is a customary practice here called *chasing the nanghait*."

"You seriously can't tell me that means what it sounds like it means."

"The opposite holds true, actually—it's usually the *nanghait* that winds up chasing the Yadoshans. Hordes bait the *nanghait* before stampeding over each other when they get its attention, trying to avoid getting themselves killed before a Dark asha can bring down the daeva."

"But that's crazy!" Likh gasped.

"Lady Mykaela had been subjected to this insanity in the past," Khalad said wryly. "It's why she killed the *nanghait* without alerting the Yadoshans the last few times, although that's never deterred them. I've heard of people camping out by the burial mound in the days leading up to its resurrection."

"But don't people die from this behavior?"

"There have been casualties. Buried with full military honors, even. Tea will need to put down the *nanghait* quickly, before any mishaps occur."

"That's easier said than done, Khalad!" I protested. "If Mykkie has been actively trying to discontinue the practice, then surely there won't be as many participants this time around?"

I was wrong. As it turned out, a lot of Yadoshans had traveled to Thanh solely for this event, which was why I was seeing so many citizens armed to the teeth. "Thanh doesn't have this many residents," Lord Besserly told me.

I was aghast. "You consider this a celebration?"

"We celebrate life in different ways, Lady Tea. Yadoshans come from a long line of warmongers. We used to rule over the parts of the continent that're now Odalia and Kion, until they decided we were right bastards and rebelled. I was told you grew up in Knightscross, milady. That's as obviously an Odalian name as any, eh? We were too busy fighting each other to notice them break away until they'd amassed a good ol' army of their own!

"We've given peace a chance for nearly three hundred years, and we've been liking it, but every now and then we get the urge to smash something. This is one of the best ways to go about it without causing anyone else too much trouble."

"But I'm not going to let you be maimed or worse!"

"We're all big boys, Lady Tea. We all know what we're getting into." The Lord Besserly was in his sixties, but the grin he shot my way was forty years younger than the rest of him. "We're not used to having other people do our dirty work, but we don't have much of a choice with daeva. We'll stay out of your way—mostly. Who knows? We've made for good distraction for other Dark asha in the past. Maybe we'll be of use to you too."

"Are we really going to do this?" I asked Kalen as we led our unlikely and unwanted "army" out of the city, toward the *nanghait*'s last reported sighting.

"You're not going to get them to change their minds," Kalen grunted. "Focus on the *nanghait*. Whatever happens to the Yadoshans will be on their heads, not yours. They're right about one thing—their ability to distract, not just the *nanghait*, but you."

We could hear the daeva long before we could see it; a low moaning sound sang through the trees, and the winds sighed in counterpoint. Kalen was quick to disseminate my orders. With the exception of the soldiers already stationed along the way, the rest were to fall back until I said otherwise.

"It sounds like that bellowing could be coming from anywhere," Likh muttered nervously.

I'd already woven my runes. Chief snorted his eagerness underneath me, pawing a hoof at the soil.

Entering a daeva's mind for the first time was always a disorienting experience, and the *nanghait* felt like it had as many minds scrambling for position in its head as it had faces. It was hard and time-consuming, trying to latch on to any one stray thought to find my leverage. Even its view of the world was multifaceted; I could see visions of the Five Rivers, visions of sky across the Swiftsea, visions of the Mithra's Wall of mountains, and more visions of endless plains. I couldn't pinpoint its location given the bizarre array of landscapes that collaged together in my mind. It was like multiple daeva minds in one body, each with its own perspective.

It didn't usually take long to kill a daeva with the *Resurrection* rune, but I'd never summoned the *nanghait* before. Now I saw why Mykaela and other Dark asha of the past struggled, why the Yadoshans had more than enough time to spread their own mayhem; it was hard to take charge of a daeva's mind when a myriad of them existed all in one head and at the same time!

I clutched at Kalen's sleeve, frantically trying to chase down the wayward, discordant thoughts. "There're too many of them," I whispered.

"Too many Yadoshans? There always have been."

"No. There are too many consciousnesses inside the *nanghait*. It's going to take me time to control it."

Kalen swore. "Which means there'll be more opportunities for the Yadoshans to get themselves in trouble, won't it? Likh, we're going to…" His voice trailed off. "No, wait. I forgot about your wards. Stay close to Tea. You too, Khalad. And by all the festering boils of the seven hells," he yelled at a few Yadoshans who were stealthily straying, hoping to escape his notice. "Keep away from the woods!"

"Be careful, Kalen, Tea," Likh pleaded.

"Always." Kalen marched forward, roaring at the others to remain out in the open, but very few of the Yadoshans were obeying him.

I latched on to one mind and fought to reach another, only to have the one I had anchored start to slide from my grasp. At the same time, the daeva's moaning grew louder. It was a challenge to corral these runaway globs of awarenesses and still keep an eye out on what was happening on the plain.

My vision dimmed. The *nanghait* had shut each of its eyes, leaving me in darkness. But its thoughts continued to stream and pivot around me. I made another grab for the nearest, trying to imagine steel ropes binding it to me. "Likh, something's about to happen. Tell Kalen that the—"

A sudden shrieking nearly made me let go of my hold altogether, and I scrambled to secure my grip as my own eyes caught sight of the *nanghait* dropping down from a nearby tree, where it had concealed itself all this time. It landed right in front of a poor Yadoshan. The beast seized the unfortunate man by the waist and lifted him up—then dropped him almost immediately as Kalen's *Fire* rune sizzled through its arm, scorching the *nanghait*'s skin.

The Yadoshans began running in all directions at once, whooping and hollering despite the fear evident in their heartsglass. The *nanghait* turned to face them, still emitting that high-pitched groaning. It reared up on its hind legs and reached down. Clawed talons dug into the ground, coming up with clumps of soil the size of boulders that it lobbed at the warriors, enraged by their antics.

There was a fizzle of magic beside me as the runic wards dissolved, and Likh extended his arms above his head. The ground shuddered again, and a pillar of earth rose, shifting into an arch above us and taking the brunt of the daeva's attacks. "Everyone, get underneath here!" Likh yelled, and the smarter of the Yadoshans were quick to follow his lead.

"Likh!" Khalad grasped the asha's hand, looking horrified. "What are you doing?"

"Tea and Kalen can't do this on their own. Not with this many people." Likh shook off his grip and ran without a pause in his weaving. The *Shield* rune he created was easily fifty feet wide. Gritting his teeth, Likh braced his shoulder against the base of the spell, protecting the people cowering underneath it even as the sod assault hammered fruitlessly against it.

As a young girl, I'd played a game called ice and fire with other children in Knightscross. One designated child would be "ice," and every person ice tagged would remain frozen until another child, representing fire, could tag them back. This felt very much like that game, with more devastating results if I didn't tag the daeva minds quickly enough.

I snagged one more wandering thought and anchored another to the bundle I'd already harnessed, but I could feel them tugging away, wanting to break free. In contrast to the creature attacking us, its mind was almost playful. *Two more*, I thought desperately. *Two more minds to secure.*

Kalen was magnificent. Spear-shaped winds sang through the air and struck with deadly precision, and the *nanghait's* voice rose to a near shriek as they cut into its form. All around us, the Yadoshans continued to scramble, some still hollering in glee. I could hear Khalad on my right, yelling at the remaining men to get underneath the protection of Likh's *Shield* rune.

A thought zipped by me, and I lunged, catching it by its tail and stacking it on the growing pile of minds I was imprisoning. Only one more remained. It was the smallest of all the daeva's consciousnesses, more adept at avoiding my grasp. I was breathing hard, the load from the others already weighing on me, my exhaustion beginning to take its toll on my strength.

"Khalad!" I heard Likh scream this time. I opened my eyes to see the *nanghait* heading for the Heartforger. It pounced, sensing victory, but Likh arrived first, throwing his arms around the stunned heartforger as the *Shield* rune stretched above their heads.

"Enough!" my mouth and my mind roared at the same time. I threw everything I had at the final untethered mind by expanding my own, filling the space until it had nowhere to go but through me. I snatched it up and yoked the minds together. "DIE!" I screamed.

The *nanghait*'s minds wobbled under my control, seeming to melt and re-form again into one. At the same time, Kalen all but lifted the *nanghait* away with wind before it could strike Likh, almost from willpower alone. The *nanghait* fell, wailed, and died, all in one breath.

The Yadoshans had quieted, staring in awe at the hideous beast, and then at Kalen and Likh. Lord Besserly turned to me, somehow managing to look shaken while still grinning widely.

"Now that," he said, "was a celebration."

*L*ORD *B*ESSERLY *ROARED WITH LAUGHTER when I finished reading. "Lady Tea was right. We were quite the idiots then. Didn't get a lot of asha in our part of the world, you know. Kion and Arhen-Kosho had nearly a monopoly on the runemakers, and the ones we did have wound up moving to Ankyo anyway. I had several ancestors who'd encountered the nanghait and lost and were celebrated for it. Sure, Dark asha bring them down faster than a Steerfall monsoon chases off summer, but it'd dishonor the people who came before me if I didn't do the same at least once or twice in my lifetime." He shrugged. "Reminds us we didn't always have it this easy, that we may not always have it so. Always been our way."*

Ankyon pale lager made the man talkative, boisterous; he'd been the complete opposite earlier, when Empress Alyx decided to have the armies wait until Lady Mykaela's body had been safely returned to Ankyo. Already reports told of the first ships docking at the harbor, of Mistress Parmina and her soldiers landing ashore, intending to complete the journey back to the city at day's end. Lord Besserly balked at that, protesting that this could delay much-needed support to King Kance should he choose to attack the Drychta within the Hollow Mountains.

"Then it would be best he waits for our arrival," Princess Inessa shot back. "Surely he's aware that reinforcements are on the way?

Surely he's wise enough to understand that mounting an assault now means he will be greatly outnumbered?"

"It's not easy to know what Kance thinks nowadays," Empress Alyx said wearily. "But spies inform me that he is keeping his distance from the Drychta, instead choosing to skirt the borders and build defensive fortresses along the mountain exits. It's a sound strategy, and the Odalians should be safe from any counterattacks until we arrive—in two weeks."

There was more to this plan than the empress was letting on. I knew there was more information she left us out of. That was not surprising, as I was a stranger by every definition, and Lord Besserly was a talker when in his cups. Still, I worried. That a new war brewed in the south made for disquieting contemplation.

Cheated of an early fight, Lord Besserly and several of his men had slouched off to the nearest tavern to drown their sorrows; I'd tagged along. Surprisingly—or perhaps not—Lord Fox joined them, buying the first three rounds much to their pleasure.

"None of us imagined that girl had so much firepower in her," Lord Besserly continued. "We knew about the azi, of course. Everyone knows that. But she was quiet and polite, even though she could incinerate the whole lot of us without batting a beautiful lash. She's a stunning woman—Lord Kalen was very smitten with her, gave us a good talking-to when he thought we teased her too much. Wasn't till later that we realized how dangerous she truly was. She was—well, my mam would have called her a lodestone. She attracted people to her, but not always in a good way." He paused. "Maybe we underestimated her because she could never hold her drink. My twelve-year-old niece took brew better than she did."

"I can't believe she did this to Kion," Lord Knox said. *"She didn't stay long in Thanh, but she left on good terms with Stefan. But she made a lot of our best warriors nervous, and not because she was a good-looking woman."*

"Her and the other asha. Likh." Lord Balfour was the quietest, almost sad, and currently the soberest Yadoshan of the lot. Lord Aden told me he'd been to see Lord Khalad, but said little of how their exchange had gone. *"Prettiest I've ever seen."*

Lord Aden downed his ale and shifted uncomfortably. *"Say, you don't think Lady Tea would go back to Yadosha and set it ablaze too, do you?"*

"She had a vendetta against Kion," Lord Fox assured him, *"not with Stefan. The chances aren't very likely."*

"But why would she turn her back on this city? Last I heard, she was friends with your girl, Fox—beggin' your pardon, Her Highness— and loyal to your empress. She left most of Ankyo alone, but she laid waste to the bulk of the Willows, if my eyes don't deceive me."

"There was a reason." Lord Fox stared into his goblet. *"She didn't betray Kion. Not in the way one thinks of betrayal. Some days, it almost feels like Kion turned her back on Tea first."* Like mine had, his silver heartsglass seemed to glitter. *"Did she say anything about Kion while she was with you?"*

Lord Knox paused. *"Not explicitly, no. But she said some things about wanting to leave and be someone else. To travel the lands without the need for a name. Where she could carve out her own peace, her words were. I remember, because she'd looked so sad and vulnerable. With all due respect, Lord Fox, it was easy to admire her,* even knowing the damage she could do, even knowing how Kalen would beat my arse. Maybe the danger was a part of her attraction."

"We all admired her, Knox." Lord Besserly raised his glass. "Let's raise our glasses to the Dark asha. As strong and mighty as we are, able warriors one and all—may nothing we do piss her off."

"Hear, hear," the rest of the table chorused, and that made Lord Fox crack a smile.

12

THERE WERE MINIMAL INJURIES FROM the daeva hunt, no thanks to the Yadoshans or their leader. The man the *nanghait* had first attacked would live with a broken leg—and despite the injury, *still* attended the party later that night where we were made honored guests, ignoring my pleas for rest.

"It wouldn't be much of a celebration if the people we were celebrating weren't present," the minister pointed out. "Tomorrow is as good a day to sleep as any. But tonight, we drink!"

And that was why I sat at the center of a very long table, staring down at a roasted hog with a caramelized apple in its mouth. Yadoshan parties were as grand and as outlandish as their hunts. While their gatherings in Kion were tame out of respect for the Willows' policies and general dislike of loud noises, the Thanh celebration was a citywide affair, spilling out of the council house and finding lodgings in the endless number of taverns and inns surrounding it. While the more influential nobles and ministers dominated the great hall we stayed at, the locals conducted their own festivities with lesser frills and more beer.

"This is ridiculous," I complained once the First Minister was out of earshot. "There's no point to all this. They deliberately went out of their way to get themselves hurt or worse, and now they're celebrating the fact that they survived?"

"Sometimes people do things because they want to, and not because they make sense." Khalad took a small sip of his ale and gingerly placed it back on the table. "It's not like you've never met Yadoshans."

I snorted. "I've never been responsible for their lives before."

Kalen chuckled, mellower than I'd expected. "One of the few rules for the hunt requires participants to take sole responsibility for their actions should they die underfoot. It's the only way they can claim a hero's burial. You may have to endure this every several years whenever the *nanghait* wakes, but I don't think the Yadoshans would oppose our staying here as normal citizens. Their policy is to never get themselves involved in southern kingdom politics—staying neutral is good for trade. Hunting the *nanghait* might actually put them in your debt."

"That's not exactly the best way to start a life incognito." Kalen was serious about leaving Kion for good, but I still wasn't sure what my own thoughts were on that the subject. I couldn't let Mykaela shoulder all the duties of a Dark asha alone.

I looked around at the throngs of men and women talking and laughing and noisily chugging down dark butter ale like tonight was their last night on earth. "Maybe Yadosha isn't the best place to settle. Maybe we should live in the frozen tundra with the Gorvekai instead."

"But you're seriously considering my proposal?"

"Would you expect me to let other daeva roam free? Even if Mykaela could no longer put them down herself?"

"Mykaela has her heartsglass back. And she can train someone else in your stead."

"Then it'll never end, will it? Endless cycles of Dark asha dying too early, teaching new apprentices the craft, so they can die too early too."

Kalen sighed. "I don't want *you* to die early either. But Mykaela has never once complained about her fate. You can't decide how she lives her life."

"You can't do the same for me either, Kalen. I would have been all right staying at Kion."

Kalen stared at me, his expression turning angry. "You want them to kill you? You're giving up, just like that?"

"What else can I do? Being a bone witch is harder to relinquish than a title, Kalen! I can't be selfish!"

"And you're implying I am?" Kalen pushed his chair back. "This isn't a game!"

"You can't tell me not to speak for Mykkie and then speak for me!" I snapped before realizing this was brewing into a fight neither of us wanted.

Kalen came to the same conclusion; he slumped and sighed. "We'll have all the time in the world to decide where to go after tonight. But it's best we stay in Thanh and wait for favorable winds. Can we at least agree to that?"

I nodded meekly. "Yes. I can."

"I'm just—" Kalen ran a hand over his dark hair. His voice softened. "I don't want to see you hurt."

"Kalen!" Lord Besserly bellowed, appearing out of nowhere to clap him on the back. "The ministers would like to talk to you about your cousin and Odalia."

"I am no longer King Kance's representative, Your Excellency."

"Ah, is Kance as prudish about nobles being with asha as his blowhard of a father? I wish Telemaine a speedy recovery, by the way, but I always figured Kance would be a lot more lenient."

"Our distance is for an entirely different matter, your lordship."

"A pity. There are talks of him sending a considerable portion of his army our way, and while I trust Odalia and Yadosha remain in good standing, we've got every reason to be more than a little uncomfortable about his decision."

"What? Kance is sending troops here? When?"

"We received a missive an hour ago. While you might not be representing Odalia in any official capacity, we thought you or Lord Khalad might be able to shed some light on his perplexing behavior."

Kalen glanced back at me.

"While we have only the highest respect for the Lady Tea," the duke said apologetically, "she speaks for the Willows, and this is a matter that doesn't concern them—yet. I know Lady Tea is as knowledgeable about the politics of the situation, but there are protocols to follow."

"We're to talk about it *here*? In the middle of all...this?"

"We never discuss politics unless we're at least half-drunk, Lord Kalen. That's how we maintain our sanity."

"Go with them," I said gently. "And take Khalad too. I don't know what Kance is doing, but you both know him better than anyone else. I'll go have a talk with Likh...and we can speak again later."

"I'll be back as soon as I can," he promised as they headed for Khalad.

I took up the empty chair beside Likh once they had left. "Is he still mad?" I asked.

Likh nodded miserably, though not without anger coloring his heartsglass. Both he and the Heartforger had been silent all throughout the meal; Likh was studiously looking down at his food and doing his hardest to not look at Khalad, to the latter's obvious displeasure. *Kalen and I aren't the only ones arguing*, I thought with a sigh.

The runic wards had been rewoven around Likh, and they felt stronger than before. "What else was I supposed to do?" the boy asha asked. "The *nanghait* could have killed him!"

"And he was scared that it could have killed you," I reminded him. "How are you feeling?"

"Not too bad for someone who's been blighted." Likh lifted a tankard to his lips. He was never this blunt, and I quickly learned why. All asha under seventeen summers were prohibited intoxicants—though like most establishments, the regulation was waived with important clients as long as the asha was under the supervision of an older mentor. The Yadoshan council house was a far cry from a conservative asha-ka, and as the only senior asha available, I wasn't sure I could do much more at this point. "I was fine. I knew what I was doing. Forging hearts is his expertise, but I know my own strengths."

I laughed.

"What's so funny?"

"Nothing. I'm just realizing how I must have looked and acted from Polaire's or Althy's point of view at your age. You do realize that he was frightened for you."

"Yeah. But that was my own decision, right? He couldn't have known Kalen would have fended off the daeva. I couldn't have known what would happen if I hadn't intervened. He keeps... He thinks that because he sees every emotion in my heartsglass, he gets to decide what is best for me!"

"He doesn't see everything in your heartsglass," I said quietly. "Khalad's a very clever man and an exceptional heart-forger. But sometimes his own feelings cloud his judgment and prevent him from seeing into heartsglass. He doesn't know that you like him."

He blushed. "And... Does he...?"

"I don't know. He's better at hiding his emotions than I am."

"Well, if it isn't the Lady Tea! Fancy meeting you here!"

I recognized the voice, but my groans were muffled as Aden,

a Yadoshan trader and frequent customer of the Valerian, bounded over and enveloped me in a hug that would have given Rahim a run for his money. Balfour and Knox were directly behind him, laughing boisterously and already inebriated. "Last time I saw you was at the Dawnbreak tearoom last month. What brings you to our part of the world?"

"I'm considering permanent relocation, Sir Aden," I said around a mouthful of arm, adopting Kalen's proposal for the purpose of this meeting.

"Ha! There are so few asha here nowadays—sent back to Ankyo, more's the pity—and you two are a welcome sight to see! Come sit with us for a little while, you and your beautiful lady friend! You *are* an asha too, aren't you, milady?"

"My name is Likh," Likh said, rising from his chair. "And thank you, kind sir. I'm an asha who's never been to Yadosha before and would love to know more about what you do."

"The more the merrier!" Knox proclaimed.

"Likh—"

"I'm only going to talk to them, Tea. Isn't that part of what we do?" The boy asha drained his mug and stood. "Where were we, men?"

Groaning inwardly, I followed them to their table. I'd known the guys long enough to trust them not to take advantage, and I'd be on hand. But they didn't know Likh, and I didn't know *drunk* Likh, and I couldn't find a way to extricate ourselves from the situation without causing a scene.

Deciding to allow Likh some leeway, I accepted a

watery-looking but sweet beverage that didn't taste like hard beer at all. "It's like mother's milk," Balfour assured us.

The innocent-seeming drink, I learned much later, was renowned for its smoothness. It was the lightest of the drinks served at that hall, that was certain, but potent enough for someone who didn't always imbibe, the kick creeping up on one unawares until it was far too late.

The men started with a toast in my honor, and then to Likh's. By then, I was still sober enough to make my own toast. "May our children one day inherit a world where they can explore the lands without the need for a name," I intoned, "and free to carve out their own peace."

The men seemed to like that. From there, we moved on to toasting the day's *nanghait* hunt, future *nanghait* hunts, and it was only when we were toasting *nanghait* hunts twenty years hence and I spilled more beer than I drank that I knew I was in trouble.

Likh handled his drinks better than I did. He flirted with the men, knew the right words to say, and was full of compliments. His training in Kion had paid off—he was better at flattery than I was, possibly on the same par as Shadi, who excelled at it.

It was easy to keep drinking. With every refilled bowl, it took less effort to forget what I'd left behind in Kion—Daisy, Fox, the elder asha, all of it.

"My great-great-great-grandfather helped build this council house," Lord Aden said fondly, patting the wall like he was stroking a pet. "See these faint markings over here? You can barely see them now. They're Gorvekan. They helped us build it, said these were protection symbols. They don't usually put them up in the places they help build, mind—they're part of some rituals they're committed to, and they don't let outsiders see their symbols too often—but my many-great-grandpa did the impossible and got 'em drunk, so they got a bit careless. Friendly people, helped us fight against the *nanghait* back when there weren't Dark asha around to contain them. Did you know they got more runebinders than even Arhen-Kosho if you take population size into account? Not something they tell you in the history books."

I stared hard at the design he'd indicated. It looked familiar, but my mind was thoroughly greased by the alcohol and its significance kept sliding away from me. "It's very pretty, Lord Aden."

"Grew up in Thanh, I did. Knox and Balfour are Steerfall natives, and Besserly's a Chittengrin, if you can believe it. Not as stuffed up as the rest of them over there, gods be good. Thanh's a good place, but starved of asha."

Likh laughed. "And now it has two! Perhaps a celebration? Should we dance, Tea?" He tottered.

"Not today, Likh. But we are quite open to more drinking."

Lord Aden guffawed. "Then more drinking it is!"

Khalad found us deep in our cups, giggling over some inanities that I no longer recall. The Heartforger didn't look pleased, barely paying attention to the men's respectful bows—the ones who didn't lose their balance, anyway. "Might I have a talk with *Lady* Likh?" he asked frostily.

Likh peered up at him from through his long eyelashes, blinking owlishly. "I'm not sure I want to talk to you," he said calmly, despite his lack of sobriety. "I much rather prefer the company of these men, if you please."

"Is this your girl, Lord Khalad?" Knox raised his hands. "We were only accompanying these lovely ladies, milord. We meant no harm—"

"I want to talk to you *now*, Likh." Khalad's tone allowed no room for discussion. The Heartforger was rarely this angry, and it startled Likh back into some sobriety. He waved cheerfully at us before marching off so he and Khalad could talk in private.

"I didn't know Lord Khalad was interested in the Lady Likh," Aden slurred. "They make a cute couple."

"Kalen and I make a cute couple too." The words tumbled out without filter, and I remembered the surge of pride at finally being able to say so out loud, here in this place, where it was easier to spill secrets to a roomful of strangers than family and friends.

The spurts of laughter didn't sound like they were directed *at* me. "I'd noticed the particular closeness between you two but did not realize the happy occasion!" Knox proclaimed. "We must drink to your health and to Kalen's! Have you been long together?"

"Not too long, milord, but I intend it to last me my days!"

"Once I traveled the Steerfall strays," Aden started to sing, "with gold to last me my days, but soon found myself on old Thanh's shore, all shacked up with a Yadoshan wh—"

"Stop!" I raised my hand before he could finish. "Kalen and I are nothing of that sort! Our Kion songs speak of it better than your bawdy tunes!"

"An asha performance!" Knox crowed. "Sing us some refrains, little miss, and let us be the judge!"

I was not known for my singing voice. Instructor Mina had been able to coax my frog-like warbles into a decent melody, but inebriation masked what little skill I possessed. Still, I endeavored.

Kiss me with your generous mouth,
That source of endless wine.
Kiss me close when season's drouth,
Your lips a taste of mine.
Through storm-led skies and sun-dried fires,
Our love 'twas meant to be.
When roses fade on funeral pyres
I'll carry your heart with me.

The men applauded like I'd danced the *darashi oyun*. "Fighting words!" Balfour said. "Softer than what we're accustomed to, but the heart speaks true! Which does raise the question: Who seduced whom?"

The men found that hilarious, and I laughed along with them. "I'm not entirely certain, Lord Balfour. It was difficult to ascertain who made the first move; we were initially on hostile terms, you see. But that might have been part of his charm."

"But surely there was a turning point, milady?" Our table was no longer my only audience. About half of the hall was silent, riveted by my performance.

I reflected, ignoring them all. "Perhaps it was when I accidentally used compulsion to save his life, Sir Balfour."

For some reason, a fresh chorus of laughter met my words.

"Surely you didn't need to compel him to be fond of you?" someone called out. "You have no need for trickeries when you look the way you do!"

"Oh, but I did, and I apologized! It took him so long to forgive me. Even after I offered for him to do the same to me!"

Balfour gaped at me. "You volunteered to relinquish control of your mind? That is quite the test of trust, milady."

That was true, wasn't it? As angry as he had been with me, I'd trusted him enough not to take advantage, even when he threatened to do just that. Even when I hadn't done the same. I drained another bowl. "He didn't like me, but I had confidence in him. That's the kind of man Lord Kalen is."

"How did you convince him of your devotion, Lady Tea?" an armor-clad woman asked.

"I'm still not quite sure. But I remember the day he convinced me of mine."

"What was it, if I may be so bold?"

"I saw him bathing in a river with his shirt off."

I was certain the tables would break; the Yadoshans pounded their fists, howling their glee. "We must demand Lord Kalen's side of the story!" Aden chortled. "Is your young beau still with the First Minister?"

"Not anymore" came the amused reply behind me. "First Minister Stefan didn't want to keep me for too long. It was a wise decision."

"A wise man, is our Stefan. Our pretty asha would no doubt be accosted by some hooligans had not our wholesome selves intervened. O' course, we would never think of stealing your girl, milord! Let's have another toast for you both!"

"How many toasts have you had?" Kalen asked, peering down at me.

"Does it matter?" My voice slurred. "I am having a very lovely time with all these genta...genner...genteel...*boys*, and they have been very kind."

"That's nice, Tea."

"I told them alla 'bout you."

"That's nice, Tea."

"I love you. I really do."

"I know. You are also very drunk."

"Whatsa sense o' drinking from Stefan's very expensive vintage if you don' get drunk off your ass?" Knox countered.

"I love him," I confided to the others. "He saved me so many times. He smells really nice."

"We'll take your word for it, little lady."

"He didn't like me at first though. I changed his mind."

"So you said."

"He would have been a fool not to," Balfour agreed.

"We fought only this evening. He wants me to stay here, but I think I should return to Kion."

"Tea," Kalen said.

"I am quite in favor of Kalen's decision, milady," Knox said.

"I have reshponsi—reshpunsib—*duties* to see to. But I would spend forever with him if I could. I would trade heartsglass with him this instant. He is *glorious* in bed."

"*Tea!*" Kalen sputtered, turning a bright red, as the roars of the other men and women grew louder.

"And if anyone here so much as touches a hair on his adorable head, I shall pull out their beating hearts and force them to consume every last vein," I added cheerfully.

"I think Tea's had enough for today, gentlemen. If you will excuse us." Kalen reached down and scooped me into his arms. Without protest, I tucked my head underneath his chin, knowing I belonged there.

"I understand, Lord Kalen," Aden said almost reverently. "I would follow Lady Tea into battle with that kind of encouragement."

"You are an idiot," Kalen said as soon as we were out of earshot.

"But do you still love me?" I asked coquettishly, kissing his neck, oblivious to the hoots still coming from the great hall. "Will you love me if I don't want to stay here in Yadosha?"

He groaned. "Of course I will, you outrageous little sot. You are going to wake up tomorrow with a terrible headache. The main reason you'll not want to stay here after this will be because of your inability to look any of those men in the eye again. What song was that?"

"Song?"

"The one you sang. You never sang for me before."

"I wanted you to like me. Nobody likes me after I've sung for them."

"You sang it terribly, and I like you just fine."

"How rude. Instructor Mia invested a lot of hours in my training, I'll have you know."

"I want you to focus, Tea. We need you alert, not with a keg's worth of Mireth Light in you."

"That's its name? What a horrible name. There was nothing light about it. Is there a doohickey you can do?"

"A what?"

"You know. A—" I began gesticulating wildly. "A doohickey."

Kalen closed his eyes. "A spell. You want me to cast a spell on you."

"You already did!" I giggled. "I'm *enthralled* by you!"

"A spell to ease your hangover."

"That's what I said! A doohickey. Is there?"

My gaze couldn't follow the weaves he made, mostly because I had double vision and he now had four hands, but as soon as he finished, I felt a warm, slow wave steal over my senses, gently washing away some of my sluggishness. I blinked, the hall coming back into focus. "It… Did it work?"

"It's the *Calming* rune. The same one I've always used. You'll still get a headache tomorrow, but at least you're coherent now. *Somewhat* coherent. It doesn't completely remove the intoxication."

"I shouldn't have gotten drunk."

"You shouldn't have."

"I didn't know *Calming* runes could do this. Did you?"

"It's one of the spells Deathseekers learn before their first night out—for reasons that have nothing to do with our training. We used to draw straws over who had to remain sober enough not to fudge the weave."

"Why didn't you do this for me before I made a fool of myself?" I hid my face against his chest with a pained groan. The Yadoshans were never going to let me live this down.

"Because I thought it was hilarious. And before you start complaining," he continued, "I had my eye on you this whole time. You might know Aden and his friends, but I don't, and if they tried anything untoward, I would have bashed their faces in."

"My hero," I purred against his neck. "You thought it was funny, but you got me out of there pretty quickly when I started bragging about your..." Perhaps I wasn't completely sober yet. "*You know.*"

He leaned close, his mouth against my ear, and I shivered. "Would you like a refresher?" he whispered. I could feel the grin curling at his mouth.

I giggled, quite liking that idea and not really wanting to go back to our earlier fight. I cast a guilty glance at the other revelers, remembering my charge. "What about Likh? He wasn't any better off than I was, and he'd been drinking more."

Kalen paused. "You're right. And he's warded, so the rune won't work. We'd best see if he hasn't killed Khalad yet."

"You noticed?"

"They weren't hiding their emotions."

We found Khalad and Likh both still in fighting moods. I'd never seen Likh so angry before. His hands were balled at his sides, and if looks could wither, Khalad would have been missing a few extremities.

"I'm sorry for interrupting." I was still tipsy and wobbled a bit when Kalen set me on my feet. "But I want to make sure you guys are okay before Kalen and I go—"

"You've been arguing," Kalen interrupted bluntly. "And we thought it was time you patched things up."

"We're not arguing," Khalad said, and his heartsglass flamed blue.

"Shut up, Khalad. I'm not here to fight." A headache was starting somewhere behind my eyeballs—not enough to put me out of action, but enough to irritate me. "Likh, drop your wards, and let Kalen make you sober."

"I *promised* Khalad I wouldn't do that again," Likh snapped, "despite not taking what *I* want into consideration, and I'm fairly sure he won't—"

"Likh, for the gods' sake." I flung out my hands, weaving a barely legible caricature of the *Delving* rune. "Look, let's conduct a room-wide search to prove it's safe to let down the barrier so we can—"

I couldn't finish. The rune showed me the lie of my own words and was glowing a dark, sooty red over one of the guests.

I swung around, and the rune followed, like a pendulum— one, two, three, four. Four guests had the *Blight* rune incubating inside them—including Lord Aden.

"Tea?" Kalen matched my pace as I marched toward the center of the room, no longer drunk, channeling *Scrying* runes as fast as I could make them. Like stationary fireflies, they shone. I braced myself for the barrage of thoughts coming my way.

       they should have *nanghait* hunts every year. I reckon
          we could convince the southerners to let us use
          their *taurvi* a time or two—
       watered down codswallop, these things are nowadays. And only two years ago we had the finest
          lager straight from Steerfall—
       gotta be heading off soon. The missus ain't gonna be
          happy I'm late, hunt or no hunt—
       Druj. It was a subtle whisper barely perceptible amid the throng of loud Yadoshan thoughts, but it stank of ugly magic and bitter spells. *King Aadil.*

There was a man, sitting off to one side, all on his own, with a tankard of untasted beer beside him. He was dressed like a Yadoshan, and he looked like one: tall with a full beard and dark eyes. Our gazes met, and the thoughts grew overpowering.

Druj, his mind seemed to snarl. *Aadil, King of the world and the Dying and the Life, may his house flourish from now until the end of eternity—*

The man sprang up, and so did I. I saw the magic fizzle from his fingertips and knew what he intended. My gestures were quick, concise, accurate, and my rune was done before his.

"*Stop!*" I yelled, and the room quieted. The Yadoshan imposter stopped, eyes wide as he choked. His hand lingered in the air, about to complete the final stroke that would have sent Aden and three other people spiraling into blighted, grotesque daeva-like transformations. With all my might, I forced the man to lower his arm, dispel his own rune.

Then I drew back my fist and punched him hard on the chin. I felt the satisfactory crack of my knuckles hitting jaw, hopefully breaking it, and the man collapsed, knocked out cold.

"This man," I announced to the rest, "is Drychta!" before bending over and throwing up all over my shoes.

*T*HE BULK OF THE *K*ION *army we had left in Daanoris drifted into Ankyo. Zoya had enlisted more asha to accompany their ships, drag them speedily back to the continent.*

Mistress Parmina headed the first regiment, and she brought with her the body of the Dark asha, Lady Mykaela. Her remains had been carefully placed in a coffin of ice, no doubt the Valerian headmistress's doing—opaque enough to see very little, but transparent enough to catch quick glimpses of what lay within: a lock of golden hair, a reposed palm, a layer of hua. The people were quiet with their heads bowed as horses pulled her coffin down their paved roads. Dark asha or not, Lady Mykaela was beloved among the Kions, and not a dry eye greeted the procession as it continued to her final resting place in the Willows.

I looked on from the edge of the crowd as Empress Alyx and Princess Inessa rode up to receive her, Lord Fox a canter behind. Both royal women wept. The daughter's slim form was racked with sobs while her mother sat, tall and erect in her saddle, as fresh tears coursed down her face.

"Your Majesty," Mistress Parmina said in a voice as clear as a bell, in a ritual as old as the kingdom itself. Her eyes were clear, and her patrician nose lifted despite the dried streaks of makeup that betrayed her poise. "Please welcome your most honored daughter to the Willows, who has served the House Valerian faithfully for twenty-six years. Now she sleeps, and we are all the lesser for her loss."

"*Kion welcomes Lady Mykaela of the Sorrows,*" the empress intoned, "*and we honor her above all.*"

I never wished for this to happen.

I startled, but the unexpected voice was quick to pacify me, taking up space in my head where it did not belong. I do not plan on staying long, Bard. I only wished… I only wanted to see… *Her voice quieted, yearning toward the carriage, where her mentor lay.*

"*Where are you?*" I asked aloud. "*And where are your daeva?*"

Have they enticed you to betray me already? Are you their agent now, set to wait for my contact, to goad me into revealing myself? It is difficult to be certain, to be careful, when there are so many schemes afoot.

"*What do you want?*"

I want to watch. For a little while. I owe her that much. I wish I could raise her. I wish I could raise Polaire. You don't die from regret, but people keep dying for it in my place.

We were silent, she and I, watching the rest of the procession pass, until the Lady Mykaela was within the embrace of the Willows. "*They will find you,*" I murmured.

I expect them to, Bard. Fox knows where I intend.

Why not maintain contact with me this way, instead of abandoning me to my own devices?

My strength is not inexhaustible, as you saw in Daanoris. The Dark pulls too much from me now, more than it ever has, and I need to survive a little longer. I have other traps lying in wait, baits to replenish, and they command greater attention.

The letters you left me—they are unfinished.

Oh?

There was no ending. You promised me an ending. There are missing pages.

Did I? *There was no surprise in her voice, no shock. But there was—satisfaction. Eagerness.* I offered you my story, Bard. I will not be held responsible for what you misplace in the interim.

And just like that, she was gone, taking more answers from me than I ever had of her.

13

"T ALK."
    Unlike in Kion, Yadoshans have little qualms about "interrogating" their prisoners, especially when said prisoner has been caught in the act. The Drychta was in slightly worse shape than when I had found him, with runic wards woven about his person as strong as Kalen could make them. Although he was initially confused, First Minister Stefan understood the situation after we explained, particularly after the man woke and began swearing at us in Drychta.

    There was a small volcano erupting somewhere behind my eyeballs. While Kalen's *Calming* rune alleviated some of the previous night's celebration, he had been right in warning me of the other aftereffects. The lack of a good night's sleep made my hangover worse. Warding off Aden and the others infected by the blight had sapped most of my energy, and *Delving* the rest of the Yadoshans had taken the rest.

First Minister Stefan and the other second ministers were in attendance, all armed to the teeth and looking ferocious, almost eager to have the Drychta escape for the chance at another hunt. There was no love lost between the two kingdoms; wars against the desert people made up a large part of Yadoshan history, and old habits were hard to break.

First Minister Stefan had taken part in the initial inter-rogations, although his was conducted in the language of fists. By the time the prisoner was brought into my presence, the man sported black eyes and a bleeding lip, and no doubt other bruises I couldn't see. My current mood gave me no incentive to protest his treatment, and even Khalad was unusually silent about the matter.

"Can't you finagle the information out of his brain?" Lord Besserly asked me. "Dark asha can do that, right?"

First Minister Stefan coughed. "Lady Tea can most certainly put him in a better frame of mind to talk," he said, rubbing at his reddened knuckles, "and she can most certainly compel his actions, but she told me the Drychta has blocks in his head that repel her *Compulsion*, like the Faceless. Unless he chooses to speak, she can do little."

"And he's tied up in runic wards, milord," Kalen reminded him. "It prevents him from attacking your minds, but also stops Tea from compelling his. More importantly, it prevents other minds nearby from gaining access to him, and he to them."

Lord Besserly swore. "Do you mean there are more of these spies in Thanh?"

"Khalad and Likh are investigating. It's best to be sure."

"How frustratingly complicated."

"I have a few more tricks up my sleeve, Your Excellency." The runes I used were not of the Dark. Hidden ambushes were planted within the Drychta's mind, that I knew. Underestimating the Faceless was the reason Aenah took advantage of me. "Is Druj your master?"

I didn't need to understand Drychta to know the words flying out of the prisoner's mouth, none of them answers to my question. First Minister Stefan responded to his impertinence with a quick blow across the face. The man sagged backward.

I fashioned another layer of spells, adding them to the glittering runes already revolving around the prisoner. "Is Druj your master?"

Blood dripped down the man's chin, but he was defiantly silent. Slowly, steadily, I added another coating of spells. Each time, I posed the question again.

Kalen stood behind the man, his hands copying my movements, adding to my strength. After five rune tiers, our prisoner began to fidget. At the eighth, he was trembling, beads of perspiration dripping down his forehead and onto his beard. By the fourteenth, he was shaking uncontrollably until, in the middle of my question, he finally blurted out a frantic, explosive, "Yes!"

"How did you do it?" Lord Besserly asked, astounded. "You never even touched him."

"The wards were customized to prevent destructive spells, milord. But there are passive runes that pose no direct danger to anyone and are easily overlooked because of it. These runes simply increased his desire to talk." I was right to be cautious. It had taken both Kalen and I together to overcome the man's resistance, and *Eagerness* was a minor spell, easy enough to impose. "What is your name?"

"Jareek of the Golden Rod, Third of the Light."

Lord Stefan sucked in a noisy breath, and Lord Besserly swore again.

"Does his name hold some significance?" Kalen asked.

"Very much so. This man is a ranked soldier and a member of King Aadil's private bodyguards. How did he come to channel Dark runes? Seems Aadil has been keeping secrets from us. Why have you come to Yadosha, cretin? To attack Lady Tea?"

"My king saw the dreaded three-headed beast flying above us into Yadosha, and so learned of the witch's presence in the north," Jareek said. "He sent me, in his infinite wisdom, to sow discord, and prevent you from assisting Odalia."

"Assisting Odalia?" I demanded.

"We seek the same thing you do, witch. When the mountains fall and we reclaim the forbidden fruit, his Highness, King Aadil—may the heavens forever bless his name—shall hold the key to immortality and rule the eons. Kance, that fool prince of an insipid king, seeks to deny us. We will prevail and crush his army. Already you are too late. We have taken the mountains. Soon, we will take the harvest."

"And what does Druj have to do with all this?"

"Druj is with us. Druj counsels the king. Druj learned of my skill in the Dark and brought the runes out of me." The man bared his teeth. "You will not stop us. My life is but a small grain in the sands of a fate you cannot hope to overturn. Drycht will rise as it once had, and there is no stopping the tide."

The next blow that came was not from Lord Stefan's hand, but from mine. My fist slammed into the side of his head; the chair he was strapped to wobbled, then overturned. I held his head against the ground with as much force as I could manage.

"If you ever harm Kance," I said coldly, "I will kill you slowly, and you will relive that nightmare in your head over and over until I snuff out your life as easily as a candle's flame. Your suffering will last a hundred thousand sunsets." I strengthened the wards, ensuring that not even a meditation rune could cross the barrier. "Take him away and do what you want to him. I have all the information I need."

"Remind me never to anger the good asha," Lord Stefan said as I stalked away.

"You haven't looked at me since this morning," Kalen observed as he caught up to me.

"I don't know what you're talking about," I said, my head down.

"Was it because of last night?"

Of course it was about last night! I had drunkenly announced my ardent love for Kalen to anyone who would listen, then pledged to exchange heartsglass while also threatening everyone at the same time. And *that* was right after a fight about returning to Kion. My cheeks colored. I'd asked him to marry me! "No," I mumbled.

Kalen stared straight ahead. "When the worst of this is over and we find the culprits responsible, I wouldn't mind."

"Mind what?"

"Exchanging heartsglass." Then he strode away, leaving me stunned.

By the time I caught up with Kalen, he was with Likh and Khalad in the now-empty great hall. Likh was bent over a cup of tea, breathing in the aroma. He looked as bad as I felt, though I suspected he was worse off. He had refused to relinquish the runic wards in light of recent news. The Heartforger had taken off his spectacles, and his eyes were bloodshot.

"The Drychta thinks the First Harvest is in Mithra's Wall," I announced, and both turned to me. "Aadil's army managed to sneak past the southern kingdoms, and they now occupy the range. Kance's army is there, trying to head them off. We must help them. From what the spy says, it seems Aadil is well aware of the shadowglass spell, and that Druj has allied himself with them."

"I thought Lord Garindor said that the First Harvest was in the Ring of Worship?" Khalad asked.

"He said he *thinks* it's there. But if Druj thinks it's at Mithra's Wall, we can't risk not investigating."

Likh started to rise, then flinched when a ray of sunlight from a nearby window glanced across his face and sat back down. "Right now?" he asked weakly.

"We're leaving, but you aren't. Don't argue with me on this, Likh. It's too risky for you, and you know it. There'll be Faceless there, and I have no doubt Druj will be in those mountains. If he's anything like Aenah or Usij, he'll find some way around the wards."

"Okay," the asha said meekly.

I raised my eyebrow. "Really? You're not going to fight me on this?"

"I'd be fairly useless, wouldn't I? It's not like I can use any spells at this point, and I haven't quite gotten the fighting part of my training perfected yet." Likh took a sip of his tea and shuddered. "I'm so occupied with trying not to throw up that I don't have much room in me to protest. I want to die," he moaned.

"Is tea the best solution?"

"It's Althy's concoction that we brought with us," Khalad said shortly, then softened his tone. "Drink up, Likh, and I'll make you a fresh batch."

"It tastes disgusting," Likh mumbled, but drank obediently.

"I want you here with him," Kalen told his cousin. "With Likh under the wards, you're the most qualified to seek out other blighted here in Yadosha."

"I take it you're off to join Kance's fight?"

"The Yadoshans are also interested in coming to his aid. They're not very happy about being fooled. But Tea and I will be faster on the *azi*. If Kance is facing off against the Faceless, then time's of the essence. And if anything happens here, we'll only be a dragon's flight away." He glanced at me, and I nodded. "Stefan is sending word to Istera and Tresea as well. They have no love lost for the Drychta. As soon as we hear word of what the Yadoshans intend to do, we'll be leaving."

"Good luck and get back safely. And send my regards to my brother."

"It might be a good idea to address some other issues while you're here in Thanh," Kalen advised gently.

Khalad looked back at Likh, who rested his head on the table. "I suppose you're right." He picked up the empty teacup. "I'll refill this."

"I'll go with you," Kalen said.

"You okay?" I asked Likh once they were gone.

The boy's head bobbed, face still buried in his arms. "I am never *ever* going to drink again."

"Is now a good time to bring up Khalad?"

"You're an evil person, Tea," he accused.

"So I've been told."

Likh jerked up. "Oh… I'm sorry. I didn't mean it like that."

"I know what you meant." I'd been so close to forgetting about Daisy, about Fox. I forced down my own melancholy, stifling a sudden spasm of grief. "Does he know now?"

"He does." Likh's face was miserable. "I…I blurted it out in the heat of anger. He just stared at me like I'd grown another head. He had no idea. He hadn't thought about me that way. That's what made me want to drink and forget last night. That's why I was flirting with your friends. I wanted to feel, for one brief second, how it would be if I were what I looked like, instead of what I really am. I know that's no excuse…"

"I'm so sorry."

He looked at me in amazement. "Sorry for what?"

"The rest of this wasn't supposed to happen. You were supposed to be accepted as an asha and be an amazing dancer and star in the *darashi oyun*, without all these other challenges. "

"No one forced me to become an asha. I wanted it. I wanted it so bad that it was obvious to you. Even when I was a zivar shopkeeper's assistant with a talent for weaves and a head full of dreams." Likh smiled. "I thought about quitting, but if I did, it would only justify what others thought about me, that I didn't deserve to be asha. There were some bad days, but there were a lot of good days too, and I won't trade any of those for the world."

He looked down at his hands. "Maybe I need to understand myself first, you know? So I can figure out what I'd like to change about me after that."

I hugged him. "You are far wiser than I will ever be, Likh. Whatever you do, I'll support you. But we must get the *Blight* purged from your system first."

"Lady Tea, Lady Likh." Lord Aden entered the hall with Lords Knox and Balfour. The big man was especially pale, and not from the Mireth Light; nearly escaping a terrible fate tended to do that, even to the bravest fighters. He also stank of his own runic wards. "I understand that I have you to thank for my life."

"It was I who imperiled it in the first place," I said, rising to my feet. As Kalen had predicted, I couldn't quite meet their eyes after my show last night. "If Aadil hadn't seen the *azi*, you all might have been spared."

Lord Knox chuckled. "How red you are, Lady Tea! What's spoken in our cups remains in our cups, milady. We've been down that road many times before."

"I don't trust that shite bastard—begging your pardon—of not blighting us, with or without your daeva," Lord Aden continued. "The first minister and the others are drawing up plans to mobilize our army and join Odalia. It would take a three days' ride to Mithra's Wall. There's no hurry at the moment, he said— King Kance's army's expected to arrive around the same time too." He looked downcast. "I'd been hoping I could still join up, but Stefan isn't seeing things my way."

"You've been blighted, and you *still* want to fight?"

"Besserly says as long as you don't eat compromised food, the *Blight*'ll fade and you'll be back to normal, right? These wards don't make me feel any different. Like a hidden shield on me, right? Wouldn't that mean I've got added protection? I mean, I can fish my own way and brew my own hops, and I can still hold a sword. What other problem ought I have if I go with the rest of the men?"

"Oh dear," I said.

Lord Knox guffawed. "You must forgive him, Lady Tea. It's the first battle he'll be missing since that wrangle with that Tresean trawler at Montvaisin a year ago, on account of him being seasick. Stefan's sending you over to Westmarchen Tower at the Finger, Aden, to keep a close eye out on any other strange ships coming in. The gods willing, you'll have your share of action there."

Aden sighed.

"I would like to apologize as well," Likh said shamefacedly. "I misled you and your friends last night, Sir Knox. You were led to believe that I was…that I was a lady. Likh…in Odalia, Likh is a boy's name. I joined the Willows out of a genuine sincerity to be an asha…but I shouldn't have withheld this from any of you. Please forgive me." He closed his eyes.

How many times had he confessed this in Kion, I thought, *only to be met with derision and disgust?* I felt terrible, not having known before.

All three Yadoshans stared incredulously at the asha before Knox and Aden threw their heads back in laughter. Balfour, on the other hand, looked stricken.

"Poor Bally here's smitten with you!" Aden explained in between chortles, forgetting his own problem. "He was all doled out, asking Besserly questions about what he needed to be your patron and worrying how he'd go about it without causing you offense! We've traveled all the kingdoms, Lady Likh. And sure, there's some right bastards, but we ain't as narrow-minded as some of our kinsmen. No harm—well, except for poor Balfour's broken heart here."

"There's a waiting period after becoming an asha before Likh can accept such offers, even if he were willing," I told the man gently, "and he hasn't quite finished his training yet."

"Would…would the rates be different if he ain't a girl?" Balfour asked, almost mournfully, and his fellows roared. The asha in question was already beet red, mouth open as he stared at the contrite Yadoshan. Khalad looked horrified. He stared at

Balfour—I was pleased to observe—with almost the same look Likh had when Lord Cyran had taken Khalad's hand back in Istera.

"Yadoshans," Kalen said again, shaking his head.

·· ⋋⫫⋌ ··

Preliminary reports told us, as Lord Aden confirmed, that Kance's army had yet to arrive at Mithra's Wall but was expected to in three days. The Yadoshan army had already moved out to add to their numbers, itching to get to the fighting before the Odalians could. At Kalen's insistence, I reluctantly agreed to spend the night in Thanh instead of setting out immediately.

"*Azi* or not, it's suicidal to face down a Drychta army and a Faceless lurking within their ranks without rest," he reminded me. "We'll get there long before Stefan's soldiers, even if you stay the next two nights. Let's not head into a potential battle before conserving our strength."

I'd fallen asleep quickly after dinner, after another round of *Delving* to ensure that there were no other traitors in our midst, but woke up around midnight, trembling. There were no visions or nightmares this time—I had not experienced those since leaving Odalia.

This time it was different. I had a strange feeling of fear and discomfort, and I couldn't shake the feeling that something bad was about to happen…and that I would be powerless to prevent it.

I stole quietly out of bed, so as not to disturb Kalen, and

hesitated before the window, looking up at the moon. Slowly, I reached for the *azi* and felt its gentle presence reach out for mine. It was soaring with no particular destination in mind, enjoying the wind billowing underneath its wings, the fresh, cool air against its three heads.

That's what true freedom looks like, I thought enviously. *Nothing but endless sky before you, as far as you dare.*

I retreated slightly. Despite my promise never to make contact with Fox again—for the fear that he would be accused of being an accessory to my actions—I stepped out, reaching across the miles between us. The door separating us that I had so carefully built in my mind, the painstaking seals I had placed to keep myself out, crumbled easily at my touch.

I missed Fox. I missed Mykaela too, and Althy and Inessa and Shadi—even Zoya and Parmina—but it was Fox's absence that grieved me. His was the voice that provided comfort and companionship during my long years of training, and I had never been apart from him this long. This might have been an exile of my own making, but knowing what I had to do was different from remembering what I was missing. *I only want to know if he's all right*, I promised myself, and believed in my own delusion.

Fox was no longer in prison, and the relief that took hold of me knew no bounds. He was in the royal chambers, standing before an open window and looking out into the city, while Princess Inessa slept nearby. It was good to see that he had retained favor with Empress Alyx. His thoughts were somber, his mood bleak.

Leave, I told myself. *You should leave.* I didn't.

There was a faint rustle, and Inessa's sleepy voice broke through the darkness. "Come to bed, Fox. I'm cold."

Fox turned away from the window. "Kance has left Odalia," he said quietly.

"I was there when Mother broke the news to us, my love, remember? Right before you saved us from my blighted maids."

Blighted maids? Visions rose in my head unbidden, as Fox gave in to his memories. Horribly transformed women with spider legs and horns gunned for Inessa and the empress, my brother fighting them off.

"If Tea knows, she'll go after him."

Inessa lifted her head. "You haven't talked about your sister since she left," the princess said gently, and my heart twisted.

"I—sometimes I feel her in my head, and I don't know if it's my mind playing tricks or if she's really there. I do my best to push her out, but she hovers like a ghost, haunting me. There is a wall between us, a wall she built, and both Mykkie and Althy tell me I must leave it that way. If I don't, the elder asha will believe I'm still in contact with her, no matter what Mykkie and the other asha offer for evidence."

"If they refuse to believe you no matter what you do, why don't you reach out to her?"

My brother was silent.

"Do you really believe that she killed Daisy?"

"I saw her, Inessa." The confession sounded like it had been torn from his throat. "I was in her head when she did it.

I've been in her head when she was controlled by a Faceless, and this was different. She was in control. She may claim not to remember, but no one was in possession of her thoughts when she killed our sister." His voice hardened. "It's her black heartsglass. I know it. Killing Aenah tainted her. The more she takes in the Dark, the more uncontrollable she becomes. I don't want to see her hurt anyone else, Inessa, even if it is unintentionally. I don't—I don't want Mykkie or anyone else to have to kill her."

"I am not going to lose either of you, Fox."

"I don't know that you have a choice." He took her in his arms. "It might be better for you to give me up. My presence is enough to cost you your reputation. Some people already see me as a traitor. You should not endure whispers for consorting with one."

"Mykaela says to be patient, and I trust her." She kissed him. "Whatever happens, I will not leave you. And if you have any faith in me, then you will do the same."

"I will do everything in my power to stay by your side. But not at the cost of your life or your honor, even if I have to slay my own sister to protect them." Then he lifted his head, startled. Before his lips could form my name, I retreated, weeping, to the other side of the door. The seals I added were more formidable, enforced by a stronger will than I had at the last undertaking. *He will be safer without me in his head*, I thought as I built. *He will be safe.*

But all I could focus on were his words. *Even if I have to slay my own sister.*

He was right. I could not blame him. It might come down to that in the end.

By the time Kalen found me, my tears had dried and I was more pensive than melancholic. "Why is it," I asked him with a rueful smile, "that you have the uncanny ability to wake when I need you, though I do my best to be silent?"

He tapped his heartsglass. Despite the cold, he wore no shirt, and my heart quickened at the sight. "It's almost instinct to close my eyes and know where you are."

"Do you know what's strange? Mykkie said something similar not too long ago. Like she could feel Polaire still, because they'd shared heartsglass."

"Can't sleep?"

"Couldn't stay asleep." I looked up at the stars. "We can't run away, Kalen," I said softly. "I can't sit by while Druj and the Drychta attempt to create darksglass. Without us, they could force Khalad to create lightsglass for them. And if they find the First Harvest, then it will only be a matter of time before they combine the two to make shadowglass. Once we've found a solution to that, we can leave. I'll go with you anywhere."

He tried to hide his disappointment and nodded. "Fair enough. Lord Garindor says a mountain must be passed to gain darksglass. There is something more to that than simply spells."

"I'm not sure we can rely on the books. Darksglass alone is enough to frighten me. A spell where *all the seven daeva are contained therein*. That must be the daeva's bezoars. And then there's lightsglass, which requires the souls of the Five Heroes or their descendants—which Khalad can do. We must prevent Druj from getting his hands on them."

"That should be easy enough. You have the *azi*, and I doubt it would willingly turn itself over to anyone else. And there's the *nanghait*'s bezoar that we've taken, and the *zarich*'s."

"And part of the *taurvi* still back in Kion. I could try to send word to Mykaela to keep an eye on it." I looked at him. He smiled, and it was like our previous fight had never happened.

"I'm not going to ask you to talk to Fox," he said. "I… don't know how to fix what's happening between the two of you, but it might be easier once we put down the Drychta threat. It was a courageous thing you did tonight, even if it was a little spontaneous."

"You saw?"

"While I was sleeping. Not all, but enough to understand. I can't explain how."

"I don't know if it will ever be the same between Fox and me." I closed my eyes and kissed him slowly. "But I have you." I burrowed my fingers into his hair. "Every path I've chosen and every decision I've made, you were my one constant. I meant what I said last night. If anyone tries to hurt you, I swear on everything that I am I will hunt him down."

"And what about the rest?" His hands moved lower. "About exchanging heartsglass?"

"In a heartbeat, if I could. When this is over, as you said."

"Agreed. But you can't control the future," Kalen reminded me gently, his breath warm against my mouth.

"I don't care. I'll bring us back from the grave if I have to, silver heartsglass or not."

"And I will kill anyone standing between us," he promised, before his lips closed over mine, "even if I have to crawl out of my grave to do so."

*S*HE SAID NOTHING OF HER *location?*" Lady Altaecia studied me like she could discern my thoughts from my expression alone. The Dark asha gave me no reason to believe that she wanted our conversation to remain a secret. She abandoned me while her brother offered sanctuary, though he had every right to turn me away. I was loyal to her tale first and foremost—let her politics hang.

"She wanted to pay her respects to Lady Mykaela, milady."

"She'll make for the Hollow ranges," Lord Fox predicted grimly. "Kance's army is there. If he'll lead the charge, so will she."

"But will it be on our side and Kance's? It's easier to treat her as a foe rather than as a friend nowadays."

"I would much rather ignore them both and attack Drycht instead," Empress Alyx fumed. "Every hour that we do not set foot in the desert kingdom gives them more time to prepare."

"I'd rather not have an army attacking us from behind, Your Majesty," Lord Fox disagreed. "We'll have to muddle through them first. I'd choose a delay over lives lost. And whatever Tea says, she believes there is a trap waiting for us in Drycht. The Hollows will be good middle ground."

Lady Altaecia turned back to me. "I don't suppose you will agree to stay behind."

"I hope you would permit me the honor of accompanying you, milady."

"You are dedicated, which is admirable. What do you say, Your Majesty?"

"We shall take Lord Knox's soldiers and half our army and make for the Hollow Mountains," the empress decided. "The rest will stay behind. I do not want to see what remains of Kion lost to either more dragonfire or blighted folk."

The beautiful woman gazed at her daughter and her consort. "What say the both of you? Whatever her intentions, Tea attacked my kingdom. Any other ruler would have considered that an act of war. What reason should I have to spare Tea's life, rather than have her hauled up in chains—or killed—before she can work her compulsion on anyone else?"

The princess spread her hands helplessly. "You trusted her once, Mother. You saw the lies the elders wrought to make her bitter. You saw her thrown out of home and kingdom, seeking refuge in other nations like a vagabond, despite everything she has done to protect us. She minimizes our casualties as she directs her anger against the elders. She bears us no ill will. Read her letters, as I have."

"Her letters could easily be a plant, created to soften our stances and put us off our guard. I understand that Tea is a friend, Inessa, but I have a responsibility to do what is best for Kion, as will you when you take my place. You cannot let your heart rule your head in these matters, especially when she has shown no signs of conciliation toward us. She may still nurse a grudge, despite her accusations. And she may *have spared most of us from death, but there were deaths all the same. She is losing her self-control. What do you think, Fox?"*

"Whatever her intentions, it is the results that matter, Your Majesty. She threatened Kion, and now she may threaten Odalia. If she turns against us when we reach the Hollow Mountains, then do not hesitate to take her down."

"You can't!" Inessa gasped.

"Is that why you're so willing to give Tea the benefit of the doubt, Inessa? Because her death will result in Fox's?"

The princess trembled. "We need to find another way."

"You have to be prepared for the eventuality that there may not be another solution." Love had scrubbed the roughness from Lord Fox's voice. "I died a soldier once. If I can protect you, then I'd do it all over again."

"Idiot," Princess Inessa lamented as we left the throne room. Already the orders for the army to start for southern Odalia had been given. "She's your sister! There has to be another option! There has to—there must be a—"

Quietly, I stole away. But before I did, I saw Lord Fox framing Princess Inessa's face with his hands, murmuring words beyond my hearing. He wore a look I have seen men adopt when they venture into the thick of war knowing they would not return—and finding their peace in it.

Lady Zoya waited at the entrance to the palace, her face set. Beside her was the largest man I had ever seen. His beard was carefully combed and long hair pulled back from his face. A wicked-looking hatchet hung from his side.

"*We leave in half an hour,*" the asha said abruptly. "*No word if you're to come with us, Bard, but it would be best to prepare anyway.*"

"*Bard?*" the tall man boomed. "*Drychta, from his looks. Will Althy allow him into battlefields in the first place?*"

"*They're allowing you, Rahim, and you aren't in the army either.*"

"*Bah. Tresean men fight whether they wield sword, hoe, or needle.*"

"*What's going on?*" I asked, alarmed.

"*Shadi went ahead to warn Fox, so he'll be hearing it soon enough. They've sighted the* azi, *and it's heading for the Hollows as well. This time, Tea's making no attempts at hiding.*"

14

PIGEONS WERE SENT TO KING Kance's army, informing them of the city-states of Yadosha's willingness to "aid the Odalians in their attempts to eradicate our misguided desert brothers and the Faceless's mortal cesspool couched in human form"—First Minister Stefan was elected for skills other than his diplomacy—and arrangements were soon underway for the rest of the Yadoshans' departure. The men celebrated preparation for war in the same manner they celebrated their daeva hunts; Lord Knox told me, only half jesting, that cheerful bloodlust was a cultural trait.

"They're able warriors, at least," Khalad pointed out. "Kance may soon find himself outmatched and outnumbered, especially with a Faceless lurking among the Drychta. They'll help to even the odds." He frowned. "I can't believe Kance would go to war without informing us. Surely he would err on the side of caution."

"I may be the reason he did not ask Kion for assistance."
I was quiet. The Yadoshans had been reluctant to give us leave
for Mithra's Wall ahead of their soldiers, as the fighting would be
much diminished after the *azi* had had its way. I'd finally agreed
to Lord Stefan's proposal to choose warriors to accompany us on
the back of the daeva, and a short brawl had broken out over who
would receive that honor. Kalen, bless him, had taken it upon
himself to sort the men to spare me the headache.

Khalad smiled at me. "Kance would never let his personal
feelings get in the way of a logical strategy. Whatever he might
think of you, he would never let it cloud his judgment, especially
if his kingdom's on the line. He doesn't think ill of you, regardless
of what he's said in the past."

"You were present the last time Kance and I'd talked. He
didn't seem ready to let go of his bitterness."

"Things change, Tea. He's changed. I've had the chance to
talk to him in the last few months. I think that once the initial
anger had passed and he had more time to assess his father's condition and understand the circumstances that led to it, he realized
why you did what you did."

"He never reached out to me."

"Kance is a kind man, but kings have pride too. He manages
it better than I ever could."

I wanted to change the subject and seized the opening. "Is
pride stopping you from talking to Likh?"

Khalad blanched. "Did he tell you?"

"I have eyes, Khalad. Remember all those times when

you chided me about *my* crush? Karma is a swift, unforgiving mistress."

He cleared his throat. "I don't understand him, Tea, and I thought I was good at figuring out people. He gets mad at me for things I have no control over, and blows up when I try to help. The runic wards are for his own protection. He can't simply undo them whenever he feels like it because he's an asha who can. You've scolded him before, and so has Kalen, but he never blows his fuse with you two the way he does with me!"

I stared at him, mouth agape. Was he seriously that oblivious? Had I been as oblivious with Kalen? That thought alone stopped me from laughing in his face. It wasn't my place to tell him. It wasn't likely he would believe me even if I did. That was Likh's job now.

"Likh values your opinion more than he does either Kalen's or mine. And he dissolved his wards to save you. I'd like to believe he was expecting a bit more gratitude than anger. Do you like him?"

Khalad looked astounded. "What? Me? I—I don't know. I'm not in the habit of thinking of people—of anyone—that way. We're... Heartforgers aren't supposed to—"

"It's not unheard of. I can cite a couple of instances of heartforgers marrying and raising children."

"Ah, I don't think the latter would be possible with Likh, Tea."

I opened my mouth but caught myself. Likh's desires weren't my business to tell either. "There can be more to a family than children, Khalad. Or you can adopt. Or there could be other ways. I think you should talk to him first. Don't start with anger or explain why he shouldn't risk his life for yours. Just talk to him. No—*listen*. He doesn't want to hear solutions. He wants you to hear him out."

Khalad sighed. "I suppose I can try."

"Lady Tea?" One of the soldiers poked his head into the room. "Stefan wants to see you immediately."

Kalen was with Lord Stefan, Lord Besserly, and the other ministers when we entered the stateroom, though he didn't look happy. "Lady Tea," the First Minister started, clearing his throat several times. His heartsglass was crystal blue. "We have news."

"I trust that the matter of choosing warriors for the *azi* has been settled amicably?"

"Yes. But that's not what I refer to. A raven arrived from Kion, from the asha association."

The room turned cold. Khalad muttered something indistinct.

"It's a bit troubling, milady. They've accused you of fleeing the kingdom after murdering some villagers, including your own sister. I trust Lady Mykaela and know that she vouches for you, but if you have been found guilty as it says, we cannot take that lightly. They request you be placed under arrest and taken back to Kion pending your sentence."

"The blighted incidents appeared only after your arrival," one of the ministers pointed out. "It *is* an odd coincidence."

"You forget that she took down the *nanghait* for us, Heathrow," Lord Besserly argued. "And had Lady Tea been the instigator of those blights, then she would have let them happen instead of preventing them. We found the Drychta responsible, in case you weren't listening."

"That could have easily been a ploy orchestrated to win our trust."

"And what did she gain by that trust? She asked for none of our secrets and made no concessions for it. I am a living testament to her loyalty. I owe her my life. The least we can do is give her the benefit of the doubt."

"If I may speak?" I asked.

"Please do, Lady Tea," Lord Stefan responded.

"There is reason to believe that the elders have been keeping secrets for years. Several asha and I believe that Kion was built on a lie. Magic was not a privilege we were given to keep, but a means to right an old wrong. Hollow Knife intended to heal a rift in the world with a rare spell, though the consequence would be to end our use of magic once and for all."

"Those are the same precepts that the Faceless prattle on about!" another minister warned.

"I will never approve of the Faceless's actions, milord. We have slain Usij and Aenah, and we will slay Druj and anyone else who would try to take their place. The elder asha want to keep the Faceless from their goal, but neither do they want to lose our magic, and so they have been doing their utmost to defy us at every turn. If you are a friend of Lady Mykaela, then you would want her to live, not die slowly from the Dark. We almost lost her. We've lost Lady Polaire already."

"I don't understand," Lord Knox said. "To heal the rift sounds like a noble endeavor. Why would you take away your own magic?"

"The rift gives daeva life, milord," Kalen said. "Without magic, the Faceless would be powerless. I don't know if the absence of magic can truly bring peace, but it can guarantee the permanent death of those monsters and benefit at least four of your citizens. The elder asha prefer an endless fight against the Faceless and their runes, rather than be deprived of their own magic."

"So you intend to rid the kingdoms of spells, Lady Tea?"

"I don't know yet," I answered honestly. "I'm as selfish as they are. I have too many friends who rely on magic, and I won't be the one to take it away from them. But for now, I want to keep it away from both the Faceless and from the elder asha, to ensure they won't misuse their abilities at the cost of anyone else's."

"Then this was all a trick?" another minister asked. "You did not murder these villagers as they claim? Or your sister?"

Kalen's gaze sought mine, and I drew strength from what I saw there. "I have no memories of committing such acts. I only know that I would never have done so of my own volition. As for the others, I *know* that I am innocent."

The First Minister sighed. "You've given us much to think about, Lady Tea. But though I am inclined to believe you, there will be many of us who disagree."

"I do not intend to stay in Yadosha, Your Excellency." I ignored the startled glances both Khalad and Kalen sent my way. "Once this business with Drycht and Odalia is done, I intend to leave your kingdom and seek sanctuary elsewhere. I have no desire to see you risk your alliance with Kion for me. Stability between your kingdoms cannot be compromised."

Lord Stefan sighed. "I am truly sorry, milady."

"I understand the politics, milord. The blight some of your citizens suffer should abate in the next few weeks. Once the asha return to Yadosha, ask my sisters to monitor their conditions. With me gone from the city-states and with both Drycht and the Faceless searching for my presence elsewhere, I doubt they will attack again."

"If there is anything else we can do for you in any unofficial capacity…"

"There's an old saying in Odalia, Your Excellency: before you weigh your neighbor's hogs, fix your own broken pens."

"Hey now. We like to muck around in the mud every now and then, but we're hardly hogs, milady."

I smiled. "It means that we must fix our own problems before we pontificate on someone else's. My friends and I are ready and will be set to leave within the hour."

"I speak not as the first minister but as, I hope, a friend, when I say I wish you all the best, Lady Tea."

"We got off lightly this time," Khalad said, breathing a sigh of relief as we returned to the great hall. The place was deserted, give or take a few people still sleeping off last night's excesses. Without thinking, I sat at the same table I'd shared with the Yadoshans; it still stank slightly of ale. "There was a good chance he'd turn us over to Kion anyway."

"Lord Besserly has his ear, and he's well aware of your role in saving his life." Kalen brushed a stray lock from my forehead. "Are you sure, Tea? If we leave Yadosha, there won't be many other places to stay. Arhen-Kosho has even stronger ties to both Kion and Odalia. Tresea isn't the safest option, and we certainly wouldn't want Drycht. Istera might be our best bet."

"I'm not sure I want to subject Istera to me either. If some other kingdom is willing to take me in, they'll eventually gain the elder ashas' ire and reprisal. Empress Alyx may try to hold them off whenever she can, but the Willows is a small kingdom on its own. It would be easy enough for them to enact their own sanctions independent of Kion." I gulped, fighting back tears. "Likh and Khalad—they can live incognito if they want to. As long as I'm not with them, I doubt they'd be targeted. But… Oh, Kalen. Maybe I really should be hidden away, tucked into some vast wilderness where no one can harm me and where I can't harm others."

"We're not leaving you, Tea," Khalad protested.

"You won't have a choice. You still have a duty to the kingdoms, and you're not the type of person to turn your back on them. You'll have hearts to forge, and you'll find your own novices to train eventually. But without me, you'll be safer."

"And can you do the same?" Likh asked shrewdly, stepping into the room. He had forsaken his usual *hua* and was dressed in dark clothes and thick breeches, his long hair pulled back. "You're not the type to turn away when you know people need help."

"I'll travel if I have to, avoid detection. I'll visit villages, treat the sick to earn money."

"And what if another daeva appears? If you take it down with the Dark, then you accomplish what the elder asha want—to have your life drained with every resurrection. And if you bond them like you did the *azi*, then you may as well shine a beacon revealing your location, because the asha will find you."

"Let's not make any hasty decisions," Kalen said. "One thing at a time. Focus on the Drychta and Kance now, and we'll weigh the rest of our options later."

"I won't let you come to any more harm, Likh," I said. "But in the end, it might not be my choice to make."

"Then for as long as we can still make decisions, I'll go with you." Likh hugged me, then turned to Khalad. "I would like to talk to you. Do you have a moment?"

The Heartforger cast a furtive glance at me and nodded.

"Did you mean that?" Kalen asked me as they stepped out. "Do you really want to spend the rest of your life living in the middle of nowhere like some hermit?"

"Wasn't that what you wanted?"

"I meant living in a small town under assumed names. I have enough funds to set us up in moderate comfort indefinitely. Complete isolation isn't what I—Tea?"

I stared at the wall, awed.

"Tea?"

"Do we have enough time for a detour again?" I asked faintly. "Before we head to Kance's army?"

"It should be another two days before the Odalians reach Mithra's Wall. Armies can't move quickly over that terrain. Why?"

"Because we need to stop by Istera. I want to have a talk with the Gorvekai. The symbol on Sakmeet's notes—I knew I'd seen it before." I placed my hands against the wall, where Lord Aden had showed me the faint Gorvekan symbols the night before. "I think the Gorvekai are the missing link in all of this, Kalen."

I CANNOT JOIN YOU," LORD GARINDOR *said regretfully as I secured my meager belongings. "There is little I can do in a war that I can do better in its aftermath, and you already serve as royal chronicler."*

"I was commissioned by the bone witch, not by Empress Alyx." I saw Lord Fox astride Chief, already deep in discussion with Lord Knox and the Kion generals. Lady Zoya was present, attending to their own preparations. Lady Shadi, who was to remain behind and oversee the salvaging of the Willows, flew to the latter's side to give her a sweet kiss, oblivious to the faint wolf whistles of the men. Lady Altaecia had already left with a smaller party to scout ahead of the main army.

"Yet you call her the slur they use to brand those of her profession. You are the closest thing to her defender among these Kions after Princess Inessa, and yet you bear a grudge," he said.

"She left me to my own devices and broke her promise, and she has never once called me by my own name. I don't see why I cannot do the same," I replied.

"Would you have preferred it if she called you by your name? Not the one you call yourself nowadays, at any rate."

I glanced sharply down at him.

"I will keep your secret, milord. We are very good at that. I wish you peace and good blessings, my esteemed brother, and when

the long day is done, may you find your way back home." Lord Garindor bowed—not in the royal Odalian or Kion way, but in the Drychta manner—his head pressed close to the ground and his hands upturned before it, then rose to leave, ignoring the curious stares after him.

Lord Khalad had reappeared, pale and wan and uncommunicative. He ignored the others and saddled his horse.

"You don't need to come with us, Khalad," Lord Fox told him, sympathy laced through his words.

"I will see this through with Tea, Fox. I have a feeling I will be needed where you are going. What do you think Tea's doing?"

The other man scowled. "She's luring us there. And she knows we can't afford to ignore her. Do you know her reasons?"

The Heartforger spread his hands. "Your guess is as good as mine. But if it's a trap, it's likely a trap for the Drychta. Why she wants us there, on the other hand, is a complete mystery to me."

"Hold!"

Lord Fox turned warily as a soldier rushed forward. A hasty conversation commenced, and Lord Fox frowned. "It's unusual to see so many of them here," he mused. "I've only seen two before, and that was when they presented Mykkie and Tea with Chief and Kismet."

"It's best to see what they want, Fox," Lady Zoya said. "We cannot linger for too long."

"They" turned out to be a group of Gorvekai. They waited respectfully while Lord Fox rode forward to greet them. Despite the heat, they remained garbed in thick woolen furs, though they took off their traditional caps as a concession. Their leader cantered forward.

"You are the General Pahlavi," he said. "Sister to the Dark asha and royal consort to the princess of Kion."

"What do you want with us, milord? As you can see, we are in a hurry."

"Perhaps it would be best then that we come with you to the southern edges of Odalia, to aid King Kance."

"You are knowledgeable of both our movements and our objectives, sir?"

"My name is Agnarr, the first of my clan. The Gorvekai have come to pledge our assistance in your war against the Drychta. We are here to see our prophecies come to pass."

"And what prophecy is that, Sir Agnarr?"

The man smiled. "The prophecy of the shadowglass, General Pahlavi. Your sister came to us once, seeking its spell as many have done before her. For so long we have kept to our community along the Ice Knife, waiting for one who might be worthy to wield it. We have pledged our service and our loyalty to Little Tears's seed, and now she has bade us to aid you in your battle against both Druj and the Drychta that the Faceless compels."

15

"Th-this wasn't exactly what I h-had in mind when I asked for a ch-change of scenery!" Likh chattered against my ear as we clambered off the *azi*. We had traded the mild Yadoshan climate for the bone-chilling winters of Istera, but the capital city of Farsun was not our destination. Instead, we had flown farther north, onto the Gorvekan steppes. The wind was harsh and biting, and not even the warmest cloaks we'd brought for the journey nor the *Fire* runes Kalen manifested to warm us could counteract the cold.

Already a group of Gorvekai gathered, watching us silently. They wore their cloak pelts loosely, but generations spent in the harshest climate meant their bodies were toughened by weather. They had no heartsglass that I could see, but I fancied they were more curious of us than anything else.

As we approached, I saw *Fire* runes blazed around the

Gorvekai as well, bright and red against the winterscape. I had only ever seen two Gorvekai in my life; they traveled to Kion during my apprenticeship, bringing with them the horses Mykaela and I would eventually love as Kismet and Chief. The latter whinnied softly at the sight of them, ears perked.

"Stay on your guard, Tea," Kalen cautioned. "It's rare for Gorvekai to allow strangers onto their soil. Not even asha and Deathseekers are permitted to stay long."

"Except for Mykaela," I whispered. "Kalen, they gave us Chief and Kismet in gratitude for something Mykkie had done for them. Surely they remember."

Their leader's gaze traveled to Chief, who was still nickering in delight. "What do you want from us?"

I cleared my throat. "We've come to talk about shadowglass."

The others took a step back, hostility replacing their polite indifference. Some of the men and women reached for bows and axes. Still others wove familiar runes into the air, which glittered against the falling snow. Likh made a startled sound.

"Wait!" I talked hurriedly. "We mean no harm. The Faceless have infiltrated Mithra's Wall, searching for the First Harvest."

A snort echoed against the quiet; one of the men snickered. Soon, another joined in and then another; until laughter surrounded us. Even the leader, so unwelcoming only seconds before, allowed a grin to cross his harsh, bearded features.

"They will find nothing in Mithra's Wall, Tea of the Embers. The First Harvest does not reside within those mountains. There is nothing to fear, and you may leave safe in that knowledge."

But I was not one to give up so easily. "As a token of your gratitude, you once gifted my mentor, Lady Mykaela, two horses, one of whom is now my constant companion. Please, I beseech you—we are dying. Lady Mykaela is dying. The Dark that we draw is killing us. I came because the old legends speak of the People of the Shadow, who know the secrets to shadowglass. That's who you are, aren't you?"

The axes and bows rose again, trained on me this time. Kalen inched closer, but I stopped him, my gaze on their leader. "I understand your suspicions. You've protected it for thousands of years. But I know you too wish to keep shadowglass from the Faceless. I don't want it in their hands either."

The man said nothing. Kalen was rigid with tension. Behind me, Likh gulped noisily. But the man lifted his hand and uttered a word I did not understand. The others lowered their weapons.

"We are of the Shadow," he said. "In your tongue, I am called Agnarr. In mine, it means the Edge of a Sword. We've shared bread with Mykaela of the Sorrows, and we extend our welcome to Tea of the Embers and her companions." His gaze moved to Likh, who was still shivering. At another gesture from Agnarr, the other warriors stepped forward, weaving. The bursts of fire they created were warmer than what most asha could channel. "Our home lies near the mountain. We shall speak there."

The Gorvekans' village turned out to be a wooden settlement protected by a wall of runes—*Fire*, *Ice*, and *Shield*—carefully maintained by watchful guards. Children scampered about, pausing to stare at us while men and women hovered near campfires. There were dark-skinned and light-skinned Gorvekai, red- and yellow- and dark-haired. The delicious smell of cooking meat filled the air, and my stomach growled, an indication that I had eaten little that day.

"For a small community, they sure do have a lot of rune-binders," Likh murmured.

"I had the opportunity of talking with Lord Garindor before we left Istera," Khalad said. "If they're the People of the Shadow, then he says they're the direct descendants of the people who lived around the same time as Blade that Soars ruled, and they're supposedly stronger in the runic arts than most. But the Gorvekai's isolation may be a problem, if it promotes inbreeding."

"Not quite," said one of the women guiding us toward the largest stone enclosure in the small town. "We travel the world frequently to trade our runeberries, and we take partners from kingdoms as far as Kion and Drycht. Look around; we are a varied people, and for good purpose. To live within our own lineage weakens the alchemy of our hearts. To survive, we exchange heartsglass with all."

"But you wear no heartsglass," Khalad said.

The woman laid a hand against her chest. "We have no need for glass trinkets to see our own, honored Forger."

The largest building lay in the shadow of Stranger's Peak, the tallest mountain among the kingdoms. Kalen stared up at the imposing ridge with an expression I'd learned to recognize. "Why are you staring at the mountain the same way you stare at *bamieh*?"

His head whipped around so fast I was surprised it didn't come off his neck. "I don't look at *bamieh* like that!"

"Your mouth waters every time I mention fried dough."

He scowled. "The Gorvekai harvest the best quality runeberries atop Stranger's Peak. I tried the wine distilled from it once. It was…more than pleasant. And very expensive."

I rolled my eyes. "Perhaps if you scale the mountain, they'll give you a sip. Stranger's Peak is not a sight everyone gets to see up close, and you're thinking about runeberries?"

"It was really good wine, Tea."

We sat on comfortable-looking bundles made from animal pelts. Our female guide and another girl stepped forward with bowls of fragrant-smelling liquid.

"My daughters," Lord Agnarr murmured. "Solveiga and Eydís—*Strength of the Sun* and *Celestial Fortune*. We have added some *kolscheya* to your rose tea, to encourage the warmth back into your bones. It is essential, living in the heart of winter." The man fixed a steely gaze on me. "Why have you come for shadowglass?"

"Before we discuss that, I have one request. My friend here, Likh—he's been blighted. We were hoping perhaps you knew of some spell that could heal—"

Already the man was shaking his head. "Not even our ancestors knew of a true antidote." Likh lowered his head. "But she is adequately shielded, and she will be safe. The effects of the *Blight* rune will pass in a few weeks, though Lady Likh must take the utmost care before then."

The boy asha looked up. "Oh…I'm not—I'm not a girl."

"My apologies," Agnarr said gently. "Your heartsglass is not afraid to speak its honesty, and I only follow what it expresses. But if that troubles you..."

"No. No, it doesn't. Th-thank you, milord," the asha stuttered.

"There are other things you are afraid of, Lady Tea, that you do not say. You are afraid for your brother, estranged as you are."

I started.

"I see it clearly in your heart. Your brother walks a thin line between the lands of life and death. To use shadowglass means to give up the Dark. But to give up the Dark means to give up your brother, and that you will never do."

I nodded, speechless, trembling at how quickly Agnarr saw through me.

"Our people guard the secrets of Hollow Knife. It is to our benefit that the world knows little of shadowglass. You have no intention of taking its power for your own—I see that much."

Khalad spoke up. "Why haven't you completed the spell yourself?"

"None of our people draw the Dark. We can channel all runes but those. It was deliberate—our blood does not share in the curse of Little Tears. We can accomplish shadowglass without an outsider's help no more than they can succeed without ours."

"Lady Mykaela helped you?" I found myself asking.

"The *zarich* rarely makes its way this far north, but on one occasion it drew close to our territory, long before the Dark asha Sakmeet made Farsun her home. I promised to gift her the best of our horses at the *zarich*'s passing. But Lady Mykaela was not fit for our purpose without her heartsglass. Though she has reclaimed it, she has been greatly weakened."

"So Mykaela knew about shadowglass?"

"No. There are trials Dark asha must agree to take before we impart our knowledge. She knew nothing." His eyes settled on mine. "You are the first to come to us armed with that knowledge. Have you come to volunteer?"

"What would she be volunteering for exactly?" Kalen asked suspiciously.

"There are two key components of shadowglass—the light and the dark. To attain the light, the essence of the Five Great Heroes must be distilled into a silver heart. We have perfected a technique over the centuries, which allows us to forge one without taking a life." He looked at Khalad. "I believe, Heartforger, that you and your master, Narel, had discovered our method."

Khalad nodded, awed. "It only looks easy in hindsight."

"The other is the dark, and that is a far more dangerous route, one that only Dark asha can safely create."

I nodded slowly. The words came easy from memory. "*Present yourself with a heartsglass of black, where love's blood had shed over, and seven daeva's bezoars. Boil the stones separately, and drink a vial's worth of their waters. Weave* Compulsion *in the air; its heart shall reveal itself to you. Take it into your heartsglass—*"

"*And be born anew,*" Agnarr finished. "*The process will not be gentle.*" He smiled at the incredulity on our faces. "We are all connected. Sea and sky can influence each other, though they never meet. The words you speak come from the same legends we honor."

Wordlessly, Khalad rose and went to our packs, rummaging until he found a heavy pouch. Returning, he upended its contents on the ground. Bezoars rolled out. The *taurvi*'s stopped beside my foot.

"Where did you get this, Khalad?" I gasped.

"From the Dawnseed apothecary. Mistress Salika's mother suffered from the early stages of dementia, and she was kind enough to give me the remains of the *taurvi*'s bezoar in exchange for a healthy heartsglass. And here is the *aeshma*'s from the year before, and the bezoar of the *savul* you fought in Daanoris. And of course, the *zarich*'s from Istera, and the *nanghait*'s from Yadosha."

"But how did you get all these?" I asked.

"First Minister Stefan didn't care about the *nanghait* bezoar, quite frankly. King Rendorvik offered the *zarich*'s back to me. And as for Empress Alyx…" Khalad cleared his throat. "She doesn't know. I swore Salika to secrecy."

"Khalad!" Likh gasped.

"They imprisoned Tea, Likh. I knew the elders would seek it out sooner or later. I couldn't talk to Alyx without one of them in attendance, so I took it before they could."

"And the *aeshma*?" Kalen asked. "It was slain in Odalia, Khalad. By rights, Kance was supposed to have it."

Khalad sighed. "He gave it to me two months ago, when I visited him last. He thought it would be more beneficial in Tea's hands than in his."

"Kance said that?" I whispered.

"But what do we do with them?" Likh demanded. "Are you going to let Tea use her own heart?"

"If I volunteered," I asked, thinking, "what can I do to keep my brother alive?"

"Tea!" Kalen exclaimed.

"The First Harvest kills those who do not bear the shadowglass," Lord Agnarr said, "not even the Great Heroes were exempted from that tragedy, and all save Rashnu the Just perished. Including Vernasha herself. But to one that possesses the light and the dark, the First Harvest is like mother's milk. *Distill the juices of the First Harvest into a familiar's heart, to take back what death had decreed.*"

"That is, word for word, the same line in a book I once took from a Faceless woman," I said.

"Words are shapeshifters. They take different forms to suit different motivations. The word for *blue* can be sifted and changed until it spells *red*. We share similar teachings with the Faceless, but what they take and learn from those teachings are different from the messages we treasure. It is why words are important, and it is why they can be dangerous."

"Do you know then where the First Harvest is located? Is it at the Ring of Worship?"

The man nodded approvingly. "We believe so. But no asha, Dark or otherwise, has ever seen it and returned alive. Only Rashnu the Just survived, and only because he was wise enough to touch nothing."

"So the only way is to acquire shadowglass?"

"A test is required, to prove one's worthiness."

"Why is this necessary?" Khalad asked.

"The road to treachery and malice has always been cobbled with the intentions of those who thought to only do what was best."

I put my hand over my heartsglass instinctively.

"There is no shame in a black heart, Lady Tea." Agnarr's fingers caressed the air. Something shimmered on his chest: a heartsglass of impenetrable black.

Likh gasped.

"There are many myths regarding black heartsglass. It is not a sign of corruption, as many kingdoms would believe. It is a sign of strength and power, the ability to harness your talents beyond the average runebinder's. Very few can manifest the black, though it is more common among Dark asha and Faceless. The Dark runes are the strongest of the magics, after all." He drew another rune, and the outlines of a strange, ever-branching tree shimmered into view.

"What is that?" Likh asked, entranced.

"The rune to summon shadowglass. You can create it before the First Harvest as many times as you desire, but without shadowglass, it will refuse your call each time. To acquire shadowglass, you must first abide by our test. *To you, seeking Hollow Knife's path: present yourself to the mountain for judgment.*"

Silently, I cursed Aenah for being right. "What is this mountain that I must pass?" I felt Kalen's hand on my arm, but I persisted. "What is it that I need to do?"

In response, Lord Agnarr turned his face to stare out the window at the looming figure of Stranger's Peak.

Likh's mouth fell open. "Tea has to climb the mountain?"

"No, Lady Likh. Our men and women scale Stranger's Peak frequently to gather runeberries to sell. It is a difficult task, but it is not impossible. To pass the test, Lady Tea must not go up the mountain; instead, she must go through it."

"YOU CAN ASK ME A *question, if you'd like,*" *she said.*

She was Lord Agnarr's daughter, called Solveiga, Strength of the Sun. It was a strange name for someone who has spent most of her years in winter, under the shadow of a mountain. "We prize what we do not always have," she responded, and I could not refute her logic.

Here, sitting on her horse in ungainly furs as we traveled to southern Odalia with the rest of the Kion army, she looked at ease with the world. I envied this skill of hers—it was one I had never been able to master.

"Did your father tell the Dark asha the secrets of shadowglass?" I spotted Lord Agnarr riding with Lord Fox, the two engaged in deep conversation. The asha's brother seemed troubled, but they were too far away for their words to reach us.

She nodded at her father. "That was the same question your general asked earlier. As Lady Tea's familiar, Lord Fox will die should she complete the spell. His courage is commendable, but he has no reason to worry. A touch of the First Harvest upon his own, and he will be saved."

I said, "He didn't want his sister to take shadowglass. He knows she will die from it."

"She's been dying for a long time, milord. There is a reason why

we keep shadowglass a secret. There is a reason why Faceless seek us out despite not truly understanding the tenets of Hollow Knife. We have been threatened by the Faceless more times than they have threatened kingdoms, and still they balk at rising against us. Once we are gone, their hopes cannot come to fruition. We cannot be compelled, and their holds on daeva have always been tenuous—not as complete as Lady Tea's. Should she join darksglass and lightsglass with the First Harvest, then she too becomes a creature of magic. Do you not see what happens next?"

"If all magic dies," I began slowly, and then understood, "so will she."

"It is a strong possibility. I suspect she has realized the same, and that is why she makes many plans. She has two familiars now, doesn't she?"

"Lord Kalen would rather share her fate than gain another lifetime without her, milady."

"Perhaps. We are wary of those who come seeking shadowglass. We trust the mountain to judge the worthy. Lady Tea will become like a goddess herself. She could choose to divest herself of those powers— perhaps sacrificing her life in the process—or use them to hold dominion over us as a god. Though the mountain rejects those who choose the latter. That is why so many runebinders fail its test. That is why so many Faceless are desperate for another way."

A yell rose from the vanguard. Clouds of dust swirled as weapons were drawn. Lord Fox swore loudly and rode on ahead, the rest of the soldiers at his heels.

A small regiment of dead Drychta littered the ground. We

could not gauge their numbers at first glance, for many had been torn apart.

Three blighted creatures crouched over the remains, the sickening crunch of sharp teeth on bone loud over the horse hooves. The smallest of the creatures lifted its crab-like head, swiveled eyeless sockets our way, and screeched.

Lord Fox was several gallops ahead of everyone else. His sword bit into the beast's armored neck, sending its head flying. The body tottered, extremities twitching, and was promptly ridden down by Chief.

The other two were not as easy to kill. The first was an eight-foot spider, half-submerged in the loam. Its head was a rotting skull, sticky silk webs spreading underneath its spinnerets. At the end of each leg was a fierce humanlike hand with hooks for fingernails. They swiped at the soldiers drawing closer, quicker than the beast's size suggested. The second resembled a giant piranha on hind legs with an upward-pointing mouth, jaws wider than the tallest man, and teeth asymmetrically pointed.

I backed away from the horrific scene, and several of the men did the same, their horses whinnying in fear. Lord Fox never faltered; his sword cut through one of the spider legs, avoiding its grasp. Lord Rahim was the next to reach them, and he hacked rhythmically at the rest of the splayed limbs like he was chopping wood. Lord Knox released a battle cry and charged forward, some of the braver Yadoshans following suit. Above my head, I saw arcs of fire as both Deathseekers and asha unleashed their spells, and soon the sky overhead was filled with lightning and the sounds of brutal fighting.

My horse stumbled. I fell, rolling across the ground, rocks

cutting into my arms and hands. Petrified, I stared into the maw of the piscine horror, irisless eyes gaping down at me.

Suddenly, Solveiga sprung into view, her palms crackling with magic. The thing shrieked its agony as it took in a gill-ful of magic that sliced its way out from within. Solveiga grabbed me, and we fled.

It was hard work, killing nightmares. By the end of the day, the grounds were littered with new, grisly dead, and the army had lost half a dozen men for their trouble. Lord Fox, covered in blood not his own, ordered his men to burn the corpses, to see to the wounded, and then to push on with the march.

"Still eager to come with us, Bard?" he asked wryly.

I was trembling, the fish creature's gaping gullet still burned into my mind. "I must, milord."

"I cannot promise you there will be no more of these abominations. I can't promise you your life."

"I must, milord. Even the dead have their stories."

"Yes." He smiled then. "And if we both survive this, we might have more to tell you."

16

A SMALL CAVE LAY TUCKED AGAINST the base of the mountain, barely noticeable amid the sleet and snow. The half-hour journey to reach the entrance did little to improve Kalen's mood. "At least let me go with you," he rasped in my ear.

"Agnarr promised that my life wouldn't be in danger, Kalen. They're a very peaceful people, and I don't think they would stand for bloodshed, custom or not."

"Just because none of the other Dark asha have ever been injured doesn't mean it's impossible. How many Dark asha have entered here throughout the years?"

"Forty-eight over the centuries," said a helpful Gorvekai woman. *Lady Solveiga*, I remembered.

"That's not an impressive statistic."

"Many Gorvekai travel the kingdoms, searching for suitable

candidates. These are forty-eight Dark asha over thousands we have assessed and ultimately rejected long before they knew of any trials."

"And what of me?" I asked. "Would I have been rejected, if I hadn't come?"

The woman shrugged. In many ways, she reminded me of Zoya. "You're here now, aren't you? The point appears to be moot."

"You don't have to do this," Kalen repeated for the eleventh time that day.

I grinned and kissed him. "You're just mad you have to stay out here in the cold while I'll be warm and cozy inside. Trust me. If this is what I have to do, then this is what I'll do."

"Are you sure, Tea? Are you sure the only reason you want to find out if you're capable of shadowglass is so you can keep it away from the elders?"

I hesitated and sighed. "What if I succeed?"

Kalen shook his head. "I trust you, but that is dangerous. There's no telling how the magic could change you."

"I know. But if there's a chance I could change the world, why not bring Fox back for good and *then* rid the world of magic? I could bring back Polaire and Daisy while I'm at it! It would solve so many of our problems—".

"That's not how that works," Solveiga said, unabashedly eavesdropping. "You only choose one or the other."

I glared at her. "Then why not change the magic to ensure it will no longer be misused?"

"That's more complicated than you make it sound," Kalen pointed out.

"Look, I don't know if I'm capable yet, right? I'll make no promises. We need options; we don't have very many left."

Kalen growled. "If you run into any trouble in there, don't hesitate to shout. Summon some dead corpses. Call on the *azi*. Cause enough ruckus for me to hear."

"I will not call the *azi* this close to Stranger's Peak unless you want a firsthand view of an avalanche." I kissed him again and turned to face the entrance. The snow had lightened, and I could make out some small torches burning inside. At least I wouldn't be in total darkness. "I'm ready, Lord Agnarr."

The Gorvekai stepped aside, forming a short line on either side of me as I walked toward the entrance, their features solemn. Despite Agnarr's reassurances, I felt like I was about to head into danger, and that feeling lingered.

Inside it was cold, but at least there was none of the swirling snow. I gingerly felt my way through the narrow corridor, the torches lighting my path for another mile or so, until I reached the final burning wick. Up ahead, darkness stared back.

I took the torch from its makeshift holder—only for the fire to go out without warning. I whirled around in time to see the rest of the torches flicker out one after the other, until there was complete darkness.

"Seven hells." I could turn and go out the way I came in, or I could forge ahead. Despite what I'd told Kalen, I reached for the *azi*, but found no consciousness other than my own. It felt like the mountain was one giant, runic ward, more complete and thorough than any I'd encountered before, and it prevented all kinds of magic, powerful and small.

I trudged on, with one hand on the wall to keep my balance. My eyes gradually adjusted; another fifth of a mile out, I found myself facing three forks in the path, all leading into further darkness.

Agnarr had never mentioned this. I paused, indecisive, until my eyes fell on three small, headstone-like markers growing before the diverging paths like stalagmites, weathered and eroding. Words glowed on each: *Duty* on the leftmost stone, *Honor* on the right, and *Love* at the center.

I had no idea what the stones meant and decided it would make no difference whichever one I picked. I made for the left passageway, cautiously passing the stone. I took several steps before finding myself blinking against a sudden glare, back in the Valerian asha-ka in Kion.

Confused, I looked around, but the cave had disappeared. Instead, there was Polaire, carrying a fan in one hand and splaying the other at her hip, smiling coldly at me. I shrank back in fear, the shock of seeing her alive making my knees buckle.

"You want to cast shadowglass, child?" Her voice was brittle, mocking. "Do you think to cast the spell and that will be all there is to it, Tea? Foolish girl. You have always been foolish. It's why Parmina rejected you all those years ago, when you first came to the Willows to make your mark as an asha, none of us knowing you would do so with soot and ash. You have always been blind to consequences. That's how you killed me."

I shook. "Who are you?"

My sister-asha grinned. "I am the truth, you stupid chit. Always have been. You traveled here to see me judge you worthy of shadowglass. I'm here to tell you that you won't be. Have a look."

She stepped out of the Valerian. I followed—and stopped.

Kion was in flames. I could hear the screams of those trapped within buildings, heard the wood collapsing under the weight of fires. I saw bodies in the streets, and smoke sending soot into the blackened sky. I saw friends, lifeless, with unseeing eyes and outstretched arms. Beyond the destruction, I could make out the shape of the *azi* as it flew overhead, breathing death down into the city. Frantic, I reached out to the daeva but could not connect with its mind.

This is a nightmare, I told myself. I reached for a burning piece of wood without thinking and then cried out in pain, dropping it. The pain was intense and all too real.

"This is what happens when you take shadowglass," Polaire said. "This is what happens when you fancy yourself worthy of a god's heart. You will bring about Kion's destruction. You will wreck the lives of everyone you have ever loved, and you will doom them to hardship until the end of their days. We of the shadow can pass no falsehood through this mountain, and you know in your heart that this is your fate.

"Your duty to the lands outweighs your duty to those you call friends, those you call allies. The world must burn in order to heal. Do you still find yourself worthy, Tea of the Embers? Do you still accept this responsibility?"

I knew then that she told the truth. Already I had ruined lives. Already I had imagined Kion burning. "Yes," I choked out, still weeping and cradling my burnt hand.

Polaire vanished, and the rest of Kion with her. I stood inside the dark cave once more, but this time only two paths remained open to me, their passages yawning into night. But my wound remained, and I had to bite my lip against the throbbing pain.

Now *Honor* lay to the left, with *Love* on the right.

Trembling, I stepped into the left passageway once more. There was another spark of light, so blinding I had to cover my eyes with my uninjured hand.

"It is time."

I gasped. King Kance stood before me, his hand held out for me, smiling gently.

"Kance? Your Majesty?" I took his hand. He was warm, solid, and reassuring. "What are you—?"

He tucked my arm underneath his. "They're waiting for us, Lady Tea. Let's not be late."

"Waiting for what?"

"For your execution, Tea." Kance's smile was soft, but it held an edge of malice. "Or have you forgotten? All the spells in the world cannot make up for your sins. Surely you didn't think you would be allowed to live after everything you've done? You killed Polaire. You ruined my father. Everything you touch bleeds sorrow and misery."

"I didn't mean to—"

"Intention amounts to nothing in this place."

He pushed open a door that had not been there before, and we stood before the gardens of the Odalian palace. A scaffold had been set up at its center, surrounded by a cheering crowd. On the platform stood a hooded executioner. The ax in his hands gleamed in the sunlight, though the blade's edge was already dark with blood.

I took a step back, but Kance's grip was steel, forcing me forward. The cheers turned to jeering as he ushered me up the wooden steps. Desperate, I glanced around, searching for a friendly face, for someone to protest and fight for me, but I saw only contempt and accusation.

"You should know by now that everything has a price, Tea. Contrite as you are, you still caused Daisy's death. You still caused the blight. Imagine the countless lives we could save after you are gone. Now, kneel. No blindfold, I think. You deserve to die with your eyes open, seeing true justice done."

"Wait," I choked. "If I die, then Fox—Fox will—"

"You have no need to worry." Kance pointed, and I saw a lifeless body nearby, matted with blood and grime.

I screamed, bolting out of his grip to reach for Fox, though there was nothing I could do to save him. "Oh, he'll be all right," Kance chuckled, hauling me back roughly. "He was dead to start with. But he'll need a better body than the one you gave him."

My knees buckled. Gently, as if he were an attentive lover, Kance guided my head onto the chopping block.

"Honor must be answered for, dearest Tea. Honor outweighs your reputation. Already you are called a villain, and for good reason—you have brought chaos into my kingdom with your petty desires, and you must answer for your crimes."

He lifted my hair and pushed it to the side, exposing the back of my neck to the blade. I could feel the edge of the ax, sharp and ready, as it came to rest against my skin. "Do you still find yourself worthy, Tea of the Embers?" Kance asked, his tone cruel. "Do you still accept?"

I closed my eyes, tears leaking onto the block. "Yes," I sobbed. I deserved to die, didn't I? Daisy, Telemaine, Polaire, Fox—

The ax fell with a *whoosh*, and I found myself on my knees on the cave's cold stone floor, my body heaving with sobs. "No more," I cried. "No more!"

But there was one more path to take.

I fled, running away from that terrible stone and the horrors that lay beyond it. Except I found myself turned and standing before the marker. I tried to escape again, only to return to the place I was desperate to avoid. I would be running within this mountain until I faced its trial.

"No more," I wept, though there was no choice before me.

This time, no one greeted me. A long, winding corridor took the place of the cavern, which had transformed into the oracle's temple. I followed the path quickly, wanting the experience to be over with, afraid of what I might find.

"No." He lay before the brazier with his eyes closed. A sword had been driven through his chest, and a puddle of blood had formed underneath him. His hair and his clothes were stained in its red.

"No!" I broke into a run, sobbing and screaming so loudly it was a wonder the walls didn't shake. I drew the blade out of him, pressed my hands over the horrible wound, and push down, willing his chest to rise, his heart to beat. "No!"

I would have gladly endured all the terrors I had witnessed in this mountain again to be spared this sight. Kalen was clearly dead. A thin, crimson line ran down the side of his mouth. Irrationally, I drew the rune of *Raising*, willed all my energy into his body, taking in so much of the Dark that my vision blurred and the air crackled. "Don't die!" I howled at him. "Please don't die! You can't!"

"It was inevitable. Everything you touch decomposes," a familiar voice murmured, sounding almost amused. I didn't look up, only continued to cry as Fox slowly crouched beside me, looking at Kalen's body with cold detachedness. "Take it from me, dearest Sister. Dying isn't all the fuss it's made out to be."

"I have to bring him back," I wept.

"You can't. Silver heartsglass, remember? Tricky stuff. Wield all the magic you want in your first life, but you don't get a chance at a second. Fair trade, I'd say." Fox picked up the sword that had stabbed Kalen and eyed it critically. "No different than the one that got me. A sword or a *savul*'s claw—as long as it gets the job done, what difference does it make if it is human or daeva? That doesn't make you a different kind of dead. Now, Kalen—that's a shame. He was devoted to you. Even now, I reckon he'd die saving your life."

"I have to bring him back!"

"You can't break the rules simply because you want to. More often than not, the rules wind up breaking you. You're gonna save the world, Tea. But you'll return to Kion to mourn on graves. Kalen's gonna have to pay the price for your impulses."

"I don't want to save the world!"

"If you don't save it, then everyone dies anyway. Then what difference will that make?" My brother grabbed my chin and forced me to look at him. "Love requires sacrifice, Tea. If it's real love, then it will hurt. You'll need to give him up. He's a distraction and a weakness, and you can't have more of those. Don't you remember? Love is what got you into this mess, Sister. Love is the reason you raised me from the dead, and we've both been paying for that ever since—and all because you couldn't let me go. Do you still find yourself worthy, Tea of the Embers? Do you still accept?"

I screamed, and this time the walls shuddered and collapsed. Rocks toppled toward us, Kalen and Fox and me. I closed my eyes. Briefly, in that expanse between fainting and waking, I saw a vision: Kance on a white horse, his army charging into an unending tide of Drychta—transformed, blighted Drychta.

When I opened my eyes again, I was sitting by the cave's entrance, my teeth chattering. Kalen—alive and breathing—was by my side. He hastily pulled the hood from my head, his worried, brown eyes staring into mine. Khalad put his hand on my shoulder, scanning my heartsglass and breathing a loud sigh. "She's scared and a little confused, and there's a burn on her hand, but there's nothing else wrong with her."

"Tea?" Kalen asked hesitantly, gently nudging my face

toward his. "Are you all right? You stumbled out of the mountain and fell. You're crying… What happened in there?"

I hugged him tightly, my tears wet against his cheek. "I couldn't accept." I touched his jaw, his nose, his hair, every inch of him that my numbed hands could reach. "I failed, and I am so, so glad I did."

*W*HY DO YOU HELP HER?" *Lord Fox was angry, his ire directed at the Gorvekai leader. Fists clenched, hands straying toward the sword at his hip, every line of his body threatened violence. "She failed your test. Why would you show her how to wield shadowglass? Are you that desperate to see your prophecy fulfilled that you would give her your secrets rather than wait for someone worthy?"*

"Why do you think your sister isn't worthy?" Lord Agnarr was calm, more concerned with the bowl of tea between his hands than Lord Fox's fury. We sat around a hastily built campfire as we waited out the night—enough time to beg mercy from whatever god would listen. We were to cross paths with the Odalian army the next day, and Lord Fox's request for at least one good night's sleep for our soldiers was a demand by the time his words filtered through the generals.

Lord Rahim had quietly volunteered for the first watch, suggesting two asha for every shift after his. Lady Zoya, however, showed no signs of wanting to rest. She reclined against a boulder, watching the exchange.

"Weren't her letters proof enough? Why do you have so little faith?" Lord Agnarr asked.

Lord Fox glowered. "I can no longer trust her actions."

"Do you intend to slay her before she finds the First Harvest?"

He hesitated. He attempted to speak, but the words died before I heard them, and he trailed into silence.

The Gorvekai glanced at Lord Khalad, who appeared deep in thought. "And what of you, Forger? You fought with her, shared her hopes and fears. Do you feel the same?"

The white-haired man blinked and shook himself out of his thoughts. "I do trust her, milord. I would not have forged lightsglass for her if I didn't."

"But you have your own motives for wishing her success, don't you?" The Gorvekai's voice was like stroking fur.

"I'd rather not talk about it, milord." The fire fanned its shadows across Lord Khalad's face.

"The night can overwhelm," the older man murmured. "There is good reason to fear those who wield too much of the Dark. I have seen many succumb to its lure, witnessed noble natures corrupted under its direction. But I have also seen some struggle to rise above its attraction. I am sorry for your other sister, Lord Fox. Lady Tea grieves too."

"I cannot forgive her." Lord Fox remained unbending.

"But do you still love her?"

The familiar looked away, and that was answer enough. "Why do you help her? She failed your trial."

The man smiled, his expression sympathetic, almost pitying. "Because she didn't, General Pahlavi. She passed."

17

I SLEPT FOR TWELVE HOURS STRAIGHT, woken only by the smell of hot soup Likh brought into my room. I feared I might wake to find myself still in that dreaded cave or that the strange visions within might somehow have escaped to find me in my nightmares. But when I woke, Kalen's fingers clasped mine, his palm folded over my smaller one.

"Was it real?" Likh asked quietly, watching me devour the meal. "You mentioned a fire in Kion. Surely nothing in that mountain was capable of burning your hand. The torches?"

My injury stung, wrapped in a bandage stuffed with herbs and other medicines. "I don't know. You'll need to question Agnarr. But I understand why so many people fail the mountain's test. I'm sorry to be one of them."

Likh scowled. "I'd like to give him a piece of my mind. Why would he subject people to that kind of trauma?"

"Because they have to be sure." I had come away from Stranger's Peak with more than a singed grip. "Gorvekai know the ingredients to shadowglass but cannot wield it on their own. The spell in the wrong Dark asha's hands makes the world worse, not better. They need someone willing to sacrifice every ambition for it. I couldn't."

"But of course you'd refuse! Kion burning, being told you would die—what did they expect?"

I was silent.

"Agnarr wants to meet with us again once Tea feels up to it," Khalad said.

"I'll be ready as soon as I change this," I said, lifting my hand. "It's starting to smell."

"I'll see to it."

"Can you accompany Khalad for a bit, Kalen?" Likh asked. "I want to discuss something with Tea."

Kalen looked over at me, and I nodded. "We'll be back soon," he promised.

"I don't trust this Agnarr fellow," Likh began heatedly after they left. "I don't care if he thinks you're not the right kind of Dark asha, even if you clearly are. We don't have another twenty years for the next one to come along and meet his requirements. There are Drychta and Faceless in Yadosha *right now*. He and the Gorvekai can afford to wait in their little corner of the world, but King Kance can't!"

I was watching the kaleidoscope of colors in Likh's heartsglass change from silver to red to blue to yellow in dizzying patterns. He was angry for other reasons. Was it because Agnarr had called him *Lady* Likh?

I didn't realize I'd spoken the question aloud until Likh froze, the scowl slipping from his face. I pushed on hurriedly.

"Is that how you want to be called? Admittedly, it feels odd to hear others call you *Lord* or *Sir*."

Likh's expression turned pained. "*Lady* puts me off guard, gives rise to other thoughts. But would it be strange to ask for that title?"

"Is that what you'd like?"

He spent several seconds in thought, then straightened. "Being a girl or a boy or a Deathseeker or an asha isn't about how you were born; it's about who you are. You had no say in how you were born, and neither did I, but my ability to be true to who I am is the reason I'm an asha, not a Deathseeker. And the reason you're an asha, not a Faceless.

"I don't want to make other people uncomfortable, but I want to be who I am, and I need to understand my pride in that before anything else. Even if there are no spells to give me that shape, it doesn't stop me from knowing I *am* a woman, whatever else they may say. Can't...can't I at least have that?"

"And I'll support you," I promised, smiling. "Every step of the way, Lady Likh."

Likh grinned sheepishly. "It sounds so much simpler than doing it."

"The best truths are always simple, I think. Life makes them complicated. Agnarr sounds like a rather perceptive person, and he seems to get to the heart of the matter quickly. I bow to his wisdom and yours."

Likh laughed, suddenly shy. "Thank you. I'm not entirely convinced of *his* wisdom yet. But back to the issue at hand—now that you've been refused shadowglass, what do we do? We're no better off now than we were before coming to Istera."

"I don't want to be their chosen Dark asha, Likh. But perhaps we can find another compromise."

"We've received word from the Gorvekai," Kalen said, returning with Khalad. "They want to see us."

"Let's not keep them waiting." Khalad treated my injury, then we stood. "Shall we see what Lord Agnarr wants, Lady Likh?"

Likh giggled. Khalad looked puzzled, but a smile tugged at the corners of Kalen's mouth.

"I am sorry," Lord Agnarr said when we had entered his hut, "that we could not come to an agreement."

"How exactly is Stranger's Peak capable of its magic?" Kalen asked. "It is unlike anything I've ever seen before. How has this been kept a secret for so long?"

"The average asha or Deathseeker may enter, but they will find nothing there on their own. Dark asha and Faceless who have attempted shadowglass have reasons to keep our secret. If they cannot be chosen, then it is to their benefit that no one else is. The legends of Hollow Knife and Blade that Soars have always been shrouded in mystery. But there is one detail that many have forgotten: where the two brothers fell, a mountain rose in their place."

Khalad stared. "Stranger's Peak marks where Blade that Soars and Hollow Knife died?"

"We are both blessed and cursed with this legacy. The visions you've seen inside that sacred mountain are truths that have not yet come to pass, Lady Tea. They show the price you must be willing to pay to accept shadowglass."

"I'm sorry I was not worthy," I said.

"There was nothing you did wrong. We each have different roles to play. A farmer cannot be asked to assume the responsibilities of the bricklayer. They may not be as powerful in the eyes of others as, say, a king, but they are important to running a kingdom."

"But what now?" Likh blurted out. "We are running out of time. Even as we speak, war is brewing between the Odalians and the Drychta. Faceless have King Aadil's ear. Nothing good will come out of this, and they will not stop until they get their hands on shadowglass. How long before they come after you to demand the location of the First Harvest?"

Agnarr smiled. "They have tried in the past and will never succeed. They have connived and schemed for centuries, always seeking a way to push past our defenses. But we will prevail."

"Will you?" Likh challenged him. "You might have bested them in the past because you outnumbered them, but that's no longer the case. They've rallied other kingdoms to their cause. Drycht was not the first to turn. Odalia came close. Aenah was only defeated through Lady Tea's efforts. You may have more runebinders on your side, but how would you fare when faced with armies twenty times your size? They will have no qualms about manipulating other innocents to wage their war against you. Can you say the same?"

Agnarr studied Likh with interest until the asha's ears turned pink. "We will fight, every man and woman, to our last breath," he said, "but the winters grow longer, and men grow more complacent. There is truth in what you say, Lady Likh. It sounds like you have an alternative proposal for us."

Likh glanced back at me.

I took over. "We do. I have no intentions of ruling or taking away magic. All I desire is that no one else does until another Dark asha is deemed worthy of the curse. Faceless know the process of both lightsglass and darkglass. What if they ignore the mountain and attempt to create shadowglass on their own?"

"One asha tried. The founder of Kion herself. Lightsglass she discovered on her own, and the bezoars she tried to collect. But when she attempted darkglass within that Ring of Worship the explosion took out much of Drycht and caused the Dry Lands. It was already an arid desert during the Great Heroes' time, but now nothing grows there. The results will be very much similar to those who attempt shadowglass without our mountain's benediction."

I gasped. "Vernasha of the Roses tried to make shadowglass?! But she tried to ban the spell!"

"Temptation is strange, Lady Tea—it crawls out of unexpected places. The idea that she could shape magic to her own desires may have held some appeal. I assume it was a cause for shame among the asha, and most information surrounding her death was buried quickly."

"That might not stop others from trying to make shadow-glass." Khalad spoke up. "People never believe paint is wet until they have touched it for themselves. Somehow I don't believe Aenah or Usij were willing to wait and let Stranger's Peak pass judgment on them."

Likh frowned. "So you're saying we need to at least hide the bezoars?"

"That's been worrying me for some time," Kalen said. "Why not collect them sooner? Surely they could have gathered all the bezoars before we ever came into the picture?"

"I think it's because of the resurrection seasons of the daeva," Khalad theorized. "They tend to be staggered—the *taurvi* takes seven years, for example, and the *nanghait* three, and so on. There's never been an occasion where all seven daeva could be resurrected to take their bezoars at the same time. When the *savul* can have its bezoar harvested, the *zarich*'s would be close to rotting. The *azi* had not been sighted since the Great Heroes' lifetimes, and gods only know where Aenah found it."

"Not anymore," I argued. "First Minister Stefan said the *nanghait* had been resurrected earlier than expected. I think someone's discovered a way to raise the daeva before they're supposed to."

"Then it must be a recent discovery," Khalad said. "Aenah and Usij never raised their daeva earlier than their cycles. Druj must be the culprit."

"Does a rune like that exist?" Kalen demanded.

Agnarr paused. "Yes, it does."

"What happens to the daeva after you incorporate their bezoars into shadowglass?"

"They fall under the thrall of whoever holds the shadowglass. Their owner's death before its completion will simply condemn them to their usual demise, to await resurrection once again. Their mortality becomes permanent only when magic truly disappears."

I considered that. "So they'll be docile if their owner commands them to?"

"What exactly are you getting at, Tea?" Kalen asked suspiciously.

"I don't know yet. But surely, *surely* there's a way we can. Lord Agnarr, I saw a vision inside the mountain."

Agnarr traded glances with his daughters. "Rarely can an asha pass one of the trials," he murmured. "Much less two. You are only one of four in history to have ever done so."

"Almost isn't the same as being successful," I said brusquely. "I saw Kance's soldiers fighting blighted Drychta. Have I seen the future? Was Stranger's Peak responsible for my sight as well?"

"For better or for worse, our mountain rewards the worthy, my lady. *Duty* offers brief glimpses of what may come, and *Honor* offers strength."

"And that is all the assistance I can expect?"

Agnarr was quiet for several seconds, his head bowed. "Yes. Your ways differ from ours. What you believe is an immediate threat, we see as history in a constant state of repetition. The Faceless Eshrok came close to killing the Odalian king for his *urvan* one hundred and twenty years ago, only to be slain by Veshyareda of the Light. The Faceless Kinma killed Brenymede the Lovely and was three daeva away from taking all seven before he was felled by the young Anahiko, a newly pledged asha of House Imperial. It is always a matter of life and death, and every time we keep our silence, the world does not end. Shadowglass is our paramount duty, not the rise and fall of kingdoms. If you wish to help, then weed out the Faceless who dare usurp the daeva and destroy him and all other armies that follow."

"That doesn't sound like a permanent solution," Khalad said.

"Nothing is permanent, Heartforger."

I turned away, disappointed. "We'll make for Mithra's Wall, then." I was angry at having come so far, at having gone through hell inside Stranger's Peak, only to find myself with nothing to show for my efforts.

"You are a wiser woman than when you entered our mountain, Tea," Lord Agnarr said. "Heed my words carefully. Magic that we cannot comprehend touched you there, left traces of itself in you. You have passed the trial of *Honor*, and your strength has grown. You have passed the trial of *Duty*, and your eyes have been opened to glimpses of what may come to pass. Only the trial of *Love* eludes you. Perhaps in the near future, it is a trial you will find worth repeating."

"Nothing within that mountain merited the price it asks for, milord."

"Our value changes depending on how we perceive our worth, Lady Tea. You will always be welcomed here, no matter how far you go."

"Thank you, Lord Agnarr. We shall leave in the morning."

"It feels like this was all a waste of time," Likh complained.

"Not necessarily. We didn't lose anything making the journey. We have time to spare to join the Odalians and Yadoshans."

Khalad shot her a careful, deliberate glance. "Do you want to talk about it?" he asked. "I think we need to talk."

Likh glanced at us, blushed, and turned to him. "Tea, Kalen. If you will excuse us?"

"What are those two up to?" I asked, watching them head off.

"A lot happened while you were asleep. Khalad hasn't voiced an opinion yet, but after the shock wore off, I don't think he's against the idea that Likh likes him."

The snow had gotten worse, and our meals were served to us in the small houses allotted for our visit—hot mutton stew and fresh loaves of bread. Kalen was quiet for most of the meal, chewing on bread and staring out the window. The *Fire* runes in the room kept us from the cold, but outside, we could hear the storm growing in strength. Above us, the wooden roof creaked.

"What's on your mind? You seem preoccupied," I said.

Kalen smiled briefly. "Just a little tired. I haven't had much sleep."

"Because you were watching over me while I did," I remembered. "Don't stay up on my behalf. Our hosts were kind enough to prepare beds for us. We have a long flight tomorrow—"

"After you answer me one question. What made you refuse the last trial?"

I stopped, looking into his serious, brown eyes. "I'm not sure why this is important," I hedged.

"It is to me. You told us everything about the trials of *Duty* and *Honor*, but you were recalcitrant when it came to the last. What is it that you're not telling me?"

I trembled, wavering between confessing and lying, though the latter was no longer an option where he was involved. "It was you. You were dead in a pool of blood. Fox was there, telling me that you were a necessary sacrifice for me to be worthy. And I couldn't—you were dead, and I couldn't…"

I saw no surprise in his heartsglass, only a quiet sadness.

"You knew?" I whispered.

"I knew it was a possibility." He gathered my hands in his. "The world is a much bigger place than the space I occupy, and with even greater consequences."

"There will be no world if you aren't here with me, Kalen." I was shocked by the vehemence of my words, my anger that he would even consider it.

"I asked you to run away with me, to make our own small mark in the world." His voice trembled, proof he was more shaken than he would have me believe.

"If I agree to run away with you, and we learn that Kance is in trouble a month later, would you stay away?"

He hesitated.

"And yet, I know you love me."

"Let me modify my original proposal, then. Run away with me. And if a daeva returns, or if Fox or Kance or Mykaela or anyone else finds themselves in trouble, then we discuss the means to aid them without attracting the elders' attention."

"That's not very fair of you," I whispered.

"I'm not trying to be. The only thing stopping you from saying yes is your guilt."

"I don't deserve a happy ending."

"You're wrong." He kissed my temple. "*We* deserve this, Tea. Come away with me. Wherever we wind up, I'll love you till the end of my days. *Please.*" His voice broke. "I don't want you to die, Tea. Don't leave me alone."

It was selfish.

I was selfish.

But I had already given up far too much.

"Yes. Yes, I'll run away with you."

The hail pounding against the roof was the only sound in the room. Kalen's heartsglass flickered from the purest silver to the deepest, darkest red.

We came together violently, a tangle of limbs, his hard frame against mine as we stumbled blindly into bed. His hands were eager, his fingers experienced from older memories of us. The robes I wore were promptly discarded, his own following after. We clung like starved folk finding safety in each other and drinking our fill as the blizzard outside increased in intensity, matching our desperation.

In the middle of it all, I began to weep. Perhaps the thought of more death unsettled me, the idea finding traction in my skin. My choices shaped the topography of some unseen map; every decision dictated a far-reaching repercussion, rippling into outcomes I did not intend. Did the summoning of an *azi* set off a king's madness or the slaying of a beloved mentor? If I had never insulted a young runeberry picker from Murkwick village, might I have not murdered my sister? Had I never raised Fox from the dead, would shadowglass be someone else's problem, or no problem at all?

If I had done none of them, would I have fallen in love with Kalen?

And that's what it all boiled down to, didn't it? *Kalen.*

"Tea?" Kalen lifted his face, wet from my tears. He brushed slick, dark strands of hair off my face. He lifted himself to lie beside and gathered me close, our fervency no longer important.

"Tea." On his lips, my name was an anguished prayer. "Don't cry." He kissed my eyelids, the salt on my jaw. "Don't cry."

Have you ever loved anyone so fiercely you were afraid it might shatter you? It was a blessing and a burden I carried.

*T*HE ODALIANS ARE SOME OF *the fiercest fighters in the world; they have to be. With the seafaring Arhen-Kosho to their west, the magic-wielding Kions to their east, and the unpredictable Yadoshans up north, their exceptional fighting prowess kept their kingdom from being whittled down to its barest parts, and in this, their defenses were second to none. I'd heard stories of fortresses built overnight on sand dunes and rocky beaches, of soldiers trained to form impenetrable barriers of shields. The first kings of Odalia famously traded the profits of their runeberry patch to hire purple-hearted craftsmen, who wove expensive spells into their shields that could deflect all but the strongest asha. It was the best investment for those early years when the continent had been fragmented into wars and territories long before the diplomacy of kingdoms.*

I'd never met King Kance, and the dark asha's infatuation was understandable. The young man was dressed not in the satin and ermine preferred by his father, King Telemaine, but in chain mail shaped to his form, decorated with the marks of previous battles and none of the shine that comes from the novelty of wear. His handsome face was molded after his notable ancestors. He had a bit of King Kareth along the jawline and Queen Bregane from his cheekbones to his brow, where King Lorek's features then found dominance. He looked nothing like his father save for his keen and intelligent green eyes. Perhaps the lack of similarity was good.

King Kalen had gathered the Isterans to his cause—General
Androvey, King Rendorvik's military commander and right-hand
man, was present, and ten regiments stood with him. Commander
Selvynt, Queen Lynoria's most trusted adviser, represented Arhen-
Kosho, and I had no doubt that his ships were stealing along the
southern coast, awaiting the order to strike. But King Kance was the
only monarch present in this unexpected alliance.

The king's expression relaxed as Lord Fox approached. "I was
wondering when you would join us, Fox. I see you've brought more
Isterans with you. How are things in Kion?"

"We will persevere, and we will rebuild, Your Majesty."

"Drychta at Mithra's Wall was troubling enough," Commander
Selvynt boomed. "Drychta in the Hollows is all but an act of war. And
Lady Tea of the Embers, somehow caught up in all this. How fares the
mad king?"

"If I am to believe the reports," General Androvey rumbled, "he
graces the mountains with his company."

"It was a mistake, taking him alive last time." King Kance spoke
softly, but his volume took away none of his harshness. I did not recognize the hardened man from the gentle king the Dark asha recalled in
her tale. "And I do not intend to make that same error again."

"The Drychta may retaliate, Your Majesty."

"They will not." I surprised myself by interrupting. "Many live
in fear of him as much as you do—even more so. The next in line to
the throne is a distant cousin, Jakova of House Gansla. He is a moderate, and wise for his age. I do not know if he is keen on accepting the
crown's burden, but at the very least, he will listen to reason."

"And who might you be?" The Odalian king's stare was hard and suspicious.

"Tea's chronicler," Lady Zoya explained. *"He can tell you many things about our wayward asha, if you wish."*

"He is Drychta."

"He is harmless, Your Majesty."

I reached into my coat, eager to show him the letters that proved my value.

"Stop!" He made a fierce gesture, and I was surrounded by swords and spears. The tip of one blade grazed my chin. *"I have heard of you. The songs you sing are popular in my own courts, a favorite to mimic among my own bards. But you are Drychta, and that does not change."*

"I can vouch for him, Your Majesty," Lord Fox said.

"And how certain are you of his loyalties?"

"You've asked me about Tea many times these last few months, and I had no answers to give. The letters he holds will alleviate some of those concerns, though I doubt you'll find all the answers there."

The Odalian king paused. He eyed the papers in my hand.

"Show me," he responded.

18

WE MADE HASTE THE NEXT day, packing quickly and making our good-byes so we could make for Mithra's Wall before Kance's army could engage the Drychta. I hurried to Likh's tent when the latter proved slow to appear. "Lord Agnarr is waiting to see us go," I said abruptly, pushing back the door. "I'm worried about Prince—King Kance, and the sooner we leave, the quicker we can get to—"

Likh and Khalad sprang apart. I stared, focused on keeping my jaw shut, while they both babbled together:

"We were already leaving—"

"Khalad was—it's cold even with all the *Fire* runes present—"

"We weren't—Likh wasn't feeling well and I was trying to—"

"—we didn't bring enough warm clothing, and Khalad was kind enough to—"

"—not sick or anything, but I wanted to check the wards in case—"

"I'm going to give you two five minutes to compose yourselves," I said gently, "and to get your stories straight, but that's all the time we can spare. We leave within half an hour if we want to find Kance before his army clashes with Aadil's. We may be in the thick of battle as soon as the *azi* lands, so prepare yourselves." Slowly, I closed the door, smiling to myself. It was a start.

"I am sorry that you could not find the answers you seek here," Agnarr told me as I returned to where he and the other Gorvekai waited with Kalen to see us off.

"So am I, milord." Likh and Khalad arrived moments later, the couple blushing and taking great pains not to look at me. Kalen raised an eyebrow.

"Your cousin finally got the hint," I murmured to him.

"Good. I was wondering when he'd work up the guts to make a move."

"I'm not sure he was the first to do so."

The *azi* was quick to answer my call. I saw brief images of forests below and bright sky overhead before the two blurred together as it sped obediently toward me. Seas glittered blue before peaks of white crystals abruptly appeared. I saw an ice fjord, a breathtaking land sculpture of ice and glass, before the *azi* veered off, making for our small encampment.

Through its eyes, I caught sight of us, small as ants, standing in a cluster at the center of the frozen tundra. The beast landed, crooning and dipping all three heads in a monstrous curtsy.

"Good boys." I stroked each head in turn as they butted one another for my attention. Behind us, the soldiers' spears and axes remained raised, unconvinced by the daeva's show of obedience.

"If I took all the daeva as pets, rather than as beasts to be put into the ground every few years, would I be worthy, regardless of what your mountain tells you?"

Agnarr bowed. "It is hard enough to war with one's own conscience, but far more difficult to deal with one's own and another's at all times. Add six more and insanity is not far off."

"But if I was successful?"

"I cannot speak for the mountain, but perhaps you can ask it again one day."

"Thank you for your hospitality, Lord Agnarr. I hope we shall see each other again under more forgiving circumstances."

"Were you serious about that?" Kalen asked me, as Khalad awkwardly offered a helping hand to the still red-faced Likh, which the asha accepted. My love didn't look happy—it was the complete opposite of what I'd promised the night before. "Do you intend to control all the other daeva?"

"No," I admitted. "It took everything I had juggling both the *azi* and the *savul*, and I'm not keen on taking on more. But if I keep my hold on the *azi*, and perhaps Mykkie or another Dark asha she trains take in one or two more, then maybe we could prevent the Faceless from taking their bezoars."

"That will make you all targets."

"Dark asha have always been targets. If we divided the tasks, perhaps it would lessen the burden."

"There usually aren't more than three or four Dark asha at a time."

"Four could be enough, as long as the Faceless don't take control of all seven daeva. It's the best compromise I can think of." I sighed. "I'm better now at *Veiling*, at hiding where people cannot find me. It's not the most foolproof plan, but at least I can spare Mykkie the exertion of a few more daeva, and both of us would draw in less of the Dark that way."

"And increase both your life spans." No longer shy about showing his affection before strangers, Kalen pecked me on the lips. "I can't think of any better options."

The Gorvekai drove the butts of their spears against the hard ground, and the others brandished their axes. It was a strange ceremony, a special farewell. The *azi* acknowledged their good-byes with a thin, approving cry. It spread its wings to full span, a majestic sight against the backdrop of ice and snow, and leaped into the sky. Soon the men and women saluting us were no more than specks as I aligned my thoughts with the daeva's, charting a new route for us, crossing continents into Yadoshan territory, heading for Mithra's Wall.

The *azi* was quick. Scarcely an hour passed before we caught sight of the mountain range destination looming ahead, and I directed the *azi* to take a circular route over it, trying to determine if there were armies on the ground already locked in battle.

What I saw froze my heart. The black-and-yellow banners of the Drychta already surrounded the base of the largest peak. I saw soldiers in armor scaling its heights, no doubt seeking a cave or entrance within. Not too far away, the gold and red of the Odalian banners marched toward the Drychta. A large portion of Aadil's troops had already turned, their intent to engage the Odalians obvious.

I felt Kalen's hands on my waist, anchoring me against him as I ordered the *azi* to make for the open space that separated both combatants, which was narrowing by the minute. The daeva dipped headfirst, barreling toward the ground at dizzying speed. Just before impact, it shifted abruptly so that its heavy, clawed talons struck up soil and dirt, sending storms of sand rising up to obscure our vision.

The unexpected appearance of the *azi* was enough to give the Odalians pause, but the Drychta showed no such prudence. They focused on the daeva, yelling battle cries as they pressed forward, weapons at the ready. Among the approaching crowd I could make out the glittering runes of *Fire*, *Wind*, and *Mud* that Drychta spellbinders hurled at us.

Kalen was busy forming a spell of his own, taking advantage of the *azi*'s speed to create the largest rune I'd ever seen across the sky. As the army drew near, he made a quick, cutting gesture, sending a concentrated wave of knifelike wind that took down whole columns of soldiers, bowling them over before they could cast their own magic. At the same time, the *azi* snarled and turned, its spiked tail whipping the nearest soldiers and tearing several of them in half. Likh made a gagging sound beside me and squeezed her eyes as Khalad held her, shielding her from the horrific view. Kalen's spell had taken out hordes of men, mowing them down like stalks of wheat, and the others immediately scrambled for safety. Several of the spellbinders had held back though, and now their spells came spiraling toward us.

I didn't stop to think. I pushed my thoughts, the *azi's* still tied to mine, and wove both the *Raising* and *Puppet* runes in quick succession. Almost immediately, the fallen soldiers righted themselves, their features blank, and rushed before us, taking the brunt of the magic that sizzled through their bodies and creating a human barrier that gave Kalen enough time to construct a *Shield* rune of his own.

I ordered other undead toward their comrades, and soon the Drychta were fighting their own previously deceased. The *azi* raised its three heads, adding fire to the chaos, and the line holding the Drychta defenses faltered. More soldiers turned and fled, leaving only their dead behind.

"How did you raise so many?" Kalen asked me, chest heaving from his exertions.

I stared at the Drychta dead. I heard their protests and sensed their resistance; I felt them struggling against me, unwilling to give me power over their bodies.

And yet I could.

I let go, and the babble of angry voices faded from my head. The soldiers dropped, dead in every sense of the word once more.

"Was this one of the gifts of Stranger's Peak that Agnarr mentioned?" he asked.

I should not have been capable of raising so many fighters, even with the *Puppet* rune and the *azi* to draw strength from.

"Let's talk about this after we see Kance," Kalen suggested, though the worry didn't leave him. I nodded and glanced back at Khalad and Likh to see how the two were faring, finding them shaken but unhurt.

The Odalians had not joined our efforts when we engaged the Drychta, but neither had they retreated. Instead, they stood some distance away, warily eyeing the *azi*, who snorted and ignored them. One of them rode forward cautiously, and I saw, to my surprise, that it was General Lode.

"Milady," he greeted us uncertainly. "This is the last place I expected to see you again." He turned his gaze to Kalen. "It is equally surprising to see the Duke of Holsrath."

"I relinquished all claims to the dukedom, sir," Kalen said irritably. "And Kance can insist that I am eligible for the throne after him and Khalad all he wants, but he needs to understand what *official abdication* means."

General Lode coughed. "I presume, then, that you are to assist us in our war against Drycht?"

"Why is Drycht even here to begin with? And why has Kance sent no word to Kion or to the Yadoshans for assistance until the very last minute? He cannot imagine that sending out armies without aid would result in a victory. King Aadil is not known for his honor. Where is he, by the way? Still at the palace?"

"That is not entirely true, Kalen," came an all-too-familiar voice as King Kance stopped before the daeva, taking his white horse in hand. His tone was how I remembered: soft, pleasant, quiet. "For one thing, I am not, as you can see, in the palace."

"Are you a blithering fool?" Kalen exploded the instant we reached the Odalian encampment. His heartsglass had been a stormy mix of silver and blue, but he had reined in his anger until we were within the safety of the improvised garrison General Lode had constructed, away from any unexpected attacks by the Drycht. The *azi* had trotted after us, settling itself comfortably outside the Odalian defenses, one head keeping an eye on the fortifications while the other two watched the horizon intently.

"I did what I had to, Kalen." King Kance had changed. He'd grown his hair longer, and he was thinner. There were dark circles underneath his eyes, more prominent than when I had last seen him. His skin was darker as well, like he'd been spending more time under the sun. He no longer made my heartsglass flutter like it had when I was a novice, but it hurt to see him all the same.

"I've had to make a few adjustments in the last few months." King Kance didn't look at me. In fact, he acted like I wasn't even there at all. "We've caught more than our share of Drychta spies skulking about Odalia, which aroused my curiosity. Mithra's Wall straddles the border between my kingdom and the Yadosha city-states, and all our information pointed to some secret goings-on there by our brothers of the south. Aadil is a crafty bastard; he'd sent a reconnaissance group at first, no more than four or five people, to infiltrate the mountain. But one of Lode's patrols caught them. We sent several Deathseekers to back those soldiers, and fortunately, they were no match for us, though the survivors chose to kill themselves before we could interrogate them.

"But rather than explain himself, Aadil responded with an even bigger army, as you can see. They spent months sailing around the Yellow Sea and skirting along Yadosha's Eternity Mountains to avoid our patrols. They want something important from these ranges to go through all this trouble."

"This is not a good enough reason to insert yourself in the thick of battle," Kalen growled.

"My father kept me in the palace for most of my life, Kalen. You know that—you were there. He laughed when I asked to be taught proper swordsmanship, and it was you who gave me lessons in secret. I am sick and tired of not knowing what is in my own kingdom. I barely knew what went on in my own palace! If I had been wiser, perhaps Telemaine would not have connived with a Faceless for so long!"

I rarely saw Kance angry. The cold fury he displayed at our last meeting had been the first and last time. But he had clearly grown accustomed to anger and could now wield it like a finely sharpened knife. Quietly, I grieved for the role I played in his change.

"I found some of those Drychta spies in Kneave, Kalen," the king continued. "*In my own palace*. If I cannot be safe there, then I will not be safe anywhere."

"Wait, Your Majesty." I didn't need him to acknowledge my presence. But talk of spies in Kneave brought to mind the vision I'd had of him in battle, and I would much rather face his icy wrath again than remain uncertain. "There have been cases of a strange new rune in Kion—they call it *Blight*. It transforms its victims into daeva-like monsters, and there is no cure, save for the early prevention and treatment of its symptoms. If I may, I would like to use a *Delving* rune on all of you, to determine if anyone has been affected."

Kance had fallen silent as I spoke, and for the first time since we had seen each other again, his green eyes were on mine, though his face was neutral. He inclined his head, barely enough for a nod. Not trusting myself to look back at him again, I wove the rune and sighed in quiet relief when it displayed none of the red glows that marked the affected.

"We need to conduct the *Delving* on all the soldiers who've come with you," Kalen said tersely. "Why didn't you ask us for help? Do you no longer trust us?"

"This is not the time, the both of you," Khalad said quietly. "We think a Faceless hides in Mithra's Wall, allying himself with King Aadil's army, and we suspect it might be Druj."

"If that is true, then we would appreciate any help you can give," General Lode said brusquely. "We have come with our own Deathseekers, but they will need updates on any information you may have, Kalen. What strategy do you propose?"

"Leave the Faceless to us. But we'll need the rest of the Drychta distracted. That's where your men come in, General. Draw as many of them away from the base of Mithra's Wall as you can and keep an eye on the *azi*. Let it fight, and retreat when it starts spurting fire. You may not want the daeva involved, but it's our weapon to use."

General Lode frowned. "It sends ice through my veins, having that beast near. I cannot guarantee that my men won't behave foolishly if it lies between us and safety, milord."

"Tea will tell it to keep its distance from your soldiers."

"A good compromise. Milady, some of my Deathseekers vouch for your trustworthiness, but many of my soldiers have not been given the same education. They might not cotton to being delved, however that works."

"I'll go with you," Khalad told me, rising to his feet. "They remember me, at least." He turned to Likh. "Will you come with me, milady?" he asked softly, humbly, and the smile that spread across the asha's face was heartwarming.

"Stay, Kalen," Kance said, and it was hard to read the intent in his heartsglass. "We need to talk."

Kalen nodded, equally as expressionless. "Tea, I'll find you later."

"Will they be all right?" I asked Khalad worriedly, glancing back to watch the rest of the generals dispersing, leaving the two alone.

"They need to talk out their issues." Khalad grinned impishly. "Stubborn mules, the both of them, though you wouldn't think it of Kance. I know it doesn't sound like it right now, but trust me—they'll reconcile. They always do."

*S*HE TELLS THE TRUTH," *KING Kance affirmed. "Kalen and I were estranged for a while. We talked of many things that day. About my father. About his life in Kion. But mostly, we talked about Tea."* He smiled wryly. *"Did you know she had a brief infatuation with me once? I never realized. She was always so quiet and polite."*

The letters had mellowed the king, and further convincing from both Lady Zoya and Lord Fox had the soldiers withdrawing their weapons from my throat. But the king was still suspicious, and a few of his men idled nearby *"for my own protection."* We were to reach the base of the Hollow Mountains in the morning, but the king showed no desire to sleep in preparation.

His distrust also did not prevent him from inquiring further about the letters and Tea, particularly the gaps in his knowledge from her unexpected disappearance to her sudden emergence in Daanoris. His hostility softened as we spoke, and I caught glimpses of the prince he might have been when the Dark asha had been new to the Willows, neither none the wiser about the future ahead of them.

"These letters," he noted, *"are unfinished."*

"We could not recover the last few pages, Your Majesty." I was still ashamed to admit.

"No matter. If the bone witch arrives as you claim, then it is easy enough to ask her what follows myself." He stared into the fire. *"That*

was another one of my mistakes. It is easier to criticize the crown when its weight isn't heavy on your head, I suppose. My father—he was not as good a man as the people think. But he was not always a villain. Tea, I believe, is the same. I wish we could have talked then; instead, I gave in to my anger and sent her away. I was inconsolable. It felt like an abyss had opened inside of me and directing my rage at her would somehow close that chasm. I had every reason to blame her. But...the situation has changed."

"You are no longer angry?"

"We have come to a...tentative understanding. I understand her better now than I did then. I am sorry about her sister. Fox thinks she can no longer be trusted. He is afraid that the Dark bides its time, waiting to take over again and find another victim. He doesn't want her dead, but he sees no other recourse.

"I think differently. She raised my cousin from the dead. It is a feat of silver heartsglass no other Dark asha has ever repeated. For that alone, she has my eternal gratitude. She loves Kalen—fiercely, wholly. And I can understand her agony. If she succeeds in her attempt at shadowglass, if she can find a way to take the Dark out of her, then I will pray for her success."

The king allowed himself a smile, grim yet full of promise, spreading across his face like calligraphy. "After all, who better to understand a kinslayer but another kinslayer?"

19

To everyone's relief, none of the Odalians exhibited symptoms of *Blight*. "I'm glad we got here in time to give them due warning," I said soberly, after delving the last of the soldiers. "I don't think I could live with myself if I had gotten Kance sick."

Khalad sighed. "Tea, Kance feels just as badly about what he did as you."

"He has an odd way of showing it. He won't even look at me."

"He's a bit awkward in that respect. Kance rarely loses his temper. That he was even this mad tells me he cares deeply for you and Kalen. Give him time."

We'd arrived at one of the two tents where Khalad and Kalen had stored their belongings. Likh and I were sharing the second. Likh was waiting for us and cleared her throat. "Tea, would you mind if I switched places with Kalen?"

"Huh?" Khalad asked, though he was already blushing.

"Please do," I said. "I was about to make the same suggestion anyway."

"Thanks." Likh shot the Heartforger an inviting, if a shade
nervous, smile before disappearing inside our tent.

"So," I continued once the asha had gone, "you and Likh,
huh?"

Khalad was still red. "The morning at the Gorvekai's…it
wasn't what you think."

"That would be a shame, because if it *was*, then I couldn't be
any happier for you two. Why so embarrassed?"

"It isn't like I've got much experience in relationships. I don't
want to move too fast. I don't want to make Likh uncomfortable."

From my vantage point, Likh was moving ten miles to his
five, but I refrained from pointing that out. "She's had a horrible
crush on you for a while, Khalad."

"You knew?!"

I shrugged sheepishly. "Just talk with her. Don't assume
what she wants. Don't make the same mistake Kalen and I made.
As I recall, you pointed out nearly the same issues about us once."

Khalad smiled faintly. "I suppose it's easier to judge when
you're on the outside looking in, isn't it? Thanks. I'll go see if she
needs help."

He stepped into our tent. I was about to enter the adjoin-
ing quarters but stopped short when I saw King Kance heading
my way.

"Wait." There were no accusations in his voice, but there

was no offer of reconciliation either. "Tea, if I might have a word with you?"

I nodded, not knowing what to say. Kance gestured toward the campsite, where the generals and soldiers sat for their noonday meal. I followed his lead.

He said nothing for several minutes, content to walk in silence, but my nerves weren't getting any calmer the longer he was quiet. "Where is Kalen?" I finally blurted out.

"He's talking strategy with General Lode and the other Deathseekers. Given his experience with the Faceless, I thought it best to trust his judgment." He glanced at me. "I hear that the two of you are together. My congratulations."

"Thank you," I mumbled, staring down at my boots. It wasn't all that long ago when I was congratulating him on his engagement to Princess Inessa and wishing it were otherwise. It was strange how a year could change everything.

We passed a few more soldiers eating their rations and trading stories around the fire.

"And where is Fox?" he asked.

"He's in Kion."

"I'm surprised. You've always been inseparable."

"Things change, Your Majesty."

He was sharp enough to take the hint. "Would you like to know how my father is doing, Lady Tea?"

"How—how is your father, Your Majesty?"

"Dead." I was taken aback by his calm. "He died two weeks ago, shortly before we left Odalia. I swore all my trusted counsel and generals to secrecy, and I intend to make the announcement once I return."

"But...Your Majesty. How—"

"I killed him." His admission was brutally simple. "I was surprised by how easy it was. All it took was a pillow over his face while he ranted and raved. Khalad was right. He was not always a good father, Lady Tea. He seemed strong and imposing, his reputation towering over me since I was a child, and that never went away as I grew older.

"Once, when I was very young, he had me watch while he put down a horse who'd been mortally injured. 'If you must kill something,' he told me, 'then you must do it cleanly and quickly. Put it out of its misery without causing more pain.' It was almost like that—putting him out of his agony."

"Your Majesty." Tears filled my eyes, my guilt bubbling within me. "I am so sorry."

"I am not. The things that he said—they were unforgivable." Kance's voice grated, ax on whetstone. "I thought at first that his rantings were the result of his madness. Gibberish that had no foundation in truth. But as time went on, he spoke of deeds I knew to be authentic. About how he collaborated with Aenah and how he was willing to sacrifice Khalad for Aenah to gain her shadowglass. He would curse my brother often, refer to him as a sodomite, as not a man or child of his.

"And you. He would scream your name like it was a curse, day and night, more than he would scream Khalad's. He'd scream about all the horrible things he'd planned to do to you, of the terrible things he still wanted to do. I realized then that he'd been insane long before you'd turned him mad. He'd learned to hide it behind hearty laughs and an occasional wave to the crowd."

"I am sorry."

"Lady Tea." For the first time in so long, Kance took my hand in his, the gesture at once gentle and achingly familiar. "I killed my father because it was the right decision, not for you. I'm not sorry for killing him. I am only sorry that I had not done so earlier. The headaches plaguing me during the months that I cared for him disappeared the night I smothered him. I slept like a baby, undisturbed by nightmares. I no longer needed Althy's herbs for sleep. My father was the tumor I needed to excise. And whenever I allow myself to feel shame for being a kinslayer, I only remember his horrid ravings, and it passes soon enough."

He dropped my hand and added quietly, "But I do not trust the Dark, nor its powers that you wield. It is too much for any one person, and possessing that power can only end in tragedy. Odalia remains closed to you, Lady Tea—for the time being. I cannot risk my kingdom. My father did enough damage to last my lifetime. I will accept your help and your alliance for this war with Drycht, but only because I intend to see every Faceless wiped from these lands. If Druj resides within those mountains, then I will see him burn myself."

"I understand, Your Majesty." *Kance is no longer a friend*, I thought with a pang of sadness. But his lack of animosity was the best I could hope for. "Thank you for your clemency."

"Make no mistake, Lady Tea. If the Dark should take

control of you—though I pray to the gods every day that will not be so—then I will not hesitate."

"Should the darkrot take me, Your Majesty, then I pray for the awareness and the acuity to lay my head on the block for your killing blow."

Much to my surprise, his hand found mine again, gripping it tightly. "Do not jest," Kance snapped. "Do you think I await that day? You were one of my trusted friends, Tea. You were the sister I never had. Do you think it doesn't hurt me to be at odds with you? That it doesn't scare me to imagine that the power you wield will wind up killing you? If there was a way to extract the Dark from you, I would do it in a heartbeat."

"The Dark has always been a part of me, Your Majesty. And it came with benefits. It was drawing in the Dark that led me to your acquaintance. It was the Dark that enabled me to raise my brother from the dead. That I have lost both your trust does not make me bitter in the experience."

Kance looked troubled. His heartsglass glowed pale red.

"And if it were not for the Dark, I would never have met Kalen, and that alone is enough to be thankful for, regardless of whatever else may happen. I am happy that you do not hold me in so poor a regard as you did in our last encounter, Your Majesty. I only hope to improve my standing with you in the coming months by proving there is more to me than the Dark you fear."

"What makes you think I shall change my mind?"

"Because you told me about your father's death. That you thought to place your trust in me despite all that has happened…I am glad. The fault has always been mine, Your Majesty, and I never once disagreed with your decision to exile me from Odalia. If anything, you were more merciful than I ever was. Should my time come, I hope to find that same mercy, undeserving as I am of it."

"Tea," Kance began, but fell silent when Kalen drew beside me.

"Kance," Kalen greeted, his gaze sliding to me curiously.

"Lady Tea and I were catching up," King Kance murmured. He offered me a bow. "Thank you for your time."

"What was that all about?" Kalen asked, watching the King of Odalia leave.

"King Telemaine died," I said, unsure if it was my place to tell anyone about Kance's hand in his father's passing, even if it was Kalen. He sensed my hesitation and didn't press for further details. "He hasn't forgiven me."

"Not yet. It's different when one's own father dies, no matter what he'd done."

I leaned closer toward him.

"Is that what's troubling you?"

"No. I'm just glad he's put aside his hostility toward me, if only for the moment. It's more than I expected."

"Having second thoughts?" Kalen teased. "Should I be jealous?"

I made a face at him. "You know I'm not. But our conversation's left me wondering—if Odalia knows of Drychta here at Mithra's Wall, then surely Kion must have had some news of it too. But there has been no word from them."

Kalen frowned. "That's true. Empress Alyx would not have allowed any interlopers here, especially if they're Aadil's men. General Lode has received word that the Yadoshans are coming to their aid and that they're expected to arrive within the next day. But they have heard nothing from her."

"I'm concerned."

"Have you thought about contacting Fox?" Kalen was gentle; my brother was a painful issue, and he knew it. "We need to know what Kion plans to do, and we have no quicker means at our disposal."

"I..." I didn't know if I could bear feeling Fox's anger and disgust again. "Can't General Lode send another raven?"

"He's sent four, but we can't expect an answer for another few days at least." Kalen kissed me. "If it makes you uncomfortable, then I won't ask again. Perhaps a messenger on a fast horse is necessary, so we can at least guarantee a reply."

I took a deep breath. "No. You're right. The situation supersedes my personal problems. Kion will know we're with the Odalians soon, so there's no point in hiding from them. Give me a minute to pull myself together and I will reach out to him."

It took me ten minutes to find the nerve to break down the door I had so meticulously built in my mind, separating my thoughts from Fox's. I resisted the urge to weep as Fox's mind flowed into mine, the familiarity of him bringing a fresh wave of tears.

Tea? I heard him ask in shock. He was, I saw, dining with Princess Inessa in her private chambers. He rose to his feet, eyes wide.

"Is that Tea?" Inessa sounded apprehensive, cautious, delighted. "Tea? Where are you? We were so worried—"

Drycht has an army at Mithra's Wall, I said bluntly, keeping my own emotions at bay, ignoring the tears spilling down my cheeks. Oh, I missed Fox, but the anger, disgust, and fear swirling inside him when we last saw each other was still there, dimmed but pulled back to the forefront when I announced my presence.

The *Calming* runes that Kalen administered to me daily could do nothing against the torrent of emotions that reconnecting to Fox brought me. Once again, I was overcome with emotion that Daisy was dead and I responsible for it. That perhaps I did deserve to die before I wreaked havoc in other kingdoms. I was a plague that infected all I touched. I deserved no mercy, only justice. Had Kance thought to have me executed for my crimes against his father all those months ago, then Daisy would still be alive.

Tea? Fox sensed my maelstrom of emotions, and his concern grew, outpacing his previous anger. At the same time, I could feel Kalen slowly seeping into my mind as he held me, stroking my hair and murmuring soft, reassuring words. His warmth seeped into my core, and I found my self-control.

Did you know about Aadil's army?

I—no. We received missives this morning about activity along Yadosha's borders, but we've had no confirmation—

Consider this your confirmation. There is a Faceless within Aadil's army, and they think the First Harvest is within Mithra's Wall. Tell Empress Alyx to send a representative—perhaps asha you

can spare from the hunt for me, as I am here with the Odalians,
surrounding what's left of the Drychta. The Yadoshans are coming,
and Empress Alyx will be left out.

Althy's already by Yadosha, scouting. We'll relay word to her to
ride to your location. Tea, I want to—

I was at my limit. The message relayed, I slammed the door
between us, cutting off the rest of his words and frantically building until I could hear no more from him. No anger, no disappointment, no sorrow.

But the dam had broken, and I cried fresh grief at losing
Daisy and at Fox's distrust, twin swords through my heart. It took
a minute for the *Calming* to take effect, and it washed over me in
waves. My sobs stifled and quieted, growing softer after every sweep.

Kalen was himself shaken. "I didn't realize—I didn't understand why you were so reluctant, until I…"

"Y-you shouldn't have been able to eavesdrop." The bond
I shared with Fox was unique as far as I knew. I looked down at
Kalen's heartsglass and then at mine. We beat in perfect synchro-
nicity. I loved Fox, and I always would, but the years-long bond
we shared paled in comparison to what Kalen and I shared. In that
moment, I understood how completely he loved me. But as the
minutes passed, the link ebbed, and Kalen's presence slid away.

"*Heartshare,*" Kalen murmured. "It's a permanent depen-
dence, isn't it? I am sorry, Tea. I won't ask you to do that again."

"No. I had to. There's more at stake than me and my feelings.
More at stake than us. I can live with Fox's anger. As long as he's
safe and under the empress's protection, then that is enough."

"You have no reason to hide your hurt from me, Tea. I'll be here for you. Always."

He kissed me as he was wont to do, slow and lingering. I returned the favor as his arms slid around me. The heartshare's effects had disappeared, but in that moment, it no longer mattered.

*T*HEY WILL CONTROL NO DAEVA *here." Lord Knox sounded pleased and disappointed all at once. The Hollow Mountains loomed before us, thin, craggy peaks that decorated Odalia's southern coastline like the lower jaws of some gargantuan sea monster. It was a natural barrier between the kingdom and Drycht, one that Odalian kings have long harnessed as a defensive position against invaders. I was not privy to the military roundtables that went on among the generals, but I could see Arhen-Koshon ships closing in on either side of the range. It was likely that they prevented Drychta ships from landing anywhere but along these mountain shores, which gave us the advantage of terrain.*

The southern outpost had been constructed many years ago by the Odalian queen, Bregane, and it has since withstood the test of time, with fortifications added to and improved by her descendants. Though simple and utilitarian in appearance, the star-shaped bastion was heavily defended. Ditches and sharpened spikes surrounded the fort, making it impassable for most attacks.

There was no sign of the Dark asha or her azi. *Lord Fox stared into the sky, searching every cloud for the telltale speck of black. I saw his mouth move and had no need to hear his whispered,* Where are you, Tea? *sent out into the air like an open secret.*

"The Gorvekai tell us that this so-called First Harvest is not

in the Hollow Mountains," General Lode rumbled, "so what devilry do the Drychta intend to do here? Invade Odalia? They no longer have the element of surprise. Draw out the Dark asha and her daeva? Surely they could do so in other territories where they could maintain the advantage."

"Reports tell me that these are Aadil's most devoted soldiers," King Kance observed. "All ten thousand members of the Golden Rod, his private army. Then another ten thousand men from his special forces, handpicked for their brutal efficiency. And there may be more."

"That might pose more of a problem than General Lode thinks," Lord Fox decided. "We expect them to leave the range and engage us in battle, but they show every indication of staying put. Our defenses amount to nothing if they do not come down the Hollows, milords."

"We outnumber them five to one," Lord Balfour pointed out.

"That makes no difference, Sir Balfour. We won't be able to keep our formation if we go through those narrower paths, and the crevices ensure archers can pick us off before we reach the bulk of their army. If we go in, they'll have the advantage."

"So this is going to be a protracted siege?" Lord Aden groaned. "I hate sieges."

"If you have any ideas for luring the Drychta out of the Hollows, Lord Aden, then I would be more than pleased to let you assume command."

"What do you think, Althy?" Lord Fox asked.

"There are enough of us asha to try and shake the mountain asunder. But it would destroy the Hollows and cause quite a few

*problems—landslides, earthquakes, and the like. I would not want to
make that attempt until we have exhausted all other options."*

King Kance turned to Lord Agnarr, who'd been silent throughout the deliberations. "You know more about Tea's intentions than any
of us. What has she told you?"

"The Faceless have allied themselves with the Drychta for generations, Your Majesty, but it is only recently that they have infiltrated
the ranks of royalty with King Aadil."

"We already knew that. But what is their purpose here? Where
is Tea? Did she intend to attract the Drychta to these mountains long
enough for us to arrive?" His eyes narrowed, studying the man like
he'd never seen him before. "Or did her lures equally apply to us?"

"That is a possibility."

He drew his sword at lightning speed, pointed it at the Gorvekai's
chest. "Why did Tea send you with us? Tell me."

Lord Agnarr took no offense. His gaze was sympathetic. "Lady
Tea sent me to ensure that you would come here, milord, and not into
Drycht, as your empress wanted."

From somewhere far off came a thin, toneless cry. It hung in the
air, and my blood chilled at the sound. I had spent weeks listening to
those howlings while the beasts frolicked along the Sea of Skulls, after
their owner coaxed them one by one into semblances of life and bottled
their essences into her soul.

From the rocky shores of the Hollows that spilled out into the
Odalian Sea, misshapen forms rose from the foam. First came the
nanghait, *its faces emerging from beneath the roll of the tides, pulling
itself through the rocks and silt. Then the* taurvi *and its crooning*

voice, and the zarich with its loping gait. One by one, the daeva washed ashore, skins and hides gleaming from the sea, and as one, they raised their heads and roared.

From above, the azi swooped down, tail whipping and talons sharp. Unlike its brothers, it made no sound. The azi had no need for those theatrics. Instead, it made straight for the Hollows, flames streaming from its three mouths.

And as our horrified eyes watched, the mountains caught fire.

20

WE EXPECTED THE DRYCHTA ARMY to attack well before dawn, so the generals spent the rest of the night planning defense strategies. Everyone was tense. General Lode predicted the army would attack the base camp in the hopes of putting King Kance in danger, and we were determined not to let that happen.

In the end, however, it was my *azi* that sounded the warning cry. I rose from bed but had no need to leave the camp. Ignoring the shouts of alarm as soldiers scrambled for armor and weapons, I entered its mind. A group of Drychta a mile away from the first of the fortified stakes had stumbled onto my pet in the darkness, and my *azi* let them know what it thought of their insolence. The middle head caught the first of the men, killing him quickly. The other two heads sent waves of fire into the others' path. By the time the Odalians joined the fight, only scorched, burned remains were left.

"They're far bigger than a scouting party," General Lode grunted. "I say this was to test our defenses. Gods be good that your daeva was here to find them, Lady Tea. How they got this close is beyond me."

"*Compulsion*," I said grimly, while Khalad examined the dazed Odalian guards stationed along the outer camp. They'd been asleep on their feet, blank eyes staring out at the plains. Had my *azi* been slower, they would have been slain. I used my own *Compulsion* to goad them back into wakefulness but found lingering traces of the mind that had been at work—more powerful than Usij's or Aenah's. "Druj."

One of the Deathseekers swore. "What good are our preparations if they can infiltrate our minds easier than they can tear down our walls?"

"The Yadoshans have arrived," another Deathseeker affirmed. "A man named Knox wishes to speak with you, General."

"My *azi* will keep watch," I said, "but I fear there may be more ambushes."

"We'll have a talk with the Yadoshans, then attack at first light," Kance decided, rising to his feet.

I startled. "Attack, Your Majesty?"

"My army outnumbers theirs. Add in the Yadoshans, and we can overwhelm them quickly. Lady Tea is right. They attacked our camp to test us, but also to delay us. If we wait for them to make the first move, it will only give them time to regroup. Fortunately, the bulk of their troops are at Mithra's base. The paths leading up the range aren't wide enough for any kind of fighting. Let us concentrate on their soldiers and have Lady Tea and Kalen focus on the Faceless there."

General Lode nodded. "Lady Likh and Lord Khalad shall remain behind with you, Your Majesty."

But Kance shook his head. "The camp will not be as well defended, and they may try again. I will stay close by you, General. My own Deathseekers will protect me, and we'll be on hand to offer Lady Tea and Lord Kalen assistance. Both Lady Likh and Lord Khalad shall come with me. With the *azi* close by, the Drychta will not be as reckless."

The older man sighed resignedly. It was clear they'd had many discussions like this before. "Very well, Your Majesty. Lord Kalen, Lady Tea—will you be needing horses? Your own may need rest after such a strenuous journey."

"I have a special steed, General, one with an inexhaustible supply of energy. But we will be doing most of our work on my *azi*."

The general shuddered. "I never thought I would see the day when those beasts could be ridden into battle like flying cavalry."

"Do you intend to confront the Faceless within the mountains?" Kance asked me.

"I would like to concentrate on decimating as many of the Drychta as we can first. Their small numbers have the advantage up the cliffs."

"We will do our best to keep the battle as short as possible. Let's go, gentlemen. The Yadoshans are waiting."

"Will you two be all right?" I asked Khalad.

The Heartforger nodded. "I am worried about Likh though.

Her symptoms should have dissipated by now. I've talked to Knox. Aden had been examined by one of the remaining Yadoshan asha who arrived from Steerfall, and it seems he's already closer to recovery than she is. We've tested all our food. If there were any spells in it, we'd be afflicted as well. I don't see why she should be recovering any differently."

"Keep an eye on her, especially today. I don't want any of those Drychta within a mile of Likh."

"I'll kill them if I have to." Khalad sounded fierce.

Both the Yadoshans and the Odalians had reached an agreement by the time we returned. Knox grinned widely when he saw us. "Lady Tea," he crowed, hefting a battle-ax. "Much better than a daeva hunt, don't you think?"

I groaned. "Only Yadoshans would look at this as a game, Knox."

"If we play to win, then why does it matter?" He bowed respectfully to Kance. "Your Majesty, we've come to lend our strength to yours. First Minister Stefan bids us to follow your orders as if they were his own."

"I am honored by the faith your leader places in me, Lord Knox. My scouts have told me that King Aadil himself is within these mountains, and that there is some unrest among his soldiers, though the reason eludes us. We aim to take advantage of their unease and attack as soon as we are able."

"Can't the Lady Tea traipse into their heads and use runes to force information out of them? She seemed quite capable of it when we interrogated that Drychta spy."

"That's not how it works, milord," I said.

"Drychta spy?" Kance asked curiously.

The man coughed, chastened. "Ah, nothing important, Your Majesty. My men await your orders."

"The Faceless will be quick to fend off any intrusions, milord," I reminded him. I'd already tried a quick *Scry* into the mountains but had detected nothing.

"Then let us begin. The Drychta are used to cavalry, and several phalanxes will be necessary. My Deathseekers shall attack first. It will be best to stay out of their way. My men shall move with archers behind them to cut down any approaching fighters. Once engaged, I would like your men to attack from both sides in a pincer maneuver. Lady Tea and Lord Kalen will direct the battle from overhead, on their *azi*."

"Done and done, Your Majesty. Though I wager the *azi*'ll cut our work for us."

"I've had my own experiences with daeva, and they are unpredictable, to say the least." Kance's voice was clipped. "I will put my trust in my men, and in yours. Let's move out, and may whatever gods listening bestow their grace on us all this day."

The *azi* was primed and ready, snorting out thick gusts of smoke as we slid down its neck. We had scarcely settled when it rose, wings flapping, sending up small tornadoes of dust, causing soldiers to scurry out of its way. Kance watched as the daeva took us into the clouds. We watched as the army pushed forward, banners of red and gold streaming across the plain to meet the Drychta's black and yellow. We circled the empty space above them, waiting for Kance's signal.

A blast of trumpets sounded below, and my thoughts spurred the *azi* into action. It swooped, and a fireball cut down a swath of soldiers in its path before most were even aware an attack had commenced. Desperate, they turned, fleeing the burning ground, many of them running straight into the Deathseekers' line of fire. The flames they channeled from their hands were smaller than my daeva's, but enough to accomplish their aims. Kalen's *Wind* runes gleamed, mapping a constellation across the sky that goaded the fires into spreading among the demoralized Drychta. The Odalian army marched forward, fresh and eager to join the fight with the Yadoshans converging, cutting down enemy stragglers too slow to move out of their way.

A terrible rumbling came from the direction of the mountains. The *azi's* heads huddled together and hissed, its mind prodding gently at mine, asking for control. I relinquished my hold, and it landed on the ground, sending troops from both sides scattering. *Danger*, it whispered to me, *dangerdangerdanger*.

"Tell the Odalians and the Deathseekers to retreat!" I barked at Kalen. "Something big is coming their way!"

"You heard the lady!" Kalen yelled back at the troops, amplifying *Wind* so that his voice carried clearly across the battlefield. "Stay back if you value your lives!"

The Odalians were quite willing to obey, the Yadoshans a shade more reluctant. "What is the *azi* telling you?" Kalen asked me tersely.

"I don't know yet, but it feels foreboding."

As soon as I said the words, I had a vision of scaled claws

fighting their way up through the surface of the ground, dripping black, acid-like vomit in their wake. I clutched at Kalen's arm. "The *indar*."

"I don't see any—"

My words proved prophetic. The ground moved beneath us without warning, a terrible earthquake that threw allies and enemies alike off their feet, as if the whole world trembled with fury. A fissure appeared before us and widened, the soil breaking apart as something black and malevolent scratched its way to the surface. The *azi* sneered, all three heads breathing contempt, as the new daeva cawed at the air with a high-pitched cry that I swore could be heard all the way to Istera.

"Back, men!" Knox shouted. This time the Yadoshans yielded, widening the distance between them and the terrible beast, which climbed out of the bowels of the earth. The *indar* was a tar-soaked abomination, and the ground underneath it sizzled as its foul-smelling secretions spread across the soil, burning the land with every drip. It was a monster with feathers and wings, if feathers and wings could be carved from stone. I knew that, like the *azi*, it could fly, though its heavy body ensured its flight was limited. And like the *savul*, its weapon of choice was poison secreted in heavy sacs underneath its limbs, serving as both projectile and armor.

"Keep away!" General Lode snapped. "Archers only! The rest, retreat and protect the king! Deathseekers, keep it busy!"

The *azi* and the *indar* circled each other. Kalen focused on channeling *Shield* runes in the air, and I added my strength to his as I burrowed the rest of myself into the *azi*'s movements. The *indar*'s mind was a swamp of putrid, undecipherable emotions, all of them hungry and sluggish, but I could detect the faintest human presence, nestled deep within the bog.

Druj. Who else could possess such skill? But while Aenah and Usij were quick to confront me head-on, using their force to barrel into my mind, overwhelm me, and take control of the *azi*, Druj's thoughts slid away whenever I drew too close, evading my prodding with ease, much to my mounting frustration. The *azi* was the first to attack, all three heads lashing forward. The *indar* was quick, despite its bulk, and evaded the attempts. Like its possessor, it was content to move out of the way rather than attack, though its poisonous sweat still presented a danger. The *azi* growled as some of the poison spattered its skin. Pain flashed through our shared link.

"Hold on," Kalen said through gritted teeth, and I felt him expand the *Shield*. I watched with amazement as his runes crept over the *azi* and covered it, a makeshift armor forged from spells.

Kalen was taking power from our *Heartshare*, I realized— and through me, the *azi*'s strength. I had linked with other asha before, but they had never been able to share the *azi*'s strength. I heard the fighting resume behind us; the other Deathseekers had banded together, attacking the *indar* with their own volley of spells and runes, though they distracted more than maimed. Some of the braver Odalian archers sent arrows bouncing off its hide, but the Yadoshans, more keen on inflicting genuine injuries, were busy sinking their swords into every Drychta they could reach.

I cursed quietly, wading through the thick mental mire to

reach the *indar*'s core. Though the Deathseekers' spells had little physical effect on the daeva, they were successful at diverting some of its attention away from me, allowing me to pinpoint the center of its thoughts. I sensed a faint struggle, some independent, reptilian aspect of its mind resisting Druj's control.

But then the *indar*'s thoughts shifted. It turned from the *azi*, no longer interested in an offensive. It turned its attentions to the Odalians, toward the circle of soldiers protecting Kance, Likh, and Khalad.

"Protect the king!" Kalen snarled, even as I ordered the *azi* to block the *indar*'s path. But the *indar* threw its head back and brought its wings down in one violent motion. A fountain of black bile spewed out, arcing forward like a sickly rainbow, showering its surroundings with its poison. I saw some of the Deathseekers switch to the defensive, forming *Shield* runes of their own, protecting a bulk of the army from the acid. But I watched, sickened, as some were not as lucky.

Screaming, those soldiers dissolved before our very eyes as the tar ate their flesh, steam rising from their writhing bodies. "Water!" General Lode roared, and to my horror, Likh leaped forward, the wards around her gone as she sent cloudbursts onto the unfortunate victims, soaking them in a sudden flood. A Drychta lunged for her, but was beaten back by a determined Khalad, who had found himself a sword amid the chaos.

I reached out with my mind and compelled every suffering soldier I could reach, sending them into blissful unconsciousness. It was the only mercy I could afford them.

My grip on the *indar* slipped as I did, and I swore again through my tears, plunging back into its head and repeating the painstaking process all over again. *You are weak*, a voice whispered into my ear, confident enough to taunt rather than take advantage. *Your compassion makes you weak, Lady Tea.*

I focused my will and tried to attack, but, laughing, he slid out of my grasp once more.

The soldiers surrounding Kance were at full retreat, but the *indar* stubbornly raced after them, knocking other Odalians and Yadoshans out of the way. My *azi* stormed into its path, crashing deliberately into the other daeva just as the latter raised its hideous wings again. Kalen grabbed me, held me close as black rain spattered around us, making harsh sizzling noises as some of the *Shield* runes melted at the potency.

I located the *indar*'s core again, reached for it. There was another mind latching on, tightening its hold as it sensed me. I shoved against that presence, only to encounter resistance. I tried again.

The *azi*'s left head snapped forward. Heedless of the acid, its teeth latched onto the *indar*'s feathered neck, fangs sinking into its jugular. The daeva shrieked with pain for the first time since the fight started, but it was not enough to shake off Druj's control. The *azi* cried out as well, and I felt the terrible sizzle of its hide as if it were my own skin. I screamed but wouldn't, couldn't, let go, even as the agony grew intolerable.

A blaze of lightning cut through the *indar*, separating it from the *azi*. "Asha!" Althy's voice sounded over the din, strong and sure and safe. "To me! Aim for its eyes!"

New arcs of lightning filled the horizon, cutting into the other daeva. I turned and saw Althy surrounded by other Kion asha, linked and sending swaths of bright light, sharp and cutting, burrowing into the *indar*'s flesh. They did little to hurt the daeva, but the light dazzled it. Yowling, the *indar* twisted to and fro, its lidless eyes unable to turn away from the brightness filling its vision.

Tea, I heard, from far away and close at the same time. A sudden spasm of strength went through me, catching me by surprise. The energy trickled up to the part of me that continued to cling to the *indar*'s thoughts, which were still under Druj's control. I seized it, pushed with all my might.

A blaze of light exploded into the abyss when my thoughts touched both the daeva's and Druj's, and it was enough to startle the Faceless into letting go. The *indar*'s mind fell into mine.

Die! I shouted. *Die, die, die, die, die—*

I don't know how long I shrieked. It was only Kalen, shaking me gently, that brought me back to myself. "Tea," he murmured. "It's over."

The *indar* lay on its side, surrounded by a pool of its own black acid. Druj's mind was gone, retreating somewhere inside Mithra's Wall. A subdued, shaken cheer rose among the soldiers as they watched the rest of the unaltered Drychta army run, leaving their dead comrades behind, while some of the Yadoshans persisted in chasing the stragglers. The Odalian banner flew over Kance's location, flapping in the wind. The king was safe.

The door in my head that separated Fox from me remained

closed, but I was sure Fox had gotten through somehow, that he had added his strength to mine to allow me to triumph over Druj. I reached for him, expecting to find my brother's warm, comforting presence. But there was nothing. The barriers between us remained intact, and I was alone.

Still holding on to Kalen, I burst into tears.

*T*HE *DRYCHTA STAGGERED OUT FROM* the base of the mountains, many on fire. I watched others jump off higher peaks, screaming as the flames consumed them until they were but balls of light, falling like rain.

As they plunged down, I saw them change. Their bodies warped and shifted. They did not hit the ground with lifeless thuds, but with raspy chitterings and undulations as their midsections broke and re-formed and gave way to new segmented bodies, horrible insect-like mutations fused with mammalian limbs. Still burning, they skittered forward, shrugging off the fires like they had their humanity, creeping toward the stricken Odalians and Yadoshans who retreated from the sight. Nothing in their training had prepared them for such macabre alchemy.

It was the nanghait that saved them. Rushing forward with its trunk-like legs, the daeva scooped up the first of the grotesque insects. Its jaws unhinged, and it stuffed the creature into its gaping maw, its crunching curdling my blood. Another insect leaped forward, but the nanghait was ceaseless, simply shifting its head to present a second hungry face to consume a fresh meal, and then another, and another.

The taurvi lifted its head and sang a lullaby, a seductive melody that should not have been possible from those ruined mandibles, those protruding fangs. The blighted Drychta slowed, transfixed by the sound, as did other soldiers nearby—including me. It stole into my head, erasing all emotions in me but rapture. All thought of fleeing, or moving, slipped away. The aeshma lumbered close, ignoring us. It rolled itself into a ball and mowed down the immobile Drychta without pause, stampeding through the flock even as they sat and listened to its brother daeva's deathsong.

But the savul was a much more brutal beast; it clawed eagerly into anyone close enough to obstruct its path, and I could hear General Lode over the din, yelling at the rest to fall back, to keep away from the daeva.

The zarich breathed ice and mist. The crackling stole up Drychta legs, rendering them useless as it sliced through their scaled bodies. And still, the azi above us continued its pillaging, promising more infernos.

The others had not been idle. Arcs of Fire and Ice and Wind and Lightning filled the sky as the asha and the Deathseekers attacked, halting the Drychta's progress. Lord Agnarr and his men knelt, hands firm against the ground. The nearest Drychta took a step and sank into unexpected quicksand. The earth shuddered as spikes jutted out without warning, impaling others.

"Tea!" Lord Fox rode into view, cutting down every Drychta in his path. His eyes were trained on the azi flying overhead, and he exchanged his blade for a bow that was strapped across his shoulders. He strung an arrow and loosened it quickly when the three-headed daeva sailed nearer to the ground. There was no visible wound, but the azi veered away.

"Tell your pet to stop burning the Hollows, you idiot!" the man roared up at the sky. "You'll burn everything!"

The Dark asha heard him. The zarich *stomped forward and took a deep gargle of air. Mist formed around my mouth even as the cold extended into the mountain, containing the conflagration for the moment.*

But her brother was far from done. He leaped off Chief and sliced his way through the rest of the Drychta. His eyes were on the savul, *still on its rampage. He cut down the remaining blighted—and drove his sword into the daeva, bloodying its shin.*

Its roar was one of surprise. For a moment, it seemed recognition blazed behind its yellow, bulging eyes. Its maimed claw, after all, had been responsible for the man's death. Still caught in its bloodlust, the daeva swung at him. Lord Fox did nothing to deter the attack. Its talon slashed through his chest.

Both reeled back unexpectedly. The savul *shrilled from some invisible pain. The undead general sank to the ground with his hand over his lacerated chest and his mouth pulled back in a snarl, gulping air he did not require. From above, the* azi's *reaction was immediate. It landed beside the* savul, *stumbling in its haste. The first to jump off its back was Lord Kalen, slamming his blade against a blighted Drychta's unprotected side when it ventured near.*

"Fox!" She had changed much since the last time I had seen her. Her hair streamed behind her like the night, clothed in the hua *of three dragons she had worn at our first meeting, dark eyes still a mystery, but her cheeks had hollowed and her skin had lost some of its luster. An unspoken thought passed between her and Fox, between her and Kalen, between her and her daeva—and both* savul *and* azi *turned to protect the three, snapping and clawing at the dwindling Drychta still putting up a fight.*

"You did it on purpose," she seethed, her voice cutting deeper than the Deathseeker's knives of wind.

Lord Fox smiled grimly before the azi obscured them from my view.

I don't remember how long the battle lasted. I cowered behind the Deathseekers as they wove rune after rune after rune, blanketing the sky with barriers invisible to my eyes. Occasionally, I caught sight of a flare of debris when it came into contact with those magical shields, the way a sword's tip might drag against another blade and send up sparks. I huddled with the wounded and injured, scrabbling to bring them closer to the blockade the Odalians had erected, hoping that no wayward rune or daeva attack would find us. I could no longer see the trio; the azi and the savul still blocked my sight, snapping and slicing at anyone or anything that drew too close.

The zarich won its war against the flames. Smoke rose from the mountains, and the Drychta who were still unchanged staggered out coughing, averting their faces, lifting their hands to plead surrender. Only the blighted continued their losing fight, assaulting the combined armies until every last one of them were killed.

Bereft of enemies, all the daeva—save for the azi—turned their backs on us and moved rapidly toward the sea. They waded in with little preamble. The waves washed over their heads, and they were gone before we could react.

Were they running away, I wondered, or toward something else?

It was only when one of the Gorvekai—Solveiga—nudged me gently with her foot that I realized that the battle was over. "The Faceless has gone too far this time," she said soberly. "To change a nation of people into abominations—now do you understand why the strongest is not always the worthiest?"

There were heavy casualties on both sides of the conflict. Many of the soldiers had been ripped apart by the beasts, but among the blighted, none survived. The still-human Drychta, now docile, sat on the ground, watched over by a group of asha. General Lode questioned one, and the prisoner was all too eager to respond.

"Aadil is missing" came his terse report. "They do not know if he still remains in the mountains."

"He does not." The Dark asha stood before us, her face smudged from dirt and ash. Her familiars stood beside her. The generals and commanders of the army lifted their swords as one, watching the bone witch with distrust. Only Khalad and Lord Agnarr were nonplussed.

The horrific wound on Lord Fox's chest that would have been mortal on anyone else had vanished. "I remembered this," the familiar said. "On Mithra's Wall—you reached out to me—"

"So it was you back then," she said, and her voice broke my heart. "I wondered if I had dreamed it out of longing. Or if I'd gone insane, as you feared."

"Tea—"

She stepped away. "Don't," she begged. "Later. Please."

Her brother's mouth curved down at the corners, scowling, worried.

She smiled wanly at King Kance. "Drycht," she says, "is kingless."

"Did you kill him, Tea?"

"We have very different interpretations of what death means, Your Majesty."

"*Tea, you look unwell. Please, let me—*"

"*Nothing is happening that shouldn't be, Your Majesty.*" She moved toward her azi. "*I must go.*"

"*No!*" Lord Fox grabbed her arm. "*You will not leave until I've had every answer out of you!*"

"*Fox is right.*" The Odalian noble was tired and adamant. "*We have many questions—*"

The Dark asha laughed. We were all taken aback by the unnaturally loud, high-pitched strangeness of it. "*Have you finally decided to take my head, Your Majesty?*"

"*I am more interested in your answers.*"

"*And if I refuse?*"

"*Do not make it harder for us, Tea.*"

"*On the contrary, it will be quite easy.*"

Lethargy stole into my bones. My lips moved, but no sound came out. I could not walk. I could not speak. Instead, my knees sank of their own volition into the hard soil. I saw King Kance's eyes widen as he did the same. So did the generals and soldiers, the wounded and the healthy, the asha and the Deathseekers. The bone witch's mark was on us all, and we were helpless in the face of her Compulsion. Only the Gorvekai remained on their feet, proving their duplicity. Lord Fox was upright too, but he made no move.

The bone witch let out a gasp, her hand flying to her chest. Lord Kalen took her in his arms, his own face grim and strained. "*You're overexerting yourself again, love.*"

She grinned wanly. "*Nothing you wouldn't have done in my place.*"

"*What are you doing, Tea?*" Lord Fox whispered.

"*What you wouldn't let me do if you had your way.*"

"*Tea!*" Lady Zoya burst through the crowd but stumbled and fell to the ground as well, her hand dropping. Still she mustered strength to blister the air with words. "*Let—us—go! You cannot do this!*"

"*Zoya. For once in your life, shut up and listen. You want answers?*" The Lady Tea's voice rose, mocking. "*You shall have them. You intend to invade Drycht after this victory at the Hollows, to depose Aadil once and for all. Instead, you will face civilians and innocents with the blight. As soon as the first of you sets foot on Drychta soil, they will turn, and you will find nothing to save, only a city of monsters hungering for your flesh. Druj has cast a large net. The Faceless will have the people suffer to kill as many of you as needed. Druj doesn't intend this to be a war—he intends it to be a massacre.*"

21

To his credit, King Kance said nothing of my pale, tear-streaked face, though his heartsglass beat quick, erratic patterns of blue. He had drawn his sword during the battle, its tip bloody, and I wondered if he'd been fighting long, though it was doubtful that General Lode would allow many to get past him.

The bulk of the casualties had fallen to the Drychta, but many of the Odalians were caught in the *indar*'s deadly acid attack. One look at their heartsglass was enough for me to gauge fatal wounds from the less grievous, and it was a difficult task to move from one fallen fighter to the next, compelling them into sleep knowing they would never wake.

Likh had the runic wards wrapped around herself again as she bustled about, dressing as many of the soldiers' wounds as she was able to. She, Khalad, and I all knelt side by side, tending to patients as Kalen and Kance remained deep in conversation, planning their next move. General Lode was coordinating transport to send the wounded back to Odalia, where they would receive better treatment in better facilities.

Althy had helped arrange most of those travel details. Now she was on the other side of the camp, healing other wounded. The older asha had taken great pains to avoid me since she'd arrived with her circle of asha, and the snub added to my worry, unsure if I would be arrested and if she would be doing the arresting.

Sadly, I wove another set of *Compulsion*, giving my patient a small measure of peace in his final moments, and tearfully closed his eyes after he had passed, mercifully, without pain. I gave quiet instructions for his body to be carried to Althy, and turned to Knox, who suffered from a broken arm.

"We were careless," Knox said hoarsely, watching the other Kion asha remove the body. "Didn't have much experience with daeva beyond the *nanghait*, and to see that black poison spurting out of that creature was a nightmare."

"I'm sorry for your losses, milord."

"No sorrier than I am. We ought to eliminate these bloody-assed demons, Lady Tea. We can't live in the same world as they. If one of us's gotta go, I'd rather it be them."

"The daeva was being controlled by a Faceless. I doubt it would attack on its own."

"The fact that it can be controlled makes it a danger. Begging your pardon, milady," he added, with a nervous glance at the *azi* flying overhead, who patrolled against any unexpected assaults. "I know you're fond of them. Or one of them."

"No offense taken, milord. I can understand the fear."

He's right, I thought, setting his splint, *I cannot keep resurrecting and killing daeva*. Fighting the *indar* with the *azi* had already made me more exhausted than I remembered being in the past. But what could I do? Now that we'd learned that I cannot create shadowglass, bonding them to trustworthy Dark asha seemed the next best thing.

Likh and Khalad spoke quietly, the former's eyes red. "Why not?" I overheard her ask. "I'm as much in danger of dying here with the runic wards as without them." The soldier she was ministering to had sustained a severe head wound but was not in any mortal danger.

"You have a higher chance of dying without the wards as with them," Khalad corrected. "We've had this discussion before, Likh. I'm not going to lose you on a maybe."

"What would you have done in my place? Would you be willing to stand by, knowing you could make a difference despite the risks?"

"Not if I trust the people with me. Not if I ask them for protection as well. Your safety makes all the difference to the people you're helping right now, Likh. You don't need runes for that."

Likh looked at him, then down at the unconscious soldier. "I just wish I could do more."

I did a quick weave on her and saw the rune glow red. "This is ridiculous!" I exclaimed. "Likh, we've been eating the same foods, and none of us have exhibited any of the symptoms of *Blight*."

Likh didn't look as distressed as I was; strangely enough,

she grew calmer the more I spoke. "Maybe the blight affects silver heartsglass more than it does regular heartsglass. We've never been able to make a comparison, and I've been the only silver-hearted victim to survive this long. But that's not as important anymore."

"But it is!" Khalad exploded. "Surely you can't think that!"

"I think that I should learn to accept that which is beyond my control and make the best of my situation. I'm not scared. This isn't the time or the place to be scared. Too much is happening." Likh smiled at him. "I'm not trying to deliberately put myself in danger. But if I'm already cursed, then the least I can do is to ensure none of you wind up the same way."

Without warning, Khalad yanked Likh to him and kissed her so thoroughly that I averted my eyes with some embarrassment. "I don't care," he snapped, breaking away, "I'll protect you because I want to believe we have more years to spend together, and anything coming out of your mouth saying otherwise is a lie."

Likh's eyes widened. Her face softened with adoration. I finished my work on Knox's dressing and gently assisted the Yadoshan back to the main camp, allowing the two a private moment. Nowadays, those were rare.

"Lady Likh and Lord Khalad?" Knox asked. "I had no idea. Isn't Likh a...well..."

"Lord Khalad finds no issue with that," I told him. "And Lady Likh is Lady Likh. That's all that matters."

"If you say so, Lady Tea. They're both fine people." Gingerly, Knox touched his sling. "Thank you for the aid. Though I fear this may render me useless should more battles break out."

The loss of their kinsmen had had a sobering effect on many of the Yadoshans, and they were more than eager to scale Mithra's Wall and avenge their fallen comrades. I drew myself up, prepared to scold their recklessness, but a new voice broke into the conversation.

"If all works out for the best, Lord Knox, then the next Drychta fight will be the last that both the Odalians and the Yadoshans shall concern themselves with. And the Kions, for that matter."

Gulping, I turned to face Althy. Zoya stood with her.

"If you would give Lady Tea and I a moment, Lord Knox?"

The man obliged. Awkwardly, I shuffled my feet. "I was surprised to see you here. I didn't think Ankyo knew about the Drychta yet."

"The pigeons we sent to Yadosha never returned. It made Empress Alyx suspicious. So she sent out a small entourage of asha under my charge to investigate. That was a week and a half ago. If truth be told, I convinced her to send us here, just in case. By the time she and Fox sent us word of your warning, we were already a day's ride from Mithra's Wall."

I exhaled in relief. So Fox *had* heeded my call. "And I suppose you're planning on bringing me back to Ankyo for my trial?"

The asha snorted. "I don't condone your decision to leave, Tea. But I am concerned with all the choices you have made since then. You were only to stay in Yadosha and lie low there until Mykkie and I could concoct a way for you to return. And now I find you here, among the Odalians and the Yadoshans, with a Faceless camped within reach."

"I couldn't sit by and do nothing, Althy." Quickly, I related everything that had happened since we had parted ways—the discovery of *Blight* runes in Thanh, my subsequent journey to meet with the Gorvekai, the trials within Stranger's Peak. Althy's brows were pinched together in concern by the time I was done.

"It is troubling," she said. "I think it was ill-advised of you to volunteer for the mountain's tests. But I'm relieved that you have emerged unscathed. And here in Mithra's Wall...you're much stronger than before, Tea. Controlling a daeva normally takes concentration, yet you were able to handle two with ease, while fighting off a Faceless in one's head besides."

"I'm almost jealous," Zoya said. "Serves me right for staying behind. Stranger's Peak would have been marvelous to see."

I shuddered. "I would have gladly traded places with you if I could, Zoya. It wasn't a pleasant experience."

"I can prepare some more herbs for you, to help calm you," Althy offered.

"Kalen has been giving me the *Calming* spell nearly every day since we left Kion."

"The fool," Zoya scoffed. "Surely he knows it saps his strength."

"I've tried. You know Kalen."

"I'll make sure to yell at him for it later. And how is Likh?"

I bit my lip. "She still has the blight, but I don't know why. We've been so careful..."

Althy mulled that over. "I'll have a talk with Khalad and see what other options we have. Perhaps the *Blight* rune affects those with silver heartsglass differently."

"That is what she said. How…how is Fox?"

Althy looked at me without saying a word.

"I see."

"Tea, he's as busy as you are, what with the princess and the—"

"There is no need for an explanation, Althy. I understand all too well."

"He believed you about Druj," Zoya persisted. "He's still in shock. With the blighted courtiers, we didn't have much time to—"

I startled. "*Blighted courtiers?*"

Althy shot Zoya a scathing look. "We've had our own share of blighted attacks. There is no reason to worry. The queen and princess are fine, as is Mykkie. Fox was instrumental in saving them."

"Lady Altaecia," Kance greeted, nearing us with Kalen and General Lode by his side, "And, Lady Zoya. Thank you both for your assistance."

Zoya curtsied. "We nearly didn't make it in time, Your Majesty, given the late start we were afforded. What do you intend to do now?"

"We need to head to Mithra's Wall and confront King Aadil," Kance said abruptly. "I will not leave until I have that madman out of my kingdom, preferably in chains."

"And I would like to have a talk with the Faceless who stands behind him," I added bleakly.

"What if they raise another daeva?" General Lode asked. "I am leery of having to face another so soon."

"How many of the bezoars do we have now?" Kalen asked.

"Five." It had taken nearly two hours and a host of *Fire* runes to evaporate most of the poisonous bile the dead *indar* excreted in death before I was able to retrieve its sapphire-blue bezoar. "Including the *azi*, that makes six. There's one more daeva not yet accounted for."

Zoya frowned. "That would be the *akvan*. But if I remember correctly, it won't be ripe for resurrection for another two years."

"Unfortunately, the Faceless may have found a way to speed up the process. The Gorvekai claim such a rune exists but refuse to divulge the secret."

"Then Druj must have gleaned it through some other text," Althy theorized. "And recently. We had no such problems with them in the past. He must have reason to believe the First Harvest is somewhere inside Mithra's Wall."

"Then we must go after it immediately!" Zoya protested.

"It's not as easy as it sounds, Lady Zoya," Kance said. "The close, cramped caves within the Wall will not be advantageous for large armies. The *azi* will not be able to enter short of burning down the whole mountain."

"Then let's level it." There was a nasty glint in Zoya's eye.

"As a last resort, yes. But I would much rather take less drastic means to lure the Drychta king out, milady."

"Why bother luring him out?" I interrupted. "I brushed against Druj's mind for a few moments while the *azi* fought his *indar*. He's smarter than Aenah, but not as feckless as Usij. I doubt you will get them out of the mountain for any reason until they find their prize, and time is running short. I understand that we might have the disadvantage going in, but with his soldiers depleted, that may be the best course of action."

"Mayhap it would be better for everyone if it did burn," Althy murmured. "Let the First Harvest burn."

"I don't think it would take to fire that easily," Kalen said. "Lord Agnarr gave me the impression that it would endure whatever we did to destroy it."

"Then who do we send into Mithra's?" Kance asked.

"Tea and me, Zoya and Althy if they're up for it, a half dozen more asha and Deathseekers. Some soldiers to guard the entrance, perhaps, and the rest to make sure the Drychta survivors don't try anything else," Kalen replied.

"The Drychta survivors are down to manageable numbers," Althy agreed. "They're the lucky ones, given the fates of their comrades. Perhaps they will be amenable to surrender now."

King Kance sighed. "This will put you all in greater danger."

"There's not a lot of choice at this point." Kalen allowed himself a smile, drawn tight at the edges. "And that's part of our job description. In fact, I'd rather start sooner than later. Once Tea has rested enough." There was a question behind his words.

I nodded. "I'm fine, and I'm ready. The Drychta think we'll be licking our wounds, and they'll surely be tending to theirs. They won't expect an attack so quickly after the last."

Althy nodded. "I'll send for the other asha."

"Are you sure, Tea?" Kance asked, momentarily forgetting to be formal. "This is…" He paused, and his heartsglass supplied the rest: *This is asking too much of you.*

"This is bigger than any of us, Your Majesty. Aadil's actions imperil the rest of the kingdoms, including his own." I cleared my throat. "We won't have much communication once we're in the Wall, and I might need someone to scry in too, so I can inform you of what happens inside. I propose that Khalad be my—"

"No. Let me do it."

"Your Majesty—"

"Khalad still has a lot of work to help the wounded, and my other generals need to focus on other matters should Aadil attack again. Allow me to be your *Scrying* vessel, Tea. Let me be useful."

I took a quick, surreptitious glance at Kalen, who inclined his head ever so slightly. "As you wish, Your Majesty."

·· ☽ ··

The planning was quick but meticulous. There would only be a handful of people heading into the mountains with us, mostly asha and what Deathseekers General Lode could afford to spare, while the rest surrounded the mountain in anticipation of further attacks. Mithra's Wall, I learned, had dozens of entrances, and Knox supplied us with most of that knowledge. He too had volunteered to accompany us despite his injury.

"Most of the caves inside are interconnected," he told us. "And from what King Kance's spies have reported, Aadil entered one of the topmost entrances. I've explored those caves before with my buddies in the past, and I'm the only one here experienced with the routes and passageways along that tier. They're not as many as the ones below it, and almost all the openings lead into a large chamber, so you should have no trouble finding anyone hiding inside."

The remnants of the Drychta army were unlike what anyone expected. All the fight had leached out of the men. They were waiting almost meekly when we arrived and, once we were near enough, deliberately threw down their spears, axes, and bows.

"They're surrendering," Zoya noted with astonishment. "But why? Could this be another trap?"

"Let's find out." General Lode strode forward and barked a command in Drychta. One of the men responded in a long, halting monologue, and all sank to their knees in unison.

"They're frightened," the man translated. "They've been worked hard and nearly starved the last few days. The blighted were the last straw. All they want is some food and water, and they're more than willing to let us pass. This man says they've been mistreated terribly. They were promised good wages for their families if they followed Aadil into battle, but they have not been paid. He says their king is a madman."

"That's horrible," Althy breathed softly.

Lode frowned. "I'm not sure if I translated this correctly, but they claim there is forbidden magic in their bones, and that they have been condemned to the seven hells by Aadil, who threatened to turn them into demons if they disobeyed."

A chill ran through me. I knew what that meant. Had Aadil allowed *all* his army to be blighted? "Stay away from them," I barked at the general and wove my *Delving*. My heart lurched at what I saw: the runes festered red in the air before them, all compromised.

Kalen was already one step ahead of the others. "Channel wards on them all!" he barked at both asha and Deathseekers alike. "Do it quickly, while we still have time!" His hands were a blur, wrapping tendrils of protective magic around the Drychta who had spoken, then hurried to the next.

The others were quick to act, and before long, the air was alive with brilliant magic, spells cloaking the poor soldiers to keep them safe from further harm. "What tyrant would blight his own people?" Kance gasped. "His own loyal soldiers? This is unthinkable!"

"I am entirely unsurprised, given all the stories I've heard of Aadil," Zoya said drolly, firmly tying off a ward around another grateful fighter. "Good thing we didn't think to wait for them to come. Aadil could have sent them after us next."

"Too late!" Althy shouted. Some of the other half dozen soldiers who had yet to be warded were starting to change. Desperate, still beseeching, their features warped, and I could only watch helplessly as their new, grisly forms sealed their fate. The other, more fortunate Drychta scrambled away from their transformed comrades, shouting frantically.

But how? Who had woven the rune? All the men were within my line of sight, and not one of them had moved.

Some instinct told me to look up. High above a ledge, a cloaked figure stood, an arm raised. There was a quick, cutting gesture, and the last of the unwarded, blighted men completed their horrific metamorphosis. The hooded shape lingered for a few moments, staring down at me. The distance was too far for me to make out any features, but I knew who it must be.

A blast of lightning erupted from Zoya's fingertips, aimed at the cowled stranger.

But the figure stepped away, avoiding the attack, almost dismissive of the attempt, and the lightning sizzled harmlessly against the escarpment. The figure twisted its head in my direction. I could not see its face but knew its eyes were on me, cold and assessing, before it turned and disappeared back into the—

*T*HE DARK ASHA'S LETTER ENDED there. *The rest of the tale was missing.*

"You were always impulsive, Zoya," the bone witch said, "though I would be a hypocrite to criticize you for something I have always been guilty of myself."

"Let me go," Zoya told her, "and I can offer you another refresher."

The Dark asha laughed at that.

"Why hadn't you thought to tell us before, little uchenik?" Lord Rahim pleaded. "Why such secrecy? Why did you have to burn a mountain?"

"Because there is a traitor among you. I discovered it only recently, after you had all left the safety of Ankyo's runic wards. I would denounce the betrayer, but what good would that do? You would have never believed me before, and it was more advantageous for me to keep an eye on her where she was, rather than have her flee once more into parts unknown."

"Who is it?" Lord Fox was tight-lipped and trembling, the sword heavy in his hands. He raised it toward the Dark asha. She did not move, did not compel him. She watched him instead, and somehow that was worse.

"Do you finally believe me, Fox? You were right. I killed Daisy. I might not remember it, but it was my hand that did the deed. But I *was not myself. I did not need someone to compel me, to carry out their orders. I made that discovery far too late." Her voice fell. "And Likh..."*

Khalad wept. His sobs were soft, barely discernible; in the quiet, they could cut stone.

"Tea," King Kance said in a soft, satin timbre. "Tell us. Please."

These were the songs they would never play at the darashi oyun, *the dances Vernasha of the Roses would have burned along with her books. All eyes were on Lady Tea as she took the stage, and a new tale lay poised at her fingertips, the missing pieces eager to fall into place.*

"Let me tell you the rest of the story," she said.

22

THE CAVES OF MITHRA'S WALL were unlike the caves at Stranger's Peak; the ground was riddled with limestone stalagmites and the lichen-covered walls were moist to the touch, sticking my hair to the back of my neck and leaving my palms sweaty from the moisture-heavy air. We had raced into the caves after the hooded figure while General Lode covered our backs, defending us from what was left of the blighted men. I could feel my *azi* already on the offensive, its three mouths aflame. We had no choice. I would be more useful confronting the Faceless inside than I would fighting the terrible beasts outside.

"I can see why these caves are free of tourists," Zoya grunted, pushing wet hair out of her eyes. The asha wore loose-fitting blouses and traveler's skirts to make the climb easier, but I smelled heavy clouds of magic wafting from the spells sewn into their clothes. Zoya was in the lead, and runes of *Light* surrounded her, glowing dimly.

"Quiet now," Althy cautioned. "It shouldn't be long before we come to the large pocket chambers that Knox spoke of."

Mithra's Wall, I remembered, had been a favorite hideaway of the great hero it was named for. The ranges had supposedly come into being when Mithra commanded the earth to rise, to stop the *nanghait* from demolishing his beloved Ashi's hometown of Thanh. But while the caves held little attraction for the average visitor, they were popular for explorers and spelunkers, and those who made the yearly pilgrimage to worship Mithra as a god in his own right.

As Althy had predicted, the narrow passageway soon opened into a large chamber, one I had seen in popular paintings and lithographs. It was the cave where Mithra famously rested after defeating the daeva, considered by many to be a holy place. Any traces of previous habitation had long since disappeared, whatever artifacts left behind no doubt stolen by adventurers over the years. There was nothing beyond a few broken pieces of wood, and a small, dark pool at the farthest wall. Neither Aadil nor the Faceless were present.

"There is something wrong here, Lady Altaecia." One of the asha, a young woman named Ginrei, spoke up. "This chamber has no exits beyond the one we entered. If Lord Knox is right, and if Lady Tea is positive this passage is where Druj disappeared, then they could not have left without our seeing them."

I cast my mind briefly toward Kance's thoughts, scrying swiftly. The decision to ward as many of the Drychta as possible had proven beneficial, I saw. The fight had been speedy, if brutal. *Did anyone leave the caves after we entered?* I asked him.

He jumped, startled by the unexpected voice in his head. "No. Khalad and I have been watching."

They're not in Mithra's chamber. They must have escaped through some other means. Please ask General Lode to guard the mountain paths and keep further watch, just in case.

"Understood, Lady Tea."

"Kance and Khalad saw nothing," I told the rest.

"Surely they couldn't have gone to another apex in the range this quickly?" Zoya asked. "It would take years to search them all."

"Can you sense Druj?" Kalen asked me.

"The Faceless is very good at masking his thoughts. I've been trying to find him, to no effect."

Knox cleared his throat. "That's not quite accurate, actually. That the chamber is a dead end, I mean."

Althy rounded on him, looking cross. "Now is not the time for riddles, Knox. Out with it."

The Yadoshan coughed. "I wasn't intending to hide it, lady asha. It's been some time since I traveled here, but I now remember. There's another way out." He pointed toward the small pool. "We were curious, milady. Nearly drowned getting to the other end, since we didn't know how long the underground spring traveled. Blacked out a bit before Aden managed to pull my head out of the water. But there wasn't anything much on the other side, only another smaller chamber. Granted, we didn't explore it much. The wind was chillier there, and we all wanted drier clothes."

Althy sighed; she could have groaned *Yadoshans*, and it would have sounded the same. "How far along is the spring?"

"You won't need to hold your breath too long. There's a fork in the spring though. Go down the wrong end and there's nothing to surface to, which was what nearly got me."

"We will take better precautions than you or your friends did, but you will lead the way. You do remember how to get there, don't you?"

"Yes, ma'am."

The other asha and Deathseekers cobbled together an ingenious combination of *Air* and *Water* runes that allowed us small pockets of air while we swam underneath the surface—more than enough to get through the underwater tunnel. Kalen and the others insisted on retaining their hold on their weapons, not wanting to emerge unarmed on the other side, and our progress was slower than I would have hoped.

It was a new experience to swim while we breathed. Zoya manifested enough *Light* underwater to ensure none of us were separated, and we resurfaced without any problems.

Kalen had exercised caution, sending *Shield* runes jutting out into the air before anyone of us left the water, but no enemy waited for us on the banks. We took our time drying off with more *Wind* and *Fire* while my love took it upon himself to explore the immediate area. "It's as Knox said," he observed. "There's a smaller passageway down to the right though, half-hidden by some formations. The Faceless might have gone through there."

"They did," I said bleakly. "Be careful, all of you. I can practically smell the wards emanating from that direction."

Zoya's nose wrinkled. "She's right. Seems like they're more concerned with stopping us from accessing our runes than they are at keeping their location a secret. Perhaps this is where they intend the ambush."

"Undoubtedly so," Althy agreed. "And it will take time to remove these barriers."

"It's not a complete warding," I said softly. "They may not have had as much time as they wanted either. These wards will prevent the rest of you from using runes, but they're not keeping me from using the Dark. They *want* me to go alone."

"Don't do it!" Zoya warned.

"I've been inside enough Faceless minds to understand a bit of how they think. This is a blatant invitation—they want to know what I know. The best course of action would be to go in and see what they want, and for the rest of you to unravel the wards while I buy us time."

"I'm not leaving you," Kalen said stubbornly.

"Neither will I," Althy decided. "Zoya, focus on the barrier with the others, then join us afterward."

"Althy, you'll be powerless beyond this passage."

The asha smiled grimly. "I still have a few tricks up my sleeve. If Tea's right, then they're not looking for a battle. Let's go see what they want."

The warded passageway led to the smallest of the chambers we'd been to, and the Faceless and King Aadil waited for us at its end with a few bodyguards. Druj was still heavily cloaked, a hood pulled down over his face, obscuring his features. King Aadil took no such steps to hide his identity. The mad king was clothed in ceremonial armor, similar to what I'd seen hanging from the scholar Garindor's walls in his tiny Isteran cottage back in Farsun. The king also wore a gold circlet on his head in place of a crown, with wings hammered on either side.

About a dozen bodyguards flanked him, all of whom moved in unison to shield their ruler. The king drew his sword and snarled a warning as we approached. I didn't need to look into his head to know his insanity; his eyes looked the same as Telemaine's had all those months ago.

"As you suspected, Tea," Althy said quietly. "They do not have the First Harvest, and the king demands that we hand it to him immediately." She lifted her voice and returned an answer to him in Drychta. The king responded with streams of abuse and stepped forward but stopped when the hooded figure raised its hand.

"Give up," I said, directing my words to Druj. "You won't find the First Harvest here."

The figure turned its face toward me. Suddenly, I was no longer standing in a cave inside Mithra's wall of mountains. Instead, I was some distance from a great city, watching it burn. The smoke and ash seared my senses, the smell stinging and acrid.

This is not real, I thought frantically, willing myself to calm down. *This is not real!*

The Faceless stood before me, but he did not attack. Instead, he inclined his covered face in the direction of the city, watching it burn.

This wasn't Kion. The buildings were different.

It is not a city you will recognize, someone said, more whisper than voice. It was soft and hoarse, pitched low. *Its name has been forgotten to all but history.*

Why are you showing me this?

I have suffered loss as you have. For you, it is visions of Kion in flames. That is your nightmare as much as this was mine. And the irony is that you shall burn Kion to save it.

Who are you?

A friend, if you are willing. The figure walked into the center of that maelstrom, wordlessly bidding me to follow. I hesitated, but there was nowhere else to go, so I trailed after the cloaked figure warily, wrapping the Dark around me should my instincts prove wrong.

The man was content to walk ahead without bothering to look back and see if I followed. He stopped before the remnants of a house whose foundation had since been given up to heat and flames. It smoldered while everything around it continued to rage.

A woman lay huddled on the ground. Weeping, she clasped an unmoving infant in her arms. Her cries were the only sounds amid the crackling of fire.

We all come from broken pasts, murmured the voice from underneath the hood. *The Dark attracts the grieving. The sounds of lament are a pleasure to its senses. All who embrace the Dark know loss before they are granted its blessing.*

Was this Aenah? I remembered a similar vision when that Faceless had briefly lowered her defenses and gave me access to her mind. She too had clung to a dead infant before a burning city, the first and only time I felt any empathy on her behalf.

Aenah knew loss, but her grief differed from yours. Your brother was old enough to be raised, had enough of his own will to be given his own freedoms. Aenah's child had no such choices. Her daughter would always remain an infant, never growing up and never understanding what had happened. That knowledge tore at Aenah. Usij may have known similar agonies, though the well of his mind had been poisoned for far too long to draw sanity from its depths.

You all worked together...

No. We shared the same goals and sought to independently attain them by all means. As do you, Tea. Your colleagues sought to hide the truth from you. They are willing to kill you to preserve their objectives. Only you, of all the asha who claim the Dark, seek out shadowglass.

This was the elders' purpose, then? To kill me under the guise of a trial and an execution? Because my death under other circumstances would incite suspicion?

Have you ever thought otherwise?

I paused. *No.*

Mykaela they can control. She is too weak. In time, they believe, opposition will fade once you are gone. There will be new empresses and new Dark asha, and the elders shall endure. That is the nature of tyranny, young Tea. Maintaining power is their sole intention. Why worry about retaliation and revolution when they have always intended to wield the sword? Such was Vernasha's dream.

You have kept yourself abreast of Kion politics.

I am aware of many things.

Why tell me this?

We share the same goals, Lady Tea. We make good allies. What does it matter the means used to bring about the end result?

You want destruction. You seek to complete shadowglass to rule. That is not the same as what I want.

You do not know what it is that you want. You wish to rid the world of magic, yet you do not wish to rid yourself of your dead brother. It is a contradiction you have not yet come to terms with. The only solution is to wield magic for your own good, to suit the world to your principles. You know this. It gives you guilt. We are the same.

We are not the same! You have killed so many! You blighted your own men!

There must be sacrifices. Already we have given up too much. What is the difference if men fall to the blight or if they fall to an uncontrollable daeva? You have sacrificed your own people too.

That's not true! I refused to think about Telemaine, dead at his son's hand, a murder I had indirectly carried out. I refused to think about poor Daisy. I refused to think about Fox, and Inessa, and Polaire.

We are the same, he murmured. *We were always the same. I knew as much the first time we met.*

Who are you?

One of us shall find the First Harvest, Tea. It will not matter who takes the prize, for the consequences will be the same. Once you hold a god's soul in your hands, you will not resist. You could make a

"The First Harvest isn't here," I said hoarsely, still brimming with the immense power that the Faceless had given me. It was too much too soon, and I had to release it. "It was never here to begin with. He fooled us this whole time. He—I—all this bloodshed, just to reach out to *me*—"

"Tea!" Kalen grabbed me as I slumped down. I could hear him barking orders at the others, no doubt sensing what was about to happen, but I no longer cared. There was a need inside me begging to be freed, the powers building until there was only exquisite pleasure until I had no choice but to burst.

And I did.

The ground before us tore open. The bones of beetles and roaches and spiders long dead scuttled out, freed by the potency of my spells, overrunning the walls. Larger skeletons followed suit, leopards and jaguars and people who had died in these mountains pushed their way out of the ground. A low moan rose from outside, and I felt rather than saw the dead blighted Drychta reconstitute themselves, this time under my reign. I heard the yells of fright, the sound of a thousand swords being drawn.

"Kalen," I heard Zoya say. "I'm sorry."

And then, without further warning, she drew back her hand and punched me.

*S*HE FOOLED YOU ALL." THE *Dark asha sounded weary. "I should know. She fooled me too."*

We remained rigid, with no choice but to cling to Tea's every word. Wasn't that what I wanted? *I thought, angry. My bitterness must have shown, for she turned back to me. "Have you found the rest of the pages, Bard?"*

"No." *The word tasted stale in my mouth.*

Her black eyes gleamed, and her satisfaction was terrible to behold. *"Good."*

"Tea," *Lord Fox began.*

"The Hollows was a distraction. I knew, and I came anyway. She hoped that one of you would fall. Kance, Khalad, anyone I cared for who had come to repel the Drychta. She sacrificed the rest of the Drychta army for the chance to kill one of you and cause me further pain. She knew I would defend you. And she was right. And if this plan succeeded, then she wanted you to enter Drycht, to face a city full of nightmares."

"'She'?" *Lord Fox demanded.*

Lady Tea ignored him. *"I weakened her, last we fought. I know I did. But she was wilier than even Usij. Usij was arrogant, not one to hide. His thoughts screamed to me all the way to Santiang, until my mind found that false pretender on the Daanorian throne and knew that it was he in disguise. But she—she was craftier. Where Usij disguised himself in the illusion of a royal emperor, she disguised herself as a woman I had loved and respected, so well that not even the Willows knew…" Her lip curled. "But then again, she always knew how to hide herself in Kion. She has been trained to hide there."*

What a sight it was to see commanders and soldiers and a king on their knees at the Dark asha's feet, even as she wavered, like a strong enough wind might send her stumbling. "I am done with setting fire to cities," she told them. "But I will bring harm upon your kingdoms nonetheless because there is no other way. Send my apologies to Queen Lynoria, Lord Selvyant, for no longer will asha be born from Arhen-Kosho—or anywhere else, for that matter. You will need to find other revenues beyond Murkwick's runeberry patch, Your Majesty. Knox—I am sorry for the nanghait that you can no longer hunt."

"Tea," her brother pleaded, pained.

The bone witch coughed. There were flecks of blood on her sleeve when her hand came away. "I will be the last bone witch, Fox. Mykaela is gone. The Faceless will win when I am dead. My daeva will succumb to their baser natures without me, and you cannot handle both them and the blight. You know that I cannot let Druj live. And as for Daisy—well, my life for hers. Was that not what you encouraged me to do, Your Majesty?"

King Kance licked his dry lips and found his voice. "I remember what I said, Tea. But not like this."

"You idiot." Lord Fox's voice was no louder than a whisper. "To hell with magic. To hell with the asha and the Willows and the rest of the kingdoms. To hell with me. I don't want you to die."

She smiled and placed her palm against his cheek. "I am already dying. There is a limit to shadowglass. It is like a hundred silver heartsglass, a hundred more ways to draw deeply of the Dark. I will not last the year. I will create shadowglass, or I will die. Sometimes it is that easy."

There were tears on his face. He moved to speak, failed, tried again. "Who is she, Tea? Who betrayed us?"

She bent her head and told her brother a name.

23

W ELL," ZOYA SAID, AS I groggily shifted into a sitting position. "That was quite a show you put on, Tea."

My shoulder hurt. It was heavily bandaged. The rest of me was numb on lemon balm and lilybrew, and I wasn't sure I could even feel my head. "How is everyone?" I mumbled.

"Doing fairly well, considering." Zoya was the last person I wanted telling me what I'd done wrong, and she was probably at my bedside for that very reason. "Considering you woke every dead critter to have ever lived inside Mithra's Wall. We had quite the time getting out of the cave with your dead weight while skeletal insects and bats flew all over the place. I reckon I'll have nightmares of beetle corpses crawling up my hair after this."

"Did I—?"

"Kill anyone? Oh, thankfully no. You did the exact opposite. We endured the half-formed bats and undead roaches and rats, and we fought our way out of the mountain only to discover that you'd also summoned the bones of every animal that had ever walked this part of the plains, including the Drychta we'd already killed."

I tried to lurch out of the cot, ignoring my burning pain, but *Wind* held me in place.

"Stop that," Zoya said impatiently, flicking another rune in my direction, "especially after all the trouble it took to get you here. Everything's under control. I thought they'd remain dead after I knocked you out and after Althy destroyed the Seeking Stone, but I guess a few corpses had a bit more agency than we thought. You've made peaceful yogis out of the surviving Drychta soldiers though. I'd bet all my *hua* they'll never lift a sword again. That's one way to scare fighters into farmers."

I touched my wound gingerly and flinched. "How did I get this?"

Zoya's mirth faded. She looked worried. "You don't remember?"

"Should I?"

"I would think so, since you're the one to go and *stab* yourself, which was why I punched you. I suppose you thought it was the only way to keep yourself from drawing in more Dark. *Never* do that again. It was rather unfair to Kalen, as he had to carry you with your blood dripping all over him. He's been guarding you the last two days, and it's only my wonderful skills of persuasion that finally convinced him to get some rest."

"I was out for two days?" I felt drained but also strangely

restless. I had taken in more of the Dark than I'd ever done, but part of me yearned for more.

"You really don't remember?"

"My memory has been bad as of late."

"Tea?" Kalen entered the tent, relaxing upon seeing me awake. He looked exhausted. "How are you?"

"Doing much better, as you can see." Zoya stood and rearranged her skirts. "I'll be off now. Althy intends to return to Kion soon, and I suppose I'll be forced to do the same." Her voice softened. "I'm glad to see you're better."

"You have to ward me," I whispered, the instant Zoya was out of the tent.

"Tea?"

"You have to, Kalen." I trembled, staring at my sheets. "I don't remember. I don't remember stabbing myself. Just like I don't remember stabbing Daisy. I seem to lose more and more of myself every time I wield the Dark, and I don't know what I might do next time. I'm starting to crave it. I can't risk…"

The bed dipped as Kalen pressed a knee onto the mattress, tugging me forward until I was in his arms. "You scared me today," he said quietly.

"That appears to be a habit of late."

"Do you really want to do this, Tea?"

I nodded, my face buried against his chest. "Just for now. Please?"

He said nothing else, but I could feel his runes wrapping around me, solidifying into barriers. The Dark slipped away. I was grateful that he didn't argue for once—perhaps he'd sensed the fear I had and understood the reality behind it.

I wanted to fuel my body with the Dark until I could lever the world with it. Druj wanted me a slave to power like an addict to opioids. Neither Aenah nor Usij would have dared. How could Druj channel that much power and not succumb to darkrot himself?

Questions swirled inside of me, then were placated as Kalen's wards did their work. The craving abated, though was not fully diminished. He said nothing, content to hold me close. And for the moment, that was all I wanted.

.. \|/ ..

Kance visited me hours later. I had fallen asleep again and woke to find the Odalian king sitting beside me, holding my hand. He allowed himself a brief smile at my confusion. "I asked Kalen to stay with General Lode while he interrogates Aadil, as he would need my cousin's expertise." He watched me relax, and a small, sad smile crossed his lips. "How long have you two been together?"

I looked away, embarrassed. "We became aware of each other's feelings in Daanoris, Your Majesty."

"While searching for a cure to my sickness?" When I nodded, he sighed. "Thank you. It occurred to me that I had not yet shown you any gratitude for those efforts."

"Many things happened in the interim, Your Majesty."

"That's no excuse. You frightened me, Tea. Kalen tells

me that you have no memories of what transpired after Aadil's capture. He also tells me that you chose to have yourself warded."

"I was fortunate that no one was injured this time, Your Majesty. I cannot take the same risks again."

"How many times have I told you not to call me by titles? 'Kance' will do."

I kept my gaze down, disentangling my fingers from his. "I didn't think I deserved that honor," I admitted. "Not anymore."

"I remain wary of your abilities, Tea. I always will. But that doesn't mean I'm not concerned for your well-being." He leaned forward and gripped my hand, refusing to let go. "I suspected that there was something between you and Kalen soon after my engagement to Inessa."

"Your Majes—Kance—I hadn't even realized then."

"But Kalen did. I know him well enough to see. He was good at keeping his emotions in check, but he always lost that composure whenever you were involved." Kance chuckled. "I teased him about you—it was a day or two before I fell sick, I think. He didn't even bother to deny it, just stared at me like I was a ghost. It made me jealous."

I looked at him, puzzled. I was certain he'd felt no romantic attachment to me before.

He clarified. "I was jealous of both of you. Of how easy it was to choose to be with someone you loved, of how there was no burden on either of you as there was on me. I would have married Inessa out of duty, you know, even if my father hadn't forced me to. But Inessa is made of stronger stuff than I. I resent her sometimes, and Fox." He sighed heavily. "You didn't choose the Dark just as I never chose to be born into royalty. Kalen told me about shadowglass. How using the spell would rid the world of all magic. What do you intend to do?"

I closed my eyes. "What do you think I should do?"

"I understand that you have a duty to the other asha, to the kingdoms that benefit from the runes they wield. You know more than I do of how heartsglass can help people, how my brother helps people. There are ramifications to losing that power, and it will affect everyone." Kance fell silent for several minutes, though his hand never left mine.

"But do it anyway," he said finally. "My brother will help people whether or not he remains the Heartforger. There will no longer be beasts to roam the land and attack people. With or without heartsglass, there will always be war. The asha and the Deathseekers will fade and become like the rest of us. They will learn in time that our existence is not so bad. I beg of you, Tea—if you have the opportunity to rid yourself of the magic that will one day consume you, then do it."

"I cannot lose my brother again, Kance." Tears dripped down to where our hands were joined. "I cannot. If you were in my place, and the price was Khalad, could you do it?" *A silver heartsglass and the* Resurrecting *rune*, Aenah's voice whispered in my head, as if she hadn't been dead all these months. *And a kiss from the First Harvest. That's all you need to bring young Fox Pahlavi his own heart, my Tea. But the harvest requires shadowglass, and shadowglass requires sacrifice. Surely he is worth the risk?*

Kance withdrew his hand from mine, his face immeasurably sad. He stood and drew his cloak around himself, but not before his heartsglass swung free. My eyes followed the movement and spotted a smaller crystal pendant that hung from the same chain. He saw where my gaze drifted and touched the smaller stone with a finger.

"You told me it would help with my exhaustion. You gave this to me the night my engagement to Inessa was finalized," he said quietly. "My anger at you in the days that followed did not prevent me from drawing comfort from your gift, and I am never without it. You are right. I could not ask that of Khalad. But had I been in his or your brother's place, I would like to believe I could offer my life willingly."

He sighed. "Maddening, isn't it? The bonds that tie us together are the same bonds preventing us from what we would sacrifice for ourselves. I will let Kalen know that you are awake."

•• ⌇ ••

"Do you mean to tell me," Zoya said much later, sounding incredulous, "that Druj intended to turn King Aadil over to us all along?"

"It seems that way." Once Kalen decided I was fit enough to get out of bed, I had emerged to find the Odalians hastily erecting makeshift prisons for the compliant Drychta. "Druj knew there was no First Harvest in Mithra's Wall yet convinced the king to invade." *To seek me out.*

Zoya scowled. "I'm not sure Aadil would make a competent ally. Perhaps the Faceless was simply foisting his trouble on us."

"Be that as it may," Althy said sensibly, "Kance has offered to assume charge of the prisoner, so it is one less burden for us. The other asha and I must make haste to Kion. Empress Alyx will want to hear what's happened immediately. The asha association, no doubt, will be very interested as well."

"Are you going to arrest me?" I asked her.

"You know me better than that. However, the *azi* has likely been sighted by now, and Kion should be receiving independent verification from other messengers soon."

"Won't you get in trouble for not bringing me in?"

"If a whole city could not contain you, then what should they expect from a handful of asha?" Althy smiled sadly at me. "Everyone misses you."

"You know that that's a lie, Althy."

The plump asha sighed. "He does, Tea. You will both heal from this one day, but you two must *choose* to. Fox has not been the same since you left, my dear."

"I cannot stay in contact with him, Althy. The elders will use our bond. They will know the instant I break through the runic wards around him again, and Mykkie has sworn to be truthful."

"Inessa is gaining ground. She is loved by the people, just like her mother, and she is fighting for you both. We all are." She hugged me. "We must take our leave soon. I will look over Likh, perhaps prescribe something stronger for him to take." Althy sighed. "Protect those two."

"You know I will."

She turned to Kalen. "And it is on you to protect Tea, or I will be very much put out."

"You know I always will, Althy."

Kance and General Lode had gone to question more of the Drychta prisoners, and they returned troubled. "King Aadil's madness is an open secret among the people of Drycht," the Odalian general said. "But they serve him because they knew no other way, even as they feared him. There have been attempts to overthrow him in the past, though all were unsuccessful, and the instigators were made to suffer horrible deaths. Some of the prisoners tell us that Aadil had once been a kind king, with the potential to become one of their greatest rulers. How that change happened in less than a decade is puzzling."

"That was Druj's doing." It horrified me, knowing that I had inflicted King Telemaine with the same madness the Faceless had on the Drychta ruler. *No. I am better than him. I am better than him.* "What do they say about Druj's role in this?"

"That he was first installed in Aadil's court as one of his closest advisers, though he never bared his face to the public. He always presented himself as a mystery. Behind Aadil's back, the people called him a sorcerer. Those who went so far as to publicly oppose him were either killed or imprisoned. All of Drycht lives in fear."

"Those poor people," Zoya said quietly. "What do we do now?"

"We are looking into who is next in line to the throne. Once we've found someone outside the Faceless's influence, we can ask neutral parties to set that person in Aadil's place as a trusted regent. I've heard that Adhitaya's son was exiled from the kingdom before the purge, and he may still be alive. Barring that, some distant relatives of the last king live, though they remain in hiding. Some of Aadil's factions remain in power, and I doubt they're willing to relinquish their control all that easily. We can hold Aadil captive for now, demand restitution for his crimes, but that's the extent of what we can do. We don't want to be accused of intervening in Drychta affairs more than we already have."

"We must leave soon," I added abruptly. "My presence complicates the situation, and I'm sure people from Kion already know I'm here, if sightings of the *azi* haven't already given me away. Althy is an ally, but the asha association will send their own representatives after me."

Kance hesitated. "You can claim sanctuary in Odalia," he said slowly. "They believe that we're not on good terms, and we can use that to our advantage."

"You told me my exile still stands, Your Ma—Kance."

"I am the king. I am allowed to change my mind."

I smiled weakly. "I'm a target in many different ways, Kance. I refuse to put your kingdom at further risk the way I did with the Yadoshans."

"But where will you go?"

"Somewhere they won't find us. It's a big world. There must be a small spot in it for us."

"But surely there's something else I can do?"

"There is." Kalen slipped his hand in mine. "Feign ignorance when you are asked where we are. Tell people we are still estranged and told you nothing. We want to live out the rest of our lives in peace, Kance, and we can only do so if we are hidden away."

"But will the elders stop sending people after you?"

"Wars come sooner or later, but they come all the same. There are no guarantees, but we have to try."

"I will do my best." Kance gripped Kalen's other hand in a firm handshake. "Blessings be upon you then, Kalen. Take care of yourselves, and look after Tea and Khalad for me."

"Without question, Your Majesty."

It took less than an hour for Likh and Khalad to get ready, both in noticeably better spirits. It was a good decision to make our departure immediate; the Yadoshans, Drychta, and Odalians were uncomfortable around me now, and even Knox seemed a shade awed, though not fearful, like most. "It was a good fight," the dark-skinned Yadoshan told us reverently. "I will remember it to the end of my days. I know I may not necessarily speak for my kinsmen, but should you ever find your way back to Yadosha, feel free to look me up. I owe you a tankard or two."

The *azi* was also eager to be off, its wings braced for flight. Once we had loaded the rest of our belongings on its back, it was quick to take to the air, and I watched as Kance stared up after us, an indecipherable expression on his face until he disappeared in the distance.

•• ⧫ ••

"There's something on your mind," Kalen said once we had set up camp. After much discussion, we had decided that time away from the Odalian-Kion-Yadoshan continent was needed, and when Likh had proposed staying overnight by the Sea of Skulls while we planned our next moves, we found little to protest. Khalad and Likh had caught enough fish for dinner, but I spent most of the evening staring into the campfire, lost in thought.

"There's something I'm missing," I confessed. "It's been nagging at me ever since we left."

"You need to give your body time to heal, Tea," Likh said with a smile, stirring a small pot.

I wrinkled my nose. "That doesn't smell like soup."

"It's some herbs Althy gave me before we left. My supplies were running low, and she offered some of her share." Likh blushed and lowered her voice. "She suggested that you take some. She mentioned that it was good for, ah...for preventing...when men and women have relations. It's for the woman to not..."

I blushed in turn. "I have my own herbs for that. But I'm not sure how you would benefit from, um..."

Likh was bright red. "O-of course not! She says it's also good for keeping up one's strength, and I thought I could brew you some as well."

"Thank you." I accepted a cup, breathing in the slightly bitter aroma. Althy had always favored quality over taste. Wryly, I recalled the terrible-tasting concoctions she had administered to me over the years, though they did a good job of healing me quickly enough, whether it was coughs or—

I froze, staring down at the herbal drink. The steam rising from the brown liquid felt hot against my face. *Fallowroot and winter ginger*, I thought almost absently, *mixed in with juniper berries and lacrow flowers...*

"It's not quite the *cha-khana*," Likh sighed, raising her own brew to her lips. "But this is better than nothing."

My arm whipped forward, dislodging the cup from her hands. The earthen bowl fell to the ground, shattering into pieces.

"Tea?" Khalad rushed forward at the sound, and Kalen turned from his cooking. "What's wrong?"

"Don't drink that!" I staggered to my feet.

"What—"

I delved. The rune stood, bleeding red, in the air. Likh's jaw dropped.

"All this time we'd wondered if the *Blight* rune affected silver heartsglass worse than it did others. We thought we were watching what we ate and drank. We were wrong." Shaking, I upended the contents of my bowl on the ground, liquid sloshing everywhere. I felt sick to my stomach, my appetite gone. "Likh, how long have you been drinking this?"

The poor girl was shaking. Khalad pulled her closer, and she all but collapsed against his chest. "Ever since we left Kion. Althy told me to take it every day, that it would be good for long journeys, especially now that I'd been blighted..."

I remembered Kance, the headaches and pain plaguing him in the days before his engagement to Inessa had been announced. How his father's death gave him the peace to chase them away;

how he stopped drinking the herbs after that. Who had brewed his tea, during those long months?

Hadn't I been drinking her concoctions as well? Strange dreams and visions had swirled my days together. Dreams that made me want to jump from high Isteran towers, that taught me how Kion should burn. Nightmares that drew my knife into my hands and stabbed my sister with my anger. Those nightmares had lessened after leaving Kion, but I had prepared my own herbs by hand since then.

Had Kance been blighted during those months as well? Was it a last resort, an unfulfilled threat?

I was wrong. I *must* be wrong. I would give up almost everything, not to be right.

"Tea." Kalen's face was strained. "Surely you don't think…"

"I don't know what to think. But you need to take the runic wards off me, Kalen. We need answers, and there's only one person I know who can give us them now."

*T*HE COMPULSION *DISSOLVED AROUND US, but the soldiers had
learned their lessons and dared not approach.*

*"You didn't believe me about Daisy," the bone witch said,
breathing hard. "You would not have believed me had I told you the
truth about Altaecia. Why would you? I had no proof. Khalad knew
then, but Altaecia only arrived back at Kion after he had left for
Daanoris. She claimed to have visited Odalian villages, it seems—a
deliberate ploy. It was my word against hers, and of the two of us, she
was not the known kinslayer, not the renegade bone witch. Altaecia
was clever, treating my mind with ills and humors until I questioned
even myself."*

*"I was stunned when I saw her at the port," Khalad murmured.
"I'd told no one about what had happened to her. I kept silent—I had
no way of reaching you with this new information, Tea, but it seemed
you knew all along."*

*"Not for a long time, no. But who would you side with—the
highly respected asha of the Willows, or a poor bone witch who'd slain
her own sister and showed every indication of losing her mind? In
your places, I would have sided against me. Poor Likh could not have
testified for my sake. Only Khalad believed me."*

*"And even then, I knew I could not speak up," the Heartforger
admitted. She thought I was unconscious the whole time back then,*

and that her secret was safe. "I held my tongue for Likh alone. I could not risk retaliation against her."

"You must have been mistaken, Tea," Zoya said, her voice quavering. "After the fight at Mithra's Wall, Althy placed me in charge of the asha and told me to return to Kion without her. She said she had mulled it over and decided to accompany Kance back to Odalia, to keep watch over Aadil. She said she would follow me in a few days. Althy...Althy would never..."

"Look around you. Where is Altaecia now? I have scried the whole area while you all stood compelled and could find no trace of her anywhere. Isn't her absence enough evidence?"

The asha sagged. "But it can't... Surely there's an explanation..."

I swayed on my feet. "She must have taken the letters," I choked out, remembering her strange insistence at seeing them, her indifference after the pages were missing. "I refused her at first...but then turned them over when she asked again. She might have..."

"Subtlety is her asset. It would be easy enough to compel you in the middle of the Willows, surrounded by asha, if she thought herself beyond reproach. And now she is gone."

"But Althy did not know compul—"

"Why would she go through all this trouble?" Lady Zoya croaked.

"This war is a farce. Druj intends to keep you occupied here while she journeys to Drycht and to the Ring of Worship, where the First Harvest lies. Shadowglass and lightsglass are the keys to unlocking its secrets, and I possess both. She has woven wards around the Ring of Worship to ensure that I cannot enter without her presence, and took on a new identity to hide herself from me. I attacked Kion *in the hopes of drawing her out, trying to dismantle the disguise she now assumes.*

"In response, she orders the Drychta to occupy the Hollows, knowing it will bring me out in the open, knowing I will not stand by and allow Kance and the others to come to harm. She knew that when I came to Mithra's Wall, to aid the Odalians and risk discovery when I could have chosen prudence and kept myself away." Her lip curled. "She knows my weaknesses, and she knows that I am aware of her ploys—and that I have no choice but to rise to her bait. But there is no turning back. She will be waiting for me now at the Ring of Worship, where she believes the runic wards will give her the upper hand."

"But if she shares your goals of completing shadowglass…"

The Dark asha laughed. "Did you believe her? Druj rages against the elder asha for usurping their powers, but Druj has known the Dark longer than they and wants it more. Should I complete shadowglass, she will find some new way to wrest it from me. I will see that monster dead before anything else."

"And how will you defeat Druj?" Lord Fox was hoarse.

The Dark asha offered her hand to her brother. "You can come with me and see for yourself." There was a quiver in her voice. "I could not tell you all this before, Fox. You testified against me in my own trial. You told them about my black heartsglass. You would not have believed me had I told you the truth about Altaecia, and you would have told her about your suspicions. That you didn't kept you safe from her. Do you understand now, Fox? Why I refused to contact you all this time?

"She thought me a powerless vagabond, and I needed her to

think that. Your trust in her would have prepared her sooner for my rebirth. I could not have asked you to choose between Inessa and me any more than you would ask me to choose between you and Kalen. But everything is out in the open now, and as I told you in Daanoris, there will be no more secrets. Please trust me one final time. Give me a good burial. I never gave you one, Fox…but oh, please give me this."

He stared at Lady Tea for the longest time before he silently took her hand.

I sprang to my feet. "Let me go with you."

"It is one thing to summon a bard to write my song. It is another thing entirely to bring a Drychta royal noble as vanguard to a fight I may not win."

Kance looked stunned. Zoya's eyes went wide.

"So you know." I understood then why she had been adamant about sending me away—not to break her promise, but to preserve a bloodline.

"I am not so arrogant as to find a bard solely for him to sing my songs. You are good at tales, but you would make a better ruler for a kingdom mistreated by tyrants for far too long. I am sorry for what happened to Princess Esther, Your Highness. We can choose who we love, but we cannot choose who loves us. Your father was a tyrant in his own way—but you are not. For the good of Drycht's future, you must be kept out of harm's way."

"I am a bard more than I am a king. And I am not the last of my lineage. Please. Let me do one last service for you."

She paused, staring at me with the gentlest look on her face.

And then, as she had done with her brother, she extended her hand.

"We will fight her together then," she said.

I nodded, then clarified, "Altaecia? She is Druj, right?"

"No." Her smile this time was grim. "Druj is a woman who has hidden herself away within the Willows for decades. A woman who has counseled me and others for so long, with none of us the wiser. Not Altaecia. Someone else."

24

DRUJ MAY HAVE INTENDED TO foist the Dark on me to instill new fears, but he underestimated my newfound strength. My mind barreled past the borders of Kion back into the territories of Odalia and beyond, and I was stunned by the impossible that I could manage. I flitted from the nearest thought to the next, using them as stepping-stones as I expanded my *Scrying* to search for one mind in particular, traveling from Odalian guard to Kion farmer to Yadoshan merchant, but found nothing of Altaecia's mind in that whole continent. Where was she?

I changed targets, and this time located Zoya's mind. She was on her way back to Ankyo with the other asha, but my mentor was nowhere nearby. Altaecia had sent Zoya and most of the other asha back to Kion, while she had remained behind…but for what? What was she waiting for?

I should have known. I *should* have known. The visions of

the future Lord Agnarr told me I would gain, the crescent symbol carved into the rock at Mithra's Wall—the same design as the zivar I had worn for so many years. How blind could I be?

Naturally, Kalen refused when I told him of my intentions. "We haven't gotten this far for you to do this alone." I couldn't blame him for his anger.

"She wants something from me, and I can't put any of you at more risk than I already have." I didn't want to return to Ankyo. *You'll return to Kion to mourn on graves*, the Fox from Stranger's Peak had told me.

"This is not up for discussion. You should know that by now."

"We're not leaving either," Likh said just as stubbornly.

"We're taking you back to the Willows," I said quietly. "You and Khalad will be safe there. Now that we know the source of your blight, it should dissipate soon enough. You won't be in any further danger." I clenched my fists, my fears running a mile a minute. "I suffered none of the blackouts I had in Ankyo after I left. You weren't the only one she'd been poisoning. I was meant to be a victim all along—not of the blight, but of madness."

·· 〰 ··

We stayed overnight at the Sea of Skulls, looking to regain what strength we could manage before our return to Ankyo, with plans to drop Likh and Khalad off at the nearest village. Likh wasn't happy, though she appeared more amenable after Khalad had taken her aside for a more private talk.

Kalen, on the other hand, was a lost cause. "You already know my answer," he growled, tossing more kindling onto the fire. "Where you go, I go."

I couldn't sleep, uneasy about what the next day would bring for us. "I don't know where I'm going yet. The asha association could hunt me down for the rest of my life. You weren't born for this, Kalen."

"Last time I checked, neither were you." He touched the tip of my nose with a calloused finger. "We'll go to Istera, find a place away from the city like Lord Garindor did. Or Tresea, where the asha's reach is paltry at best and everyone would much rather mind their own business. We'll find our own house and garden." He smiled. "They're always looking for people who're good with their hands, ready to do hard work."

"I can sew," I volunteered, hungry for this dream that he wove. "Enough for a livelihood, I think. And I know enough to treat the sick. I can use *Illusion*, change our appearances. They'll never find us that way."

He bent closer, brushed his lips with mine. His hands trailed to my stomach. For the first time that I can remember, his touch was awkward and unsure. "When we're sure they won't find us, if they do stop looking, I wouldn't mind having some… They'll be looking for a couple, not a family. If you would one day want to—"

My heart was full. "You'll need to make an honest woman out of me first."

"If you'd let me, I'll find the nearest judge between here

and Kion. Likh and Khalad could even attend to us before we send them back to Ankyo." He kissed me longer. "You propositioned me, remember? You asked me for my heartsglass in a room full of Yadoshans. If we'd had another day to ourselves, I would have married you right there and took them all for witnesses. You would have enjoyed some of their raunchier wedding customs."

"Even if the bride was an asha?" I was horrified. He laughed, and I was on his lap in an instant, kissing him eagerly, my hands running through his hair. "I was drunk and out of sorts," I whispered to him, but found myself liking the idea more and more. Surely I had nothing left to lose. Surely I could start a new life, not as one, but as one half of two…

"I regret nothing I said. Marry me, Kalen. Take my heartsglass and honor me with yours."

His arms encircled me. "You already do."

From behind us, Khalad cleared his throat. "I, uh…I'm going to take the rest of the utensils. Just go ahead and—"

He crumpled abruptly. Stunned, we broke apart and rushed to him. "What's wrong with him?" I asked in a panic, immediately *Delving* him and finding nothing.

"Have no fear, Tea. He's only asleep. He's too important a person to kill, but I would like him unconscious for the rest of our conversation."

A figure emerged from the darkness, and only then did I sense their presence. There were two of them: the mysteriously cowled figure that looked down on me from the cliffs of Mithra's

Wall, and—*no, no, no*—Altaecia. Kalen let out a growl. Likh stumbled toward us, shock clear on her face.

"You don't seem as surprised as they are." Altaecia greeted me with a smile, as if she had not just gone out of her way to betray me, to betray everything the asha and Kion had stood for.

"I should have known sooner. There were signs, but I refused to believe them." I was angry, horrified. "Why, Althy?"

"It was for you, my dear." Her voice was as I remembered it, patient and kind and wise, but a strange tremor lay tucked behind it. There was sadness in the way she walked and sighed, a peculiar regret that I could not understand. "And for Mykaela, surely you didn't think you were the only one who wanted to save her? To find some method to keep her from drawing in the Dark and prolong her life?"

"I had hoped I was wrong. That someone else had contaminated the herbs when you were unaware of it. But you gave us a fresh batch back at the Odalian camp, and the rune was just as strong there. I could have explained away the first, but not the second. Surely you wouldn't have been so careless."

"I had no intentions of hiding any longer, Tea, and hoped you would discover it once you had left the Odalians and Yadoshans. I encouraged you to leave quickly, as you'll recall. After learning you had gone to Stranger's Peak and endured the Gorvekan trials, I knew it was time for us to join strengths."

"You could have killed Likh!" Kalen all but snarled.

"We needed collateral, a contingency for occasions like these. Tea was our priority, but another asha would do. I trusted that you would find a means to stay Likh's condition, and I was right. I could not have taught you so much of what I knew only to see you fail."

"And what can you offer me that Aenah could not?" I asked bitterly. "Did you think our previous friendship would be enough for me to accept your offer when I rejected hers?"

"This is not a betrayal, Tea. I do this to save your life. I was complicit long before you were asha, almost twenty years now, in fact. I was too late for Mykkie—I had no idea where her heartsglass had gone, you see. That was Aenah and Telemaine's doing, and the elder asha exacerbated the matter by refusing to investigate. I would not have been complicit in something that would so affect her health that way.

"I raged when Polaire died—if there was a way to bring her back, I would've done so. It was always about her, about Mykkie, and, then later, about you. I knew the Dark would claim your lives as it has everyone it was unfortunate enough to touch. But shadowglass would ensure your survival. We have no need for magic, child. I would destroy every rune to keep you both safe."

"How? By *Blighting* everyone else? By putting Likh in danger? By corrupting Aadil and starting a war among the kingdoms? That's your idea of helping?"

"Yes. What better evidence to show how easily spells are abused than by demonstrating them in all their corrupted glory? Runic magic was not made for us mortals. No person should hold this much power. It will be used to destroy people as much as help them, as you have already seen. We must start anew—in a world without magic, with nothing but our own will."

"I can't. Fox—"

"You know as well as I that there is a way to save Fox. The juice of the First Harvest, wasn't it? Failing that, well, perhaps shadowglass can be used to shape the world according to how we want it to be. As a god, you would have no limits. We could remake the world, make it a kinder place."

"Are you insane?" Kalen shouted. "You cannot build a kinder world on the blood of innocents!"

"Can Tea tell me, with yourself as the exception, if there is no other heartsglass Tea would value more than Fox's? Is the price too great to see him alive in the truest sense? Ask her if I lie, Kalen. Her heartsglass tells me all I need to know."

"I can't do that," I choked out. "So many lives already— Yarrod, the Drychta, Aadil's madness, Knightscross, Kance and Telemaine...Daisy..."

"Daisy was an unfortunate accident. The Dark was stronger in you than I thought."

"I escaped the blight, but your medicine made me weaker, more complicit to accept the Dark. You plagued me with fevered dreams, made me doubt myself, made me think I was falling into darkrot. You did it so that Kion would turn against me, to make me more susceptible to join your cause. You offered your services to Kance under the guise of healing, but instead you gave him nightmares and headaches. And you gave him *Blight* for a time, in case I needed further persuasion."

She offered no defense, and my rage grew. "And Daisy—why did you make me kill her?"

Altaecia gazed serenely back at me. "I did nothing of the sort, Tea. My herbs may have given you greater cause to take in the Darkness, that is true, but your actions have always been your own."

"And what of this Faceless?" Likh demanded, staring at the figure. "Druj committed countless atrocities. How could you stoop so low as to ally yourself with him?"

Laughter, nearly hysterical, bubbled at the back of my throat. "Because we trusted Druj ourselves. Didn't we, Althy? How many times had we gone to her, asking for advice? I should know—I went to the temple more than anyone else."

"Tea." Likh quaked. "What do you mean?"

"Nobody knows what Druj looks like, because Druj had always lived inside Ankyo. What better sanctuary than in the Willows itself? Hadn't Aenah taught us that even Ankyo can be compromised? And yet, we made the same mistakes we should have learned from when she posed as a young servant of the Valerian. How would Druj know to carve out a moon-and-crescents symbol in a Seeking Stone for me to find—a symbol that resembled a crescent pin I own? A pin that I had tried to sacrifice to her sacred fires not long ago and was refused?

"Druj too went through the same trials I had at Stranger's Peak—and failed. What were the gifts that mountain granted? Greater strength in the Dark—and the ability to look into the future. Perhaps Druj was better at prophecy than I am, with more years to hone her foretelling. Isn't that right, Oracle?"

The figure removed her hood, revealing features only previously hinted at during my visits to the temple: long, flowing hair the color of corn silk, so light it was pale under the moonlight; bright-green eyes no longer hidden under a thick veil; pale, unblemished skin; a wide, lovely mouth. "I had hoped you would know me," she said. Even out in the open air, a faint chorus of voices echoed her words.

"But how?" Likh stuttered. "I—we trusted you. Everyone in the Willows trusted you!"

"The trust has not been in vain, young Likh. My duty in the Willows was always to serve as a balance to the asha association. To ensure they did not go astray, did not go beyond their own selfish desires. It was a responsibility passed down to me from countless oracles who had served before, harkening back to the days of Vernasha herself."

"Impossible!"

"Vernasha was our greatest asha, yet her greed was as deadly as her power. Many of her colleagues knew what she had tried to corrupt, the legends she tried to undo. But they too were weak. Magic was not a drug they could give up so easily, no matter their fear of damnation.

"But the strongest-willed of them, a Dark asha whose name had long since been lost to time, learned of the Gorvekai's trial and sought to be worthy of shadowglass, only to fail as you and I had, Tea. But the trial imbued her with the powers of prophecy, and she knew one day there would be one worthy to fulfill Hollow Knife's wish.

"And so she imposed a balance of sorts: by installing herself as an oracle, her precognition easily won Vernasha's trust. But her purpose was different from the rest of the Willows; she would serve as a gatekeeper to shadowglass, to prevent the unworthy from attaining that knowledge, and to pass on these learnings to Dark asha brave enough to take her place as a new oracle. Bone witches died quickly even then, and it was simple enough to stage their deaths one day and resurface as a new incarnation of the oracle the next.

"Our veils and seclusion made for easy camouflage. We knew that one of us would eventually find favor at Stranger's Peak, and it is she who shall remove the dishonor that all Little Tears's descendants share.

"But there are many others who seek shadowglass. We soon found it easier to fight against them under the guise of another Faceless. And so we adopted the moniker of Druj, 'the truth,' as oracles before me had. We have many followers among the Willows, Tea, silent and unseen. Althy is my most trusted confidant. We hope to invite you into that same circle."

"She is right, Tea, and you know it," Althy added gently. "Mykkie was too weak without her heartsglass, and we could not risk her health to enlighten her to our cause. But when you arrived, the oracle took one look at you and knew you were worthy. She is never wrong."

"She *is* wrong. I failed." To gain shadowglass, Kalen would have paid the price. Even if they could bring Fox back to life without killing anyone else, I would have refused from that alone. "I am not worthy. I never was."

The oracle—Druj—sighed, and unseen voices sighed with her. "Most Dark asha do not pass one test, let alone two. That you have is telling. The trial for *Duty* grants one the power of foretelling. The trial for *Honor* grants expanded abilities. But the third—the third trial is *Love*, isn't it? No asha has ever passed it. It was always the last test we choose. Perhaps, instinctively, we know it would be the worst of the lot."

Kalen growled.

Druj ignored him and continued, "I know your strength. I was within the *zarich*'s mind when you explored it, and in your fear, you killed it for my sin. I know how powerful you can be, Tea. I cannot allow a millennia of efforts by Dark asha who have slaved and sacrificed to come to naught. I have lost so many to the cause, so many Dark asha have gone mad and withered trying to reach this moment. The prophecy will be fulfilled, regardless of what you believe. We are so close. We are so close! We have angered the Great Creator for so long. We will not allow you to prolong our torment."

*W*E WERE SIX ON THE azi: *the Dark asha and I; Lords Kalen, Fox, and Khalad; and the Lady Zoya, who insisted on coming despite all opposition. The flight to Drycht was brief. We bypassed the populated cities of the desert kingdom: Rasha, Karinsha, even my once-home, Adra-al. There were no other civilizations to the east of the continent; a slew of mountains surrounded the dried lands, unfit for living for several thousand years. There was a reason they call Drycht "the Impenetrable Kingdom." If the harsh, unforgiving sun did not bake you dry, then the absence of water, runes or otherwise, made death long and lingering.*

We flew past the Dry Lands and into the Ring of Worship: a mountainous posy of craggy peaks and unscalable heights that protected a small, barren circle of sand. There was little that could be called life there; nothing but tiny, horned lizards and unhealthy shoots of brown moss. An unknown cataclysm—Vernasha perhaps, as Lord Garindor believed and Agnarr claimed—had corrupted what history swore was a lush, fertile greenscape, and four of the Five Great Heroes had met their ends here. How, no one had ever been certain.

The rest of the daeva were already present, but they gave the broken circle of mountains a wide berth, their reluctance to draw closer obvious.

"She is here," the Dark asha murmured as we disembarked. "She is not even hiding it."

"What happens now?" Zoya asked.

"Say and do nothing until Tea orders it," Kalen told her. "You could have stayed with Kance, you know. Shadi would not be happy, you coming along."

"Shadi isn't here. And we need a representative from Kion to see this through. Empress Alyx would appreciate my efforts." She leaped to the bone witch's aid when the latter stumbled, her breathing uneven. Kalen sprang to her other side, arm hooked underneath hers.

"Are you sure about this, Tea?" the Kion asha asked, biting her lip. "You aren't well. You cannot think to go there and confront Druj in your weakened state."

"I am not going to get any better, Zoya." The Dark asha straightened. "It would do you and the bard well to stay outside the ring and let the rest of us enter."

"I didn't come all the way here to be banned from fighting. I can feel the wards, and they're far too strong to unravel." Lady Zoya paused, looking down. A sob rose from her. "I'm sorry. I haven't apologized, have I? All those years waiting for the right time, never realizing there would never be one until I made it so. I'm sorry."

The Dark asha laughed her little, golden laugh. "You've apologized many times over with actions rather than words...but I am happy, all the same."

"We'll go in with you, and we'll come out together. Years from now, we'll laugh about our foolishness. Just you wait."

"But how?" Lord Khalad asked. "With the wards in place, none of you can use spells."

"There's one more way," Lady Zoya said. "We can link with each other to overcome the wards. Linking with all the daeva will be more than enough to counteract those barriers—not even a Faceless of Druj's caliber could withstand all seven. But with such potential for destruction, Tea isn't in any shape to confront Druj on her own. If the rest of us could tap into the reserves she holds, it will be enough. But we'll need to lure Druj out of the ring and into the open. If we can't bring the daeva to her, then let's bring her to them instead."

The daeva retreated farther as we approached the ranges. "Garindor was right," Lord Kalen said. "There is something within these ruins that they fear, and I suspect it isn't Druj's wards. We can convince them to linger by the entrance, but they'll take no further steps."

There was nothing majestic or breathtaking about the Ring of Worship. There was only a long stretch of sand within that circle of mountains, no more than one or two kilometers in diameter, with only a narrow passage as entrance and exit. The sky was a giant, blue eye above us, peering in. Strange, yellowing plants—pale and unhealthy looking yet thriving despite the lack of rain—crept along the edges where the mountains threw meager shade.

There were no stones or monuments to decorate this place, no inkling that four great warriors had entered here and never left. Rashnu's accounts of his comrades' fates had talked of a sacred tree, of a light so fierce that it had turned able warriors into nothing in an instant. I stepped warily inside, searching for unseen dangers I knew I had no skill at sighting.

Druj showed no such prudence. She stood at the very center with her back to us, staring down at her feet as the Dark asha approached. The strange woman wore a cowl to obscure her vision, carefully wrapped in heavy robes to deter the sun's heat. Beside her was the only patch of green on the desolate field—a paltry festering of weedy plants with tiny, apple-shaped fruit that swayed gently in the wind.

Kalen signaled for us to stay behind, letting his beloved walk on alone. "Whatever you do," he muttered tersely, "do not stray too close to those runeberries."

"They're unlike any runeberries I've ever seen before," Lady Zoya murmured.

Lord Khalad grunted in understanding. "The First Harvest, aren't they?"

"I would have thought they'd look more impressive..."

"So did four of the Great Heroes, I'd wager, and it cost them their lives."

The Faceless spoke up. "I take it you have saved your Odalian king and other kingdoms besides."

"You wanted them to invade Adra-al," the bone witch responded. "You wanted them to watch in horror as you transformed the people there into your blighted pets. No doubt you had already killed Aadil."

"I must plan my own precautions. But their lives are spared now that you are here. You were victorious at the Hollows. Isn't it nice how things work out?" She turned to smile at us, and she wore the face of the asha Altaecia. Zoya's breath left her in a soft, shuddering gasp.

"Assume your own face, you scum," the Dark asha snarled. "You aren't worthy of hers."

"Even knowing she betrayed you, Tea? You still harbor fond memories of my ward?"

"She did what she thought was right, misguided as she was. You convinced her that you would rid the world of magic. You lie. I know better."

"How do I lie?" The Faceless's face rippled, her own lovely features supplanting the other asha's. She was a breathtaking beauty, as the bone witch had described, though there was a cruel tilt to her mouth. "We want the same thing. You will not live for much longer, and you must make a choice soon. Will you take the First Harvest and save us from magic, or will you subvert it to create a paradise of your own making?"

The bone witch hesitated.

"It is not so easy, is it, to talk of saving the world before you've experienced true power coursing through your veins?"

"You do not want to rid the world of magic," Lady Tea declared. "You will fade in influence and position, just like the elder asha you suspect. If you cannot complete shadowglass yourself, then you seek to influence the one who can—or will attempt to steal it."

"I am far too cautious to do the latter. But my advice will be worth your while," the former oracle promised. "I vow on the graves of Ashi, Mithra, Anahita, and Sraosha underneath my feet that I will protect Kion. I will guide King Kance into a golden age of prosperity, and Empress Alyx and her daughter as well. I will take care of Likh, Lord Khalad."

The Heartforger bared his teeth. "Like hell you will."

"You lie," the bone witch repeated. "Once I create shadowglass,

you will take it from me, weak as I am, and force your own will into the world. You know the original legends better than anyone else. Blade that Soars proved capable of seizing shadowglass, and he would have, had not Hollow Knife chosen to halt the spell. You of all people know that shadowglass can be wrested away from the one who creates it."

"You blighted people on a whim," Lord Fox snapped. "You can no longer resume your place in Kion society after this unless it's in chains. You have no plans of letting us leave this place alive."

"I trusted Althy!" Zoya cried. "Shadi, Mykkie—everyone trusted you! How dare you? How could you?"

"Do you not believe my intentions?" the Faceless implored the Dark asha. *"How could I be so strong as to steal shadowglass in the face of you all? I am powerless now, as I will be then, and I will choose to be so willingly."*

The Dark asha looked back at her, stared hard. She folded her hands behind her. "Where are the letters you stole?" Lady Tea asked. "The ones you took from the bard?"

Druj drew the papers from within her robes. "I had to take them, of course. I could not have my disguise revealed, not then. The dead Altaecia in your story would have turned suspicion against me. I could not learn of Kance's plans while I was the oracle, so I had to adopt Altaecia's—"

She broke off. The former oracle smiled, and a peculiar sleepiness overcame me.

"I do not know how you learned of the Blight rune, for the Gorvekai never told you," the bone witch all but purred. "But they *told* me *many things after I emerged from my second trial at Stranger's Peak. They told me of more uses for runes that not even you know of and modifications to the runes you do. Did you know that the* Scrying *rune can be woven into common items, not only a person's mind? In letters, for instance? Did you know that the spell can be modified to find one specific individual and not the others who touch it? Or that it could serve as a beacon for me to find you?"*

A sharp gasp left the oracle.

"You knew you could hide your mind from me. You were clever. I would not have thought of using Althy's face for your disguise, to strut about like she was still alive. You wove wards around Kion to prevent me access, convinced Alyx it was necessary. Even with the daeva, I could not find your thoughts, and so I relied on other means. Did you not realize the uselessness of your camouflage the moment you abandoned the Hollows and sailed to Drycht? That I knew who you were hiding as, where you were, the instant your hand touched the parchment?"

The papers fluttered out of the Faceless's grasp and drifted to the ground.

Immediately, a foreign presence pushed into my mind, frantic, seeking leverage. But the bone witch's presence was already there, forcing her out—though not without some effort. Lord Kalen moved, the Wind *he conjured holding the Faceless motionless. Lady Zoya lifted her hands, no doubt adding to his strength.*

But the Faceless attacked again, with both her mind and another weapon. A roar thundered behind me.

A terrible beast climbed out from the sand, blocking our

exit—not a daeva, but with a daeva's height and breadth. It was a corpse with a skeleton-like face, sharp bones jutting around it like a lion's mane. It sported eight legs like a spider, each tipped with cruel hooks. It snarled at us with dead eyes. I knew who it was.

The blighted King Aadil leaped, too quickly for me to antic- ipate, but Lord Kalen stepped into its path, taking the blow meant for me. There was a sickening crunch as its hooks closed on his shoul- der, tearing through flesh. Lord Fox dashed forward and swiped at the beast's head, slicing off the top of its skeletal cranium. The gaunt creature skittered back, shook itself, and jumped again.

"Thanks." The Deathseeker sent a wall of wind knives digging into its bony midsection, slicing off more limbs. Aadil howled.

The Faceless was relentless, burning a vision in my head, digging into my psyche, trying to mark her victory. But the Dark asha was just as obstinate. I felt her mind pushing out Druj to prevent her from wresting control. I saw the others struggle with the same assault, protected only by their strong willpowers and the asha's assistance.

How Lord Fox and Lord Kalen could still fight was bewildering to me; I could feel nothing but pain radiating from inside my skull. I understood why the bone witch feared the woman's skills; to attack us all at once while still maintaining command of the blighted Aadil was not an easy feat—one the Dark asha could only do with darksglass.

Both familiars moved in unison; blades snapping, their feet quick and agile, they circled Aadil on either side, some unspoken strat- egy passing between them. Lord Kalen was the first to attack, worry- ing at the shinbones that kept the beast upright. The demon snapped at him, giving Lord Fox a chance to swipe at its rib cage. The former king staggered; the Deathseeker took out its right shoulder, and the Kion general cut through a hip bone.

Lady Zoya had been sidestepping the fracas, zigzagging as she ran from one section of sand to the other. Her actions confused me until the ground gave out underneath the Aadil-beast without warning, sending it scrabbling for a fresh hold. But it was a mere distraction for the beast, and the asha swore. "I can't draw Water here or channel it with other runes," she rasped. "There is something in this place that absorbs the spell before I can unleash it!" She cursed again. "And look!"

Her spell had uncovered corpses buried within the sand—not four of the Five Great Heroes I expected, but men in Drychta armor.

"This is blasphemy," Lord Khalad hissed. "To bring them to this sacred place!"

"I have no need for courtesies, Forger." The Faceless was clearly struggling, but she had enough strength to sketch a new symbol in the air. With low groans, the fallen warriors rose, staggered to their feet, sunken eyes fixed on us.

"Not today!" The Dark asha whipped out her own sword. Her heels dug into the rising sands as she fought her way toward the Faceless. The other woman raised both arms as if to ward herself, and several corpses rushed to her side. But the Dark asha was almost as quick as her familiars, and she mowed them down easily, driven by her anger. She employed a combination of blade and spells, chopping her way through the crowd as some of those corpses turned on each other without warning, egged on by her compulsion. She sliced a path through the masses of bodies and swung her sword at

the Faceless before the other could muster more of the undead to shield herself.

Lord Fox's blade sank into Aadil's hollowed chest. Lord Kalen's sword whirred through the air and neatly sliced off the blighted's head. Lady Zoya kept the other fiends at bay, grunting as runes tore into them, one after another.

Druj was gasping for breath, her hand clasped over her now-bloody stomach. The Dark asha stood over her. "You will regret killing me, Tea," she snarled, though the fear in her eyes was clear to all.

"I do not have the strength to engage you in direct confrontation." Sweat beaded at the bone witch's upper lip, and she was panting. "I presumed that you were sent word of my bard when I was still in Daanoris. You knew I planned to tell my story. How quickly did you meet my brother at Ankyo's port, wondering if it was already too late—if I had told all? What relief that must have been to discover they had not yet read my letters. Did you perhaps compel some of them from reading the final pages, to keep your secret a little longer? Even from across a sea, you've always had a long reach."

I gasped, remembering.

"You were meant to read them," Tea of the Embers declared. "Even with my shadowglass, you are cleverer, craftier in the Dark. You will wreak havoc with or without magic. You will never again have the opportunity."

She brought her sword down in a swift gesture.

The Faceless screamed, and her fingers moved one final time.

The blow should have killed her. It did not.

Druj's features warped. Her transformation was swift and

merciless. Her legs fused together to create a long, serpentlike tail. Her face was a terrifying specter; her hair lengthened and then darkened as brown sap dripped from it, acid hissing steam wherever the drops landed. She was almost as tall as a daeva, with insect-like eyes and incisors growing where her mouth once was. Unlike the other blighted, she retained some of her female features, a mother of some new species that no god should have ever brought to life.

The Dark asha reeled back, stunned, and the newly blighted Faceless wailed, a heartrending sound, and bounded for her throat.

25

ALTHY MOVED SO QUICKLY THAT I wasn't aware of the thick bolt of lightning she sent arcing toward Kalen, but he was just as quick. The jolt sizzled against his *Shield* rune, glancing harmlessly against the barrier. With mounting horror, I realized they intended to see the last of the Stranger Peak's trials fulfilled, which Kalen put together before I did. "I don't die so easily, Altaecia."

"I know." Altaecia sounded so sad. "But you will die all the same. It hurts me to do this, Kalen. Dark asha were not permitted familiars until they presented themselves to the oracle. Dark asha were to be feared and hated to prevent them from forming attachments. My inability to prevent Tea from both shall be my shame and is a mistake I intend to rectify. I am sorry—more than you will ever know."

She struck again, and Kalen parried. Druj's eyes seemed to glow. She raised her hands and a new bezoar, the final stone not yet accounted for, beamed with an unearthly light. Somewhere in the empty shore lay the *akvan*'s burial mound, the beast doomed to slumber for two more years.

Why had Likh suggested we make our camp here, in the Sea of Skulls, when I should have known better? Had the idea been planted in her head when Altaecia had refreshed her stash of herbs? Why find refuge near the daeva whose bezoar I had not yet taken? The former oracle saw the question in my eyes and smiled, pleased at her culpability.

I threw myself forward, my mind colliding with hers, but as before, she evaded me with practiced agility, as elusive as fog.

The magic took hold, swirling around the bezoar. Rays of light burst forth, and we all stumbled back. Only Kalen remained unmoved, his eyes locked on Althy's regretful gaze, even as she continued to attack, and he continued to shield us. "This isn't happening," I heard Likh whimper behind me.

Druj's spell had prematurely willed the *akvan* to life, and it was angry. The stone vanished abruptly, and the newly formed daeva clawed its way out from the retreating waves. It was a terror, and the heaviest of all the daeva; an elephant-like abomination with a mouth made entirely of tusks and teeth. It lumbered toward us, but the *azi* was quick to wing its way between us, its three heads primed for violence. It hit the ground between its daeva kin and me, tail lifted and swinging. The *akvan* ducked, agile despite its bulk and, oddly enough, shied away.

"We have no need to fight, Tea," Druj said. "We share the same goals."

"I cannot condone what you've done!" The idea that she would deliberately put innocent people to the blight—the idea that Altaecia could have put Likh to the blight!—made reconciliation impossible. "Get out of here!" I rasped at Likh, who was already dragging the unconscious Khalad away.

Altaecia was as skilled as Kalen; she had decades of experience on her side. While Kalen deflected her attacks, she gave him little time to muster up his own offenses. The older asha never let up, peppering him with fire, lightning, ice. "Don't make us do this, Althy," he said, as close to begging as I had ever seen him.

"Our lives are inconsequential in the grand scheme of the Creator's plans, Kalen. The Dark ashas' short life spans have always been their punishment. We will save Mykaela. We will complete the shadowglass with your help or without."

"But all the people you murdered!"

"What of it? I cried many nights over Polaire, Kalen, but her death will not change my mind. If you will not yield, then you will meet her very soon."

The *azi* showed none of the hesitation the *akvan* displayed. With its three heads lunging and snapping, it advanced. But the other daeva avoided its blows. The *akvan* willingly relinquished ground.

My mind continued to struggle toward Druj, only for her to counter and dodge in much the same way. The *akvan* concentrated mainly on defense, Mykaela told me once. But at the hands of someone as powerful as the oracle, it was difficult to best the beast, even with the *azi*, the strongest of all the daeva.

"We could be very powerful together," Druj said. "I can show you how to become the most powerful woman in the Willows—in all the kingdoms."

"Do the elder asha know your secret?" I demanded.

"No. The oath of the oracle is a much different path from an asha. For as long as I continue to provide counsel, the elders take little interest in my affairs. They are not a group to question custom or tradition. They believe I have no power beyond the walls of my temple, yet many of my steadfast followers—like Altaecia—are eager to carry out my orders without question. The elders have no inkling of how much we have accomplished under their noses."

"You personally inflicted people with the *Blight* rune."

"An unfortunate necessity. A secret passed down from the first oracle, should another Dark asha prove too intractable. In the past, such insubordinations were taken care of quietly, without drawing attention. But with the time for shadowglass close at hand, I no longer see the need to hide."

They killed asha, I thought. They used *Blight* to kill Dark asha who knew the truth but spurned their offers. I redoubled my efforts, the *azi* lurching forward. It paid off, and two of the three heads found daeva flesh, biting into the *akvan*'s neck.

The *akvan* wailed, but one of its tusks pierced the *azi*'s hide, preventing it from retreating. The *azi* struggled, but it was too strong. I pushed back, frantically searching for another way to disentangle it from the *akvan*. Without thinking, I drew my knife.

And then, to my shock, I threw it in Kalen's direction. He

whirled, deflecting the unexpected attack with another *Shield*, but his distraction was costly. One of Altaecia's cutting winds sliced at him, and he stumbled backward, gasping for breath as blood pooled from his stomach.

"No!" I was immobile, compelled without my knowing it. I couldn't move my hands, my feet. Druj spoke again, but this time she was the only voice inside my head.

I have been doing this for a very long time, Tea, she murmured. *I have been given instruction by teachers greater than Aenah or Usij. Did you think you could overcome me so easily?*

The *azi* slipped from my grasp and collapsed. The *akvan* continued to wrap itself around its brother, rumbling.

Kalen was down on one knee, his hand pressed against his midsection. "Tea," he rasped. Altaecia stood over him with one hand raised over his head, her face sorrowing. "Don't listen to them."

There is still time. Pledge yourself to me, and I will promise to heal Kalen. I will promise to keep him safe from what follows.

"Listen to her, Tea," Altaecia said. "We can do more as allies than enemies, and I do not wish to kill any more friends today."

"Did you kill Sakmeet?" I demanded.

"Does it matter?"

"You killed her." Althy'd betrayed us from the very start. "You were never a friend," I spat.

Althy, teaching me how to cook, her patience while she instructed me in the use of herbal remedies. Althy, bringing me to the marketplace in the mornings, her justified anger at those who would swindle others out of their hard-earned savings. Her compassion for the poor. Her desire to heal everyone she touched. That was the Altaecia I knew. This was not the Altaecia I wanted.

Druj shrugged. "Sakmeet served her purpose. The destiny I told her proved true—her writings will change the world. They brought us here, together. We are a powerful team, Tea.

"I have always been the same woman you knew. I do love you, and Kalen and the others. And that is why I do not wish to end it like this." Altaecia's face was streaked with tears. "Please, Tea."

"You drove me mad. You made me kill my own sister! You hurt so many people, including Mykkie and Polaire."

"As did you, Tea. In our quest to protect those we love, sometimes we end up hurting them worse. But we will solve all that. No more magic. No more hatred. Fox will live. I will make sure of it."

"Not at the price you're asking."

"Then I have no choice, my love." Althy bent over Kalen, and her fingers moved.

A pure burst of *Wind* tore through the air, sharp as a sword's blade and just as deadly. It was Althy's turn to fall to her knees, gasping in shock as blood dripped from the wound across her chest.

Likh was crying, her hands raised as another *Wind* rune formed against her palm. "We loved you, Althy," she choked. "Why would you do this?"

My sister asha laughed weakly. "You are far too young to understand, Likh."

"You tried to kill me. You blighted me, knowing what it would do. You are trying to kill us now. There is nothing else to understand." Another sliver of *Wind* sliced at Altaecia's knuckles, and the woman cried out in pain. Khalad grunted. He was still out on the ground, breathing hard like he'd been running. His face was strained from sweat and exhaustion, though I was certain he had not been hit. *Heartshare*, I realized. Like Kalen and I, like Mykaela and Polaire, they had…

I struggled against Druj's control, but she held fast with little effort, staring in fascination at the scene before her without bothering to intervene. *Well now*, she enthused, *shall we see what unfolds here?*

Frantic, I grappled for a way out. Her possession of me was complete; there were no weak spots in her compulsion that I could find. But even at this most vulnerable moment, I could sense Kalen faintly, a remnant from our own heartsharing. I tried to move toward him. Our connection had saved us in the past. Surely…

Tea.

"You are powerful, Likh," Althy complimented her. "Tea was right. You would have been one of our best asha."

"Please don't make me do this," Likh begged, as sharp *Wind* brushed against the older woman's neck, ready to strike the killing blow.

Altaecia closed her eyes. "If I have to sacrifice my life for you to understand, Likh, then I will gladly do so, with all my being."

Wind died down. Likh made a strange choking noise. Her hands fell against her own neck, her eyes wide. And then I saw the *Blight* rune surrounding her. *No!* I screamed, as Druj lifted her fingers, prepared for the last stroke.

The *Heartshare* rune shone, bright and beautiful. Asleep or not, Khalad's strength was counteracting Likh's impending transformation. But it was taking far too much from him, and I knew with sudden clarity that he too would die.

No! I struggled to break free, finding enough strength to redirect Druj's attention back to me. For the first time, I could feel her difficulty restraining me, the *Blight* rune forgotten in her desire to overwhelm me again.

No! I cried out. Kalen struggled to his feet despite his injuries. His *Wind* rune was deadlier than Likh's, with none of her hesitation. Altaecia raised her hand to construct a *Shield* of her own, but Kalen's rune sliced through hers like there was no barrier. The woman screamed as it chopped off one of her hands, the useless wrist dropping to the floor.

The *Blight* rune flickered and faded. The young asha had not yet transformed, and I had no idea if she was dead or alive, or if the Heartforger was all that was keeping her from her horrific change. I could see the *Heartshare* rune wrapping itself around them without anyone's direct guidance. And Kalen doggedly constructed more wards around them both despite his own injuries.

Still, I was trapped. I pushed and shoved against Druj with all my might, but it was like fighting a brick wall with bare fists. She wasn't just controlling me; she was depleting my strength. I could feel my energy draining from me and adding to hers as she greedily consumed my Dark like a parasite. Severely weakened, I could only watch helplessly as Altaecia rose to her feet, clutching her stump, and turned toward Kalen.

Tea?

No. There was one thing I could do.

I turned toward another brick wall in my mind, planted there not by Druj, but by my own resolve. Desperate, I took hold of the wall I had painstakingly built and clawed my way through until the *Veiling* broke from the force of my despair, until the door opened.

Tea!

A familiar and warm feeling took over. For a brief moment, I could almost imagine that Fox was beside me, so overpowering was his presence. I pushed with all my might and tore Druj's grip from my thoughts. I felt her stunned surprise as her presence faded from my mind, replaced by the warmth of my brother's. The backlash was horrible. Druj flung herself away with a short scream, crumpling onto the ground.

The *akvan* reared up and screeched. No longer under anyone's control, it thrashed across the shoreline, its head shaking in agony.

Kalen had already collapsed, gasping into the sand. Altaecia staggered forward. Her uninjured hand was tracing another symbol. The *Wind* rune appeared around Likh.

"I am sorry, my dear," Altaecia said sadly. "But we do what needs to be done." She raised her arm.

The blow never came. Her hand dropped uselessly to her side as she stared down at her chest, where my knife had run her through.

Blood bubbled from her mouth, and my mentor fell. Weeping, I removed the dagger from her body, sinking to my knees before her. She had been responsible for so many atrocities.

She had poisoned me, doomed Likh, caused so much death… Still, I couldn't stop crying.

Altaecia made a soft wheezing sound and turned her face toward me, an eternity of regret etched onto those well-loved features. "Oh, my dear," she sighed, and died.

I wept, huge, wrenching sobs that shook me to the core, a sudden grief that I had not felt since Polaire's death. Except Althy didn't deserve my tears. She didn't deserve anything.

And yet…

Likh continued to sleep, her face pale but still human. When Altaecia had died, the remaining tatters of the *Blight* rune surrounding her had died along with the older asha. Druj collapsed, unmoving, and I prayed she was dead.

I felt weak, drained of energy. It had taken everything I had to break free from her control, and even more to kill Altaecia.

"Tea." Kalen crawled toward me.

"Y-you're hurt," I stammered.

"I'll live. Likh and Khalad—"

"They're breathing, at least." But Likh's heartsglass was palpitating wildly, silver blending into yellow and brown and red.

So complete was our focus that there was no sound but our beating hearts. Neither of us was aware of the *akvan* until it was upon us, when it was almost too late. The *akvan*'s deadly tusks sang through the air and I only had time to see its roughened mouth and teeth coming at us before everything became a blur.

Kalen was faster. He rolled over, placing himself between me and the *akvan*'s yellowed incisors.

Though no longer under my conscious control, the *azi* also planted itself in the path of the *akvan*'s attack. Teeth tore through its body, and my daeva shrieked. At the same time, its own three heads pitched forward, and its tail whipped, snapping into the *akvan* with such force that its neck was nearly severed by the attack. The other daeva fell to the ground dead. Then the *azi* collapsed. One of the *akvan*'s tusks had struck true, goring into its body and finding its heart.

The pain was overwhelming. I shrieked, clutching at my own chest as the agony tore through me as I felt the *azi*'s death throes. My nails dug into my own skin and drew blood. I could not bear this. I would die here, gasping and bleeding into the sand, though it would take so very long to die.

But as I spasmed, I felt the *azi* nip between us, at the bond we shared, and gently break free from my grip. The pain faded immediately, but the *azi* continued to shudder. Fatal as its wound was, it continued fighting for life.

Tea!

Fox was still in my mind but fainter, weaker. His thoughts could not gain enough traction to fall into mine like they once could, but I ignored him. I couldn't concentrate on him now. Not when everyone was dying. And Kalen—

At the *akvan*'s final gambit, Kalen had time to set up only one small *Shield* rune. His wounds were too deep, too severe. I pushed my hands against the injury, trying to stanch the blood spilling out of him.

Not Kalen. Never Kalen.

"Tea," he choked.

We were so close to escaping. We were so close to Tresea, to starting new lives...

If I had ignored the Odalians' war with the Drychta...

If we had never gone to Mithra's Wall...

If I had never stood before Stranger's Peak and asked the Gorvekai if I was worthy enough...

"Tea..."

"Don't move!" The words came out angry, panicked. I would not lose Kalen. I had refused shadowglass, refused the mountain solely so I could keep him. I would not lose him now. The visions promised I could keep him if I refused shadowglass. I looked around for something to aid my efforts.

Druj was gone. Sometime during the fight, she had fled, leaving only the dying and spiriting away Altaecia's body as she did.

"I told you," Kalen managed to say, coughing up blood, "that I would protect you."

"Not like this," I sobbed. "Don't move. I'll heal you. I will."

His smile was beautiful. He'd seen enough bloodshed and injuries on the battlefield to realize what was coming. "I know you will."

"We'll hide." So much blood. "Let Mykaela find another apprentice. Let them take care of the rest of the daeva. I want a small house by the shore, where no one can bother us." I couldn't stop the bleeding. I pressed harder. "Or by the forests. We'll grow our own food and herbs. No one will know our real names."

Harder. "Or we can travel. We'll see the rest of the world and wear different faces." *Harder.*

"I would like that," Kalen whispered. "A house with you. Traveling. Everything, with you." He laid a hand on top of mine. "I would like…daughters, with your eyes and your terrible singing voice. I am so sorry, Tea."

"I'll give you everything you want, Kalen," I said fiercely. "I will—" My voice broke, and I could no longer find the words.

"No grave will hold me, Tea. I swear it. I'll never leave you."

"I love you," I sobbed. "I will love you for the rest of my life."

"And I will love you for the rest of yours." He sighed, long and low, his voice growing weaker. "The song you sang once. At Thanh. Sing it again."

I held my hands over his heart, kissed him on his bloodied lips, and sang for him.

*O*NLY *L*ORD *F*OX'S *TIMELY INTERVENTION saved her. The former Faceless's teeth had sunk into the man's neck, which spurted jets of blood. He tried to push her off, but her grip was a vise.*

Lord Kalen's blade was true. It slashed across her face, forced her to drop her hold on the other familiar. The Deathseeker attacked again, in a combination of flame and fire and steel, and the blighted was forced back. Her serpentlike face was a ruin; the man had succeeded in taking out an eye, but she showed no outward pain or dismay, only hate.

"Fox!" The Dark asha went down on her knees beside her brother as the latter struggled to stand, hand clasped over the side of his neck. "I'm fine," the man said through gritted teeth. "Are you hurt?"

"You cannot be reckless here, Fox! She is stronger than most!"

"She's right," Lord Kalen supplied grimly. "Remember the elder asha in Daanoris—stronger, faster, angrier."

"She blighted herself?" *Lady Zoya breathed out, staring in horror at the new abomination. "But why?"*

"Her last resort. Because she'd rather be damned than give Tea what she wants."

"From where I stand, she already looks the part."

"We need to get out of here. Outside of the range, where we can use the other daeva against her."

The blighted Druj lashed out again, a coiled strike, but Lady Zoya clapped her hands together, and the sand sank beneath the creature again, putting her off balance. A whip of fire struck the abomination across the chest, and she keened.

"Run!" Lord Kalen roared, and we obeyed without question.

We were about a hundred or so feet away when the entrance leading into to the Ring of Worship collapsed, sand and rock and great portions of mountain toppling down in a terrifying avalanche. Druj slithered toward us, hissing, whispering, yellow, irisless eyes trained on us.

She came at me, the weakest of the runners, and my life would have ended there had not the indar dropped from the sky, its hideous talons crushing the former Faceless—only to release her with a pained scream as its talons burned from her poisoned hide.

"She can kill even daeva," Lord Khalad growled.

"Better them than us," Lady Zoya barked back. "Keep those shields ready, Kalen!"

"Everyone has a weakness. Where's hers?"

"There." The bone witch pointed at the monster's midsection, where something gleamed in the light. "Her silver heartsglass," she noted grimly, lifting her sword again. "If we could cut it out of her—"

"Stay where you are." Lord Fox rose to his feet, wincing. "If she takes you out, two of us fall with you, and she knows that. Zoya, protect them."

"And leave you two to have all the fun?" But the asha was already weaving strong runes of Shield over us, and I watched small pieces of dislodged rock bounce harmlessly off her barrier.

The Dark asha paid us little attention. It was her turn to sink to the ground with her eyes closed, her expression intense. The Heartforger knew what she intended to do but didn't enlighten me. Instead, he sat down beside her and took her hands in his. He closed his eyes, and their silver heartsglass glowed together.

The bone witch's familiars adopted the same tactic they used with Aadil, though with greater difficulty this time around, for when Druj faced one of them, her tail still posed a threat to the other. Her poison was another obstacle; it dribbled down her body like silky, black ichor and fizzled in the sand. Lord Kalen grunted as drops of it sprayed against him, though he remained as quick as ever. His sword ravaged the horrific tail, and he wove more Fire to shred the stump. But when he attempted Wind, it sent bile spurting in our direction.

"No Wind!" Lady Zoya shouted. Her defenses kept us from a grisly fate, though the poison left the unshielded ground around us black, the bile quickly dissolving the rock and debris.

The other daeva were warier. They circled the Faceless, occasionally snaking out with fangs and talons, but hesitant to commit to a full attack. The zarich tried, but the magic of the place affected it, and its breath barely conjured enough ice to frost the ground.

The savul also made an attempt but shrieked when a swipe from the Faceless soaked its limbs in the bile. It pawed at the ground in a desperate bid to wipe it off. The Dark asha hissed in pain, nails digging into the soil. Fire blazed out of the azi's mouth, but the Faceless lifted its tail, and the flames glanced off the rough scales.

An unspoken command passed through the daeva, and they all attacked as one. Their own poisons may as well have been perfume in comparison to the Faceless's and served the daeva no true defenses. They retreated but fought on as the bile ate down to bone. The Dark asha was shaking, her palms streaked with blood where her nails gouged her flesh.

Lord Fox avoided the beast's long arms as she swiped at him. He feinted to one side, waiting for the blighted to snap at him, then dodged right, shoving the tip of his blade forward. It sank deep into her chest, where her heart should have been, but the creature only yowled. When the man removed his blade, it had melted from the strength of her poison. He now carried only a hilt. He swore.

"Keep her distracted," Lord Kalen grunted, still slashing at her tail between the daeva's flurry of assaults. The thick scales were as hard as the finest armor, and he left little more than nicks and small cuts in his wake. "Tea, fall back!" His voice was raw. "Let us…"

"There's no time! Tea can't keep this up!" Lord Fox discarded his sword and barreled toward the blighted, runes protecting him as he climbed up her legs to her waist. She shrieked and scratched at him, but his hands were already digging deep into her stomach, seeking the heartsglass encased within.

"No!" ripped out of the Dark asha's throat, and the earth shuddered beneath us. The ground rose, a tsunami of dirt and soil, and as I stared at the crest of a sand-wave, I realized that the dead around us were rising along with it. The Drychta men who had served Druj were turning against the Faceless; undead hands grabbed at her, ignoring the hiss of acid as it burned through their rotting flesh.

Still wailing, the Dark asha raised her palm, and the daeva attacked. The Druj beast attempted to fend them off, but they were too many, even for her.

Lord Kalen abandoned his assault and rushed to his brother familiar's aid, but a flash of the blighted's tail put him back on the defensive. I heard Lady Zoya panting, struggling to extend her shield toward the two familiars.

The dead soldiers distracted the blighted woman, but her tail was unguarded. It sang through the air, dripping black, aimed toward Lord Fox. None of the compelled soldiers were close enough to stop her blow.

There was a blur of red and gold, then the tail struck the ground harmlessly, missing its target. The Dark asha had dashed forward and dragged her brother to safety, but not without a price.

Another howl cleaved the air, but this time it was from Lord Kalen when he saw her stagger and fall. The soldiers surrounding the Faceless stumbled, a few disintegrating, but Lady Zoya was quick to take advantage. Despite her earlier warnings to Lord Kalen, Wind curled around Druj's tail, forcing it deep into the sands to keep it from seeking out another target.

The daeva hesitated, and while I could tell the asha remained linked to them, she no longer had a hold over them. For a moment, they twisted their heads to and fro in confusion, not used to the lack of Compulsion that goaded their actions. The Faceless shrilled, shaking off the rest of the undead Drychta.

The azi attacked the Druj beast first. Its three heads sank down, heedless of the poison and its own pained roars. The decision made, the rest of the daeva joined in, teeth snapping and limbs flailing as they fought to defend their mistress.

Part of the Dark asha's hua had dissolved, and she was clearly in pain. The flesh on her shoulder had been burned off, and I had little time to see how deep the damage went before Lord Khalad appeared, blocking her injuries from my line of sight, frantically working to heal her with the Deathseeker.

Druj's bile stripped the Drychta of their flesh and charred their bones, but despite the agony, the daeva hung on, grips tightening. For now, with the daeva attacking all at once, the creature was immobile.

"You idiot." Lord Fox's face was a wreck; the poison had eaten into his cheekbones and the curve of his jaw, showing more bone than skin.

The bone witch's quiet laughter was tucked in between soft mews of hurt. "No more than you."

"Hush," the Heartforger instructed, ripping cloth from his own robes, mopping up as much bile as he could and tossing the remnants away as the poison burned through the fabric. He ripped more strips.

"C-can't," the Dark asha gasped, gently pushing herself out of Lord Kalen's embrace. "Khalad, see to Fox. I have to end this, as I promised."

26

I CONTINUED TO SING FOR WHAT seemed like hours, long after Kalen's body turned cold. The *azi* had quieted, watching me with golden eyes, tired of taking so long to die. Its body continued to spasm, and it wept.

As my song drew to a close, the beast drew a deep, warm sigh. *Good-bye*, it whispered into my head, and then it crumbled into ashes. All that remained of it was the bezoar at my feet, shining a bright, immutable silver.

They found me shortly after that, exhausted and weak, Kalen in my arms, with Likh and Khalad still unconscious nearby. "We could arrest you," Hestia said. Their retinue was a small affair, a cluster of old women bereft of bodyguards. During the chaos of Mithra's Wall, they had left Ankyo unannounced to hunt for me themselves. I did not know how they achieved this without

Empress Alyx knowing, but that didn't matter anymore. "We could bring you to Ankyo and charge you with murder."

They intend to keep this a secret like they do everything else, I thought, and a sudden urge to giggle overcame me. "Do whatever you want. I don't care."

"Princess Inessa, however, is a hindrance. She and her mother do not wish you dead, as to spare your brother's life. I will be honest, Tea. When you fled Ankyo, we had intended to kill you the next day. We have had time to discuss the matter and recognize that would have been a rash decision. To carry out your execution will invite hostility and retaliation from she who will one day become empress."

"*I don't care.*"

"Neither do we. We are willing to wait for you to live out your natural existence, however short or long that may be. We release you from all ties to the asha and to the Willows. You shall be exiled, free to wander and die as you see fit. But we want your silver heartsglass. We will not tolerate any more of the chaos you've spread through the kingdoms. In exchange, we will allow you to continue on for your brother's sake."

I wanted to laugh. I wanted to weep. It was the best offer I've ever had. Had I been given it earlier, perhaps I would not have left Kion in the first place. "Will you protect Khalad and Likh?"

"They will suffer no punishments for their decision to follow you."

I thought there would be more fanfare. That my heartsglass would spark a protest. That it would take more than a sea of salt and skulls to break my spirit. But that was a different Tea's concern. I had nothing left to feel.

Wordlessly, I handed over my silver heartsglass, and my strength along with it. It made no difference. My heart had died with Kalen.

Tea? It was Fox's voice, distant and tinny. But when Hestia's hand closed over my heartsglass, his voice disappeared completely.

I watched the elders weave wards around my heart. Hestia nodded at the others. "Take the other two. Do not injure them."

One of the asha trotted off to inspect the rest of my belongings and returned triumphantly with the pouch that held all my bezoars. The others wove *Wind* to lift Likh and Khalad gently off the ground. When they turned to follow suit with Kalen, a sob rose in my throat. "No. He stays with me."

The asha paused, uncertain. "Mistress Hestia," one of the elders worked up the courage to say, "Lord Kalen is of Odalian royalty. Surely King Kance would want his body returned to—"

"He stays with me!" I shouted.

Hestia gestured for silence. "I will grant you your wish. Let it not be said that I am not charitable." She stared at the silver heartsglass in her hands for several seconds, then back at me, with the barest hint of pity in her gaze. "All this trouble," she said, "for something so insignificant."

They left me that way, alone and already forgotten, cradling Kalen underneath a murky sky.

I FELT YOU," GENERAL PAHLAVI SAID. "I know that now. I felt shock and pain, and I reached for you on instinct. You took a lot of strength from me, and I could barely stand when it was over. But when I tried to seek you out again, your thoughts disappeared from mine. And when we learned Kalen died and Likh was injured beyond healing…I searched for you for months. I didn't know if you were hiding yourself deliberately, or if you were being held against your will."

"I am sorry. I thought to do what was best for us. We both did. I had no other recourse. The elders would have hunted me down. Druj would have done the same. I am sorry for causing you pain, but I am also glad for it. My choices were not kind to Mykkie or Polaire or Kalen, but I can save you at least. That's all I want."

The bone witch staggered to her feet and, with Lord Kalen's careful guidance, approached Druj, who was still being restrained by both the daeva and the fallen soldiers. Painfully, she crouched beside the creature, who snapped in vain at her face. The Lady Tea's hands plunged into the creature's chest and plucked out the blighted's silver heartsglass. Druj howled.

"Well now," she mimicked the Faceless's words from a lifetime that had been folded between the pages of an epic letter. "Shall we see what unfolds here?"

She wove a rune invisible to my eyes, and Druj screamed, horrific, bloodcurdling screams that bounced from one mountain to the next, until the Ring of Worship echoed with the sounds of its torment. Before the sounds died, I watched her body crumble to ashes, borne back into dust to mix with the dark sand surrounding us.

Wordlessly, the bone witch walked back to the ruined entrance of the Ring of Worship, and we followed closely. This time, the daeva showed no fear, limping at our heels. At Lady Tea's gesture, we halted on the edge of the corpse-laden sand, remaining in the shadows of the mountains that surrounded us while the asha moved into the circle of light.

She stumbled. Lord Kalen caught her before she hit the ground, and Lord Fox clambered forward despite his own injuries, the rest of us not far behind.

"Stay there!" she commanded. "I do not know how far down the roots of the First Harvest goes. Should any of you come into contact…"

"And why should you take the risk?" Lady Zoya shot back.

"The First Harvest can only be reaped in the radiance of both lightsglass and darksglass. Only Kalen and I are protected." She gestured at her own black heartsglass and that of Lord Kalen's heartsglass, the same silver that the Faceless Usij once wore. "Stay there, and let me end this."

She sank to her knees before the strange, withering plant. One of the berries broke off easily in her hand, its juices seeping into her palm. "Rashnu the Just talked of a powerful sound like thunder," she wheezed in between deep breaths, her strength seeping more quickly than any of us feared, "and saw his comrades disappear in a cloud of *light. How many Dark asha have traveled here, hoping to bring back their loved ones with the juices of this accursed plant only to join them in death? What were Vernasha's final words? But I—I've done it." Her voice lilted, softened—a happy sound. "Fox, I did it."*

Tea of the Embers walked toward her brother, knelt. The unseen rune she created in the air sent blood dripping down her finger, mixing with the fruit's dark juices. Lord Fox inhaled sharply, and his face changed, healed. His horrific burns faded, replaced with unblemished skin, and healthy flesh once more crept over the bones of his jaw, repairing his deformity until he was the royal consort of old. Her purple-stained hand pressed one of the berries against his silver heartsglass. "Let it work," she pleaded. "Please—by all that is holy and good, let this work…"

The runeberry gleamed brightly, leaching into the silver. Lord Fox's eyes widened, and for the first time in years, his lungs truly took in air. His nostrils flared, and he made a gagging sound.

"I can breathe," he gasped, bending over from the rush. "I can breathe…" And then, pained, horrified, "I can't feel you with me."

"Kalen," the bone witch said, "you could—I could also be—"

"You idiot." *Lord Kalen had never sounded more affectionate.* "I crawled out of my grave, as I promised. Do you think I'd let you get away again? You promised me daughters with your eyes. Where you go, I will follow."

A sound between laughter and crying tore out of her. Another rune flickered against her palm. I could almost see the edges of it, a symbol like the branches of a heavy oak, the magic so concentrated that even a red heartsglass could perceive the enormity of its strength.

It braided itself around the runeberry patch and, for a moment, the world stood still.

Then the plant grew. Budding shoots sprouted out from hidden seeds, the fruits growing plump. Vines wrapped around a rapidly forming trunk, which rose out of the sands until a fully formed tree was splayed proudly before us. Silver leaves fanned from multiple branches, rich and bright against the glare of the Drychta sun.

"The Sacred Tree," Lord Khalad whispered.

The Dark asha dropped a hand to her side. She was deathly pale now, her black heartsglass pulsing erratically against her breast. Lord Kalen held tightly to his lover, face strained as his own strength battled to support her a little longer. Lady Zoya began to cry.

"I have to finish this," the Dark asha murmured, feverish. "You understand, don't you, Fox? I can't stay here. Not like this, not after knowing who I am, not after what they did to Kalen. But I wanted to make sure you could. Are you still angry at me, Fox? About the wars, about Daisy?"

Weeping now, Lord Fox lifted her hands to his mouth and kissed them. "I've always loved you, Tea. Even though I was too foolish to show it. There must be something else..."

"I had months to understand that there is nothing else. Don't you see, Fox? I'm happy. This is what I want. Zoya, it won't do Shadi any good to see you blubbering on like this."

"You fool," the other asha sobbed. "They will write songs about you, even if your bard will not."

"I will." My own words were choked, wrung from my throat. "I will honor you, milady. I will spend the rest of my life singing."

"Perhaps one day you will do more than sing, Your Highness."
She focused on the Heartforger. *"Khalad. She will be safe now."*

There were tears in the man's eyes. *"I didn't help you solely for
Likh, Tea."*

*"I know. I will always be grateful nonetheless. Give her my
love when she wakes."* The bone witch tried to stand, but Lord Fox
wouldn't release her. *"I can't let you go. I can't. We have to... It isn't
fair. You gave up everything and now you're—"*

She touched his face affectionately, and his hold on her tight-
ened. *"I'll go with you."* He cried against her unharmed shoulder.
*"Don't tell me to stay. You can't order me around anymore, Tea. I can't
ask you to do this without me. We've been by each other's side for so
long. You've given me a new lifetime, so let me spend it apologizing.
Let me make it up to you. Please. I can't... Tea, I can't—"*

"Fox," her voice was soft, sweet. *"Let me go."*

He froze.

"Inessa would hate me." She pressed a kiss upon his stricken
face. *"And I would hate me as well. I love you, Fox. And if you want
to prove that you love me, then live every day with meaning. Wherever
I am, Kalen and I will watch over you."*

Lord Kalen offered her his hand. *"Are you ready, love?"*

Her smile was blinding. *"Always."*

The azi approached them, its three snouts nuzzling against her,
protective. Like her, it was dying. They were all dying, bone showing
and blood flowing, maimed deeply by the Faceless, but all seven of the
great beasts looked at peace as they began their final journey.

"Are you scared?" I thought I heard the Deathseeker ask, but I

could not hear her quiet reply, her laughter the only sound floating back to us.

We could only watch as they and their pet daeva walked toward that beautiful tree. Lady Tea and Lord Kalen turned back to smile at us, and then he bent down to kiss her, fiercely and ferociously and lovingly, until they were swallowed by the holy light.

The tree continued its upward spiral into the sky, climbing higher into the clouds until I thought it could reach the heavens. The landscape changed. Streaks of light shone around us, and for the briefest of moments, I felt serenity within the depths of my soul like I had never known before.

Then the light disappeared and the tree along with it. We were left in the empty field of sand, which started blooming to life as ponds of water formed and small green shoots grew around us, restoring the place to what must have been its ancient beauty. I looked down in wonder and discovered the Lady Tea's letters at my feet.

27

I COULD HAVE BATHED HIM IN my tears.

I had no oils to anoint him aside from asha-ka perfumes, no ceremonial robe to clothe him, but an extra cloak. I brought his body to the banks of the sea and dug at the hard sand until my hands bled, until I had uncovered a hole wide enough to hold him. We had talked about living by the seashore, but this was all I could afford him. I had no strength left to give, but everything I had was for him still.

I tried to will in the Dark, tried to wrap it around me as I always could before, direct it with all the love inside of me.

"Rise up."

I could no longer feel the darkness. I could no longer touch the runes. My chest felt bare without the weight of my heartsglass. *Wasn't that what I wanted?* I thought, and hysterical mirth bubbled from my lips, desperate for an outlet. *Didn't you want normalcy, to be free from the burdens of the Dark?*

"Rise. Rise. Rise! *Rise!*" I pounded the ground with fury. "Rise! You promised me! You promised you would crawl out of your grave! You promised me, and I…and I—"

The bones of other skeletons watched me silently, and the waves crashed against the shore.

I spent two nights by his grave, unable to move as the sun turned into moonlight into day. By the third sunrise, I had lost all sense of self. Perhaps the elder asha expected this when they abandoned me here. Perhaps they knew that the most fitting punishment was to die by my own hand.

Let me prove them right for once.

I waded out into the cold deep. The tide had arrived, and soon the waters had risen to my chest.

It would be so easy. To immerse myself in the quiet, to close my eyes, to let out one final breath.

It would be so easy to die.

It would have been easier to have never known the Dark. It would have been easier if Mykkie had never found me, if she had left me to live and die in Knightscross, never the wiser so that I could never be the fool.

Life without the Willows. Life without being an asha. Life without Polaire or Mykaela or Likh or Kance or Khalad…

Life without ever having known Kalen…

I surfaced abruptly, gasping for air, expelling salt water from my lungs. I staggered back toward the shore and fell to my knees before Kalen's grave, sobbing harder.

I had to live. I had to live for Fox. He was all I had left.

But when I opened my eyes, I saw a vision.

I saw Kalen, alive and well, standing before me, holding a light so bright and lovely. He smiled and extended his other hand toward me, eyes full of love. I had my heartsglass once more, the silver having given way to black. But instead of the dark and matted luster I had feared, it was as bright as an ebony night filled with pearly stars. It was beautiful.

"Are you scared?" he asked me gently, and I laughed. Once upon a time, my sister Lily had promised me a prince.

"Never when I'm with you," I whispered to the fading vision, as it gave way to black sands and the roar of the surf.

I should not have had that vision. My heartsglass was now locked away by the elder asha to prevent me from touching magic. So what did this mean?

I felt a warmth against my breast, a familiar weight. I looked down.

Hovering above my chest, small but growing in size and form, was the beginnings of a heartsglass, bright and black.

•• ❃ ••

There was a cave along the Sea of Skulls, small and cool, hollowed from heavy stone. I stood by the entrance and watched as the figure approached. His face was wrapped in a heavy scarf to keep out the sun and shield his face from view, but I knew him by the way he rolled his shoulders and leaned forward to squint.

"You're late," I said softly as he neared.

Slowly, Khalad pulled back the head covering. "How did you know?" His eyes drifted to where my half-finished heartsglass glowed in the glass case I had compelled a passing merchant to sell to me. "I thought... The elders—"

"My strength is not up to par yet. I can scry upon those who wander close to the beach, but the Dark grows in me every day. How is Likh?"

Khalad's eyes looked tired. "She hasn't woken up. Not since the elders brought us back. I... Nothing I did could wake her."

"Is that why you're here?"

He seemed taken aback by my quiet, gentle tone. Had he imagined he'd find a madwoman lurking along the Sea of Skulls, haunting her lover's tomb like a forgotten ghost? "Yes and no. I was worried about you."

"Do they know where I am?" *Does Fox know where I am?* was what I meant, and he understood.

He shook his head. "No one but the elders. They knew well enough to swear me to secrecy, in exchange for Likh's treatment. They know I never break my oaths, and I know they could not afford to spare me, now that Master is gone."

I murmured my sympathies.

He continued. "I wasn't sure if you wanted me to come. The only reason I knew you were alive was because of Fox. He believes that I don't know where you are. I said nothing because of my oath. I...I told no one about Altaecia either. No one's seen the oracle, but people think she's ill. I said nothing about her as well. I couldn't... I knew I had to talk to you first."

"You made the right choice. Druj might have given up her disguise as the oracle, but she is still dangerous."

"I'm not even certain there isn't a spy on my back tailing me. My leaving Kion would make the elders suspicious."

"They have someone. I turned him away at the borders, sent an illusion of you down to Amarai for him to chase."

He stared. "You've gotten stronger."

"Black heartsglass takes in more of the Dark, or so some Gorvekai say," I said.

His gaze traveled to my regenerating heartsglass again. "How?"

I smiled brightly, bitterly. "Aenah knew something the elders didn't. *Black heartsglass will always come back to you*, she told me once. That is why the Faceless prized it above all. No matter what spells they cast, my heartsglass will always come back to me. It has been two months, and perhaps it will require another two before I take back all that is rightfully mine."

Aenah told me it was acts of violence that turned one heart's black. What she failed to elaborate on was that violence *against* me would have the same result. I should have known—hadn't I seen Aenah's grief over her dead child and her burning city, watched that instant when her own heart had succumbed to black? Hadn't Druj shared a similar story of loss?

"What do you intend to do, Tea?"

"What do you want me to do, Khalad? Isn't that why you've traveled all this way? You would not have left Likh's side if you didn't believe her situation was hopeless. Where do you plan to go?"

The Heartforger hung his head. "Daanoris, to start. Master

kept many books there with notes on heartsglass. There might be something I could find for Likh."

"And you chose to pay me a courtesy call along the way?"

"I was worried, Tea!"

I smiled sadly. The time for worry had passed. "I know you, Khalad. I may not have all my heartsglass yet, but I can read yours. There's something you want from me."

The Heartforger paused and reached into his rucksack. He pulled out a familiar pouch, and all seven bezoars spilled into my hands.

"I'm glad there are still things I can hide from you." He smiled grimly. "I left Kion for good. The elders thought Likh would keep me there and out of trouble. Instead, I snuck into their study like we had all those months ago and took back the bezoars they stole. I couldn't find your heartsglass—no one but Hestia seems to know where it is."

I burst into laughter, and Khalad looked startled. "Probably buried somewhere so they never have to look at it again. Why are you giving these to me?"

"Because I am going to help you. Druj is still out there. You can still complete shadowglass if you want to."

"Stranger's Peak rejected me—"

"There is no rule about taking the test a second time. As I recall, Agnarr himself invited you to return. The final test—Druj said it was for love. Was it about Kalen?"

I nodded, my gaze sweeping, as it often did, to the small, makeshift cairn I had fashioned over Kalen's grave.

RIN CHUPECO

"I want to know if there's anything in Master's notes that will help me save Likh, but even I know the chances of a cure are small. The only way I can think to lift her curse is to rid the world of magic like Druj and the Gorvekai wanted." He clenched his fist. "It's a selfish desire, I know. But if that's what you want as well, then I'll help you. I'll forge whatever you need, whatever you want. Just please—" His voice cracked. "If you love Likh, then help me save her."

The bezoars glittered in my hands, and my black, half-finished heartsglass pulsed in answer. "Do they ask for me?"

Khalad nodded. "Fox was—is—frantic. He's in Yadosha searching for you. He's being watched closely, but I don't think the elders believe he's in contact with you."

He paused. "Do you—do you want me to tell Fox where you are?"

I shook my head. He would not believe me about the oracle or Altaecia. Not like this. "No. He will learn soon enough. Thank you for keeping my location a secret. You've placed yourself at great risk for me."

"Do you mean to stay here forever, Tea?"

"On the contrary." I lifted my hand and traced a rune in the air. The ground beneath us shuddered, and several of the ancient skeletons that slumbered nearby moved.

"Go to Daanoris, and see what help your Master's notes reveal," I said. "I have my own trials to complete."

I knelt on falling snow before the entrance to Stranger's Peak. Lord Agnarr of the Gorvekai stood before me. His face was wooden and expressionless, but I saw sympathy in his gaze. "You are Little Tears's salvation, and ours," he said. "You have passed our trials as no other asha has done before you. I will teach you the secrets of shadowglass, to unmake the magic of the world. Do you accept, Tea of the Embers?"

A new vision swam through my mind. I saw all seven daeva bowing to me, with Kalen, smiling and alive, my hand in his, while I stood surrounded by light. *You were right, Lily,* my heartsglass wept. *A prince on my arm, surrounded by silver. You were right.*

"Are you ready, love?" the Kalen of my vision asked again.

I stood, and darkness swirled. There was no darkrot in me, only purpose. "Always," I said.

*D*O YOU THINK TO STAY *long, milord?" the lady asked me, smiling brightly.*

Representatives of the seven kingdoms had traveled far and wide to Ankyo, to celebrate the marriage between Princess Inessa and her royal consort, General Fox Pahlavi. I was still unused to the dazzling displays of courtiers and ornate coaches as noble guests and emissaries clustered around the palace entrance, offering well wishes to Kion officials. Conscious of my simpler garb, I excused myself and retreated to the nearly empty royal gardens, seeking a few minutes' respite. The gardens were open to those curious enough to explore, though the fanfare at the castle gates proved more popular. I could sing before a crowd without fear, but to mingle with the nobility as one of them was distressing.

Without thinking, I sought out the twin statues at the center of the carefully manicured garden. It had been completed only a month before, though a few elder asha still protested its inclusion on palace grounds. But General Fox had insisted, and Princess Inessa seconded his wish. She was the reason, she had argued, for Fox returning to her against all odds, even after magic had ebbed away from the lands. The bone witch—no, Lady Tea—was right. The loss of the runes would not stop the tide of politics, but they no longer had the poisonous bite they once did when they came armed with spells.

I liked the monument. Even the best sculptors could not completely copy her true likeness, but it was a beautiful attempt. In it, I could see the familiar contours of her lovely face, her black hair whipping behind her, frozen in time by metal and bronze. The rendering could not accurately portray her flashing, dark eyes, alive with anger or grief or warmth or whichever mood took her, but no likeness could. Her lover stood silently beside her, clad in black, with his fingers wrapped around hers. He gazed down at her, and it softened the inexorability of his countenance.

A girl stood at the foot of both statues, gazing earnestly up at them. She was still dressed in an asha's hua, *though it was rapidly growing out of fashion in the wake of the runebinders' waning influence; still, it suited her well.*

"I wish I could have said good-bye to them," she mourned. "Khalad says they were happy in the end, and that's all I could've ever hoped for. But is it selfish of me to wish for more?"

She was a miracle, they had told me. On the day Lady Tea and Lord Kalen died, she had woken from her months-long sleep, disoriented but healthy, no longer blighted. When the news from Shadi first reached us, Lord Khalad had broken down in King Kance's arms and wept like a young child.

I looked up at the Lady Tea's statue and felt my own eyes fill. "It's never wrong to wish for more happiness," I said hoarsely.

She knelt and pressed a chaste kiss against Lady Tea's foot. "We miss you every day. Wherever you two wander, I hope you are at peace, as we are."

"Likh?" Lord Khalad idled in the garden, King Kance by his

side. *"Are you keeping His Highness from Inessa and Fox? They've been searching for him."*

"Acting regent for Prince Jakova," I corrected him. *My distant cousin would make a better ruler for Drycht. My time with the asha made me realize I had neither the patience nor the aptitude for politics. "And I arrived here of my own volition but found Lady Likh ahead of me."*

"I wanted to pay my respects," the beautiful girl said.

Shadows crossed both brothers' faces. *"But of course,"* King Kance assented, smiling sadly at the statues.

"Of course," Lord Fox repeated, arriving behind them. There were no more heartsglass left, but emotions were easy to read on his face nowadays: wistfulness, sadness, pride, love. *"Inessa is going to kill me if we delay the ceremony any longer, and I would like the wedding over and done with before I lose more of my sanity."*

Lord Khalad laughed and linked arms with Lady Likh. *"The princess'll kill you if she hears you now."*

The friends moved away, heading toward Ladies Shadi and Zoya, who were about to enter the castle with Councilor Ludvig and Lord Rahim waiting for them by the entrance. General Pahlavi stayed. There was a faint cut on his chin, barely noticeable.

"Shaving," he said, a wry smile. *"I'm still remembering how to heal properly, like a normal man."* He looked up again at his sister. *"Do you know,"* he asked, *"where the term 'seven hells' come from?"*

"Not quite," I confessed.

"There are no legends about seven hells. Not even an epigraph or a footnote. No one seems to know its origins, though we use it often

enough as a curse. And yet Lord Garindor tells me it was a common expletive even among Vernasha's contemporaries. I'd like to think that there are more stories than we can ever know in our own lifetimes. Perhaps there really are seven hells. Or perhaps there are seven heavens. Perhaps they're in one of them."

I nodded silently, not trusting myself to speak.

The man leaned his forehead against his sister's likeness. "I miss you. I'm getting married today, Tea. Married! You should be here with me and Mum and Dad and the others. You—you gave me everything. You were always the stronger of us. So why am I the one standing here, with this the closest we'll ever get to be? I've never been able to keep you from doing what you wanted, and I know you're with Kalen, and I know with him you're happiest. I didn't show my love as well as I should've, but—" He swallowed. "I'll find you again. I know it. What's one more impossibility when it's you?" His eyes traveled to the statue beside her.

"Take care of her, Kalen. Because when my own time comes, you'll be answering to me." He leaned back and blinked away his tears.

"Fox?" A soft voice came from behind us. Princess Inessa stood, hopeful and sad and unsure all at once.

He smiled. "You're not supposed to see me before the wedding," he chided and kissed her.

"I've never been one for custom." She sighed against him. "If you'd like a few more minutes…"

"No, my love. I'm ready now."

I assured them I would be along shortly and prayed silently for a long, more lasting peace to make up for everything they had lost.

"It's a nice enough piece." I whirled around, my heartbeat quickening. But I was disappointed to find an unfamiliar face. The woman had a freckled face and bright, brown eyes, tufts of short, red hair escaping from her bonnet. The man beside her was tall, sandy haired, and darker, with green eyes. They were clad in the heavy wool that was typical among the Gorvekai.

She nodded at the retreating royalty, curious. "Are they part of the wedding? Was the lady their friend?"

"Yes." It angered me sometimes, to know the extent Lord Fox and Lady Tea had gone for the kingdoms, only for very few people to recognize them or their efforts. "The wedding will be a happy affair… but they are still grieving."

The redhead squinted. "She's the one to kill the magic, wasn't she? Made things harder, even for us common folk."

"With runes, we took things for granted. I doubt most people would even begin to understand their sacrifice. There is more color to life than in a heartsglass. You may not understand today, but your sons and daughters might one day."

The woman smiled. "Well, if there are enough people like you to remember her, then she'll always be alive, won't she?" She looked at the monuments again, a most peculiar expression on her face. "Sons and daughters," she echoed, "sons with my fire, daughters with my eyes. Mayhap one day, they will. A life worth dying for is a life worth living after all." She laid a hand on her companion's shoulder, squeezing. "Let's go, my love."

I gazed up again at the bone witch's likeness, so lost in my own thoughts that it took a few seconds for the woman's words to *seep through. When they finally did, I turned, a low cry leaving my mouth.*

But I was alone in the royal gardens. The young girl and her companion had vanished.

The World of the Bone Witch:
The Eight Kingdoms

ISTERA

- The coldest among the eight kingdoms
- Has gone to war with Tresea over the Heartsbane Islands in the past and still shares some animosity
- Separated from Tresea by the River of Peace

CAPITAL: Farsun

CURRENT RULER: King Rendorvik of House Petralta

TRESEA

- Composed of mostly dense woods and wide plains
- Population is concentrated mainly in cities, with small scatterings of villages throughout

CAPITAL: Highgaard

CURRENT RULER: Czar Kamulus of House Ambersturg

DAANORIS

- Mild to moderate weather, most-populated kingdom

CAPITAL: Santiang

CURRENT RULER: Emperor Shifang

YADOSHA CITY-STATES

- The whole continent was originally the kingdom of Yadosha, but infighting among the royal descendants soon splintered it into several warring states and shrunk their dominion into only its upper continent
- While each city-state maintains a high degree of independence, all share one main government to foster ties and maintain diplomatic missions
- Each city-state has a second minister to govern them; every seven years, a first minister is elected among the second ministers to represent Yadosha as a whole

CAPITAL: None

CURRENT RULER: First Minister Stefan

KION

- Once a part of Yadosha; many kingdoms conquered and fought over this land before Kion was able to achieve its independence through Vernasha of the Roses, a legendary asha
- A melting pot of culture and the main headquarters of the asha
- Smallest land among the kingdoms

CAPITAL: Ankyo

CURRENT RULER: Empress Alyx of House Imperial

ODALIA

- Composed of plains and forests
- Originally a part of the kingdom of Yadosha but was the first in the continent to rebel and break off into its own kingdom

CAPITAL: Kneave
CURRENT RULER: King Telemaine of House Odalia

ARHEN-KOSHO
- Large group of islands on the Swiftsea, near Odalia and Kion
CAPITAL: Hottenheim
CURRENT RULER: Queen Lynoria of House Imperial

DRYCHT
- Desert kingdom
- Also notable for its austere and extreme perspective generally held in contempt by most of the other kingdoms, but tolerated for the runeberry cloth they provide
- Only the western continent of Drycht is heavily populated; the majority of the kingdom is made of sand.
CAPITAL: Adra-al
CURRENT RULER: King Aadil of the Tavronoo clan

Acknowledgments

I don't make it a habit of extending this particular page, as writing books has always been a solitary journey for me. But *publishing* them—that's a different story. As always, I cannot even remotely begin to express the amount of gratitude I feel for the people who have made all this possible.

For Rebecca Podos, my agent of more than six years and first cheerleader, who has stuck by me through many books and, I hope, for even many more.

For the Sourcebooks team: Annette Pollert-Morgan, Kathryn Lynch, Alex Yeadon, Cassie Gutman, Sarah Kasman, Gretchen Stelter, and everyone else who worked hard to make this a reality—thank you from the bottom of my heart.

I started *The Bone Witch* with the intention of writing about a girl and the brother she raised from the dead, and realized in the course of three books that despite the necromancy and the corpse-eating and the fighting, I was also writing about love in its many-splendored incarnations. Love for siblings, romantic love, platonic love. Love for the family you grew up with and love for the family you form with others. Love for country, love for yourself, love for people you've never even met. And, more importantly, about all the great things you can be capable of because of those loves. Take a moment to hug someone you love today—they will always appreciate it.

And to complete the trifecta of my thanking celebrities, I would also like to thank Terry Crews for being a perfectly sculpted angel the world does not deserve.

About the Author

Rin Chupeco wrote obscure manuals for complicated computer programs, talked people out of their money at event shows, and did many other terrible things before becoming an author. She now writes about ghosts and fairy tales and is the author of *The Girl from the Well*, *The Suffering*, and the Bone Witch Trilogy. Rin lives in the Philippines with her family. Visit her online at rinchupeco.com.

COLLECT THE
ENTIRE STUNNING

BONE
WITCH

TRILOGY

A world split between day and night.
Two sisters who must unite it.

Don't miss *The Never Tilting World*, also from Rin Chupeco!

FIREreads
#getbooklit

Your hub for the hottest in young adult books!

Visit us online and sign up for our
newsletter at FIREreads.com

 @sourcebooksfire

 sourcebooksfire

 firereads.tumblr.com